BREAKING POINT

BREAKING POINT

KRISTEN SIMMONS

TOR®
TEEN

A TOM DOHERTY ASSOCIATES BOOK
NEW YORK

BREAKING POINT

Copyright © 2013 by Kristen Simmons

A Tor Teen Book
Published by Tom Doherty Associates, LLC
175 Fifth Avenue
New York, NY 10010

www.tor-forge.com

Tor® is a registered trademark of Tom Doherty Associates, LLC.

Library of Congress Cataloging-in-Publication Data

Simmons, Kristen.
 Breaking point / Kristen Simmons.—1st ed.
  p. cm.
 "A Tom Doherty Associates Book."
 ISBN 978-0-7653-2959-2 (hardcover)
 ISBN 978-1-4299-4945-3 (e-book)
 1. Government, Resistance to—Fiction. 2. Fugitives from justice—
Fiction. 3. Science fiction. I. Title.
 PZ7.S591825Bre 2013
 [Fic]—dc23

                                                    2012037365

First Edition: February 2013

Printed in the United States of America

0 9 8 7 6 5 4 3 2 1

FOR MY PARENTS,
ANN AND DAN,

who taught me to love stories
even before they taught me to love books

BREAKING POINT

CHAPTER
1

THE Wayland Inn was behind the slums, on the west end of Knoxville. It was a place that had festered since the War, buzzing with flies that bred in the clogged sewers, stinking of dirty river water brought in on the afternoon breeze. A place that attracted those who thrived in the shadows. People you had to seek to find.

The motel's brick exterior, veined with dead ivy and pockmarked by black mold, blended with every other boarded-up office building on the street. The water was ice-cold when it ran at all, the baseboards were cracked with mouse holes, and there was only one bathroom on each floor. Sometimes it even worked.

It was the perfect location for the resistance: hidden in plain sight, on a block so rotten even the soldiers stayed in their patrol cars.

We met outside the supply room before dawn, when the standardized power resumed, for Wallace's orders. The night patrols were still out guarding our perimeter and those with stationary posts—the stairway door, the roof, and radio surveillance—were awaiting relief from the day shift. Curfew would be up soon, and they were hungry.

I stayed back against the wall, letting those who had been here longer settle to the front row. The rest of the hallway filled in quickly; if you were late, Wallace assigned you extra duties, the kind no one wanted. The supply room door was open, and though I couldn't see our hard-nosed leader from my angle, the candlelight threw a thin, distorted shadow against the inside wall.

He was talking to someone on the radio; a soft crackling filled the space while he waited for a response. I thought it might be the team he'd put on special assignment two days ago: Cara, the only other girl at the Wayland Inn, and three big guys that had been kicked out of the Federal Bureau of Reformation—or, as we'd called the soldiers who'd taken over after the War, the Moral Militia. Curiosity had me leaning toward the sound, but I didn't get too close. The more you knew, the more the MM could take from you.

"Be safe." I recognized Wallace's voice, but not the concern in it. Never had I heard him soften in the presence of others.

Sean Banks, my old guard from the Girls' Reformatory and Rehabilitation Center, staggered out of his room, pulling his shirt down over his ribs. *Too thin*, I thought, but at least he'd slept a little—his deep blue eyes were calmer than before, not so strained. He found a place on the wall beside me, rubbing at the pillow marks still on his face.

"*Always am, handsome*," came Cara's muffled response, and then the radio went dead.

"Handsome?" parroted an AWOL named Houston. His red hair was growing out and flipped in the back like the tail feathers of a chicken. "*Handsome?*" he said again. The volume in the hall had increased; several of the guys were snickering.

"You called?" Lincoln, whose freckles always looked like someone had splashed black paint across his hollow cheeks, appeared beside Houston. They'd joined together last year, and in my time here I'd yet to see one without the other.

The chatter faded as Wallace came around the corner. He needed a shower; his shoulder-length peppered hair was greasy in clumps, and the skin of his face was tight with fatigue, but even in the muted yellow glow of the flashlights it was obvious his ears had gone pink. One pointed glare, and Houston melted back toward Lincoln.

My brows rose. Wallace seemed too old for Cara; she was twenty-two while he might have been twice that age. Besides, he was married to the cause. Everything else, every*one* else, would always come second.

Not my business, I reminded myself.

The narrow corridor had crowded with eleven guys awaiting instruction. Not all of them had served; some were just noncompliant with the Statutes, like me. We all had our reasons for being here.

My heart tripped in my chest when Houston moved aside to reveal Chase Jennings, leaning against the opposite wall ten feet down. His hands were wrist-deep in the pockets of his jeans, and a white undershirt peeked through the holes of a gray, threadbare sweater. Only remnants of his incarceration in the MM base remained, a dark half-moon painted beneath one eye and a thin band of scar tissue across the bridge of his nose. He'd just gotten off the night shift securing the building's perimeter; I hadn't seen him come in.

As he watched me, the corner of his mouth lifted ever so slightly.

I looked down when I realized my lips had done the same.

"All right, quiet down," began Wallace, voice gruff once again. He hesitated, tapping the handheld radio, now silent, against his leg. I caught a glimpse of the black tattoo on his forearm that twisted beneath his frayed sleeve.

"What happened?" said Riggins, suspicious only when not outright paranoid. His fingers wove over the top of his buzzed, can-shaped head as though he expected the ceiling might suddenly cave in on us.

"Last night half the Square went without rations." Wallace's frown deepened. "Seems our blue friends are withholding."

Pity was a hard sell. Most of us went straight to anger. We all knew the MM had the food; our scouts had counted two extra Horizons trucks—the only government-sanctioned food distributers—entering the base just yesterday.

Houston balked. "If they're hoping to clear town, they're outta luck. Tent City'll starve to death first. People got nowhere else to go."

He was right. When the major cities had been destroyed or evacuated in the War, people had migrated inland, to places like Knoxville, or my home, Louisville, in search of food and shelter. They'd found only the bare minimum—soup kitchens and communities of vagrants, like the city of tents that had taken over the lot on the northern side of the city square.

"Thank you, Houston," said Wallace. "I think that's the point."

I shivered. Chase and I hadn't left the Wayland Inn since we'd pledged to the resistance, almost a month ago. If possible, the city seemed even bleaker than when we had last seen it.

"Now," continued Wallace. "Billy caught a radio thread yesterday on an upcoming draft in the Square. We don't know when, but my guess is it'll be soon, and they'll be offering signing bonuses."

"I didn't get a bonus," someone whispered.

"Rations, jackass," muttered Sean.

A collective groan filled the hallway. Soldiers using the promise of food to recruit more soldiers. They'd have a whole new army in a week.

"And forgiveness of Statute violations, of course." Wallace smiled cynically. More groans followed.

Work was slim these days. The only businesses still running required background checks, which meant applicants had better be compliant with the Moral Statutes—a list of regulations that took away women's rights, mandated a "whole" family, and prohibited things like divorce, speaking out against the government, and, of course, being born out of wedlock, like me. This had always been one of the MM's prime recruiting strategies. Men who couldn't get a job because of their record could still serve their country. And even if it meant selling their souls, soldiers got paid.

"What're we going to do about it?" Lincoln asked.

"Nothing," said Riggins. "We hit something like that, they'll smoke out this whole town till they find us."

I straightened, envisioning the MM coming here, raiding the Wayland Inn. As far as they knew, Chase and I were dead, "completed" in the holding cells at the base. I'd made certain of it before our escape. We didn't want to give them reason to believe otherwise.

Without looking over, Sean elbowed me in the ribs. I deflated, a shallow breath expelling from between my teeth.

"Quiet," said Wallace when several people objected. He shook his head. "Riggins is right. They plugged up the soup kitchen for seventy-two hours after last month's riot. Soon they'll be compensating anyone willing to sell us out. We've got to be smart. Think." He tapped his temple. "In the meantime, Banks has a report to make."

I glanced over, surprised, as Sean shoved off the wall beside me. He and I had been up late together scanning the mainframe for facilities in Chicago, searching for Rebecca—my roommate and his girlfriend—who had been beaten and arrested the night I'd tried to escape reform school. He hadn't mentioned that anything out of the ordinary had happened during his earlier shift in the Square.

"Yesterday on my way back from Tent City, I ran into a guy looking for trouble over by the Red Cross Station," said Sean.

"What kind of trouble?" Chase's dark gaze flicked to mine.

Sean scratched his jaw. "The kind that makes me think he was looking to join us. He was trying to convince a group of guys to take out the guards posted at the soup kitchen. Talking loud—*too* loud. Said he'd been in the base lately, that he knew things about it. I very politely told him to keep it down, and he called me a—"

"What did he know?" I interrupted.

"A lot," said Sean. "He was just discharged last week. *Dishonorably.* He didn't seem too pleased about it either."

I could feel Chase's tension from across the hall. A recently discharged soldier could have important information about the Knoxville base, he might even know how to break back in, but what if he recognized us? We'd only been there four weeks ago. He could have been one of those who had beaten Chase or even killed another prisoner.

"It's a con," said Riggins. "Banks is getting played. The FBR's sending in a mole."

Wallace, who'd been silent while Sean had spoken, cleared his throat. "That's why we're going to tail him. If he gets within ten feet of a uniform, cut him loose. I don't want to take any chances with this one."

"Then don't," I said before I could stop myself. "Maybe Riggins is right." Riggins snorted as if to say he didn't want my help.

"You think he didn't say the same about you when you came here?" Wallace asked.

I felt myself shrink under our leader's stare. Sean had

brought Chase and me to the Wayland Inn with no more than his word that we weren't going to spill its secrets.

"Besides," he continued, patting the radio against his leg again. "If this guy can get us access into the base, imagine the damage we could do."

The following silence was filled with consideration. The MM was stockpiling food—we'd seen the delivery trucks go in—and there were weapons, not to mention the innocent people being executed in the holding cells.

I shivered, remembering how I'd nearly been one of them.

Lincoln and Houston shoved each other excitedly, but several of the others didn't seem so convinced. Clusters of arguments broke out, which Wallace silenced by assigning a detail to keep tabs on the new recruit. He tasked Sean with bringing him in.

Sean fell back beside me, grumbling something indecipherable. The more time he spent away, the less we had to focus on breaking Rebecca out of rehab in Chicago. Still, Sean was smart enough to know that in order to use the resistance's resources, the resistance had to use *him* as a resource, so he did what he was told.

Over the next several minutes Wallace began assigning people to daily duties: patrol, motel security, and finally, distribution of rations. I paused when he gave this duty to the two brothers who bunked across the hall from the bathroom. For the last few weeks it had belonged to me. I'd just gotten used to the routine, and now Wallace was changing things up.

"We've got supplies coming in from a raid last night,"

Wallace said, and I realized this must have been what Cara and the others were doing. "The truck's parked at the checkpoint and needs to be unloaded. And there's a package in Tent City waiting for delivery."

I still hadn't gotten used to people being *packages*. Fugitives were moved for their safety to a checkpoint, a secret location where they could hide until a driver for the resistance, called a carrier, could transport them across the evacuated Red Zone lines to a safe house on the coast. Once we helped Sean rescue Rebecca, Chase and I would be going there, too.

My breath quickened. The checkpoint was across town, past the Square.

Two eager hands rose.

"Good. Inventory?"

On impulse, I raised my hand. Inventory kept me here, and kept everything on the outside, lurking just beyond the rain-stained windows.

"Miller," said Wallace slowly. "Right. Miller on supplies."

Chase's brows lifted.

I dropped my hand and picked at the peeling yellow wallpaper behind my lower back. Houston whispered something to Riggins, who shot a mocking glance at me over his shoulder.

"What about next door?" Fourteen-year-old Billy spoke up from behind Chase. "You said you'd post me there today." He shoved a mop of mousy brown hair out of his eyes.

Wallace's thin mouth drew into a smirk—an expression reserved for the youngest here.

"Billy, so nice of you to join us."

"I been here!" His claim was cheerfully denied by those closest.

"You been here?" Wallace mocked. "You *been* sleeping late, I think. You're on the latrines, kid, and Jennings and Banks will clear the abandoned buildings next door."

Jennings? Chase was leaving the building? He hadn't even slept yet. I tried to glance back over to him, but now other people were blocking the way.

Billy's chin shot out indignantly. "But—"

"How about tomorrow, too?"

Billy threw his head back and groaned.

A buzz, one that made my spine tingle, and the overhead globes flickered with light. Curfew was over. The day had begun.

The hall began to clear. I looked for Chase, but found my path blocked.

"Inventory, huh?" Riggins smirked. He had a sorry excuse for a moustache, which landed directly in my line of sight.

I planted my feet, not about to let him get to me. The guys here were rough, they had to be, and living with them meant having a thick skin sometimes.

"That's what Wallace said," I responded.

"Let's get some food." Sean tried to move between us but Riggins stopped him with one solid hand.

"Watch out in the supply room. There's *rats*, you know." He grinned, the plucky hairs on his upper lip thinning.

I wasn't sure if he was serious or just trying to make me squirm. "I've seen rats," I told him.

"Not rats this big," he said, stepping close enough to force me back again. "These rats hide in the uniform crates. You can hear 'em sometimes. They squeal, real loud."

Two hands closed around my waist from behind and pinched my ribs. A short scream burst from my throat. When I spun around Houston was cackling. He took off after Lincoln, toward the radio room.

Before any coherent words filled my mind Chase was there, his fist twisted in Riggins's collar as he shoved him into the wall. Because Chase was several inches taller, Riggins was forced to lift his dimpled chin to return a hard glare.

"Temper, temper," Riggins rasped.

"What's going on?" Wallace's voice broke through my surprise. He had rules about fighting. We were family here, that's what he always said. All Chase and I needed was to get kicked out, to be out there again running from the MM.

I squeezed Chase's bicep, feeling the muscles flex beneath my fingers. His grip eased, and finally released.

Riggins smiled before sending Wallace a no-problem-here wave.

"Come on," said Sean. He grabbed my elbow, towing me down the hall toward where the brothers were distributing dry cereal for breakfast.

Riggins leaned close as I passed. "You actually gonna do something useful today? Or just disappear again?" When I turned around he was sauntering toward the west exit, chuckling to himself.

My whole body burned.

It was no secret that Chase and I hadn't left the motel

since we'd escaped the base, but I didn't know anyone had noticed that sometimes, when the fourth floor grew too confined, I'd escape to the roof to clear my head. It wasn't like I was hurting anyone, and we pulled our weight where we could. We passed out rations, and Chase took shifts securing the building, but it wasn't the same as pounding the pavement, holding up supply trucks or helping those in danger. Riggins and I both knew it.

It wasn't like I didn't want to do more. I did. I wanted to make a difference, to help someone, the way no one had been able to help my mother. The MM may have thought we were dead, but I remembered too well what it felt like to be wanted. First as a Statute violator when my mother had been charged with an Article 5, then as a reform school runaway. Chase had been charged with everything from his AWOL as a soldier to assault. Sometimes I could still feel the MM breathing down our necks.

But those things didn't matter to people like Riggins. He hadn't trusted me since Sean had brought us here for shelter. And hiding while he and the others risked their lives did nothing to prove my dedication to the cause.

Fury stoked through me, sudden and sharp. I'd survived the MM's unforgiving rules, escaped execution, and come here, to the resistance, where we were all supposed to be on the same side. I didn't need Riggins making me feel weak, or anyone else doubting me.

I shook out of Sean's grasp and spun around—right into Chase, half a foot taller and broader even with his shoulders hunched forward. Quite a pair they were, like my own personal bodyguards. I should have been grateful for their help, but instead felt small, too in need of their protection.

"I'll talk to Riggins," said Chase. "He doesn't know when to quit."

"It's fine. He's just messing around." My voice was too thin to be believable, though, and I could feel the terror and the emptiness pushing back from behind my thin veil of control. It had been this way since I'd learned of my mother's murder. Sometimes the wall felt thicker, sometimes I felt stronger, but it was all an illusion. It could break through at a moment's notice, just as it was threatening to now.

Chase took a step forward. "Look," he said, leaning down so that our eyes were level. "We don't have to stay here. We can catch the next transport to the safe house. Put all this behind us." His voice was filled with hope.

"Not yet. You know that." We had to find Rebecca first; if I hadn't blackmailed her and Sean into helping me run away, they would still be together, and she wouldn't have been hurt. I could still hear the baton coming down on her back as the soldiers dragged her away.

"You guys go on. I'll catch up later." I cleared my throat. My walls were cracking. Chase sighed, and after Sean's prompting followed him down to breakfast.

Before the despair could take over, I fled down the corridor toward the supply room. It didn't matter if I skipped rations; the hollowness inside had nothing to do with hunger. It wasn't until the hallway was quiet that I remembered that Wallace had assigned Chase to clear the empty office building next door, that he was leaving the Wayland Inn without me. Even if he would be off the main streets, the thought of him out there alone made me sick.

BY midmorning I'd rearranged the boxes of used clothing and boots to clear space for the new shipment. I'd stacked the toilet paper into columns and consolidated ammunition into four large cardboard boxes. The small silver cartridges I'd learned belonged to our stolen 9MM's were running low, and I made note to remind Wallace of that later.

The uniform boxes stayed against the back wall, untouched.

"You put the cans in alphabetical order."

I jumped back when Billy appeared in the doorway, brows arching beneath his shaggy hair, a Horizons bottle of bleach and a shredded sponge in each hand. I pointed him toward the metal rack where I'd moved the cleaning supplies. He'd recently switched hand-me-down jeans to a pair that was too big, and I spun away as the waistband dropped below his hips.

When I turned back, he was attempting to tape them in place.

"Stop," I said, unable to hold back a laugh. "There's a belt. Over there. By the uniforms."

"You put the clothes in alphabetical order, too?"

I grinned. "Give me time." I sobered as he made his way over to the crates, one hand holding his pants in place.

"Um, Billy?" I stayed back a few steps. "I heard there might be rats in there." I was pretty sure Riggins was just being a jerk, but it couldn't hurt to see if he'd been lying.

"There are," said Billy. "Why? Did one bite you?"

I cringed. "No, I just . . . thought I saw one, that's all," I lied.

"Oh, hang on." He backed out the door, smiling broadly. The hall was quiet—the night shift was sleeping, and most of the day shift was out on assignment. Billy's feet slapped obnoxiously all the way down to his room.

He returned a few minutes later holding Gypsy, the mangy stray cat he'd pulled out of the stairwell last week. She was mostly black with missing clumps of hair on her hindquarters, but less emaciated than before.

"She's letting you hold her." She'd done nothing but hiss and scratch for days, and on cue she began to meow furiously until Billy dropped her on the floor.

"Rats, Gypsy," he said. "Yummy rats."

Gypsy didn't look so different from a rat herself, and when she curled around my calf I stifled the urge to jerk away.

"She likes you," he said.

I offered a weak smile.

Other footsteps came from the hallway, these slower and heavier, and I rushed toward the door hoping Chase and Sean had returned from clearing the building next door. Instead, I came face-to-face with Wallace, the handheld radio now tucked in his front pocket. He must have seen my face fall because he cocked his head to the side and said, "Don't look so happy to see me."

"No word from next door?" I asked as Billy joined us. The new belt worked wonders.

Wallace shook his head. "Did you want to go check?"

Yes. The word was simple, the building was only next

door, but the word stuck on my tongue. As Billy offered to escort, I shifted from foot to foot. The thought of Chase in danger, or even Sean, forced my decision, but before I could answer, Wallace had moved on.

"Billy, if you're done scrubbing the toilet I need you on the mainframe." Though his mouth was set, Wallace's eyes betrayed his pride. Billy had assembled a makeshift scanner from pieces the guys had picked up outside the base's incinerators. A small television screen had been rigged to show the MM bulletins and lists of Statute violators in cryptic black-and-white type—it was the most use I'd seen out of a TV since the end of the War.

"Right. I'm searching for news on the sniper," Billy told me importantly.

Outside on the street, a dog barked. I chewed the inside of my cheek.

Someone had murdered two FBR soldiers last month, in March, and then disappeared without a shred of evidence. Two weeks ago the sniper had struck again in Nashville: a soldier outside a Horizons distribution warehouse. Wallace was trying to find out his identity so that we might protect him, but I didn't like the idea of bringing such a high-profile criminal back to the Wayland Inn. Not when the MM was on a manhunt.

"Anything new come up?" I asked.

"Nothing." Wallace looked past me, out the dirty window behind the uniform crates. "Local news says the FBR is close to solving the case, but they've been saying that for weeks."

The radio reports we monitored made it clear they were chasing their tails.

"There's nothing new on your friend either. I looked this morning," Billy added, cheeks flaming. He'd been helping Sean and me search the mainframe for any rehab centers in Chicago where the MM might have sent Rebecca, but our searches kept coming up blank. Even Chase, who had trained there during his time as a soldier, could not recall such a place. I was seriously beginning to doubt that the tip I'd gotten in the Knoxville holding cells had been reliable.

"Go," prompted Wallace. "And it's about time you got a belt."

Billy turned to leave, grumbling, but before he did he spun back and playfully swatted Wallace across the face. A second later he was sprinting down the hall, cackling.

My mouth fell open.

"Little bastard," said Wallace affectionately, rubbing his stubbly jaw. I doubt he would have responded the same to Houston or Lincoln, or anyone else for that matter.

Gypsy hopped onto the crate of uniforms below the window and curled into a ball, assessing us with her yellow eyes. In the silence, I became acutely aware that Wallace and I had not spoken alone in weeks.

"I . . . I think we're low on bullets," I said. "I put what we had in these boxes. . . ."

"Come talk with me, Miller."

Wallace turned without another word and left me trailing him toward the stairway door. The moment came when I thought he was testing me, leading me outside to see if I'd really go, but he didn't; he shoved through the exit and went up, boots clanging on the metal steps.

Worry gnawed at me. I tried to anticipate the reason for this meeting; I didn't know any more about the sniper, and I hadn't been the only one to voice my doubt about Sean's new recruit—Riggins had spoken up, too. Surely I wasn't in trouble for that.

My thoughts turned to the MM base. There was no way I knew to break back in; we simply didn't have the manpower to take the entrances, and soldiers—even those in disguise—couldn't pass through the exit by the crematorium where Chase and I had escaped. Wallace knew this. He and I had beaten the topic into the ground, until the conversation had stalled and left us both disappointed.

Was that what he wanted to talk to me about now, my lack of contribution? My failure to save the others in the detention center? Because I knew I'd let them down. Wallace, the resistance, those prisoners I'd left behind. They haunted me, and maybe I deserved it. I'd saved Chase and myself, knowing others in the neighboring cells would die.

I tried to swallow, but my throat had tied in knots.

Wallace shoved through the heavy metal door on the tenth floor, flooding the shadowed interior with light. It wasn't a bright day, but on the fourth floor we kept the curtains drawn, and my eyes took several moments to adjust. When they did I scanned the familiar cement patio, empty but for the cave-like entrance to the stairs and the park bench behind it, and the resistance guard overlooking the streets to the west.

The air wasn't fresh, but it wasn't stagnant like inside. Breathing it raised my awareness, made me feel exposed. Being here with Wallace didn't feel as safe as when I came up here alone.

He strode toward the edge at the front of the building, to the elevated lip of red brick that stood like a battlement from an old-time castle. I followed him into the shadows, glancing up at the towering empty office building adjacent to the Wayland Inn. Though the structures didn't touch, they were close, and I wondered if Chase could see me now from one of those high, dark windows.

"Look, out there on the freeway," Wallace said, pointing around the neighboring building past the slums that had once been a college to the raised highway by the river. A few scattered cars traveled there, but the haze made it impossible to tell if they were cruisers.

"There are people in those cars who can go anywhere they'd like. People who aren't starving and freezing like the folks in the Square. Men that still have jobs. Girls that still go to school." He leaned down to rest his elbows on the ledge and glanced my way.

I felt a sudden trembling in my chest, cracked with a blow of all those things I'd been trying to shut out. Home. Beth with her wild red hair. I'd be a senior this year, graduating in June.

"Sometimes I come up here and watch them. I don't know,

I guess I come up here to feel sorry for myself." He sighed. "I never knew how good I had it, back before all this. How easy it was to walk down the street without worrying someone might turn you in."

"Yeah." I kept my eyes on the cars.

"You know what I always realize?" he asked.

I shook my head.

"I feel sorrier for them."

A siren cut through the air, drawing my attention to the alabaster fortress, crouching within its high stone walls twenty miles to the east. The FBR base.

"What do you mean?" I asked.

"My house may not look like much, but it keeps my family safe. I've got food in my gut and a roof over my head." He lifted his arms out before him, like he was holding something precious. "But more importantly, I'm free, Miller. All those poor folks who follow the rules are trapped in a prison of fear."

"You're *not* free," I said, frustrated. "You're trapped, just like they are. I don't like it, but it's the truth. The only way you're really safe is if you're compliant."

But the words suddenly sounded hollow. How many hours had my mother and I spent applying for meal passes, doing paperwork to apply for the mortgage freeze? Bending over backward because every job in the city discriminated against my mother's tarnished record? And what good did it do? They took her, they *killed* her, anyway.

"*Safe*," Wallace repeated. "That's the same thing Scarboro said when he became president." When he sensed my concern he smiled. "Don't worry, more than half the country believed him. It's what people do when they've been through war."

A memory filtered through from another time. My mother, balking at the television while the man on the screen promised safety through unity. Freedom through conformity. That traditional family values and a streamlined faith would restore our country to greatness.

I rubbed the heels of my hands into my forehead, feeling like I had so many times over the past month: too full of something, too empty to name it. Whatever small part of me believed that I still belonged in the same world I'd grown up in, the world with Beth and school and home, had been cut loose. I could never go back.

"What do I do now?" I asked feebly, twisting the gold ring—the fake wedding ring Chase had stolen for me—around my ring finger. I didn't need to wear it if I never left, but I did anyway.

Wallace sighed. "You figure out what matters. And you do something about it."

CHAPTER
2

THE field team returned to the Wayland Inn late in the afternoon. From the back stairway window I watched three men who'd left early yesterday in ragged street clothes emerge from the cab of a Horizons distribution truck in taupe, one-piece uniforms, complete with the Horizons logo spanning the widths of their shoulders, and efficiently unload boxes from the back. The engine never stopped running, and they drove away the instant the task was completed.

Cara, having stowed away in the back of the truck with the boxes, was the first to return to the fourth floor. She carried nothing, breezing in with a satisfied smirk, tugging the kinks out of her dyed black hair. I knew she kept it braided in town as an attempt to appear more conservative, but I doubted it worked; Cara could never, even in jeans and a men's sweatshirt, be accused of looking plain. It didn't take listening to the running commentary of thirty males to pick up on that.

She didn't say hello, even though she'd clearly seen my wave. Instead, I was acknowledged with no more than an arched brow as she ducked into a room and left me standing, with my hand still awkwardly half-raised, in the hallway.

Several of the others had surfaced by that time and were making their way toward the stairs to help unload. I approached the surveillance room, noting the familiar stack of handheld radios and batteries strewn across the center table. Against the back wall were Billy's patchwork computer and a black receiver board, yanked from the incinerator pile outside the base. Cara and Wallace stood beside them, speaking in hushed tones.

As her cool gaze found mine, I was reminded of our first moments within the resistance headquarters, when she'd recognized Chase and me by name. I knew it was because she listened to hacked MM radio signals religiously—at that point the MM had been tracking us for days already—but I couldn't shake the feeling that she, and maybe Wallace, too, had somehow been waiting for us.

I hustled toward the supply room to inventory the new provisions.

SIXTEEN boxes of canned food. Two boxes of liquid soap. Washrags. Clean Towels. Flats of bottled water. Matches. All in all, it was a jackpot. Of course, Wallace would review what I'd inventoried, and determine what we would siphon back into the community, but for now the mood was celebratory.

I worked alone, comforted by the sounds of the others playing poker in the hall. It distracted me from the fact that Chase and Sean had yet to return.

"Did you see the present I brought you?" Cara swung into the room, an enormous bleached sweater hanging carelessly off one shoulder. Somehow, she even looked pretty in that.

"Not unless it was soap." I smiled, trying not to sound as guarded as I felt. For weeks I'd been playing nice, attempting to make an ally of the only other girl here, but her mood swings didn't make it easy. She rolled her eyes and tipped a stack of smaller boxes so that they spilled out over the floor.

"Hey!" I jumped forward to right them.

Beneath those she'd overturned was another box that I had yet to sort. She peeled back the cardboard and lifted a pleated navy skirt.

A punch of memories: the reformatory, the last time I'd seen Ms. Brock, the headmistress, preparing to punish me after she'd ordered soldiers to beat Rebecca. The sound of the baton striking my roommate's back as she demanded to know what had become of Sean.

I fixed the fallen boxes, lining up the corners perfectly.

Like everywhere else, the Sisters of Salvation had gradually infiltrated the city's charity scene. They were what another Article violator had once called the MM's *answer to women's liberation,* and ran the soup kitchens here, the orphanages, even the school system.

An unexpected tremor of excitement passed through me. Cara could wear this out into the community on assignment. *I* could wear it out. Sisters could go places civilians couldn't, just like the guys in the resistance who wore stolen soldier and Horizons uniforms. It was the first time I'd seriously considered leaving the Wayland Inn, and it felt liberating. Empowering.

But mostly impossible. I couldn't do the kinds of missions Cara did. I'd already been caught. The next time I wouldn't get the luxury of a needle full of strychnine like the condemned soldiers in the holding cells at the base. I'd get a bullet in the head.

"See, now you can play dress up with your boy toy," Cara said with a plastic smile.

Her words brought on a sudden surge of humiliation. I was about to say something I'd probably regret later when Billy's shouts from the radio room intervened.

"Sniper! *Sniper!*"

We were both out of the room in a shot, bolting two doors down to where the guys playing cards had gathered. Everyone shoved at one another, trying to get closer to the confiscated switchboard Wallace was manning.

"Shut up!" Wallace roared. As the chatter died, the serious voice of Janice Barlow, a local reporter for an MM-run news station, filled the room.

". . . *indicate that the four soldiers were shot several hours after curfew, from a distance of at least one hundred yards. FBR sources revealed early this morning that they are very close to finding the Virginia Sniper, whom they believe to be responsible for a running tally of seven soldiers.*"

"Yeah, right!" called one of the guys who'd returned with Cara a few hours ago. He was immediately shushed by the two brothers who'd rationed out breakfast.

". . . is the second shooting in the state of Tennessee, the first being fifty miles south, in Nashville. In response to the crisis, the Federal Bureau of Reformation has lowered the local curfew to five P.M. until the culprit can be apprehended. Citizens are reminded to observe curfew hours and report any violations of the Statutes to the crisis line or a nearby FBR officer."

At her pause, the hall erupted in cheers. A twitchy guy not much taller than me spun Cara around in an impromptu dance. *Four*, people kept saying. *Four*, when the sniper had only hit one at a time previously. I tried to grin, but my insides were stretched taut.

"Quiet! Quiet, there's more!" Billy hollered. He leaned down while Wallace adjusted the volume.

". . . determined that the bomb, made of household appliances, was a direct attempt on the Chief of Reformation's life. Chancellor Reinhardt's condition is stable, and he is recovering at an undisclosed location. Of the attack, the president made this statement late yesterday afternoon."

There was another pause, but this time no one spoke. No one dared to breathe. An attack on the president's right-hand man made the work of the sniper seem suddenly insignificant.

The reception grew fuzzy as a man's voice filled the room.

"The work of radicals does not, and will not, represent the majority. What happened yesterday to Chancellor Reinhardt is a test. Of our faith. Of our morality. And of our freedom. It is a chance for us to prove our unity and bind together as one country. To finally purge the hedonism that led to our fall, to dispel the chaos that gripped us during the War, and to remove every *terrorist that stands between us and a safe, peaceful future. No one said reformation would be easy, but have faith when I say that it is possible, and it is right."*

It had been a long time since I'd heard him speak. My mother and I had watched him on TV during the early years of the War when he'd been a state senator. I could picture him now, a tuft of silver hair atop an enormous forehead, jaw drawn tight with concern, and a gaze so piercing, it seemed to reach straight through the television into our living room. My mom used to say you could never trust someone who talked to a camera like it was a real person.

Later, I'd learn in school that Scarboro's movement, Restart America, had been around for years, preaching strong traditional morals, censorship, and a removal of the separation between church and state. One Faith, One Family, One Country, had been their motto, one that would later change to One Whole Country, One Whole Family when he was elected president. In his campaign, he'd cited the existing administration's moral weakness for the attack on our nation, and the citizens, desperate for change, had believed him.

He'd always had a cadence to his words. It was almost mesmerizing until you listened to what he was actually saying.

Bind together. Remove every terrorist.

Well, I knew what he meant by terrorist. He meant people like my mother. People like me. Anyone that stood between him and his perfect, compliant world. He'd reduced our country to obedient house pets and unwanted strays, and I had a bad feeling things were about to get a lot worse for us.

Ms. Barlow signed off with the FBR motto: One Whole Country, One Whole Family.

"Someone tried to take out Reinhardt?" Cara finally said. She looked shocked, just like everyone else. I tried to picture the man, but couldn't. He'd come into power post-TV, during President Scarboro's formation of the FBR, to oversee the functions of the soldiers.

"Wonder how he got close enough." There was a definite edge of scheming to Wallace's tone, but he did make a point. The president and his advisors traveled in secrecy, never taking up a permanent residence, never staying anywhere too long. As far as I'd known, they'd done this since the War, when the threat of attack on any politician had been high.

"Who cares, someone did it, that's all that matters!" yelled the guy behind me. The others agreed.

"Next is our move," said Cara. "Now's the time for something big. We've got to hit them while they're limping."

It was all too much: the nodding, the bloodthirsty grins. They were getting swept up in the momentum of a new war.

"Hit them back, and they'll take it out on everyone else!" I shouted above the noise. "You heard the report, they've already extended curfew. We know they're withholding rations. It's only going to get worse."

"Aw, that's sweet," said Cara. "Shouldn't you be making dinner or something?"

I glared at her, fuming while the others laughed.

"Our actions send a message," explained Wallace. He didn't look particularly patient, as he had on the roof.

"What message? Look, we got seven of you? They've got thousands of soldiers to replace each one of them!" My voice grew thin.

"It's not a message to the FBR. It's a message to the people."

I spun toward the door and the low voice I'd recognize anywhere. My gaze swept over Chase quickly. No blood. No bruises. When I found his eyes, that part inside of me that had been clenched in his absence released. *You're back,* I said to him in my mind, and as if he could hear me, he gave a barely discernible nod.

"A message to the people," I repeated, irritated that I was the only one who didn't seem to understand. Sean had elbowed in through the back row to stand beside us.

"It says there are more of us than of them," said Wallace. "That we don't have to take what they give us. That some of us are not afraid."

"You want all those people, who have *nothing,* to fight against men with guns? They'll die." The people in this room, we were different. We'd signed up for this. But what about my friends from home—Beth? Ryan? My mother? There was a time I would have found the thought of them in a place like this outrageous; now it was just sobering.

"They're dying now," Cara pointed out. "If they fight back they won't have nothing, they'll have each other. And that, little girl, is the FBR's biggest fear."

I resented her tone, but Wallace looked positively proud. I remembered what he'd said on the roof about making your own values, but sacrificing yourself for a cause didn't make you realize who you were. It just made you dead.

"No one's doing anything, not yet anyway," said Wallace, in answer to my earlier question. He breathed in through his nostrils, as if annoyed by his own proclamation.

"Come on," Billy whined.

"I mean it," said Wallace as the others settled down. "Much as I want to ride this wave, you know the drill. We hold until Three gives the go-ahead."

I glanced at Chase, but he was looking to me for the same answers. Subtly, I snagged Sean's wrist and pulled him down to my height so that Cara and the others couldn't hear.

"Who's Three?"

Chase edged closer.

"Three's not a who, it's a what," Sean answered. "It's the center of the web—the piece that ties the underground together. All known branches, like this one, report their operations to Three, and Three tells them where to go from there."

"How do they make reports?" Chase asked.

"Through the carriers," said Sean.

"The carriers work for Three?" It made sense that they would be connected to some branch of the resistance, rather than risking their necks on their own.

Sean shook his head. "It's all top secret, hush-hush stuff. The way I heard it, the carriers don't know *who* works for Three, they just collect messages when they go to the safe house and deliver them back to their local setup. The carriers, they're more like independent contractors."

"So Wallace reports to someone." I'd thought the Wayland Inn acted on its own, independent from the rest of the *underground*, as Sean had called it. Now that I knew differently, the whole operation seemed a little bit sturdier, like we weren't a tiny boat floating on the ocean anymore.

"Thanks for the vote of confidence," Wallace whispered beside me, making me jump. "But yes, believe it or not even I report to someone. As all of *you* report to someone," he called out for the rest to hear. "And in case you've all forgotten, we've still got packages to deliver, people to feed, and a recruit to keep tabs on."

Cara groaned. "Can we *please* stop being so serious? We've just been upgraded to terrorists! We should be celebrating!"

And just like that it was over.

It shocked me, the elation over the sniper and the assassination attempt on the Chief of Reformation, but more the way everyone returned to business as usual, as if someone had pressed the off button. That they weren't thinking, as I was, of reinforcing our security, or avoiding the Square or anywhere crowded with soldiers.

They moved on. Maybe that was how they survived this life.

Wallace announced dinner and the others dispersed, leaving the radio room empty but for Chase and me. He leaned against the outer wall, looking distracted, and as I settled beside him I became aware that we hadn't been alone together for some time. As the new guy, he was often assigned the late shift securing the perimeter. Technically, we shared a room, but that didn't mean we saw much of each other.

Now that the others were gone, his guard lowered, and he rubbed his eyes with the heels of his hands, the exhaustion from his double shift breaking through. But something else was bothering him, I could tell.

"What is it?" I asked.

His eyes rested for a moment on my collarbone, and I realized the men's shirt I wore had slouched down to reveal the top of my shoulder. I righted it slowly, and he blinked and glanced away.

"Probably nothing, it's just . . ." He shrugged. "When I was fighting at the base in Chicago, there was this medic. An old guy, officer age. They'd send me to see him if I got knocked around too much, and he'd always hold up three fingers and say, 'How many fingers do you see?' I told him once it didn't work if he always held up the same number, and he said, 'Three's the only number you need to remember, sergeant.' I figured he was crazier than me."

Chase had only once spoken to me about when the officers had made him fight at the base, and even then he'd told the story from another's perspective. I knew his time in the FBR was something he wanted to forget, especially his stretch at the Chicago base, so I'd never pushed him. I'd always figured if he wanted to tell me, he would.

Now my curiosity was piqued. Could the resistance have infiltrated the MM? If so, we'd have access to FBR plans, strategies, supply shipments. . . . It seemed too much to hope for.

"What happened to the medic?" I asked.

"I don't know. They stopped the fights after I"—he stretched his shoulders back, as though his chest had suddenly constricted—"after I agreed to stop writing you. I didn't have much need for a medic after that."

He glanced over to me, and for a moment, our gazes locked. It made me remember things I didn't want to remember. All the letters I'd written that had gone unanswered. The pressure he'd gotten for fraternizing with any girl, much less one with a noncompliant mother. How they'd made him arrest her anyway.

How he'd witnessed her murder.

I believed him, that he couldn't have saved her. But even though it was useless, sometimes I wondered if he'd really done everything he possibly could—everything *I* would have done. Thoughts like this led me nowhere, of course, and only made it harder to be close to him. He was both the cause of my pain and the cure.

"So how are you?" He cleared his throat. "Really," he added.

I felt my skin stretch tight at his words, like all the anger and fear was expanding. It was pressing at my lungs, making it hard to breathe. And he must have felt it, too, because he pushed off the wall and stared a hole through his boots.

"Hungry," I said. "What do you think it'll be tonight?"

A beat passed. Then another.

"Pizza," he said finally, and I breathed out a sigh of relief that he'd changed the subject. "Maybe spaghetti. And ice cream for dessert." The corner of his mouth quirked up.

"Sounds delicious," I said. Canned ham and beans were more likely, but sometimes it was easier to pretend.

"WHO *wants ice cream sundaes?*"

I buried my head under the pillow. Was she seriously going to pretend that we had ice cream, when we didn't even have a freezer?

"Too bad. I guess I'll have to eat it all myself."

I groaned. The blank tablet of paper lay beside me, untouched. How many letters had I written to Chase in the last six months? Twenty? Thirty? And not one response. Not to say he'd arrived in Chicago and started training. Not to say he missed me.

He'd promised he'd write, and I'd believed him.

I shouldn't have.

I ignored my grumbling stomach as long as I could, but facing her was inevitable. I pushed off my bed and dragged myself into the kitchen.

She sat at the table, hands folded neatly behind a heaping bowl of instant mashed potatoes, the powdered kind that came out of a blue box. There were two spoons, one directly before her, the other in front of my seat. She'd fashioned some kind of triangle-shaped sailor hat from a brown paper bag and placed it regally on her head.

"You have got to be kidding me," I said.

"Oh, did you want some ice cream? I'm not sure there's enough to share," she taunted.

Just to humor her, I sat. I couldn't look her in the face though; the hat was too ridiculous.

She lifted her spoon, filling it with a huge dollop of mashed potatoes, and stuck it in her mouth, making all sorts of satisfied noises.

I smiled.

After a moment I picked up my spoon. Took a bite.

"Tell me that's not the best ice cream you've ever had," she said.

"It's not the best ice cream I've ever had," I said, trying hard to swallow without giggling.

A look of disbelief spread across her face. Then she slung a spoonful of mashed potatoes across the table, and splattered them all across my shirt.

"HEY."

I jolted up straight in my chair as Sean snapped his fingers in my face. My chest still ached with the memory. If I had known my mother would be dead three months later, I never would have fought with her over something stupid, or yelled at her when she'd gotten a citation. I would have packed our stuff and we would have run, and we'd both be at the safe house now.

I tried to hold on to the sound of her laughter, but it blended with the others down the hall. Cara's soprano rose above the rest. They were probably playing poker again, competing for something someone had picked up in town. Candy maybe, or cigarettes. I cringed. They might as well invite the whole base over with all the noise they were making.

Billy pushed away from the computer, shoving back his hair absently. I'd zoned out while we were scanning the mainframe for more information on girls' reformatories in Chicago. There wasn't much for me to do while Billy hacked into the server and Sean scanned the lists.

"Go to bed," Sean told me, squinting at the screen.

"I'm fine," I said, yawning. "And anyway, you're not the boss of me anymore."

He tossed me a pointed look over his shoulder. "Was I ever the boss of you?" When I grinned, he said, "That's what I thought. Go away, you're making me tired."

I did what he said, but only because I wasn't helping any. I took one of the candles; its wavering yellow light made the walls look that much more decrepit. When I got to my room, I paused outside, listening through the door for the sound of Chase's breathing. The noise in the hall seemed amplified; the guys that had left before curfew returned. Houston and Lincoln were arguing about a cute girl they'd seen in the Square. Someone was singing in the shower. The walls were way too thin.

I tried to imagine Chase lying on the bed, but the thought made me nervous. I wondered if I should go inside at all. He didn't sleep well—I knew the nightmares still plagued him, though he never talked about them. I could crash in the supply room and let him catch up on some much needed rest.

Before I could change my mind, I inched the door open and slipped inside, careful to cover the flame with my hand. It didn't take long for my eyes to adjust, to find him stretched out over the moth-eaten velvet chair, placed strategically in front of the window—the same window I'd escaped from when he'd told me about my mother. He'd left our blanket folded at the foot of the sagging mattress, empty in the center of our tiny space.

Empty, just like me. Lost without my mom, without any lead on Rebecca, without any sense of purpose here.

The yellow light was small and didn't grant much visibility, but even so I could tell he wasn't moving. Barely even breathing. He was too still to be anything but awake, and I matched his stillness, feeling his eyes graze over me, conscious of my breathing, too shallow, and the hot wax that dripped on my thumb.

I blew out the candle.

Crossing the room, I placed it on the window ledge, and before I knew what I was doing, I'd climbed into his lap. My palms searched through the dark to grasp his face, and my thumbs raced over his cheekbones, rough from not shaving, to his lips, parted and soft. There was no time to question how he'd respond, or think of how we'd barely touched these last few weeks. I needed this, needed him, and he needed me as well. His arms surrounded me and pulled me close, and then I was kissing him and he was kissing me back, his lips pressed hard into mine. He was alive and warm, smelling vaguely of sweat and mint toothpaste, and I told myself his touch would make me warm, too.

I squeezed my eyes closed and kissed him with that kind of pressure, begging him to make me forget, to feel anything beyond this bottomless, irreconcilable black hole that had torn open inside of me. His teeth skimmed my jaw, nipped my ear, and the groan he drew from my throat made his own breath stutter. He crushed me against him then, closer, impossibly close, scooting to the edge of the chair. I thought he meant to lead us to the bed, but he paused, and in those damp, trembling moments, something between us shifted.

I clung to him. Like a strong wind might whip him away.

And he must have sensed it, because I could feel his fists knot in the back of my shirt and his ragged breaths heat my neck.

"I'm sorry," he said, voice strained. And then again, "I'm sorry," only this time more desperately.

He lifted me and placed me on the edge of the bed, and then backed away so fast he stumbled over his boots. I didn't understand. All I knew was that the emptiness inside of me was filling with something else, a great impenetrable sadness. Cold and unyielding. It was growing fast now, seeping through every part of me.

I couldn't see his face in the dark, couldn't read his expression. I didn't have much time to anyway. A second later he left and closed the door behind him.

I fell back on the bed, my lips swollen and hot, my eyes burning with stubborn tears that refused to fall. I drew my knees into my chest and tried to make myself as small as possible. After a while I pulled the blanket over me, but all the heat in the room had left when Chase had.

I'm sorry, he'd said. Just as he'd said the night he'd told me he couldn't save my mother. I remembered how broken he'd been then, and as I lay awake, I couldn't help wondering if he wasn't still. If either of us would ever really mend.

CHAPTER
3

THE next morning Wallace reported that the MM had set the draft in the Square for that afternoon.

The euphoria of the previous night was absent now; what remained was a hushed anticipation. Some still wanted to take the soldiers by force, but Wallace insisted we not act without Three's orders. Instead, he composed a team—Houston, Lincoln, Cara, and three others—to dissuade the crowd. Scattered voices to object to the MM's control and abuse of power and direct the flow of conversation. Subtle enough not to get Wallace in trouble with Three, but a definite show of resistance, nonetheless.

In holey shirts and ragged jeans, they departed down the long corridor to the stairs. I watched them disappear beneath the red exit sign, unable to shake the feeling that something bad was going to happen. To make matters worse, Riggins was staying back, staffing the radios with Wallace. I'd heard from Billy that our paranoid hallmate was looking for me again, which was ridiculous with everything else going on. I avoided him all the same.

With everyone loitering outside the door, the fourth floor became cramped and tense. The waiting was too much, and before Riggins could start something I escaped to the roof for some fresh air.

I wasn't the only one with that idea. I found Chase sitting alone behind the fire escape on a bench that sank in the center from too much wood rot. When he saw me he rose, thoughts hidden behind a carefully practiced mask. I hated that he could do that; he could save it for the others if he wanted, but not for me. My gaze lowered to the tattered thermal stretched tightly across his chest, and I smoothed down my own shirt in response.

"I thought you were sleeping," I said. "You don't have an assignment right now, right?"

He shook his head.

Tentatively, I moved past him and sat on the bench. After a few seconds he sat beside me, a few inches away. We stared at the base, pristine white buildings cutting through the mid-morning haze twenty miles over the rooftops, and let the minutes tick by.

"Did I do something wrong?" I asked bluntly, and watched his guard drop.

"You? *No.*" He shook his head. "No. Last night . . . I didn't mean . . ." He scratched a hand through his black hair, then laughed awkwardly. "I shouldn't have left."

"Why did you then?" I asked.

He leaned forward, elbows on his knees. The heels of his boots made an audible tapping against the cement.

Fresh air was overrated. I rose to go back downstairs, but he grabbed my hand.

"You're grieving," he blurted. "I didn't want you to think, I don't know, I was taking advantage of you." The words were obviously tied up inside of him, and he sighed, frustrated.

"I think I was the one taking advantage of you." I returned to my seat and looked down, but looked down a little ashamed. I hadn't thought he might feel that way.

He snorted. "In that case, please. Go right ahead."

We both laughed a little at that, but I remembered the way he'd held on to me, just as raw and afraid as I was. I wasn't the only one grieving, and I wasn't the only one who felt the weight of my mother's death between us.

With the air less tense, I wanted to ask him about the building next door and tell him more about the Horizons truck, and the supplies we'd confiscated. Once, talking to him had been as easy as breathing, but things had gotten complicated.

I stood up. "Teach me to fight," I said.

After a moment, he followed, head tilted in curiosity.

"What are you talking about?"

I raised my fists. "To fight," I said, throwing a fake punch. "You know. Fight."

He laughed, and something inside me fluttered.

"You don't need to know how to fight."

I lowered my hands, placed them on my hips. "You're

kidding, right?" We were under constant threat of attack, even here, surrounded by resistance.

"You don't need to fight like that," he clarified, and laughed again. "Unless you're planning on taking up boxing."

I tried not to smile, but it was hard when he was so clearly amused.

"How, then?"

"Well." He took a step closer and my heart stuttered. His hands shot out and gripped my wrists. Not tight enough to hurt, but enough so that I couldn't automatically jerk away. "What's your plan?" His smile had melted.

I struggled for a few moments—trying to bring my fists together, to pull out of his clutches, to turn my body away— but he was too powerful. I conceded with a huff of breath.

"Most people coming for you will be bigger and stronger," he said, moving even closer so that I had to look up to see his face. His chest bumped against mine and I swallowed, feeling every place we connected. "But you're quick. You're not going to beat them in a slugfest, but you can get away if someone grabs you."

"How?"

"Where do you break a chain?" he responded. "Look at me," he said when I glanced down at our hands.

I pictured a metal chain, one link after another. Staring into his brown eyes I answered, "At the weakest link."

"Between my thumb and my fingers is a breaking point." His thumbs rubbed the sensitive skin of my wrists. "Break out."

I took a deep breath, and then as quickly as I could, twisted my wrists and pulled them together, right through the gap in his grip.

I beamed. "Now what?"

"Now you run," he said, grinning back. "But if you can't, go for soft spots. Eyes, ears, mouth, neck . . ." He gestured lower and I averted my gaze. "Like I said, you're quick. Don't think twice. Hit a soft spot and get out."

He grabbed my wrists again, and this time I didn't hesitate. I twisted out, then turned to run, but before I'd made it two steps he'd caught me, his forearm pressed lightly against my neck so that if I moved forward, I'd choke. My hands went straight to his hold, trying in vain to pull it down. His muscles flexed against me, but didn't tighten. My back rested flush against his chest, which was warm and solid, and pressed more firmly against me with each breath.

"Tuck your chin," he whispered. I could feel his lips move against my neck and shivered.

Giving up on moving his arm, I did as he said and burrowed my chin into his muscle. When I'd succeeded on sliding beneath his hold, I could breathe easier, though still not escape.

He told me I could kick back with my heel, drag it down his shin, and stomp on his foot, but when I tried he sidestepped out of the way, pulling me like a rag doll with him.

"Get as much air as you can," he instructed, "then, all at once, shove your hips back and lean forward. It'll throw me off balance."

I breathed in as deeply as I could, and pushed back against him.

It didn't work. We straightened, struggled, and then at some point became still. Every inch of my skin heated. I could scarcely breathe, feeling his heart pound against my shoulder.

"Not fast enough," he said, voice thick.

Though his hold loosened slightly, his forearm stayed pressed to my throat, but the other hand holding it in place lowered, fingers inching down my waist to drag across my stomach. I gasped.

"You can get away any time you want."

I could, but I didn't want to. His nose nuzzled my neck, then drew up behind my ear. My knees weakened, and my eyes drifted closed.

Someone broke through the stairway. The door clanged so hard against the metal stop we both bolted apart.

Sean. He closed the distance between us, his hair disheveled and a wild look on his face.

"Lincoln radioed from the Square," he said. "You should hear this."

One unsteady breath, one last look into Chase's eyes, and I followed.

SEAN didn't hesitate. He flew down the stairs, leaving us scrambling in his wake, the worry over what had happened increasing with each step.

"You two picked a great time to disappear."

"What is it?" I called after him. "What happened? Is someone hurt?" I pictured the faces of those that had left this morning.

"Not us," he said. "Them."

"What?"

We'd reached the fourth floor, and instead of answering, he pushed through into the hallway. It was like stepping into a party. People were cheering; even Riggins had taken on both brothers in a play wrestling match.

He paused when he saw us. There was a strange look on his face as he approached, almost curious, but for the ever-condemning speculation in his glare. I blushed, wondering if he knew what Chase and I had been doing upstairs, and braced for him to say something nasty.

"Where've you two been?" he asked.

"Not now, Riggins," warned Chase. To my surprise, Riggins nodded slowly and backed away.

Billy elbowed in beside us, face flushed. He was carrying Gypsy, who was practically screeching from all the noise. "Can you guys believe it?" The cat sank her teeth into his wrist and he wailed, then dropped her on the floor. She darted away between our legs.

"What's going on?" Chase was not entertained.

Sean led us through the crowd to the surveillance room, where Wallace was pacing from one corner to the other. If not for the grin plastered across his face I would have thought him seriously distressed.

Chase grabbed a radio from the coffee table and tuned it to the right frequency. We held it between us and cupped our hands over our opposite ears to drown out the noise. It was the FBR channel, and a male voice crackled through.

"All units to Market Square. There is a code seven in progress, repeat, code seven. Four soldiers down. Fire taken from above, single action, long-range sniper assault. All units cleared to return fire."

"They've been repeating the same message for the last hour," said Sean.

"The sniper?" I felt the blood rush from my face. "What's a code seven?"

"Code seven is a civilian attack on a soldier." Chase's expression was grim. It seemed like he and I were the only ones who found the event sobering. "Any word on our people?" he asked Wallace.

"Not yet," Wallace said. His grin had faded. "They'll come home when they can."

I closed my eyes. "They're probably right in the middle of this."

I didn't even want to say it, much less visualize it. But it was too late. Maybe we all weren't the best of friends, but I didn't want to see any of them dead.

"These are the risks we take," said Wallace simply.

However much I wanted to argue it, he was right.

"We need to double the perimeter guards," Chase said to Wallace. "Now, before soldiers start digging around the slums and Tent City."

Wallace slowed to a stop and shook his head, as if waking from a dream.

"Very good, Jennings," he said.

SECURITY was increased, as Chase has recommended. Nearly everyone was cleared from the building, assigned to tasks that secured the safety of our refuge. Just a few were left behind, Billy, Wallace, and me. Even Chase was detailed to the motel lobby.

I'd stayed on the fourth floor, itchy since the report that the sniper was so close. I wanted to do something, too, though I didn't know what.

Four hours passed with no movement. I listened to the radio reports, which confirmed that four soldiers had been killed by sniper fire from a rooftop overlooking the Square. A riot had flashed only briefly, and nine civilians had died in the crosshairs. I prayed none of them were our people.

In the fifth hour three of our people returned, smelling strongly of sweat and streaked with grime. They hadn't seen the others, but brought word that the Square had been locked down by soldiers, who'd made everyone lay across the bricks until the rooftops were cleared. Tent City had been over-turned in the search.

In the seventh hour Houston and Lincoln came back. They laughed about how crazy it had been. It was a little too forced maybe, but they laughed.

No one said Cara's name. Not even Billy, who had a hard time keeping his mouth shut.

I grew annoyed with the radio reports. They were running the same message, over and over. The sniper's tally was up to eleven. The highways had been closed, cutting off access in and out of Knoxville to anyone not working for the FBR.

Things had changed—the city, even within the Wayland Inn, felt different.

That night no one said a word at dinner. Not even to complain about the peas, which had gone yellow sometime since they'd been canned.

LATER, I would look back on the next morning's meeting and be able to count a dozen clues that should have made me realize everything was about to change. The way Billy refused to meet my eyes, for instance, or the way Wallace stared at me, lost in thought, and then blew off Riggins when he asked if Cara had called in. The way the radios, which had been covering different channels all night, were all silent.

"Quiet down," Wallace said. His face was a mixture of awe and concern, like he was surprised about something. It made my stomach tighten involuntarily. Wallace was never surprised about anything.

"It's Cara," I heard Lincoln whisper to Houston. His face was ashen, his freckles that much more severe.

"I lost sight of her," said Houston more to himself than anyone else. "Before the shooting even started." He swore, angry with himself.

"She does that, man," said one of the other guys. "Don't worry about it. Cara follows Cara's rules. Doesn't mean anything. She always shows back up."

I cranked my head toward the guy who'd spoken. Not much taller than me, with a patchy beard and a pointed nose, Sykes they called him.

Wallace lifted the handheld radio. "They started looping a new feed about twenty minutes ago," he said. "You're all going to hear it eventually, we might as well get it over with together. As a *family*."

The radio hissed with static as he adjusted it to the right frequency.

A familiar male reporter's voice filled the quiet hall, where the grieving for Cara was threatening to spill over.

". . . *the Bureau's office of intelligence has issued a list of five suspects thought to be in collaboration with the sniper. All bases in Region Two-fifteen have orders to post photos of these individuals in the community and offer rations passes in compensation for legitimate leads. A code one is called into effect for the following fugitives:*

"John Naser, aka John Wright, religious extremist in violation with Article One. Robert Firth, former FBR captain suspected of selling arms to civilians. Patel Cho, political rights activist who escaped capture during Long Distance Explosive Device demonstrations in Red Zone One."

I glanced across the hall to Chase, whose expression had gone grim. I hadn't heard of Long Distance Explosive Devices, but I knew what bombs could do. I'd seen the aftermath on the news as a child.

"Aiden Dewitt, former doctor of medicine, responsible for the murders of five FBR officers during a routine home inspection."

I remembered Dr. Dewitt. He was from Virginia somewhere and had been all the talk at the soup kitchen about five years ago after news of how he'd flipped out had reached my town. Some of the others were whispering; I guess they'd heard of him, too.

"Ember Miller, responsible for multiple counts of treason, escaped the Knoxville FBR base after faking completion approximately four weeks ago. All suspects should be considered armed and dangerous. Ending report now."

You could have heard a pin drop the room was so quiet. The FBR reporter went on to say a few more things—roadside patrols were still posted around the city of Knoxville, more information could be found on the mainframe—then his voice faded into static, in much the same way that I wanted to fade into the floorboards of this cheap motel.

"Wow," I heard Sean say.

"No knee-jerk responses, anyone. Got that?" Several people muttered agreement. "Jennings? Miller?" Wallace asked specifically. "You're both grounded until further notice. That's an order."

Chase was right at my side, ignoring Wallace. He didn't need to say a word. I knew exactly what he was thinking. Tucker Morris, his one-time partner, the soldier who had killed *my mother*, had broken his word and turned me in. It was the only explanation. How I could have trusted him not to rat us out in the first place, even if it did mean his precious career, now seemed a mystery.

A small sound of panic siphoned out of my airway. I blinked and saw a flash of his face—those sadistic green eyes and his perfect, golden hair. The casted arm Chase had broken and the scratches on his neck from my fingernails. I'd had the chance to kill him, to clear our names, to avenge my mother. And I hadn't.

Words echoed in my mind. Words like *coward*.

"Don't worry," Billy said, trying too hard to sound like he knew what he was talking about. "No one's going to believe a girl had anything to do with it."

His words were like a slap to the face, and he wilted under my heated glare. For the first time that morning I noticed Riggins, standing within the surveillance room behind Wallace. His buzzed head was tilted slightly to the side, but when our eyes met he quickly glanced away.

"Here," said Chase, pulling me by the elbow into the privacy of the supply room. He wanted me to sit down, but I couldn't. I navigated through the boxes of stolen uniforms and food to pace near the window. It felt safer to be close to an exit.

"This is crazy, right?" said Houston, following right on Chase's heels.

"Because you would've said so if you'd done those soldiers," finished Lincoln. Billy snuck in behind him, acting as though he needed a towel.

"I've been here for the last month!" I erupted. "How could I *possibly*—"

"Get out," Chase said to them.

"What? I didn't mean . . ." Lincoln shuffled.

"Get. *Out*. You, too, Billy."

"What did *I* do?" Billy whined as Chase pushed him out the door.

Alone, the room seemed too quiet. Too still. So opposite the pull within me to run, or fight, do *something.* Sweat dewed along my hairline. It felt like a great spotlight had been pointed in my direction; it was just a matter of time before every soldier in the city arrived.

Chase watched me warily, like I was a water balloon filled a little too full. It was always terrifying to see my own insanity reflected back in his cautious stance.

"What's a code one?" My voice sounded low and unfamiliar. When he hesitated, I added, "You promised you'd tell me everything. No secrets."

I realized it was a double standard; I hadn't told him everything that had happened with Tucker at the base, but I didn't care. His secret about my mom's murder had been far more destructive than that.

"Code one means a lethal finding. They can fire on suspicion alone. They don't have to question you. They don't have to bring you back to the base for trial with the board."

Everything within me dropped, pressed down by a greater gravity.

"What if they mistake someone else for me?" I whispered, horrified.

Chase grimaced, his copper face pale. "It's bad."

I felt my eyes widen. I could barely breathe. He reached out to touch me but I jerked away.

"Wallace is right. We have to stay," he said between his teeth.

"*We?* I didn't hear your name on that report!"

I didn't know why Tucker hadn't turned him in, too, but

it didn't matter. Everything bad the MM had ever done to us was because we'd stuck together—his torturous fights during basic training, the overhaul in which they'd arrested my mother for an Article 5 violation, the escape from the base—all because we couldn't let each other go. Now, this fact became clearer than ever. If we stayed together, we were going to get each other killed.

I wanted him gone. At that moment I wanted him a thousand miles away from me. I wanted him at the safe house. In Tent City. In some other resistance. I couldn't save my mother, but maybe I could still save him.

"We have to split up," I said.

He scoffed. "Now *that* is a knee-jerk reaction."

"They're looking for me. You heard the report. What?" I asked when he shook his head. "I can make it just fine on my own."

"You . . ." He made a frustrated sound in the back of his throat. "Of course you can. I was there, at the base, remember? You saved my life."

"And left how many more to die?"

It scared me how easy that decision had been. I would have let Tucker kill everyone on that base if it meant Chase would live.

His face darkened, and his forehead scrunched. His thumb kneaded his temple. "There was nothing we could have done for them."

"Nothing? Just like with my mom, right? There was nothing you could have done."

The words lashed out of me, as if they had been tearing at

my insides for weeks. He took a step back, allowing the space between us to grow thick and solid as glass.

I swallowed an unsteady breath and tried to stand tall. "You don't need to look out for me anymore. Things have changed. I'm not who I used to be. I don't even *remember* who I used to be."

He winced as though I'd struck him, and when he tried to come closer I fell back one step, then another. If he touched me I'd fall apart, and now I needed to be stronger than ever.

"Please go away," I said. "*Please*," I begged when his arms reached out to hold me. They dropped to his sides.

Without looking back, he stalked out of the room and disappeared down the hallway.

I COLLAPSED on a box of uniforms. My chest grew so tight I could hardly breathe. I didn't know where Chase had gone, but wherever he was, I could feel his hurt within me, magnified by my hatred for Tucker Morris, who had lied, just like I should have expected. Why was I surprised that he had turned me in? How could I ever expect my mother's murderer to do anything right by me? Now I was stuck here, endangering everyone. I was the gasoline on a pile of sticks, and Tucker, he was the match. It was just a matter of when he would strike.

"Quite a morning."

I jolted up again, ready to tell whoever it was to get lost until I realized it was Wallace, leaning casually against the doorjamb. The handheld radio, which never seemed to leave his grasp, swung, from his hand by the antennae like a pendulum.

My throat was too dry to answer him.

"You know, when you came here I had Billy look you up on the mainframe. I'm curious, do you know the list of accolades they have under your name?" When I didn't answer, he continued. "Attacked a soldier during an overhaul, ran away from a rehab facility, linked to an AWOL with everything from assault with a deadly weapon to terroristic threatening. The files had you both listed as completed—dead. That's no easy feat. The photo doesn't do you any favors, but hey."

The picture had been taken at the reformatory, right after they'd taken my mother. This was not the first time it had been posted on the MM's computer database.

"Your escape from the base was just added recently. Combined with all the rest, it's no wonder they think you're the shooter."

I swallowed over the lump in my throat. A couple days ago I'd felt a strange kinship with Wallace, but now, I felt just as defensive as I had the first time we'd met.

"I'm not a killer," I said. I shouldn't have to explain that to someone who already knew.

"That's not what the Bureau's saying."

"The Bureau lies!" I shot back at him.

"Ah," he said, smiling now. "That feels better, doesn't it?"

He turned to leave, but just before he did he stopped.

"Ember, I didn't need your résumé on the mainframe to tell me you belong here. I knew the second you walked in the door."

He left me fuming. I didn't belong here, not now that every soldier in the region was looking for me. I didn't belong anywhere. I was a danger to our cause, to Chase, to Sean and Billy. I was a danger to myself. It was just a matter of time before the MM caught me.

I spun away from the door and kicked the first thing within reach: a cardboard box. Pale blue blouses and navy pleated skirts toppled over the dirty carpet. The Sisters of Salvation uniforms Cara had brought back.

Frustrated, I grabbed a towel and escaped to the bathroom. I washed my hair with an almost frantic need to cleanse myself. I cut it to chin length, and then dyed it black with a bottle of what looked like molasses beneath the sink. Temporary color, meant to wash out so no roots would show and draw the attention of those looking for such frivolous behavior. I knew it mattered little. They had to know my appearance was subject to change, and even with a pseudonym, my photo from the reformatory was going to make it to print. Still, I had to do *something*.

I looked in the mirror at my altered reflection. At the big brown eyes that looked so much like my mother's, and the ski-slope nose we shared. I wished now, more than ever, that I could talk to her.

"YOU *can't serve them first," the man complained. He looked like every other displaced businessman pounding the streets for work: glasses askew, tie loose, collared shirt untucked. He had a canvas tote bag slung over his shoulder and was pointing to a sheet of paper while he yelled at the soup kitchen attendant.*

"*See? Just look at it. That's right, tilt your head down, that's a good girl.*"

The woman behind the counter looked like she might cry. I was five people behind the man, but the line had spread out when he'd raised his voice, and now everyone was listening.

I watched my mother hustle over from her volunteer position, outside the cold truck holding the perishable foods. She wiped her hands on her apron.

"What's the problem, sir?" I stiffened at her tone; it was generally one step before she said something snappy.

"Oh, thank God. Someone reasonable. Look, these guys are up front getting the same rations as a family. Like they're a family."

My mother's glance flickered to the two young men to her right. One was pulling at the other's shoulder, saying "Come on, let's just go, okay?" The other was red in the face and shaking his head.

"And?" Mom asked.

The man snorted. "And clearly they're not. Look right here. Article Two. Whole families are to be considered one man, one woman, and children. All other combinations are not to be considered under the title family," he air-quoted, "and should receive no tax, occupation, education, or health benefits otherwise."

"Ah. The Moral Statutes." She took the paper, and the man nodded righteously to those around him. I glared at his back while my mother read. "I don't see anything about not receiving meal rations," she said finally.

I froze. I willed her to close her mouth. This man wasn't a soldier, but he could easily report her if he wanted. He could jump over the table and attack her if he wanted.

The man laughed, then realized my mother wasn't joking. The

two men in question went still. I pushed my way to the front of the line, not sure what I would do if he flipped out.

"Clearly that's implied," he said.

"Clearly not," she answered, leaning forward over the table. "Let me tell you what is implied. Respect. And if that bothers you, I would be happy to recommend another soup kitchen which accommodates people who are obviously better than the rest of us."

My face flushed, some with fear, mostly with pride. It filled me up, that pride. She was so alive and powerful just then—the look on her face daring him to say another word. I felt my face, so like hers, mimic that expression. I thought of checking it in the mirror when I got home to make sure I had it right.

The man turned, as if to stomp away, but then grimaced and returned to his place. My mother was the one to deliver his rations.

"MILLER, don't be such a girl." Sean beat his fist against the door, snapping me from my trance. "You'll be lynched if you hog the john much longer."

I swallowed a deep breath, knowing I couldn't hide forever, and pushed through. Sean's face changed when he saw me; he blinked in surprise.

"Who the hell are you?" he said when he recovered. "I'm looking for this brunette, sort of short and moody, disappeared in there about an hour ago."

I leaned past him and searched the hallway for Chase, but he wasn't among those loitering outside Wallace's office. My heart lurched at the thought of how we'd parted.

"So," Sean said carefully. "Pretty crazy, everything that's going on."

"Yep."

"Want to talk about—"

"Nope."

He hid a smirk in a well-timed cough. "Becca says if girls don't talk about their feelings they keel over dead or something." He waved one hand flippantly through the air, and I nearly laughed at how well my old roommate had him trained.

"I'm not most girls."

"Too bad," he said, slinging an arm over my shoulders. "I always wondered what that would look like, death by emotional overload. Sounds brutal."

"And messy," I agreed, glad he was around, even if I didn't feel like talking. I changed the subject. "Any news on your recruit?"

He seemed equally glad for the switch. "He's still alive apparently. I'll bring him in tomorrow."

I nodded now wondering if this new recruit might have information on Tucker, or why he turned me in.

"Billy says he thinks there's resistance in Chicago," he added with more enthusiasm. "He found some FBR wanted lists for the region. Most of the guys are suspected of 'terrorist activity.'" He air-quoted the words.

It relieved me some that there were things I had to do. We had to find Rebecca. Somehow, even with my name smeared all over the FBR report, I had to break into a town with the biggest base in the country. Which involved walking outside of this hotel, getting through the blocked highways, and not getting shot.

No problem.

"How do we find them?" I asked.

He shook his head, suddenly tired again. "I'm working on that part. In the meantime, Wallace called a meeting. He's waiting for you—Chase is already there."

So Sean had come to find me rather than Chase. I probably deserved that.

Wallace's room was only two doors down on the right. Cautiously, I followed Sean through the entry, which gave way to a low-ceilinged room that seemed a lot bigger than mine without the bed. The walls were lined with overflow contraband—weapons and damaged electronics mostly—and several mismatched chairs had been dragged in to join the moth-eaten couch. They arced around a dinged-up coffee table cluttered with batteries, half-burned candles, and ammunition. The ranks were already assembled. Houston and Lincoln were there, as were Riggins, Billy, Wallace, and half a dozen others.

And Chase. His jaw fell slack when he registered my presence. I smoothed down my short, black bob self-consciously, and tried to stand a little straighter. When Lincoln whistled at me, Chase bit his knuckles and looked away.

"Congratulations, Ms. Miller," said Wallace. "If I hadn't already assigned latrine duty to Billy for the rest of his life, the job would now be yours."

I chewed my cheek, but didn't feel like apologizing. Lincoln pointed at Billy and laughed.

"We have ourselves a unique opportunity," Wallace started. "Ms. Miller has magically reappeared on the mainframe. Now, we can let this opportunity pass us by, or we can do something about it."

I had a bad feeling about that word: *opportunity*.

"I want to send Ember out into the city," Wallace said.

CHAPTER
4

"*WHAT?*" Chase jumped from his seat, the muscles in his neck twitching. In contrast, I went absolutely still.

"It's not an order, it's a recommendation," Wallace continued calmly. "But before answering, know that this may be the biggest chance we've had to prove to those blue bastards that there are people brave enough to stand against them."

"They'll know who she is," said Chase. His hands had formed into fists. "Her photo's already being posted."

"Exactly," said Wallace. "What better ID than the FBR's own mug shot?"

It took a moment for me to realize that the point was for me to be recognized, to show that I'd escaped, and lived, and was fighting back, unafraid. It seemed so contrary to everything Chase had taught me while on the run.

Out of the chaos in my head, I pictured my mother, standing up to that man at the soup kitchen.

"What would this entail?" I heard myself say.

Chase turned to stare incredulously at me.

A smirk lifted Wallace's unshaven face. "Nothing unusual. Same mission I would have sent Riggins and Banks on tomorrow. We've got a package in Tent City that needs to be delivered to the checkpoint. No fancy speeches, no dramatic unveiling. Just let a couple of people see you."

"What's the package's name?" I asked. "It's a person, right?"

The room grew stiff with discomfort as eyes darted and people shifted. Putting a name on the package made him real. Made him live and breathe, and die, if we weren't careful. I wasn't so sure I wanted to know after all.

Wallace hesitated, caught off guard. "She didn't say. All we know is that the carrier needs to get her over the lines to the Red Zone ASAP."

There were many Red Zones declared after the War, but the Eastern Seaboard was the first and by far the largest evacuated space in the country.

"Soldiers after her?" Riggins asked.

"Probably," said Wallace. "You'd know a thing or two about that, right, Miller?"

I swallowed.

"No," said Chase adamantly. "There's a code one in effect. Anyone can turn her in for a food pass. And once a soldier sees her . . ."

"You never seem so worried when Wallace sends me out," said Riggins.

Chase ignored him.

"There's always a code one in effect for people like us," said Wallace. "Besides, I'd wrap her up with everyone we can spare. Banks has to tail that recruit in the Square, so he'd be with her. Houston and Lincoln can go, too. Riggins will follow."

As if leaving the Wayland Inn wasn't dangerous enough, Riggins, the one person I was sure hated me, would be assigned to keep me safe. Great.

"I don't do Tent City," said Sean. He was watching me warily through the corner of his eye.

"And I don't wash windows," said Wallace. "Tomorrow you will."

Chase leaned toward Wallace, but spoke loudly enough that we could all hear.

"Don't do this."

Wallace scraped a hand over his scruffy jaw. "You'd rather hide your whole life? Waste away here?"

"Isn't that what *you're* doing?" Chase countered. "Why don't you ever leave, Wallace? Is your life so much more valuable than hers?"

An electric silence filled the room. My cheeks burned, as though Chase's outburst had been my own. No one challenged Wallace like that, even if the point he made was true.

"That's bordering on insubordination," said Riggins.

"You're damn right it is." Wallace stepped up to Chase, shorter, narrower, but unafraid. "Someone's got to stay behind, Jennings. That's the way this works. You think you're man enough for the job, by all means, sit back here and wait. See how easy it is."

"I'm in." I didn't realize I'd said it until Sean whipped his head toward me.

"You're kidding, right?" he asked under his breath. "A new haircut doesn't make you bulletproof, Ember."

"When do we leave?" I was beginning to tremble in anticipation. I wanted to go as soon as possible so I couldn't change my mind. Riggins clapped, looking genuinely impressed. Chase's gaze was boring a hole through me, but I couldn't look in his direction.

Wallace's thin lips stretched into a smile. "When curfew lifts."

"Sounds like fun," said a female voice from the doorway. "Where do I sign up?"

I spun toward the sound. *Cara.*

She looked only slightly worse for wear—her clothes were marked with dirt like the others' had been, and her hair was stiff from dried sweat. Though she barely acknowledged me, I was relieved to know she was alive.

"What happened?" Lincoln launched himself across the room and lifted her into an embrace. She laughed and patted his back.

"Just laid low for a while," she said. "I lost you two, and then the sniper hit the draft setup, so I locked down and waited it out."

"Clever girl," said Wallace. Discussion of tomorrow's mission was over for now. Before I left the room I looked once more at Chase, now staring out the window alone. I thought he'd try to stop me; I *wanted* him to try to stop me. But he didn't.

It probably wouldn't have changed my decision anyway.

·   ·   ·

"**EMBER?** *Ember!*"

I raced toward my mother's voice, near the front of the house. I'd followed the two soldiers to her bedroom, where they had opened her dresser drawers and were rifling through her clothes.

"Mom!" We collided; my arms locked around her waist, and I buried my tears in her blouse. She shifted me to the side as the soldiers came into view.

"What's going on?" she demanded.

"Routine inspection, ma'am," said the first soldier. His navy uniform still had the press lines across the shoulders, like he'd just pulled it out of a package.

"How dare you come into my house when my daughter is home alone!"

He passed a nervous look to his partner, who stepped forward. There was something familiar about him, something I couldn't place. "According to the Reformation Act we don't need your permission, ma'am. Besides, if you need child care, the Church of America provides services, free of cost."

I detached from her side, arms bolting down. I was eleven, I didn't need a babysitter.

My mother's face was positively livid. "Don't tell me how to raise—"

"Now," continued the soldier. "Is there someone I can talk to? Your husband, maybe? When will he be home?"

I'd never seen her speechless before. The soldiers looked at each other, and the first made a note on the clipboard he was carrying.

"Very well," said the familiar one. "You're out of compliance with the Moral Statutes on seventeen counts today. Since it's the first time we're just going to issue a warning, but next time, it'll be a citation for each one. Do you understand what that means?"

I kept staring at him. His features were too sharp, his hair too golden. His eyes were emerald, and hypnotizing, like a snake's.

"What's he talking about?" I asked. But I remembered the assembly we'd had last week at school, when a soldier, older than these two, had come to talk to us about the Federal Bureau of Reformation and the Moral Statutes. "New Rules," he'd called them. "For a better tomorrow."

I'd told my mother about the new rules, and she'd laughed. That bitter laugh, like when she'd lost her job. Like all of this was some kind of sick joke, one that would never actually be real. I knew right then that I'd have to pay more attention to them, for both of us.

"Of course, we could always make a deal," said the soldier with the green eyes. He leaned forward and reached for my face, thumb trailing gently down my damp cheek. My gaze lowered to his gold name badge, where MORRIS was typed out in perfect black letters.

I know you. I should have been afraid, but I was so mesmerized by his touch that I didn't feel his fingers slip around my throat until it was too late.

I WOKE like a shot, gasping and writhing, ripped from the nightmare by a hand closing around my ankle, evoking another wave of panic. The thin, shredded blanket tightened around my waist. I scrambled back until my head cracked against the wall and I blinked back stars.

"Ember." The familiarity of Chase's voice tempted me to lower my guard. "Easy. It's okay. It was just a dream."

A dream? I couldn't trust it. I could still feel that oppressing weight, pinning me in place. I could feel the voice within me, drawing my tongue against my teeth to scream.

It was the last sound I'd heard before Tucker Morris's fingers tightened around my throat.

I was sitting on the upper corner of the bed, knees locked into my chest. Without the candlelight I could only see a slight differentiation of shadows from where Chase sat on the opposite edge of the mattress.

He flipped on the flashlight, laying it at my feet like a peace offering. In its glow I could see the room clearly. The lumpy, bare mattress and the old chair where he slept. Our shoes and backpack ready by the door. The crumbling drywall wearing away to reveal the wooden bones of my sanctuary.

Tomorrow I'd step outside the front door for the first time in a month, and I might not come back.

"It's okay to be scared." It was as if he'd read my mind.

"I'm not," I lied. I don't even know why I bothered.

"All right," he said slowly. "I'm just saying that if you were, it would be okay."

I rested my chin on my knees, longing for the familiarity of my own bed. The smooth feel of my own sheets and the perfect weight of my blankets. I missed home.

"Why'd he turn me in and not you?" I whispered.

"I don't know," he answered with a sigh. "But he wouldn't have if it didn't benefit him somehow. I'm just surprised he waited this long."

It did seem strange that someone would sit on this kind of information for a month before talking.

"How would it help him to fess up that I escaped on his watch?" I wondered aloud. Maybe someone had found out, pressured Tucker to talk. My mind flashed to the civilian woman who'd worked at the detention facility—Delilah. She'd been the only other person to know we'd left, but I doubted she had leaked the information. She was too afraid of Tucker to say anything that might get him in trouble, like the fact that we'd escaped on his shift.

Chase shook his head. "I can't figure it out."

We remained quiet, listening to the sirens downtown rounding up the curfew-breakers, and the bursts of raucous laughter from a room at the end of the hall. He shifted, and the rustle of fabric reminded me of the last time we'd been alone together in the dark, of the distance that had settled between us since. I wondered with a pang if he was going to return to the chair or even leave, but instead he faced me, all of him now on the bed. The flashlight made his white socks glow.

"I know this story," he said with some uncertainty. "Sometimes it helps me sleep."

I nodded my consent.

"Okay," he began, inching closer. "I was . . ."

"Once upon a time," I prompted. He looked down and smiled, pulling at the strings hanging off the end of his pant leg.

"Right. Once upon a time there was this eight-year-old boy, who had to move to . . . this faraway town. This all happened a long time ago, when people had lots of junk to cart around, so they had to rent this big truck to carry it all."

I thought of how all the things we owned could now fit into one bag. He turned so we were facing the same direction, and settled back on his elbows, two feet away. His feet hung off the mattress.

My clasped hands loosened.

"We . . . I mean *they*, drove for two days until they got to the place in the pictures his dad had shown them. It seemed all right; big at least. The boy got his own room. But the best part was that there was this old haunted house up the street." He grinned. "Classic haunted. It even had an old cemetery outside. So he went to check it out but this other boy—in a pink shirt—jumped out of the bushes and told him to get lost, because, get this, the place wasn't safe."

Hazily, that shirt appeared in my memory—an artifact from another life.

He laughed dryly, collapsing farther and rolling onto his side so that his head was resting on his knuckles. Tentatively I mirrored his position, laying my head on my bent arm. He was still a couple feet away, but now looking down on me.

"Turns out *he* was a *she*; she'd cut her own hair. Something about falling asleep chewing gum. All I'm saying is it must have been *a lot* of gum. . . ."

I kneed him in the ribs without thinking. He winced. I'd forgotten they'd been broken during his arrest, but he began to laugh, so I didn't feel the need to apologize.

His hand stayed on my calf though, holding my shin

against his body. I swallowed. I could feel him, not from be-hind a sheet of glass, but here.

"Anyway, this girl was clearly crazy, out there all alone with her pink shirt and boy hair, so our hero let it slide that she was trying to boss him around, and told her she'd better let him in because obviously the place was haunted, and he needed to investigate or else . . . I don't know, who *knows* what would've happened. So, they went inside. . . ."

I smiled.

"And it turns out it was the scariest damn place he had ever been in his life. Not safe at all for little girls. He was fine, of course. *Perfectly* fine. But it wasn't right to make a girl stay there, so he told her he heard her mom calling. Just so she didn't feel bad for being such a baby."

A giggle bubbled up inside of me.

I'd never been brave enough to go into that old house alone, but when Chase had shown up, intent to see beyond the splintering white columns and broken shutters, I couldn't say no. I hadn't known that the sour smell was asbestos and the raised veins in the wallpaper were termite highways. You didn't think of those things at six. You only thought about how fear could be split down the middle like an orange, so both of you could eat half.

He pulled me a little closer and I didn't even tense.

"You'll never guess where she lived."

As our smiles faded I noticed that his hand had moved up to the outside of my thigh, and his fingers were drawing small, slow circles that seared through my jeans. It had seemed logical to be ready to go at a moment's notice, but now I wondered what his touch would have felt like on my bare skin.

His fingers brushed the dark, cropped bangs away from my eyes, and his lips pressed softly against my brow.

"I remember who you are. Even if you forget," he said.

My eyelids weighed down, and in my last conscious moments I felt the warmth of his hand on my leg, the pressure of his touch, making me real. Not just a shadow. Not just a memory.

I DRESSED alone in our room, facing the blank wall, wishing it would inspire a clear mind. My thoughts raced with anticipation of what the day might bring, always returning to the same image: the holding cell in the base. The sterile floor, the threadbare mattress that smelled of bleach and vomit, the overhead lights that buzzed and flickered. And Tucker Morris leaning in the doorway, his green eyes saying *I knew you'd be back*.

I reminded myself that I'd lived through his internment before, and focused on the mission.

My hands shook as I buttoned up the starchy blouse, as I zipped up the itchy wool skirt and tied the triangular scarf in a sailor's knot around my neck. I wondered what Ms. Brock, my evil headmistress at the Girls' Reformatory, would think if she saw me now, back—by *choice*—in a uniform I'd resisted so fervently.

Curfew ended with a sputtering of yellow light that had me jumping out of my skin.

Houston and Lincoln had already left with Cara, scouting our path for any positioned FBR. We would go next, followed by Sean, dressed as a soldier, and Riggins in street clothes. Sean would meet us outside of Tent City, the others would keep to our shadows and watch for trouble.

I walked out of the room and came face-to-face with Chase. A look of disappointment crossed his face when he saw that I'd actually changed; clearly he'd been hoping I wouldn't go through with it. He straightened to his full height. The MM insignia—the U.S. flag flying over the cross—branded the pocket of his navy flack jacket, just above the name badge VELASQUEZ. His pants bloused over newly greased black boots. In the stolen uniform, Chase looked almost exactly as he had when he'd arrested my mother.

I realized he'd never said he would come. Some things he didn't have to say out loud.

The next thing I knew, Sean, Chase, and I were in the empty lobby, standing before the double doors. It was still dark on account of the thick rain clouds, and I was glad for the added cover. I put my hand on the glass, edging it open, feeling the cool, misty morning air seducing me out into danger, just as the familiarity of the fourth floor pulled me back.

"The Sisters are different here," Sean said. "Remember Brock? She had full authority over the soldiers at the reformatory—you'd never see her back down. In the cities, Sisters are charity workers. Models of obedience. They've got power, but not over the FBR. They're the kind of women the Statutes intended them to be, got it?"

Subservient. Respectful. Spineless.

"Got it," I said.

He paused, and then squeezed my arm. "You better go."

I swallowed. "Bye, Sean."

"I'll be right behind you." He hesitated, and then turned away from the door, as if he didn't want to see us step outside. I was glad for the privacy. He was making me nervous.

"Ember," Chase started, then shook his head. "Just stay with me, all right?"

There was something else he wanted to say, but I didn't give him the chance. I nodded and pushed the door open.

For a moment I stood on the dark street, holding my breath, expecting something earth-shattering to occur. As if the whole MM was just waiting for me to show my face so they could shoot me. But nothing happened.

Beside me, Chase transformed. His expression grew grave, his eyes daunting. When we began to walk, each long purposeful stride had me hurrying to keep up. I dropped my gaze, and kept several feet behind him, because no woman walked side by side with a soldier.

A light rain had started by the time we reached the corner. It lowered the bruised sky, coating my forearms and the back of my neck with a prickly layer of moisture that made my skin feel itchy and somehow foreign. Without hesitation, we turned into a dank alley, garnished by overturned trash cans and stray animals. I nearly tripped over a man's foot that stuck out from beneath a flattened cardboard box. Each sound—the flapping of a pigeon's wings, a clatter from within a Dumpster—shoved my heart into my throat. My gaze roamed, but no one seemed to see us. Which was good. For now.

Finally, the alley opened to a street, kitty-corner from Knoxville's city square. Two soldiers were positioned at the entrance to the Square, distracted by the words SAVE US SNIPER spray-painted across the front of an empty shop. The neon green letters drooled down the wall. I stared at the scene, wide-eyed, surprised by my own approval, before fixing my gaze on the ground.

Hastily, we moved past. The soldiers didn't even turn their heads.

I padded around the empty Contraband Items bins and condemned buildings, trying hard to shut out the chorus of groans and steady whimpers from the shapeless piles of tattered clothing strewn across the red bricks. Homeless civilians, maybe a thousand of them, immigrants from the fallen cities who'd come here for help or pity. They huddled together against the gusting wind to conserve energy. The last time I'd been here, Sean had been inciting a riot, but now the place was as somber as a funeral. With the MM's lockdown on rations, there was little to do but starve.

I glanced back, but the soldiers weren't following. We passed the abandoned shops filled with squatters. Passed the large painted sign over an empty store that read: SEVEN P.M. WORSHIP SERVICE—MANDATORY. I remembered the church I'd made us go to back home after we'd received an Article 1 citation for failure to observe the national religion. While I gave our names to the church recorder, my mother would steal cookies from the welcome table.

The way cleared for Chase; no one looked at us twice.

I turned left, focusing on Chase's heels. On the sidewalk before me a group crowded around a rain barrel, fishing out the cloudy liquid with a peeling, tin cup, fastened to the wood by a metal chain. Most bore the signs of malnourishment. Hollowed cheeks. Ashy skin. In contrast, their bodies looked bloated, loaded by layer upon layer of clothing. Trust ran thin these days; any possession left unattended was fair game.

A skin-and-bones tenant broke from the pack and approached me, sunken eyes searching hungrily over my disguise. A girl's summer dress fringed out beneath his holey sweater, and for a fleeting moment I thought of the Statutes that had been hammered into my brain at the Girls' Reformatory. Wearing clothes inappropriate for your gender could mean an Article 7 violation.

I prepared myself for recognition, panicked that the unveiling would not occur on our terms.

"You got any food, Sister? It's been two days. . . ."

He didn't know who I was. I found myself both relieved and disappointed.

When my escort backtracked, the man slumped and scurried back into the anonymity of the makeshift shelters. I wiped my sweating palms on my pleated navy skirt, then squeezed a single finger along the tight collar of my button-up blouse.

"Not yet," Chase said under his breath. He tilted his head toward a unit of soldiers standing outside a cleared area contained by yellow caution tape. The cement within that circle was stained red and black. The table where the soldiers had signed people up for the draft was broken in the center, and painted a sticky burgundy that attracted particles of dust and leaves. The MM had left it there in defiance of what had happened, as if daring a civilian to celebrate the death of a soldier.

Behind it, against the side of a building were three single lines grouped together, painted in the same neon green as the Save Us Sniper sign.

A bell resounded from the back of the Square, startling me. Though most people had given up on breakfast, it seemed there were to be some rations after all. With renewed energy, the starving sprang from the bricks, and stampeded toward the soup kitchen lines.

I ducked out of the way of a sprinting family, and aimed for a silver bus in the opposite direction, where volunteers could donate blood in exchange for rations vouchers. It was parked sideways between two buildings, marking the entrance of Tent City, just as Sean had said. A CLOSED sign hung low enough to have been spat upon multiple times.

We followed the length of the bus to a large Dumpster, overflowing with the last bits of trash that people couldn't use for shelter or warmth: broken glass, damp paper, and food too long gone to provide any nutrition. It smelled rank, like mold and vomit. My nose scrunched up involuntarily.

Hidden in a nook between the bus, the building, and the trash was the rendezvous point, and a quick scan told me that we were the first to arrive.

"Sean should be here by now." My heels tapped impatiently.

Chase's gaze darkened, and I followed it to the bus window where five printouts had been posted.

John Naser, aka John Wright. Robert Firth. Dr. Aiden Dewitt. Patel Cho.

Ember Miller. And there below my picture, in bold letters: ARTICLE 5.

A tightness stole my breath, like a fist squeezing my lungs. It was one thing to know this picture existed. It was another to see it for myself. Part of me wanted to tear it down, to burn it, but I couldn't, because that was the whole reason we were here.

Movement at the end of the bus snapped me back into the present. Chase and I spun toward the sound, expecting the rest of the team.

"S-sister?" a small female voice squeaked.

It was a small, lumpy woman, no more than twenty, with a face as pale and cratered as the surface of the moon. Her eyes were round, and her hands latched in place over her mouth. My insides knotted when I recognized her navy uniform matched my own.

We'd wanted a couple people to see us, but not those employed by the MM.

Chase's hand rested on his gun. He glanced behind her for soldiers. The Sister's gaze lifted from me, to him, and back to me. *She knows our faces,* I thought, but then remembered that she'd called *me* Sister. She hadn't studied our mug shots. I nearly laughed as I realized what she must be thinking: a FBR soldier and a Sister of Salvation, sneaking off to a deserted area. Not. Good.

There was no time to strategize. We had to act before she did. Sean was minutes behind us, and if this Sister called her friends, we'd have only moments before the soldiers arrived.

With only a fleeting look at Chase, I rushed toward her, taking care to let my shaggy black hair fall over the side of my face.

"Are you g-going to the soup kitchen?" she stammered.

"Yes," I said, trying to sound relieved. "I was just on my way." I thought if I told her to meet me there my intentions to ditch her might be too obvious.

"Are you all right?" she whispered, grasping my elbow. Sean was right—the Sisters here were different than at the reformatory. They were afraid.

"I am now, thanks to you!" I fisted my left hand so she couldn't see the thin gold band on my ring finger. There was a lesser chance of getting cited for an inappropriate relationship if people thought Chase and I were married, but Sisters were only Sisters because they weren't fortunate—or *compliant*—enough to be wives. How could I have missed this detail? Covertly, I switched the ring to my right hand.

I could lose her in the Square, I thought. Distract her in the crowd. Though I'd been around Sisters at reform school, I'd never worked as one, and didn't know the ropes. If she tried to do a secret handshake or something, I'd be busted.

"Where'd he go?" she asked, frightened. "He was so big!"

I looked behind us, feeling my stomach lurch when I didn't see him either. Where *had* he gone?

When we reached the brick paddock, we ran into three of her friends, already doubling back for their lost companion.

The masses congregated at the far end, where the Sisters had been heading to assist with breakfast.

"Peace be with you," a wide-eyed blonde said to me. The apples of her cheeks were pink from the wind.

I smiled demurely, feeling my hairline dew with perspiration.

"And also with you," came the canned response from my captor. Immediately, I parroted the phrase.

The crowds were still too sparse here for me to disappear, but if we got too much closer to the pack, Chase was not going to be able to find me. I was already kicking myself for separating. We would each be more vulnerable left out in the open alone.

We can rendezvous at the Wayland Inn, I reminded myself. I hoped we'd get there. Soldiers crawled all over the place. Wallace had said there'd be more here since the attack the other day, but that didn't calm my nerves. I was glad now for the cover these Sisters provided.

The smell of unwashed human bodies thickened as we drew toward the rations lines, overriding the burned oatmeal in the air. People watched us hungrily, and in self-defense I hung my head and kept close to the other girls.

The next time I looked up was to catch myself before running into a soldier.

My heart tripped hard in my chest. A squeak came out of my throat as he bumped my shoulder. I stumbled to the side.

"Watch it," he said. He didn't even glance my way. An unexpected rage slashed through me. I didn't want another soldier pushing me around as long as I lived.

Seconds later a woman screamed, her voice feral and high, clawing at the base of my brain. The soldier, still beside me, jerked his head up like a fox, sniffing the air, and then he unhooked the gun from his belt and raised it toward the sky.

"He's been shot!" I heard a man in the direction of the soup kitchen shout. But the soldier at my side had not yet fired. He was talking about someone else.

More voices joined his.

"Sniper!" they cried. *"Sniper!"*

CHAPTER
5

I JOLTED back, slamming into someone behind me, then was shoved back into the Sister who'd dragged me out here. Her broad cheeks had turned a dark shade of pink.

"Oh no," she was repeating. "Oh no oh no oh no."

I heard the shot this time, a loud crack that resounded through the air and ricocheted off the buildings. The soldier that I'd nearly run into was nowhere to be seen.

Code seven, Chase had said when the sniper had struck before. *A civilian attack on a soldier.* During a code seven all FBR units had been permitted to return fire.

"Get down!" I shouted, remembering what Houston and Lincoln had said about the civilians being forced to lay on the bricks. If they rioted now, the MM would kill them.

Two men near me ducked, only to be trampled by the crowd. A crack of bone, a blunted cry. Horror turned my stomach. The Sisters bolted, scurrying away like mice. I kept low, scanning furiously for Chase, searching for his hard features, his copper skin, his serious eyes, but every face was a blur.

Another shot, this time followed by a chorus of shrieks. Ahead, near what had been the front of the lines, came a loud clang, and through a sudden window between bodies I saw that the giant black cauldron of oatmeal had been knocked to the ground. Half a dozen men and women fell to their knees, scooping the dirty mush into their mouths and their cupped shirts.

Someone called for a Sister—for me—but I was already taken by the stampede, and had to hold onto the back of a woman's jacket just to stay upright. We were going backward, toward the entrance to the Square. The bricks had become slick with the light rain, and I slipped. A hand gripped my forearm, wrenching me sideways, where I banged into someone and nearly fell again.

The navy jacket nearly burst the panic swelling inside of me, but when Chase turned around, I almost sobbed with relief. He blocked the others with his body, holding me tight against his chest as he carved a path toward the alley where we were supposed to meet the others. I could feel each time someone rammed into him, see the flash of his teeth as he grunted against the pain.

Minutes passed before the way cleared. I looked up to see more soldiers racing past us toward the Square. Chase pushed me back like he meant to go after them, but at the last minute dragged me behind the Dumpster. Another clatter of footsteps had us flattening against the rusted metal.

"What part of stay together didn't you understand?" His tone may have been sharp enough to wound, but it was fear that came off of him in waves, not anger, and that was worse.

It made everything seem even more dangerous. Less than thirty minutes had passed since the Sister had caught us here, but it felt like a lot longer now. "Never mind," he muttered. "You all right?"

I nodded. His lip was bleeding, and I removed the handkerchief from around my neck and dabbed it with a trembling hand. I couldn't bring myself to meet his eyes.

"What happened?"

"Another sniper hit," he said. "I think. I saw a soldier go down."

The sniper was still here. Never before had he stayed in the same place after an attack. I couldn't contemplate what this meant, all I knew was that Chase was in a uniform—a target for this attack—but just as much in danger from the real soldiers without it.

We needed to get out of here fast.

I cringed when more shots came from the Square. One. Two. Three. Four. Five. All in quick succession. More screaming followed, sharp and bright with terror. Chase grabbed my hand, still holding the handkerchief, and pulled me down to a crouch.

We waited, listening to the tapping of the rain against the Dumpster, and the shouts from the Square. After a little while the chaos stopped, and a man's voice crackled over a bullhorn.

"Face down on the bricks," he ordered. "Move and you'll be shot."

I shuddered to think how many had already been shot. Had any of our people been among them? Had Sean?

An eerie silence came over us, punctuated by the sound of

a baby's fearful cries. At the sound of footsteps Chase stood, and motioned for me to be silent. He leaned out from behind our shelter, then gave a short whistle. A moment later Sean appeared. His chestnut hair was disheveled, and his uniform jacket had been ripped at the shoulder. The top two buttons were missing.

I jumped up and wrapped him in a hard hug, then pushed him back into the wall.

"What took you so long?" I said.

He choked out something indecipherable and jabbed a thumb over his shoulder in the direction of the Square, as if this were the stupidest question he'd ever heard.

He turned to Chase. "Is your radio working?"

Chase had left it turned off in his belt for fear anyone might hear it and find us, but now he flipped it on and lifted it to his ear, keeping the volume low. Nothing but static—on every channel. The MM wasn't broadcasting what had happened in the Square, which meant we couldn't connect to one another, or to Wallace back at the Wayland Inn, either. There went our chance for backup.

The patter of footsteps outside had him quickly switching it back off. We froze, waiting for whoever it was to pass, but the footsteps came closer. Chase reached slowly for his gun and nodded to Sean.

"There room for one more at this party?"

Cara appeared between the Dumpster and the wall, her once long locks cut to chin-length and redyed black, like mine. *Exactly* like mine, I realized. Another layer of protection so that people might even mistake us for each other. Her Sister ensemble fit more snugly across the hips and the chest to accommodate for her curves, but apart from that we were practically twins.

My blood was still thrumming as Chase's hand dropped from his holster.

"You could have just said no," she said, feigning annoyance.

"Get down here!" Sean motioned for her to come closer, which she did with a smile that made me wary.

"Oh," she whispered. "It's a secret party. You should have said so."

"What are you doing here?" I asked. "What happened to Houston and Lincoln?"

"We got separated," she said, the seriousness finally catching up to her. "What happened to you two? I saw you get ambushed by the Sisters."

So she *had* been watching us. I glanced at Chase. "We got separated."

"Radios are out," Chase interrupted.

"It's the storm," said Cara. "There were severe weather reports on the back channels earlier."

"We'll hold until this clears up," said Chase, nodding toward the Square. "Then move out at nightfall."

The disappointment weighed down on me; I did want to go back, but we hadn't accomplished anything yet. No one had recognized us. We hadn't even picked up the package.

Cara shook her head. "My guess is we've got fifteen, twenty minutes before those soldiers back there start combing every block in a ten-mile radius looking for the shooter. We need to move."

"She's right," said Sean. He didn't look happy about it. "With the radios out they can't call for backup. This is the best chance we have to get out."

I took a deep breath. Chase's expression turned hard and unreadable. He finally nodded.

"We'll go through Tent City," said Cara. "Might as well pick up our package since we're here."

"Forget the package," said Chase.

"No," I said, ignoring his scowl. "We're here. We came here for a reason. Like Cara said, soldiers are going to be coming this way soon." This person, whoever it was, needed our help now.

I stood.

"Well, boys," Cara said. "Safeties off. And remember, we're all wearing blue today, so watch where you're shooting."

AS soon as we left the shelter of our enclosure, the evidence of just how severe the weather would be became apparent. The air smelled electric, and the wind and rain were gusting. They drowned out the sounds from behind us, in the Square, where the civilians were still being searched for weapons.

Just past the donation bus, the alleyway revealed a bottleneck of makeshift shelters, corked at the closest end by a table where, Sean informed us, two armed soldiers usually sat. For now, the way was clear, and we moved fast, heads down, looking back as often as we could spare a glance.

As we passed through the barrier, the air whooshed out of my lungs. It seemed a great accomplishment that we were still alive.

Tent City was meant to be a temporary housing settlement, set up during the War when people had evacuated from the major cities on the Eastern Seaboard. In the beginning, the Red Cross had provided supplies, but over time, as it became obvious that the occupants had nowhere else to go, they began building shelter with whatever they could find. Tent City became as much a fixture in the city as the Wayland Inn. I could see that now, as the street opened up into what Cara termed blocks. The stalls contained within each were no more than six feet wide, and made of anything people could get their hands on. Car doors. Trash can lids. Piled stones. Cracked windowpanes and scavenged pieces of plexiglass. All latched together by spare twine or even leather belts.

People peeked out of their flimsy thresholds, having no doubt heard the ruckus from the Square. They regarded us with suspicious glares, and I felt the hairs on the back of my neck rise. I hadn't considered that we wouldn't be well received—we were here to help—but now of course it made sense. We looked like government employees; clearly they wouldn't trust us. We rushed down the main drag, feet shuffling through the cyclones of trash that swirled around our ankles. The guys took the lead, weapons in hand, directed by Cara's subtle instructions. We were given a wide berth. Even though the entire Tent City could easily overwhelm two soldiers, they were afraid. Should the MM have reason, this whole colony could be gunned down in an hour, tops.

It worried me that given the sniper attack, it still might be.

I looked up, scanning the rooftops on either side of the road for movement.

Four blocks down, a boy, no more than ten, with a dirty face and a greasy mess of strawberry hair popped out in front of my path, and I jumped back in surprise. One bony shoulder stuck out from his collar, and his hands were gripped before him like he was pointing a gun, aimed directly at Chase. Chase blocked me automatically, and Sean slid in at my side.

"David!" a woman hissed, ushering him away. "Sorry to bother you, sir," she added desperately over her shoulder.

"Move along," said Chase. I knew he had to play the role, but my teeth still ground together at the lack of compassion in his tone.

"No place like home," Sean muttered.

"You lived here?" I said, keeping my gaze ever moving.

"St. Louis."

When Sean had told Wallace he didn't want to go to Tent City, I'd thought it was because the place made him nervous. I should have guessed his reasons were not so simple.

"It gets old, you know," he confessed, and when I glanced over I saw that his cheeks had grown ruddy. "Freezing and being hungry all the time. Lots of guys joined when the recruiter came through. I wasn't the only one." He kicked a can across the walkway.

There was more to this story, more hidden behind his creased brows, but now wasn't the time to ask. My hair was now dripping from the rain, and I swiped it out of my face.

"How much farther?" I heard Chase ask.

Even Cara had started to jog. The urgency hummed through us. It wouldn't be long before the soldiers infiltrated this place.

We turned right. Three blocks down we reached a slightly larger shack, made of loosely bound, serrated sheets of yellow plastic and broken wooden pallets. It was bigger than its neighbors, about eight feet by eight feet.

Sean pulled aside the door flap and ducked within. When he unfolded from the shelter a few seconds later, his expression was far graver than before. He nodded once.

Silently, Cara and I moved inside, eyes watering from the smoke that emanated from a small fire in the corner. The plastic wall behind it was the density of molding Swiss cheese, blackened by smudges from where the flames had burned through. An old woman in rags with frizzy silver hair squatted beside the fire, roasting what looked like a charred rat on a skewer. I swallowed hard.

"Don't know nothin' about what's going on out there," she said gruffly, setting the rat directly on the dirty asphalt ground. She clutched her lower back as she rose, then shuffled back a step. "Oh, it's you."

I swallowed the lump in my throat. She didn't recognize me, she recognized Cara. I nearly opened my mouth to tell her my name, but with a new possible sniper attack, that seemed like a bad idea.

"We don't have a lot of time," Cara said. "Soldiers are coming. Better drop anything that's going to get you locked up."

The woman's leathery face drew tight. "That'd be you, Sarah girl."

She stepped over the rat to the opposite corner, where I'd previously only seen a stack of dirty laundry. Now it was a clear there was a person beneath it.

"Up you go. Get up now." She swatted the girl's bare leg, which emerged from beneath the covers. "Soldiers had a field day with this one," she said quietly to us.

Sarah groaned.

"I know, dear," answered the woman, sympathy cutting through her rough exterior. I bent to help her hoist the body from the floor. When I came close to Sarah's face I gasped and nearly dropped her.

One cheek and brown eye remained perfectly intact— I could see the way her full lips could easily be dazzling—but her other cheek was black and yellow and swollen an inch off the bone. Just below her jaw line was a fist-wide arc of stitches, and her left eye was completely swollen shut. Even her brow was distorted by bruising and a missing hunk of skin. I was glad I was standing on the side that was wounded. I wouldn't have wanted her to see my reaction.

Sarah was pregnant. The FBR had beaten a pregnant girl half to death.

"There we go," the woman said when Sarah stood. I kept a steadying hand beneath her elbow and glanced down, shocked by her outfit: a low-cut, cream-colored dress that blossomed around her hips and the swollen bump below her ribs. Blood stained the front of her chest and left russet streaks down to the seam. Her shoes looked like dancing slippers.

Cara seemed to notice the absurdity of her appearance as well and scowled.

"Great," she breathed. "Can you run?"

The girl nodded timidly. There was something about her demeanor that seemed entirely too innocent for the violence surrounding her. How old was she? Sixteen? That would have put her a year under me.

The wind rattled the roof, lifting it completely off its base for a few seconds of howling, then the rain began to pelt the metal, making my ears ring.

"Here's how it's going to be," Cara told her. "We're going to bring you to someone who'll take you somewhere safe. You're going to keep your mouth sealed tight until you get there. All the way until you get there."

"Yeth, ma'am." Sarah dug her heel into the ground, and a new wave of pity rose within me. "William didn' mean to do it, you know," she said. "He loved me. He *picked* me. At the thocials."

"That's enough," snapped Cara. She stuck her head outside and motioned for Sean.

"The socials?" I asked, confused.

"FBR pays top dollar for primo entertainment," said the woman under her breath. "I'll bet Officer William didn't think she'd get knocked up."

All new FBR recruits signed a contract dedicating themselves to Reformation when they entered the service. They weren't allowed to date. I knew this intimately; it was one of the violations they'd used to try to break Chase during our year apart. But I hadn't thought that they'd find other ways to keep their soldiers happy.

I forced myself not to wonder if Chase had gone to socials; we had bigger things to worry about. But the thought of him lonely, needing someone to talk to, crawled under my skin. It was then that I realized the woman was staring at me.

I was grateful when Sean entered the compartment. He winced when he saw Sarah's face.

The woman kneeled in the corner, poking around a junk pile near the clothes. When she stood, she was holding something small and silver in her hand, something I mistook as the contraband Cara had warned her to dump until she placed it between her thumb and forefinger and held it up to the firelight.

A thin chain hung from a medallion of some sort. On it, an angel wielded a knife overhead. If I squinted I could make out something beneath it, too: a demon with horns and wings. It didn't look like something that came out of the Church of America, and since I hadn't been raised with a religion prior to the War, I didn't know what the token was supposed to mean.

"I know who you are," the woman said with a tight smile. "And I'm glad. I'm glad it's you. It's good to see a woman fighting back."

I froze. I knew I should say something confirming, that the time had come, but I couldn't. My mouth had gone bone dry. Sean glanced between us, unsure, as I was, of what to say given the new circumstances.

"There's rumors you're hunting the soldiers that gave you that Article Five, is that true?" she asked. Sarah flinched beside her.

Whatever relief I'd felt faded.

"I . . . I didn't shoot anyone." *Even if I should have.* My jaw snapped shut as Cara's fist closed around my forearm. I could feel her fingernails digging into my flesh.

"Right. Of course." A wicked gleam lit the woman's eye. Though part of me wanted to make her understand I was innocent, the rest of me saw the bigger picture. This was why Wallace had sent me out: to stir things up. Few things got as much attention as claiming you were the sniper.

I shoved the necklace she'd given me into my skirt pocket and mumbled, "Thank you."

"You're in my prayers," she said. "But be careful. Not everyone will feel the same. The world's gone hard these past years."

I thought of the boy who had pretended to shoot Chase outside. When I was little we played cops and robbers. Now they played snipers and soldiers. Everything was changing.

Chase stuck his head through the door. "We've got to move."

Sean took Sarah's wrists gently and fastened them together with a neon green zip tie—a necessary protocol to deflect any suspicion. As far as everyone outside was concerned, we were here to make an arrest. Still, my wrists tingled, remembering the discomfort of restraints, and Sean scowled as he grasped her bare upper arm. I knew he was thinking, as I was, of what had happened these past weeks to Rebecca.

"Let's go," I said as soon as he was done.

We exited the shelter, Cara and I walking on either side

of our prisoner. Sarah hung her head and refused to glance up at the murmuring crowd. I didn't look up either, though I was now more concerned about the sniper than everyone else.

The wind was whipping now, and a plastic sheet that had served as someone's roof came slicing through the air. I hopped nimbly out of the way, but not before Chase had reached out to steady me.

"We've got to hurry!" I shouted. The sky was growing black. A strong enough storm could level this place, and then there'd be nowhere to hide from the MM. I wished I could unfasten Sarah's restraints, or at least shelter her beaten face from the weather, but I couldn't, not while other people were watching. A new thrash of wind knocked us both back a step.

We pushed on toward the back exit of Tent City, away from the Square. Behind us came the crackling of the bull-horn; the soldiers were sending a team to search the alley. It was too much to hope that the guards at the back gate had been called to the disturbance; as soon as the way cleared we saw the flashing blue lights. The exit, a chain-link fence broken in the middle by two vertical poles, was blocked by an FBR cruiser.

Two soldiers sat in the front seats.

"Keep moving!" Cara shouted. I hadn't realized I'd frozen.

The rain had thickened into sheets, and people were retreating to their shelters or cramming up beside the solid walls of the neighboring buildings to avoid the worst of it. By the time we reached the fence, it had already begun to hail.

The pellets made a tinny crackling sound as they bounced off the cruiser's roof, like a popcorn machine full of bullets. Just above the back tire was that dreaded insignia. The flag and the cross, and the mocking cursive message: One Whole Country, One Whole Family.

The tinted window rolled down, and a uniformed soldier with a dark complexion waved us over.

"Pick this one up in the Square?" he asked, and grimaced as the moisture that had gathered on top of the car doused his shoulder. He jutted a dimpled chin toward Sarah.

I swallowed, but my heart had lodged in my throat and would not go down. The Sisters were one thing; a secondary threat at best. They couldn't harm us themselves. But soldiers were an entirely different matter. I raised a hand to shelter my face from the rain, praying they would not recognize us.

"Sisters found her at the soup kitchen," said Sean in a voice loud enough to cut through the hail. "The tower still down?"

The soldier raised the small black radio and made a show of pressing a button on the side with his thumb. "Complete silence. Unbelievable timing, isn't it?"

Chase subtly repositioned himself between me and the car, blocking my view.

Every sane thought in my head told me to bolt, to grab him and run, just like we'd done time and time again, but I couldn't. The soldiers didn't recognize me, at least so far. Taking off now would be fatal, not just for us, but for Sean and Cara, too. We had no choice but to play this out.

"Why are you bringing in the whore?" the soldier pressed. "She the sniper?" His partner laughed.

Sean floundered. I glanced to Cara, who was flexing her hands against the sides of her skirt. Obviously she wanted to say something but couldn't. A real Sister wouldn't undermine a soldier's authority.

"Says she might have a lead," said Chase. He, too, guarded his eyes from the rain with his hand.

"We've got to get her back to base," said Sean. "Command's going to want to hear this."

The driver said nothing for several long seconds.

"We'd give you a ride, but someone needs to watch the gate," he finally answered.

"We're fine," said Sean. "Our car's just around the corner."

We were just about to pass when he called out to Sean one final time.

"Watch your back," he said, rolling up the window as he spoke. "One of those maggots in the Square reported he saw a uniform on the roof after the sniper attacked in the Square. Thinks it was FBR."

A spy within the MM. I almost liked the idea until I realized that every resistance fighter in a blue uniform was now in double the danger.

"Really," Sean said flatly.

Without another word we passed and made our way to the sidewalk, keeping a brisk pace for five blocks until it was clear the streets were empty. Then we ran for five more. At the sound of a siren somewhere nearby, we took refuge beneath the awning of an old abandoned clothing shop. Sean kicked the boarded-up door, but it didn't budge. Chase called him back, and with one hard kick he split the wood just above the handle. On the second try the door swung inward, and we all piled through.

CHAPTER
6

WE held still in the dark, barely breathing. When the siren faded into the distance, we relaxed a little, enough to catch our breath. Sarah was whimpering, and jerked her bound hands away from Sean's grasp. He looked to me to smooth things over.

"No one here's going to hurt you," I said. She kept her hands over her distended belly like a shield and continued to cry, anxious gaze traveling from one of us to the next. Cara sighed dramatically; something about this girl obviously rubbed her the wrong way. I remembered that the soldier had called Sarah a *whore* without a second glance and wondered if she was really a prostitute.

"It's okay," I soothed. "We made it." But though my voice was calm, my blood was buzzing like I'd just been struck by lightning. Over her shoulder, I caught Chase's gaze just before he slammed the weather outside; in his eyes simmered a mixture of astonishment and unease, the wordless language we'd both learned to rely upon.

"We made it," I said again. But we were far from safe.

A knock came at the door, and Chase peeked through the crack, one hand on the gun hanging from his belt. My breath caught as he stepped aside to let a shorter man in a cap and ragged clothing in.

"Did you think they got you?" Riggins smirked at me, wringing out his hat. The water streamed from the ends of his shirtsleeves. A tense breath squeezed from my throat.

"I saw you across the street," said Sean. I wasn't so sure that was true, but didn't say anything. I certainly hadn't remembered Riggins was on our tail. It wouldn't have made me feel safer, given our history.

"I knew the shooter was still here," Riggins said.

"Oh yeah, how's that?" Cara asked.

He placed his first finger in the center of his forehead. "Call it my sixth sense." He turned to me when Cara rolled her eyes. "For a greenhorn, you're not easy to follow. Kept Jennings in my sight the whole time, but I blinked and you were gone." It was a reprimand, but I didn't care.

"They got *separated*," Cara interjected.

Riggins's brows quirked. "Right before the sniper hit. That's unfortunate."

"What's your problem?" I was so tired of his accusations.

"Not the time," called Sean.

"Two minutes," said Chase firmly. "Then we're out." He disappeared in the shadows to search the back.

I looked around for the first time as Cara quickly repeated what the soldiers had told us about the sniper. The room was almost completely empty and held the sharp twinge of black mold. The metal racks that had once held displays of color-ful, folded clothes were all absent. The dressing rooms in the back were empty but for the glimmering cobwebs that stretched from wall to wall. Though the room held evidence of past break-ins, no one had been behind these locked doors for a year, maybe longer.

"I bet it's true," I heard Riggins say. "Enlistment is a per-fect cover, think about it. You could tear the infrastructure down from the inside, and no one would ever know." I was sure he'd raised his voice on the last bit so I could hear.

The wind brought a new wave of hail slapping against the front of the building. As I made my way back I was surprised to see that Riggins and Sean had switched clothing. Already damaged from the Square, the uniform jacket was a snug fit over Riggins' thicker torso, but though the existing stitches strained they would hold as long as he didn't move too much. Sean placed the wet cap atop his head.

"Riggins is taking my place," Sean said, in answer to my baffled expression. "The new recruit's supposed to be waiting at the Red Cross Camp. I've still got to bring him in."

"Sean, maybe you shouldn't . . ." I couldn't help thinking Rebecca would want me to stop him somehow. "We can all go later. Together."

He sent me a tight smile. "It's better I go now. Before the radios are back up and the city's swarming with units on foot looking for the sniper." He made a point, but that didn't mean I liked it.

"Time's up," Chase called from the back of the room. "The alleys are clear."

I looked at Sean, wishing I could say something more to convince him to stay. Odd how much had changed between us in such a short time. Once I'd thought him just another vacant, shallow soldier, but so much more existed just beneath the surface. He was a good friend, and I worried for him.

"Be careful, okay?" I said. "The radios are still out."

"Sure, Mom," he said. I narrowed my eyes, but pulled him close and wrapped my arms around his shoulders all the same.

"Keep your eyes open," he said quietly before he drew away.

We made our way to the back exit, Sarah hanging close to my side. I patted her shoulder. The unbeaten corner of her mouth lifted a little.

"It's not far," I said. But though I'd seen the checkpoint on a map, I had no idea how long it would take to actually get there.

Chase kicked out the back door just as he had the front, with a grunt and a powerful thrust that sent the wood crackling and the remaining glass shattering across the black pavement. The pressure from the storm had increased. I used the handkerchief to latch my short, black hair down, and grabbed a ripped poster outlining the Moral Statutes off the ground to hold over Sarah's head.

Then we ran.

We raced through the narrow alleys, silent but for the patter of hail. Riggins took the lead, gun drawn but down at his side. I glanced back every few steps to make sure Chase was still behind me. My heart was pounding. *No more soldiers*, I prayed.

We crossed one last major intersection, beneath a dead traffic light, but found it deserted. The main roads had been cleared of abandoned cars when the area became a Yellow Zone, but cruisers still patrolled this area so we had to be watchful. I held my breath until we reached the back lot of a closed drugstore.

Past the barred back door, surrounded by overgrown hedges, was the vehicle entrance of East End Auto. Three metal garage doors were corroded by orange rust, and on the customer entrance beside it was an OUT OF BUSINESS sign in bold, red letters. Just below it, a message was hand-painted on a rectangular scrap of tin: One Whole Country, One Whole Family. The FBR motto, minus the flag and cross emblem.

Chase and I had seen this on the side of the checkpoint on Rudy Lane. We'd seen it again tagged on a grounded eighteen-wheeler when we'd found out about the Knoxville carrier. It was everywhere there was resistance, inconspicuous to those expecting to see MM propaganda, but obvious to anyone searching for those six words alone.

Cara stepped to the front, turned her back on the garage, and kicked it with her heel three times in quick succession, three times slowly, and three times quickly again. I could barely hear the clang over the whipping wind.

I gave Chase a puzzled look as he moved beside me. His jet-black hair was dripping tiny streams down his jaw, which he wiped on his shoulder irritably.

"SOS," he answered. "Morse code."

Nothing happened.

I ran my hand over Sarah's arms, trying to keep her warm, but the cool air had prickled her skin with goose flesh. Behind blue lips her teeth chattered.

Riggins grabbed the Statute poster I'd taken from the store to shield Sarah. The paper was already translucent and turning to mush.

"Hey!" I said, pulling Sarah as close to the building as possible to shield her from the weather. It wasn't yet safe to remove the cuffs; someone could spot us. Chase was eyeing the alleyway we'd come from apprehensively.

"Article Nine," read Riggins, and I stiffened. Last I checked there were only eight. This new addition had been added recently.

He laughed caustically. "*Citizens knowingly or unknowingly assisting those in violation of the Moral Statutes are hereby denied trial and shall be punished to the full extent of the law.* Now isn't that ironic?"

My stomach dropped. Sarah made a small gasp, and I refocused my attention on her so she wouldn't feel as afraid as I did.

I told myself Article 9 didn't matter. They had already posted my name on the five most wanted. It was just another Scarlet Letter. Just like Article 5. But though it shamed me, it helped to think that everyone else in this room would be in just as much trouble as me if we were caught.

"Hurry up, Tubman!" Cara yelled. She kicked the garage again.

Before she'd finished, the door rose, just to hip height, and she disappeared beneath it. Riggins followed, as did Sarah.

Chase and I gave each other one last glance before the plunge.

As soon as we were out of the storm, a skinny man with dark brown skin in a Hawaiian shirt slammed the metal door down and chained it to a metal hook in the floor. He had a crooked nose and a jagged taupe scar that ran from the corner of his right eye down to his mouth. When he smiled, crooked white teeth broadening his face and flattening his nose, my shoulders dropped an inch, but I didn't breathe until he'd set down his pistol on a metal cart of mechanic's tools.

There were two cars in the garage. To my right was a dark blue FBR delivery truck. I imagined this was what the carrier used to deliver fugitives to the safe zone. Beside it, in the center of the garage, was a Horizons shortbed distribution truck with a perky yellow sunrise emblazed across the metal siding—the same one the team had hijacked two days ago.

"So this is where you stashed it," Riggins said to Cara, who grinned.

It was hard to believe that I used to worry about the morality of Chase hotwiring cars when here I was standing with a bunch of felons beside two stolen FBR vehicles. I removed the handkerchief on my head and shook the hail out of my hair, knowing I looked much like a dog coming in from a snowstorm. Chase had already removed Sarah's zip ties.

"Hope you didn't pull a muscle sprinting to the door," Cara said, reminding me of the other man's presence. She punched his arm and he staggered, feigning injury.

"This is Tubman," Cara said to us. "Carrier extraordinaire."

He stuck out his hand, and I reached to shake it. A shiver of fear worked through me as his amber eyes lit with recognition.

"Your mug shot doesn't do you justice," he said, and raised my knuckles for a lingering kiss.

Chase cleared his throat. The room felt very warm all of the sudden.

"Big guy," Tubman observed, moving to Chase. "I know you. No, not quite." He continued to scrutinize Chase's features. "You got people on the coast?"

"My uncle," Chase said in awe, and any resentment I harbored for his mom's brother was overridden by sheer shock that he had survived.

Chase's uncle had taken him in when his parents and sister had died in a car accident, then abandoned him during the War when he'd no longer been able to provide. They'd reconvened only once since their separation; just after Chase had been drafted. It was during that chance meeting that Chase had learned of the safe house.

"He's about my size," Chase continued. "Has a tattoo of a snake on his neck and long hair, at least the last time I saw him. His name—"

"Wouldn't know it," Tubman interrupted. "You're right. I've seen him. Can't forget a brand like that." He placed a thumb on the left side of his neck thoughtfully.

I felt a staggering clutch in my belly. Chase's uncle could have been my mother, waiting at the safe house for word from us. Instead we were escorting someone else to the checkpoint, where they would await transport, and we were stay-ing here.

Until we get Rebecca, I told myself. Then we would go, too.

"So he made it," Chase said with a relieved smile. I hadn't seen him that happy in some time.

Tubman laughed dryly. "Oh, he made it all right. Not by me though. Another carrier, maybe Baton Rouge or . . ."

"Or Harrisonburg," Riggins said in a low voice, causing my stomach to sink.

Riggins knew that Chase and I had been in that check-point on Rudy Lane the night the carrier had been murdered by MM soldiers. We'd told Wallace as much when we'd joined, and if any proof was needed, my size seven footprints had been found on the scene.

I wanted to close my eyes, to erase the last few minutes, but I didn't. I kept them wide open, otherwise I'd be back in that house, I'd see the carrier's legs spread across the floor, hear his rasping voice as he told us the location of the next checkpoint.

Tubman's eyes had pinched around the edges. "Yeah. Or that."

So he'd heard. It wasn't hard to see how it affected him, and no wonder, given their shared profession.

A crack of thunder hit so hard that I cringed.

"Can you take him a message?" Chase asked.

"Save it," said Tubman. "I ain't goin' back for a while. Hear that, Ladybird?" he called over his shoulder to Cara.

His words tripped the conversation, and everyone paused,

waiting for an explanation. My gaze fixed on the scar on his face, and I wondered if it was the Harrisonburg carrier or the posting of Article 9 that had gotten to him. Maybe both.

"What's that mean?" Cara appeared, scowling, from around the cab of the Horizons truck.

The thunder cracked again; the hail and rain beat so hard against the garage doors that we could barely hear one another. I glanced at Sarah, noting the way she was drawing closer to me, away from the other men. We needed to get her out of here as soon as possible.

Tubman grabbed the battery-powered lantern, sitting beside his weapon on the tool cart, and motioned toward the left side of the garage, where the floor opened up to reveal a red metal staircase. Downstairs was a darkened concrete room—the "grease pit"—where at one time working mechanics did oil changes. Most of the tools were cleared out now though, and in their places were boxes of nonperishable food, a few black plastic trash bags likely filled with clothes, a fold-out table and chairs, and several cots. On one wall I caught a glimpse of a stack of blue cards I knew to be U-14 forms, the documentation one needed to cross into a Red Zone.

People congregated warily against the back wall in the shadows; a man, and beside him a woman, holding a baby in her arms, and five or so guys—probably draftees, looking for sanctuary at the safe house. They watched us cagily, sticking close together for support.

"At ease, puppies," Tubman told them. He pointed at Chase and Riggins. "They're fakes."

A violent shiver shook through me, despite my attempts to stay collected. I was freezing.

"You talk," said Cara. "I'm raiding your stash." She revealed a box of crackers from a bag on the floor and tossed it to the man with the family, then rifled through a bag of stolen clothes.

Tubman sat on a metal fold-out chair and leaned back on two legs. "Highways are closed, have been since the sniper hit the draft. Or don't you remember?" He laughed like this was somehow funny.

We looked to one another—Tubman had yet to hear about the newest attack at the Square.

"They're not closed to Sisters," Cara said, fanning her skirt out in a curtsy. "And they're not closed to soldiers. And our best chance of moving is now, before the radios go back up and broadcast the newest sniper hit. Riggins, strip."

"Yes, ma'am," said Riggins eagerly.

"And give Tubman the uniform," she finished. "We'll take the blue truck."

Tubman threw his hands up. "Wait, hold on, the newest sniper *what?*"

"A soldier, maybe more than one, was shot in the Square today," I found myself explaining. I thought of the woman in Tent City, how she'd thought I'd killed those soldiers, and cringed. "We don't know it was the sniper yet," I added.

"Oh, right," Tubman scoffed. "Who else could it be?"

"A copycat," said Riggins, and I braced for the challenge, but it never came. "A rogue civilian. She's right. We don't know anything yet."

I didn't know why he was suddenly agreeing with me. It didn't suit him.

"Anyway, how are we supposed to tell Wallace we're taking his truck if the radios are out?" Riggins asked.

"Wallace and I have a little deal worked out," Cara said suggestively, making him howl. She turned back to the carrier. "Come on, Tubman, please? Pretty please? Don't make me ask three times." She batted her eyelashes. Her playfulness dug under my skin.

Tubman laughed dryly, then stopped short and blinked, as if he'd just remembered something. "Yeah, all right," he said. "We'll go through Virginia. Say we're delivering supplies to one of those boarding homes for Sisters and keep our fingers crossed they don't search the trunk. If we go while the radios are down, they can't call their friends. We could be back home by tomorrow night."

"What about curfew?" I said.

"Curfew doesn't apply to soldiers," said Cara without looking up.

"These are people's lives!" I snapped. "The carrier in Harrisonburg died because he wasn't careful!"

I remembered how it felt, slipping on the blood that coated the kitchen floor. My face buried in Chase's arm as he hid my eyes. I remembered the copper smell that permeated the air. I could smell it still.

Cara stopped rummaging through a donation bag and tilted her head curiously toward me.

The four feet of Tubman's chair came to rest on the floor. "He died because he got caught," he said.

The grease pit seemed to grow smaller, and my chest tighter. The infant was crying—a soft, low cry, that didn't at all sound healthy. I wished the mother would make it stop, and that Sarah would stop staring at me with her swollen, frightened eyes.

I glared at Cara. She may have Tubman, Riggins, and everyone else at the Wayland Inn charmed, but not me. Her recklessness was putting us all in danger and if she wasn't careful, someone was going to get killed.

Chase approached and stood beside me, waiting for me to speak first. I rubbed my thumb over my scrunched-up brows, and finally blurted, "We should stop them. The highways aren't safe."

"Nowhere is safe," he said. "At least this way gives them hope."

Clearly Chase thought this was valuable, but I wasn't so sure. Hope made you infinitely more devastated in the face of disappointment.

CLOTHING from the donation bags was distributed. I was given a sweatshirt and some old-fashioned cargo pants that were large enough to fit Chase. After our escape I'd had to start fresh with whatever was lying around.

Because my head was now pounding with too many memories and unanswered questions, I grabbed my things, told the others I'd take first watch while travel arrangements were made, and headed back upstairs into the garage. Chase watched me go in silence.

The noise from the storm helped to distract me some. I

hid behind the MM truck, setting a flashlight upright on the bumper, and began to peel off the navy skirt and blouse. The angry weather had soaked me straight down to the marrow.

But I was still alive.

We'd accomplished our mission, despite derailments. No one had tried to kill me; no civilian but the woman in Tent City even recognized my face, and she had treated me like some sort of hero. Like someone who could lead an uprising. My mother would have loved that.

Hopefully the woman had started spreading the word throughout the Square that she'd seen me. Seen the *sniper*. How many others would believe her? It occurred to me that maybe the real sniper would be angry that I'd stolen his glory; maybe he *liked* the attention. I wasn't sure though; if I were the sniper, I'd want all the help I could get. Maybe he'd even hear how I helped Sarah, and the people downstairs, and want to work together or something.

Which of course I'd politely decline, because he was obviously off his rocker.

"Oh. Hey. Sorry."

I jumped straight back into the humiliation of reality, acutely aware of my ratty bra and cotton underwear. Some watch I had been keeping. I hadn't even heard Chase climb the stairs until he was standing in the shadows, eight feet away.

If I'd been cold before, I wasn't anymore; my skin was practically glowing with heat. I tried to pretend I didn't care, that now that we'd finally slowed down I wasn't remembering how he hadn't wanted us to come on this mission, or how we'd been separated in the Square, but pretending made my movements so jerky that I ended up tying both sides of the fly into a knot rather than zipping up the baggy cargo pants.

"It's just me." Chase had quietly faced the opposite direction while I finished.

"You just scared me," I said. That was truthful at least.

He began checking the exits; the doors, the garage window, mostly blocked by a black trash bag but for a peephole in the corner.

"I said I'd take the first watch," I said, more harshly than I intended. He clawed at his scalp with one impatient hand and scowled.

"Wait," I said as he headed back toward the stairs. "Stay?"

He turned slowly, a small smile taking the edge off my nerves.

A necklace fell out of my folded skirt pocket and bounced off the oil-stained concrete floor as I hoisted myself into the open bed of the Horizons truck. He picked it up on his way back before sitting beside me. Our legs were close enough to touch, but didn't.

"Where'd you get this?" he asked, using the flashlight to discern the details.

"It was a gift from the lady hiding Sarah." I forced a yawn; my jaw had grown tight.

"You should hang on to it." He handed it over, his fingers lingering in my palm a few seconds longer than necessary. His skin was always so warm, like he had an internal furnace, and his touch made the hard angles of the world soften, like a shadow at dusk.

"I don't even know what it is," I said, withdrawing my hand.

"It's Saint Michael. The Archangel. He led the good angels in the fight against evil."

I didn't remember hearing about Saint Michael at the mandatory Church of America services. Chase must have learned this before the War.

Thunder struck again, and I ducked reactively. I felt the rough edges of the contraband silver pendant, watching the light play across the tiny winged figure and the chain shift over my skin. As the seconds passed it grew heavy, but I couldn't seem to put it away.

"Do you believe in heaven?" I asked.

I didn't know if I did. I'd accepted it before as a reality; just as blindly as I'd believed in Santa Claus as a child. But since my mother had died, a festering desire to know the unknowable had gnawed at me. I wanted so desperately to believe in something concrete. I wanted to know that somewhere there was peace.

Chase leaned forward, elbows on his knees, his face hidden in the shadows.

"You mean, is it just for the *reformed*?" The last word was bitter and drawn out.

I cringed, imagining the angels at the pearly gates checking our compliance status before letting us through. *Redemption can only be found through Reformation. Redemption can be earned through rehabilitation.* That's what the Church of America ministers liked to preach. The FBR, the president, they all gave the same message: you aren't good enough the way you are.

Every Sunday, as we walked home from service, my mother would make a point to tell me the opposite.

My chest tightened.

"For anyone," I asked again. And when he hesitated, I said, "Well, do you?"

He picked at a frayed spot on his jeans.

"I believe bad things happen to good people. And good things happen to bad people."

He was evading. "That wasn't what I asked."

"I know," he said finally. His shoulder jerked up, reminding me of the boy he'd once been before the world had hardened him. "I used to believe if you were good, good things would happen to you. I don't know what I believe anymore."

"So that's it?" I said. "You die and that's the end. There's nothing else?" The panic swelled inside of me. I could barely keep my voice from breaking.

I watched him try to swallow. "My mom said there was more. She called it the spirit world. She said death is just the bridge there, that souls stick around to guide us."

That felt truer than anything could at the moment. I felt my mother's ghost constantly. I felt it now, in the space between Chase and me.

He reached for my hand, holding it between both of his.

"Ember, I think if there is someplace like that—someplace good—I think that's where your mom would be."

It was instantaneous. The pain, the fear, the loneliness,

all balled together inside of my gut and soured. My eyes burned, but not with tears. I wanted to cry. I'd wanted to cry for days, especially when this happened, but I hadn't since our escape from the base. My tears had been choked off, and all that remained was anger.

Nothing felt right. My thoughts didn't feel right. My *skin* didn't feel right. Even Chase sitting beside me made me claustrophobic. I wanted to run away. Disappear. Forget myself.

I couldn't stop the questions: *Did you do enough? Could you have stopped him from killing her? Why couldn't I stop this? Why couldn't I see this coming?*

I didn't want to grieve my mother. I didn't want to wonder if she'd been hauled to the crematorium outside the base like any other bin of trash. I didn't want to remember that she loved pancakes and hot chocolate and contraband books. I didn't want to remember her at all, because I *didn't want her to be dead.*

It wasn't fair. My mother had been murdered simply because I'd been born.

At that moment I could see exactly why someone would snipe off soldiers.

I shook Chase's hand away. He looked intolerably sad, and that infuriated me, too. What was wrong with me? I was taking it out on him, even when I didn't want to. She was gone and he couldn't change that. *Nothing* could change that.

I shoved off the tailgate and paced around the garage.

"Maybe if you talked to me," he suggested tentatively.

"I'm talking! We're talking! It doesn't fix *anything!*"

He was standing now, too, hands hanging limply at his sides. He moved closer.

"I don't know if it works exactly like that."

"What are you, my damn therapist?" I fumed, fists balled at my sides.

"No!" His hand raked through his hair, but it was so short, his hand slid back to the collar of the holey, borrowed golf shirt. "No, I'm just your . . ." he shrugged. "Neighbor," he muttered, his face darkening. His eyes fixed on a particular spot of oil on the floor.

"My *neighbor?*" I said, and the laughter that bubbled out of my throat sounded so evil I turned away so I couldn't see my own cruelty reflected in his face. Not his best friend. Not his *girl*friend. Just the neighbor. My mind flashed to Sarah, and her once-pretty dress, and suddenly I was sick with wonder of how Chase had spent his nights in the MM.

The silence grew thin and was punctuated by another clap of thunder.

There was something in the way he looked at me then, as if he'd asked a question and were waiting for an answer. As if he were *willing* me to answer, but how could I? I didn't know what we were, even if what I felt was strong enough to die for.

"We're loading the truck," announced Riggins from the stairs. I jumped at the sound of his voice and noticed that Cara was with him. I wondered how long they'd been standing there.

Chase pulled back, averting his gaze.

"Right," he said.

An hour later, Cara and Tubman, in the MM uniform, took the stolen government truck filled with refugees east under the guise of delivering rations to a soup kitchen in Maryville. I prayed the guards on the freeway would see the MM vehicle, see Tubman and Cara in uniform, and usher them through without question. With or without the instatement of Article 9, they were as good as dead if caught.

CHAPTER
7

AFTER the carrier's transport had gone, I'd crawled back into the cab of the yellow Horizons truck to wait out the night. Chase had watched me cautiously, but we hadn't spoken anymore. There were bigger things to worry about; like how we would get back to the Wayland Inn, or whether Sean had made it safely across town and found the recruit. Still, I hated the distance between us. It left me unsettled, unbalanced. Like the good parts of myself were fading.

I wished I could talk to Beth. I missed her, and I missed home, at least the way home used to be. That all seemed a long time ago now, like something out of a different life. Still, thoughts of my redheaded friend brought a smile to my lips. The MM could ruin lots of things, but not my memories of her. As long as she kept her head down, she'd be safe. Her family was compliant, after all.

By dawn, the weather's tantrum was over and had left the garage eerily silent. The cool air made me shiver, and when I drew my knees to my chest, the St. Michael pendant slid to the floor mat.

I went to retrieve it, hand searching blindly beneath the seat, and came up with more than just the necklace. A cartridge shell. I rolled it over my palm, curious as to why a food delivery crew would have need for this kind of ammunition. I hadn't heard there had been any weapons fired when the resistance had hijacked the truck.

Something wasn't quite right with this bullet. It was pointed at the end, copper, not silver, and almost three inches long. The cartridges that filled the 9mm were no more than an inch, and rounded on top. I was no weapons expert, but I'd inventoried our supplies at the Wayland Inn, and it didn't take much experience to figure out that this was for a much larger gun than the typical resistance-issued pistol.

"We're moving," called Chase from the outside of the truck. I shoved the cartridge in my pocket, and with a conceding sigh, slipped the necklace over my head.

"Can't hurt," I said aloud, remembering what Chase had told me about protection.

CHASE stayed close as we raced west toward the resistance hideout. Both our uniforms were slung over his back in a black trash bag, but the gun, I knew, was still tucked in the waistband of his pants beneath that holey sweater. Up ahead, Riggins scouted the way for soldiers, but I remained watchful anyway. I was pretty sure my safety wasn't his top priority, despite his show of support at the garage.

The streets were littered with storm debris. Tree limbs, broken glass blinking in the early morning sun, sopping Statute circulars. Fallen power lines that probably were out of commission in this area anyway. I could only imagine what had become of Tent City or the Red Cross Camp in the park, and again felt concern for Sean tingle at the base of my neck. The air smelled like dirt and moisture, cleared, finally, of the crematorium's thick white smoke that hung like death over the city.

I tried not to think about that place.

My pulse didn't slow until we crossed the threshold of the Wayland Inn. The foyer was thick with bitter cigarette smoke, emanating from a man sitting on a stool behind the counter. Orange hair, bright as a flame, leapt from his head, and his eyes were bloodshot from too much gambling with the boys.

His name was John, and he was the landlord at the Wayland Inn. I'd only seen him a couple times in the past month, as I so rarely left the fourth floor.

"Your rent's due for next month, darlin'. Can't hide forever." His words flowed with a faint Irish rhythm.

I winced. Though his other tenants had to pay, those in the resistance fed his nicotine addiction, and we had returned without a carton of Horizons brand cigarettes.

"We'll get you next time," said Chase. He switched the bag of uniforms to his other shoulder.

"I'd always take a kiss," he said with a devilish gleam in his eye.

"You're not really my type," said Chase.

John laughed. "You'll come around." He winked so pathetically at Chase that I couldn't help but laugh.

We bypassed CJ the stairway guard—a seemingly drunk, homeless man with dreadlocks—and climbed the stairs to the fourth floor. Each step closer to resistance headquarters brought more relief. I couldn't wait to tell Wallace and Billy of our success. I hoped it would overshadow the fact that Tubman and Cara had left without his approval. I wasn't yet sure how we were going to break that to him, but I had a feeling it wouldn't be pretty.

With Chase on my heels, I pushed through the stairway door, which led to a long corridor lined by old beige wallpaper and stained blood-red carpet. Billy's mangy black cat curled around my calf, purring her greeting.

Home. It wasn't the home I'd always dreamed of, but the feeling was there, nonetheless, and I smiled, because I'd finally earned the right to stay here.

Raised voices in the hallway drew my attention. We weren't the only ones back. Chase veered into the surveillance room to see if there were any new updates to the mainframe, but I wasn't ready for bad news, not after completing my first mission. I sped toward the supply room, netted by the gathering crowd blocking the way, and warmed at the sight.

Sean was standing just outside the supply room door, hands behind his head, stretching his back. He looked worn out and dirty, and as I pushed through the others I could smell the mud and sweat on him. It didn't matter; I was glad he was safe. Without a second thought, I wrapped my arms around his waist.

"You're back," I said, relieved. "God you stink."

He squeezed me tightly, ruffling my hair into knots. "Like you smell so much better."

The greeting party made for a tight fit in the hall, and when he tried to avoid my punch he backed into Lincoln, who, when he saw me, said, "Hey, you're alive," and slapped me on the back. Houston, just behind him, offered his congratulations as well.

Sean pulled me off to the side. For the first time in weeks he looked genuinely happy about something.

"The new guy remembers Becca coming through the base," he said. "He never saw her before she went to Chicago, but he remembers her name from the inmate roster."

A smile spread across my face. Finally we had a lead.

The way cleared momentarily, revealing the recruit within the supply room. I could see only his profile, but his face was scruffy, his blond hair oily, and his muscular shoulders bowed. He wore donation-bin black slacks and a gray, long-sleeve thermal, rolled up to the elbows to reveal a scuffed cast half-torn off one arm. From where I stood I could see the faint pink lines of three parallel scars clawed from ear to collar.

Fingernails had scratched those marks.

My fingernails.

Tucker Morris.

There was a moment of fear. Crystallized, unbreakable fear, that congealed the blood in my veins and iced the breath in my throat. A moment where the frenzied images petrified me. The arrest. The hatred in his eyes. The taste of his breath. Those words I'd heard over and over again: *I'm a damn good soldier. I did what needed to be done.*

And then fury consumed me, and without another thought I pounced. He'd followed me. He'd come to finish the job. Well, I was going to finish it first. I was going to tear him to pieces. But Sean had grabbed me around the shoulders. I fought him like a cornered animal, no longer seeing my friend, only seeing danger. Feeling it rip through my limbs. My elbow swung back and connected with his jaw and a string of curse words tore from his mouth.

The breath released from my lungs in one burning strike: *"Run!"*

Wallace burst through the door of the supply room, but there was another person blocking my way. Riggins. I jerked to the side. His fingers caught in my clothing, but maybe it was deliberate. Maybe he was holding me back purposefully.

"Ember! Where is she?" I saw his black hair first, the glint off the silver gun barrel a moment later. The way cleared as those nearest to him contorted out of the way. Billy jumped on Chase's outstretched arm, but it was too late. The trigger had already been pulled.

A *crack* of gunfire had me hitting the deck reactively. A flash of a red sweatshirt fabric and my fingers were smashed under someone's shoe. The next thing I knew Sean's fist was in my collar as he was shoving me farther down on the floor.

Chaos. Shouting. Running feet, echoing in my eardrums.

"Chase!" I screamed.

I got away from Sean. I shoved past Riggins. Tucker had ducked back into the supply room, and for a brief moment I panicked, realizing he had access to more than one weapon inside. But I had to find Chase first; everything else came second.

I could barely see him. He was beneath at least four other men. One of them was Houston, and he was slamming Chase's forearm repeatedly into the floor to get him to release the gun.

"Stop it!" I jumped on Houston's back and he burst up, spinning me into the wall. I grunted as all the air fled from my lungs at the impact. But I didn't let go. I held fast to his neck.

Hands gripped my waist, pulling me down, squeezing me into submission with one arm locked firmly behind my back.

"Stop!" Sean ordered. "I don't want to hurt you, okay?"

"Then let go!"

He released my arm but trapped me in a bear hug against him, where I struggled until his knees locked my flailing legs in place.

"Ember!" I heard Chase yell.

"I'm here!"

"THAT'S ENOUGH!" roared Wallace.

Houston and Lincoln hauled Chase to his feet, and I glanced fleetingly over his body to assure he wasn't badly harmed. They pointed guns at him. As if *he* were the danger.

I smelled it now. Gun smoke. Just like in the house on Rudy Lane. Where had the bullet lodged? Somewhere in the floor. Every muscle pulled taut, like frayed twine, ready to snap.

"You and your damn hot head!" Wallace was shouting. "You had it, Jennings. You had it, and you threw it away. *Dammit.*" He got right up in Chase's face, and I had the sudden image of a drill sergeant yelling at his troops.

Chase spat a mouthful of blood on the maroon carpet. His white teeth were stained red, and for some reason, of all things, this frightened me the most.

"Tucker and I have business," Chase said.

"Not here you don't," said Wallace furiously. "You come here, into this family, and draw on one of your brothers? You're *out,* Jennings. Clear your effects and get out of my sight."

Silence.

"*What?* Hold on a second." Sean was the first to speak. He loosened his hold for just a moment, and in it, I dove in front of Chase, blocking Wallace's words with my body.

"You want a gang, go find one," said Wallace sharply over me to Chase. "There're lots of them, right outside. You can shoot anyone you want."

"I don't want to shoot just anyone," Chase said.

"There's a reason," said Billy in a tenuous voice. "There's a reason, right, Chase?"

Chase didn't answer.

"There're a lot more than one."

The way parted, and Tucker was revealed, one hand in his pocket, the casted arm hanging limply at his side. I immediately scanned for weapons. None that I could see, but that didn't mean there wasn't one in the back of his waistband.

"But one main reason, I suppose," he finished flatly.

"Care to elaborate?" challenged Chase.

"Not really," he said. And his head hung down, as if in shame. As if he were capable of such a human emotion. "But for the record, *she* kissed *me*."

The shock exploded within me.

"You . . ." I began, ready to spring on him again. To scratch out his eyes and choke him with my bare hands. He spoke as if my mother's murder held the same gravity of some stupid, fraudulent kiss! As if either one of these occurrences could be the reason Chase might want to kill him.

"Stay back," Chase whispered to me. I felt a string break somewhere inside, beneath the hardened exterior of fury. That kiss was a secret I would have taken to the grave.

I stood as tall as I could, feeling Chase warm and solid against my back, and Wallace just inches in front of me. I placed my hands squarely on his narrow chest and pushed him away.

"We have to get out," I hissed at Wallace, every muscle braced to defend myself. "He's brought others!"

"He's brought no one," said Wallace.

"I got kicked out," said Tucker. "Because of you." His voice was rougher than the last time I'd seen him, but it still sent waves of dread through me. A hateful, green-eyed gaze met mine.

"Hey, come on, man," said Sean, nursing his jaw and grimacing at his recruit.

Wallace put one hand on my vibrating shoulder and clamped down slowly, like a tightening vise. Then he turned around to Tucker and told him authoritatively:

"We play nice around here. We play nice, or we don't play at all."

Tucker scoffed, then stared at the wall beside him, as if it might burn him to look at me one second longer. The air hummed with tension.

"I don't know what he told you," I said, voice shaking with adrenaline. "But he lies. That's all he does. He's here to take us down."

"Don't be dramatic," said Tucker, his face dirty, his expression flat. "I liked you better when you thought you were dying." He turned to Sean, who was now snarling in my defense. "If she and Jennings are here, forget it. I'm out."

Every nerve crackled within me like the end of a live wire. The hallway thickened with spectators, but I couldn't take my eyes off Tucker. I had to watch him, be ready for anything.

"Cool off," said Wallace loudly. I tried to jerk away but his grip on my bicep did not loosen. "We knew he was coming, remember? The recruit from the Knoxville base. Billy retrieved his discharge papers from the mainframe after he made contact with Sean last week."

I lowered my center of gravity, ready to punch, kick, bite, whatever I had to do should Tucker spring on me.

"We need him, Miller. To get into the base. He's got information no one else has. And now we have you to back up if it's legitimate. We need to make this work."

It took me a second to grasp what he was saying. He meant for Chase to go, but for me to stay. With Tucker Morris.

"Make it work without me," I said.

"Don't be stupid," said Riggins, face grim. "You know what it's like out there. You're wanted in connection with the sniper murders." He sounded genuinely worried.

"I'm only wanted because *he* turned me in," I spat, jerking my head toward Tucker.

"That, actually," ticked Tucker, "is *not* true."

"Like I believe you!"

"I'm guilty of most everything she'll accuse me of," said Tucker, now speaking to everyone. "But not that. They arrested me before I made it back to my office. You remember Delilah, don't you, Ember? You should. You tied her up and locked her in a cell."

An image came before me of an elderly woman with white hair and blue, translucent irises.

"Did you kill her, too?" I asked. "You said you would if she ever told anyone."

"I never said that." He glanced at his feet. I couldn't deny he looked beaten down. I reminded myself this was all part of his plan to lure us in.

"The guard on rounds found her. Lucky for you, she'd refused to talk, but they had a whole team waiting to question me when I got back. I said you were dead, *completed*, just like Jennings." His expression turned sour. "The gatekeeper didn't agree."

The gate guard at the back of the complex had let me out to deliver the body—Chase's body—to the crematorium, just as I'd done the days before. He would have seen Tucker follow me, then return alone.

"And they decided to kick you out, but not report me missing for another month? Let me guess, they wanted to give me a head start," I said.

Tucker scoffed. "You think they wanted the region to know someone—a *girl*, no less—escaped the holding cells? How do you think that makes them look? At least now they can build you up as accessory to a serial killer."

I had no retort. Tucker's story was actually possible. And now it made sense why I'd been listed with the other four suspects. The MM wanted me dead, and linking me to the sniper made me appear dangerous, reckless. Capable of escape. They could justify admitting I bettered them if I was a hardened criminal.

"But . . . he's a murderer," I stammered.

"Do you think he's the first person here to be called that?" Wallace was wild-eyed now, and shaking. "Do you think I'm so different?"

Every voice was silent. Every eye on Wallace. Even mine, which had torn away from Tucker's petulant form.

Wallace had killed people. Maybe Article violators. Maybe people just like my mother. And others—Riggins, Houston, Lincoln—they might have, too. Not Sean, Rebecca had told me, but he had taken girls at the reform school down to the shack. Girls like Rosa Montoya, who'd ridden beside me on the bus. Who'd turned hollow after the torture Sean and the guards had inflicted upon her.

I'd lived here for weeks feeling safer than I had since my mother's arrest, avoiding the most obvious fact in the world: I didn't talk about my past, and *neither did they*.

It isn't so bad, I told myself, even though I trembled with this new reality. They'd done bad things; they weren't bad people. Hadn't Chase been just inches away from that cliff as well? And he'd come back to me, redeemed himself. As had Wallace, and these others, too.

But not Tucker. Tucker Morris could never be good.

He was sulking now, but that was just pretend. He was trying to pull me in with his tattered street clothes and his dirty face. With his fake discharge that Billy had supposedly seen on the FBR mainframe and his anger, like I'd ruined his precious career. I wouldn't fall for it.

"It's him or us—*both* of us—Wallace. Make your choice," I said firmly, but my thoughts begged him to see reason, to believe us about Tucker and to begin a full-scale evacuation.

"I should go," said Tucker. "I'll go . . . I don't know. I'll go somewhere."

"You're staying," Wallace told him.

I felt my knees shake for the first time.

Wallace had chosen. *For the resistance,* I told myself, *nothing personal.* But it felt personal. He'd hooked me with that family talk, and like a sucker, I'd bought it. As though it could fill the void within me. I had to tell myself three times to move before I finally did.

"Can I get our things, please?"

Wallace's face twisted. "Someone get their bag. Just what they came in with." He turned back in to the supply room.

A minute later Billy appeared, our backpack in hand. He didn't look up at me. Better that way. I hated losing friends.

Sean swore a lot, but couldn't leave while information

about Rebecca was on the line. Riggins tried to reason with Wallace. In the end it was Lincoln and Houston that escorted us downstairs, past the smoke-filled lobby. Past John the landlord, who unknowingly reminded us to bring back a pack of smokes. And then we were outside on the street in the unfriendly morning light, exposed to whomever challenged us, barred from the only place that had felt like home in a long time.

CHAPTER
8

CHASE and I made it to the Red Cross Camp just before noon. We didn't have any other options. The safest place was a crowd. The biggest crowd was the Square, and we weren't about to risk that place again.

We crossed Cumberland outside the tall wrought-iron entranceway to World's Fair Park, the location of the camp. Suspended above the white circus tent patched with blue tarps was an enormous copper globe—the sunsphere, a structure that Billy had told me was built for the World's Fair in the early 1980s. Now, half the panels were missing, and it served as a marker that temporary relief—not the actual Red Cross, they'd gone under during the War, but the Sisters of Salvation—waited below.

Chase motioned me through a long line and I followed him in shock, reeling from my latest encounter with my mother's killer. From letting him go *again*.

What lies was Sean being fed? All Tucker had told Sean was that Rebecca had been in the holding cells a very short time before being transferred to Chicago. But what if he'd seen her? What would he have done to her?

And how could Wallace be so stupid? He'd always put his home, his family, first . . . yet here he was, letting the most dangerous person I'd ever met sneak past his defenses.

I told myself not to think about it. He'd kicked us out and that was that. Adapt. Move on. Get over it. It wasn't like we were going to stay there forever anyway. We'd have to find a way to meet Sean and figure out what evil scheme Tucker was devising.

Chase stopped suddenly and snagged my elbow. He jerked me away into a crowd of people waiting for the medical clinic to open.

"What is it?" I asked.

"Soldiers." My mind immediately shot to Tucker, but no, Tucker wasn't here. Tucker was with the resistance.

Chase carved an exit, not forcefully enough to cause a fight, but definitely with purpose. I kept my eyes on his heels, half skipping so I didn't step on them. When I ventured a glance over my shoulder, I saw that there were soldiers swarming the entire compound.

Across the street, where we'd been standing five minutes earlier, another patrol team started picking through the huddled groups of vagrants. One officer had a clipboard and was showing photos to a feeble old man who leaned against a half-collapsed bus shelter. Above, on every rooftop roamed a soldier with a shotgun.

We would have been safer hiding out in some dark alley.

"Come on," Chase said. "We've got to keep moving. Let's go inside; people are thinning out here."

The Red Cross Camp was comprised of over a hundred cots, shoved into even rows and covered by drooping canvas tents. There were no walls, no privacy, no heat in the winter or fans in the summer. It was fenced off by removable chain-link partitions, which boasted cracks large enough for any thief to sneak through. The sign-in station at the front was manned by a Sister of Salvation, and behind her, attached to a metal pole was a sign: 4 HOURS ONLY.

Below it, on a large plywood board, were five photographs. The five suspects wanted in conjunction with the sniper murders.

"Chase," I whispered. He squinted across the distance.

Despite this, he made his way toward the entrance, where a line of twenty or so people waited to get a four-hour bunk. A warning within me screamed that this was wrong. We couldn't go inside and pin ourselves down; I would be recognized.

"Stay in line," he said, and headed toward the sign-in station. I saw him glance quickly at the board. His back straightened, and that was enough to say he'd seen my photo. He leaned forward to talk to a Sister at the desk who was wearing a white paper surgical mask.

The line moved forward. My gaze was drawn to a woman who'd moved in front of the board. Her green collared shirt made her skin appear ashen, and the long denim skirt was black where the seams dragged through the dirt. Though probably only in her early thirties, her hair had gone almost completely gray. Two soldiers, both younger than she, flanked her on either side.

"Listen up!" one of them shouted. I bumped into someone as I stepped back. For the moment I still blended with the crowd, but it wouldn't stay that way for long. I stared at Chase's back, willing him to return.

The woman stepped aside and revealed a boy maybe five years old. He had red dashes on his cheeks, not just from a recent tantrum but a long season of crying. The fingers of one hand twisted his mangy, shoulder-length hair. The other hand was missing.

The woman approached the boy and opened his shirt. His skin was scarred and warped by past burns, red with infection. She lifted him up for everyone to see.

"Oh God," I said before I caught myself. Chase approached, eyes betraying no shock.

"Here." He was holding a surgical mask like the Sisters were wearing. Hurriedly, I looped the elastic bands around my ears and felt my breath warm the covered space over my nose and mouth. This shield would hide my identity at least for a little while.

"There are . . ." The woman's voice trembled. Her eyes darted around the crowd of onlookers.

"Louder," prompted the soldier.

"There are worse ways to live!" she cried. "You think it's bad now, but you have no idea. If you have information on the sniper, if you've seen the criminals from the wanted posters, tell a soldier right away!"

Rampant whispers flew around the circle.

The soldier unhooked the strap locking the gun in his belt. He toyed with the boy's hair, like a father might, but for the threat so obviously posed by his weapon. From his blank expression, I knew he'd have no trouble hurting this boy to get what he wanted. I shoved back, but those behind me held solid.

"Do you think the soldiers did that?" I whispered to Chase.

His expression remained flat; only his eyes showed his rage. He didn't answer.

"Now, who has information for me?" the soldier asked.

"Someone's got to stop it," whispered a man beside me. He was right. My blood was boiling again.

"I heard that Miller girl was in Tent City yesterday after the attack," a woman to my right confessed.

I went absolutely rigid. I didn't dare breathe. Chase's shoulders rose. He shook his head as if to say *don't move*.

"Come with us. We need to ask you a few questions," said the second soldier. The mother was now grasping her child against her chest, though she seemed too petrified to move.

"That's all I know," said the confessor, her voice faltering. "I swear, that's all I know."

"Come with us," he repeated. "Or you'll be charged with withholding information."

"I told you all I know!" she screamed as one of the soldiers hauled her away.

My mouth fell open in horror. There were hundreds of people within earshot. Hundreds who could take down these two soldiers, but no one moved. I wanted to stop them myself, to say, *"I'm the one you're looking for!"* but I couldn't. They'd kill me on the spot.

"The sniper did this to us!" The mother finally set her child down, close to where we stood in the arc surrounding her. She wept bitterly. "We were fine before he got here!" People murmured their agreement.

I wanted to shake her. I told myself she was scared, that's why she was saying this. Things were just as dangerous before. But the woman in Tent City had told me not everyone would see the good of the resistance, and she was right.

The second soldier lifted his baton, and a path cleared back into the medical station. I followed Chase's gaze to the little boy, who was now bawling quietly and trying to close his shirt with his single hand while his mother ushered him away.

"What was that?" I whispered. I felt exposed; every sideways glance prickled my skin.

He swore, obviously agitated. "Advertising. Nothing puts people in their place like the threat of pain. I saw it in Chicago. It's sick."

It was not so unlike Wallace's plan to let the people see me in Tent City, I thought. Only that message was meant to inspire hope, not fear.

The world was coming unhinged. I could feel it, like a great crushing weight on my chest, pushing me into the ground beneath my feet. I'd been linked to a serial murderer, my name slandered across the country. My mother's killer had infiltrated the resistance. Girls like Sarah were being beaten by their MM boyfriends and left for dead. Moms were using their kids to spread the MM's tyrannical message. I'd lost Rebecca all over again, I didn't know what was happening at home with Beth, and poor Rosa was probably still a zombie up at the reformatory. If there was ever a time to push back, it was now, but how?

"Name?"

My eyes refocused on a woman in front of me. A Sister. The light blue knot in her handkerchief was tied perfectly. She wore a paper mask over her mouth and nose, like mine.

I felt a surge of panic and blurted, "Lori Whittman."

"Lori Whittman," she read down the list on her clipboard. "Have you been here in the past two days, Ms. Whittman?" She didn't look too closely at my face.

"Mrs.," said Chase, tearing away from another masked Sister and moving to my side. "My wife is sick," he said. "She needs to rest."

I coughed for effect, adjusting the mask to cover as much of my face as possible.

"If they're married . . ." began the one who had asked my name. She was halted by the other's dubious expression.

"We're married," I said defensively. I held up my left hand, thankful for my stolen wedding band.

"Fine," huffed the one, still unconvinced. "Remember you'll be issued a citation if the FBR finds out otherwise."

I felt myself stiffen, wondering if the MM was going to be dropping by to question us, but I didn't see anyone in a blue uniform within the tent.

The cranky Sister led us inside the flimsy chain-link barrier to the right, where we passed a bin for contraband items and cot after cot of sleeping individuals. There were three empty bunks in the back, these bigger.

The pungency of human sweat was nearly dizzying. Someone hacked up a lung to my right. We picked a cot beside a family of four, all sharing a space smaller than a twin bed. I thought of the woman outside with her son and wished they would come rest here instead of continuing their campaign.

I sat on the filthy canvas cot, avoiding a black spot near the edge that still looked damp. We'd had it good at the Wayland Inn.

I sighed, unwilling to pull the mask down on my chin. They hadn't recognized me, but I wasn't feeling particularly relieved. Chase sat next to me and placed the backpack down beside his feet, avoiding a puddle of stagnant rainwater that had blown in. He took a slow, deep breath.

"Tubman should be back in town tonight. We'll stay with him until the roads are clear." He kept his voice low so as not to wake those around us.

He wanted to go to the safe house, to abandon Rebecca and everything we'd come here to do, and though I wasn't proud of it, part of me did want to run away and hide.

Who was I kidding? The chances of me making it that far were slim. Any one of these people might turn me in. Any one of the soldiers prowling around the city might shoot me without question. I knew this; it scared me to death. But not as much as Tucker handing over the entire Knoxville resistance to the MM.

"We can't leave," I said resolutely. "Tucker's planning something."

He flinched at the name. "We have to leave. It's not safe here for you."

"It's not safe here for anyone."

"Wallace made his decision." Chase's hand swiped along his temple, and he held it there in pain. The earlier fight must have triggered his injuries from the arrest. When he saw my concern, he dropped his arm, as if embarrassed.

"It's a bad decision and you know it," I said, wondering how much of his distance had to do with his new knowledge of me kissing Tucker.

"It doesn't matter what I know."

I felt my shoulders bunch defensively. "We've got to stay. Sean's still there—I have to help him get Rebecca—and Billy. . . ."

"They're big kids." His voice was strained.

"They're our *friends*," I said, exasperated. "When people don't do what's best for themselves, you've got a responsibility to do it for them." I'd learned that lesson with my mom.

He laughed wryly.

"Just so we're clear, this rule doesn't apply to you, right?"

I glared at him.

"That's what I thought." He made a frustrated sound in his throat, then mumbled, "I should've put you on that truck to the safe house when I had the chance."

I balked. "Well, you don't have to worry about that. I wouldn't have gone."

His brow quirked, and his eyes sparkled with challenge.

I shifted my legs to the opposite side of the cot so that we could watch each other's backs.

"So, is it true?" he said, gaze roaming.

He didn't have to qualify it. I knew what he meant. My damp hands clasped, unclasped, clasped again.

"Did he hurt you, Em?"

"No," I said quickly.

Chase's jaw twitched. He didn't say anything.

"It was the only way to steal his gun." My voice was all but a whisper now. It was impossible to explain how logic changed in the face of death, but still I felt ashamed.

After a moment, he touched my arm. It was a gentle move, a move of apology and support and question for what might become of us, and I stared down at his fingers, feeling my heart crack.

"I wish Billy hadn't messed up my shot," he said.

I wasn't so sure I disagreed.

I adjusted the mask and focused on the bag, careful not to showcase Chase's old MM nightstick and radio against the back. The batteries were dead, but I thought we might have some cash left. It would be good to be able to follow any new developments in the nightly report. My hands wandered over our extra change of clothes, a toiletries kit. A worn copy of the novel *Frankenstein* filled with the letters I'd written to Chase during his training, all rubber-banded together.

"Keep your head down."

At Chase's order I froze. Down the row, in the direction of the cougher, was a soldier—the same one with the clipboard from across the street who'd been talking to the old man. He was shaking the sleepers and checking their faces.

"There's a hole in the fence we can fit through," I whispered. I'd seen it when we came in. The soldier reached the family of four and poked the father's shoulder with his baton.

"Get up," he said gruffly. "Look at these pictures."

The man blinked and rubbed his eyes. His wife woke their two children and pulled them behind her.

"Stand up," Chase breathed. I rose and zipped the bag, pretending to keep myself busy with the contents. He stayed seated but moved to the edge of the cot, ready to follow.

A low beep cut through the coughing. The soldier's radio.

"Hold it," said the soldier. For a second I thought he was talking to us and fought the urge to run. I adjusted the paper mask. My knee brushed against Chase's.

The soldier's radio hissed, then clicked, then went clear as a woman's voice came through.

"All units be advised. Fire at 1020 Franklin Station Way, ten-story motel identified as the Wayland Inn. Emergency crews called to attend have found evidence of rebel activity. All units, including road patrols, reroute to Franklin Station Way immediately. Repeat, all units reroute to Franklin Station Way immediately."

CHAPTER
9

I HELD absolutely still, the breath locked in my chest, as the operator repeated her report.

A fire in the Wayland Inn. Not a breach in Wallace and Chase's imposed security, not an MM attack on the resistance stronghold, but a fire. Was it as simple as John the landlord failing to put out one of his cigarettes? It seemed entirely too coincidental that there should be a problem now, so near to the arrival of Tucker Morris.

The soldier abandoned the family without a word of explanation and jogged to the main entrance of the compound. As soon as he was out of sight, Chase grabbed our bag and pulled me toward the hole in the fence.

No one bothered looking up as we passed, or as we separated the chain links to sneak through. Halfway through the metal snagged my shirt and made a ripping sound as I jerked free.

The thoughts raced through my mind. Sean was still at the motel. Had he made it out? What about Billy?

It took only a few steps before I realized Chase was leading me in the wrong direction—toward East End Auto and Tubman's checkpoint.

"Stop!" I dug my heels in. "What are you doing? We have to go back!"

"We can't go back." His expression was grim. When I whipped my hand out of his grasp, he blocked my way, steeling himself for a fight. His hands were down and loose, as if ready to yard me should I bolt.

"They're sending every unit that direction." He gaze darted behind me, sharp and focused, before returning to my face. "Who do you think they're hoping to find?"

The sniper. They were looking for the same five people as the soldier who'd just been combing through the Red Cross Camp. They were looking for me.

"They won't find us," I said, ignoring the dread sticking to my insides. "But they might find Sean and Billy and Wallace, even stupid Riggins if we don't help."

He flinched.

"Tucker did this," I said. "You know he did. We're the only ones who know him. We're the only ones who can stop him."

I placed my palm on his chest, feeling his heart hammer beneath his threadbare sweater. Slowly, his fingers closed around my wrist, his thumb gently sliding over the sensitive skin covering my veins, before pushing it away.

"We stay together."

I nodded.

We kept to the shadows when we could, avoiding the beggars and working girls in the alleyways. The warm day was humid enough from the week's rain, and the sweat coated my skin and ran freely down my chest and back. We ran until we came to Church Avenue, a street still in use by the public, though not heavily trafficked.

An MM cruiser drove by with its lights on and siren blaring. My heart skipped a beat. I looked down and felt my hands grow clammy.

"Not for us," Chase said.

We followed the smoke toward the Wayland Inn. People who had wandered from various areas of town had gathered on the surface streets surrounding the structure. Transients and drug dealers, unemployed scavengers, and even some curious workers from the west side of the city. They kept coming. With so little to occupy their days, a burning motel was prime entertainment.

Chase led the way through the crowd. As we came around the side of an old boarded-up Chinese restaurant we saw the flames, rising a hundred feet in the air, just below the line of windows on the tenth floor.

Instantly I became aware of the smell—sharp and suffocating. It made my eyes burn, even from my place across the street. A blast of sirens came from the two fire trucks parked in a V in front of the motel's entry. The firemen had begun piping water from a nearby hydrant.

Soldiers arrived, marching in from the northern side of the street. Black, bulletproof vests covered their blue canvas uniforms, and Kevlar helmets shaded their eyes. They carried weapons—guns, nightsticks, and long plastic shields.

No rescue teams entered.

A man stumbled out the front door carrying a woman on his shoulders. They were both black with soot and coughing. No one I recognized. Three soldiers were on them immediately, and they were cuffed and led away.

A loud burst of gunfire elicited screams from the crowd. It sounded like fireworks; shots popping off one after another. My throat tightened, though not from the bitter smoke. I knew that sound was coming from the fourth floor.

"Ammunition caught fire," Chase said, leaning close to my ear so that no one around us heard him. I searched in vain for Sean, but instead focused on a lone Sister of Salvation, speaking to a soldier near the front of the crowd. He gestured for her to back up with the others, and while he was distracted by another volley of gunfire, she slipped into the crowd, coming our direction.

Fearing she had recognized us, I backpedaled into Chase, and was just about to tell him we had to beat it when she appeared at my right side.

"Where's everyone else?" I blinked and refocused on her blue eyes and the short, black hair that matched my own.

Cara. I couldn't make sense of why she'd been talking to a soldier.

"What are you doing here?" A new dread washed over me as my mind flashed to Sarah and Tubman. Something had happened to the convoy.

"Where is Wallace?" Her voice was raw.

"Where is *Tubman*? Did he get caught?"

"I don't know."

"What do you mean you don't know?"

"I don't know!"

Her cryptic answers stoked my irritation. Something had happened for them to separate, but there wasn't time to ask now.

A man I didn't recognize was shouting from a third floor window. In only his boxer shorts, socks, and a dirty T-shirt, he attempted to climb out using only the moth-eaten curtains as a ladder. The top of them was already on fire.

"Hey! There's a guy up there!" shouted someone.

"Help him!" begged a woman. None of the soldiers moved to assist.

More gunfire from upstairs. My heart kept time with its tempo.

This time the rear line of soldiers—those closest to the building—turned around and, as one unit, fired at the building. The discharge of weapons was muffled by the roaring spray of the hoses and the sirens; the bullets disappeared into the smoke. The man trying to escape through the window slipped in his surprise, and fell three feet before catching the tearing curtains.

"We need to get out of here." Cara's voice wavered. She was backing away, face pale. "Out of town."

I grabbed her arm. "We don't know if they're still alive!"

Her gaze landed on mine. "All units are called in to contain the fire. Every head is turned this direction. This is our chance."

A chill zipped through me. "How are we supposed to get out?" The highways were still blocked.

It started from the back, a wave of bodies shoving one

another into the front line of soldiers. The soldiers pushed them back with their shields. Cara bumped into me, but when I tried to pull back she held on.

"The other truck at the checkpoint. If you're not there in an hour, I'm leaving without you."

Before I could respond, she'd disappeared into the crowd.

Chase's grip tightened around my hand.

"Over there!" He pointed at a man in a singed sweater on his hands and knees at the corner of the building, by the Dumpsters. He'd somehow avoided the main entrance and the fire escapes.

"John!"

We shoved through the crowd toward the motel manager. His eyes were bloodshot and his teeth stained gray, like he'd been eating smoke.

"Guess I . . . don't need a cigarette . . . now," he huffed as I helped him up.

"Did you see if anyone got out?" I asked urgently.

"Heard 'em leave . . . through the west exit."

My mind flashed to the blueprint of the building posted above the couch in Wallace's room. There were several marked exits. The MM had covered the front, the fire escapes, and the two back doors. The side route was thirty feet behind the Dumpster, tucked within the building's maintenance area. It was blocked by the looming stone office building Chase and Sean had searched. The alley between them was only wide enough for one person to sneak through at a time.

I ran in that direction, toward the Dumpster, behind which waited the narrow leaf-carpeted alleyway. Leaning against the outside of the entrance, a black cat tucked under his arm, was Billy.

"You're okay!" I shouted, grateful that he was alive.

He nodded weakly, wiping his mouth on his shirtsleeve. His face was beet red from the heat. "I think Gypsy's dead." He lifted the cat, and I nearly vomited. Her head was indented, as if something had smashed it.

"The others?" asked Chase, helping Billy lay Gypsy on the ground. "Billy!"

The boy shook his head, propping his dead cat against the side of the building, where she wouldn't be stepped on. "Most are out. Wallace and Riggins went back for Houston and Lincoln. No one could find them."

"And Sean?"

"He's . . . he was right behind me!"

I froze.

For one instant I saw Sean as he had been, in those woods behind the reformatory, hiding my intent to escape from the guards who had caught me, who meant to kill me. I felt the shudder tear through my body when he'd shielded me from the blows that had hit him instead.

No. Sean could not be left in this building to burn.

There were no more thoughts. I pushed past Billy and ran down the narrow alley. Someone grasped my shirt, but I slipped away.

"Stop!" shouted Chase.

But I didn't stop. I ran until I passed the broken water heaters and the metallic switchboards, until the alley opened to reveal a cement patio and a side door below an emergency exit sign.

No soldiers. Not yet anyway.

I placed my hand on the handle. Immediately it singed my palm. A putrid smell filled my nostrils—my own charred flesh.

I swore, gripping the hot doorknob with my shirt and turning it. It pulled out, revealing a great tidal wave of smoke that nearly bowled me over.

I sputtered. The poison siphoned down my throat and grasped my lungs. I covered my mouth with my hand and ducked, trying to remember what I'd learned in elementary school about stop, drop, and roll. I had to stay low.

Sure enough, the first onslaught of smoke left a thick cloud grazing over the ceiling. It was a petrifying sight—swirling like the vortex of a building tornado. I kicked a rock into the jamb, kept my body hunched down, and pushed inside.

"Sean!" I shouted. Then coughed. I breathed in through my teeth, as though they might serve as a filter. "SEAN!"

I'd entered into the stairway. Where we'd first been searched by CJ, the guard posing as a homeless man in the lobby just outside the door. I glanced up the metal steps, but the white plumes wound up in a spiral, disappearing into the next floor. It was so hot; sweat immediately began to drip from every pore in my body.

Something broke upstairs. A wooden crack, a faint explosion, and then the building groaned so loudly I was sure it was going to topple down over me.

A hand smothered my face. Through the haze I saw Chase, squinting, eyes red. He was wearing just his T-shirt, his sweater overtop now ripped in two and held against both our faces. Billy was right behind him, the sleeve of his shirt tied around his nose and mouth.

"Get out of here!" Chase shouted above the crackling. "There's no time!"

I didn't know if he meant until the MM took the building, or until the building took us all, but I wasn't about to wait around and find out. I took the stairs two at a time to the second floor, feeling his grip slide off my sweat-slicked arm.

No sign of Sean.

"Sean!" I tried again, but my shouts were getting progressively weaker. The urgency made me tremble. Sean had risked his life to help me at the reformatory. I owed it to him to return the favor.

The smoke took on an orange hue. It became so thick I could barely see right in front of me. My boots began to stick, like I was walking on gum. In horror, I realized that they were beginning to melt on the stairs. We were running out of time.

"Over there!" Chase shouted, sprinting past me to the top of the third floor. Sean was lying on his back on the landing; someone was desperately trying to hoist him up. The smoke made him weak, and he fumbled around like a drunk.

As I got closer, I saw that the person trying to help was Tucker.

My temples throbbed from the smoke and surprise. He

had started the fire, I was sure of it, so what was he still doing here?

"Help me get him up!" shouted Tucker, struggling to grab Sean with the cast on his arm. His words spurred us back into motion. Chase pulled Sean's arm over his shoulders and began lugging him down the stairs. Sean's head hung limply; his feet dragged behind. The fear began to take over. Sean couldn't be dead. Not here. Not like this.

On the second floor, Tucker lost his footing and dove into the wall. Without thinking, I grabbed his arm to steady him. We locked eyes for one short moment.

Don't help him!

But the larger voice inside yelled *we have to get out*! And somehow right then "we" included Tucker Morris, too.

"Chase! Soldiers!" cried Billy, coughing with his mask lowered. He was standing in the stairwell, pointing out the blackened window. Soot couldn't hide the fear blanketing his features.

Chase was beside him, scraping a clear spot in the glass to check.

"Exit's blocked!" I could barely hear him. He turned fast, sweat streaming off his face. "Up to the roof! Go! Go!"

Billy went up first. Then Chase heaving Sean. I tried to help, but he wouldn't let me. "Go!" he kept yelling. Tucker was right on my heels.

We were halfway up the seventh set of stairs when another eruption of gunfire came from just below. I braced reactively, and as I did, a piece of flaming drywall came crashing down from the ceiling and landed at my feet. My body twisted backward, slipping on my sticky soles. Tucker caught me beneath the arms; I could feel the sweat soaking through his shirt. In horror, I looked up, hypnotized by the fiery board on the steps that now separated us from the others. Sparks and burning ashes exploded from it, pinching my bare arms and neck in a dozen different places.

Tucker returned the cloth to my nose and mouth.

"We have to jump!" he yelled.

It was at least four steps up, and my muscles were burning. The fire was suffocating my strength from the inside out.

"Chase!"

He stopped at my voice and turned, terror lighting his face.

Balancing Sean on one shoulder he held his other arm out toward me, urging me to jump the four steps up to him. It wasn't far, but it could have been miles. Sweat and smoke blocked my vision. The roar of the fire muted whatever words he shouted. I trembled, seized by fear.

"Jump!" Tucker ordered. I took a step back in order to shove off from a lower step. A sob raked my throat.

I hesitated.

Tucker rammed into me hard, sending me careening up the steps and into Chase's chest. He grasped my shirt, pulling me the rest of the way. I screamed—for a moment I thought my pant legs were on fire, but they were only scorched at the bottom.

"Keep going!" Chase said. Billy ran ahead, disappearing into the mist.

A second later Tucker came colliding into the three of us.

The door was three feet away. Tucker shoved past and kicked the door, once, twice. It burst open, and he disappeared outside.

Chase grabbed me around the waist and threw me after Tucker, into a day turned dark by black smoke. Sean's limp form followed. Just outside the exit, Chase fell to his hands and knees. Billy was before me, shaking his head, as though waking from a dream.

The world spun. The clean air seemed just as poisonous as the smoke. I collapsed into the lip of the roof, hacking up black ooze, sliding down to where Chase had dumped Sean.

"Sean!" I croaked, eyes streaming. He was breathing, however shallowly, and in a burst of movement, he rolled on his side and vomited violently. I sobbed with relief.

And then Chase's hands were on my face, my hair, my shoulders and legs.

He swore sharply, snatching away the hot St. Michael medallion from my skin. It stuck, but when I tried to cry out, I coughed again. Exhaustion made my vision waver. My eyes streamed with tears.

"What were you thinking?" he shouted furiously. The world behind him spun. I felt another urge to be sick. "You could have been killed! You *never* listen!"

"So what!" I was drained and scared and burning everywhere. I didn't care what happened to me.

"So *what?*" he repeated, as if I'd struck him. He looked like he didn't recognize me.

"Take it easy," said someone behind me. Tucker.

Chase rounded on him fast, and instantly the teams

shifted. Not the resistance against the MM. Not Chase against me. But us against my mother's killer.

He hit Tucker square in the jaw before he ever saw it coming. Tucker flew back, spitting blood on the deck. The exertion toppled Chase, too, and he fell forward.

"You two are still trying to kill each other?"

I looked up. A lanky man with long, peppered hair was pulling Tucker off the ground.

"Wallace!" croaked Billy.

Wallace's face was smudged with smoke and sweat. He crouched beside Billy, first slapping him on the back and then pulling him into a tight embrace. "You're all right," he said several times. "Just a little smoke is all."

Chase swore, and I followed his eye line to a crowd of our people—Houston and the brothers and Riggins included—all gathered around the bench where I'd sat with Chase yesterday.

All gathered around a body, lying still upon it.

Lincoln.

"Gone," I heard Wallace say grimly. "Gone when the boys found him."

Choking. Coughing. My beaten heart twisting. *Think about it later.* We had to get out of here.

I knelt, glancing over the edge. The riot below had grown, and the soldiers were trying to contain it. The line closest to the building was waiting for us.

"We're done," said Riggins, hands on his glistening head. "We're done."

"You did this! They came here for you!" Houston approached behind him, eyes red, but not from the fire.

I couldn't answer, lost to another coughing fit. *Me?* If Wallace had only listened! But then again, Tucker wouldn't be beside us if he'd turned us in.

"We're not done," said Wallace. There was a crazy light in his eyes when he stood from Billy's side. He removed a gun from his waistband—the black pistol he carried—and chambered a round. It was then that I noticed the crate he'd left when he'd found Billy. It was filled with ammunition and firearms.

My burning eyes widened.

"Think!" said Chase. "Fire escapes are blocked. Boiler exit is blocked. Front and rear doors are out."

"No!" Wallace shouted. The others had left Lincoln now, and were gathered in a tight half circle around those of us still on the ground. Eight from the resistance had made it to the roof before us, Wallace included.

"We've lost!" shouted Chase.

"We've lost when I say we've lost!" Knoxville's leader roared back. "We have rules, Jennings! We don't abandon our brothers! We don't abandon our home! This is our chance to take a stand—"

"We can't fight if we don't live!" Chase yelled.

"This *is* the fight," Wallace said with finality. "This is the only fight that matters. The one we fight today."

Then he grabbed a pistol out of the crate and shoved it into Billy's trembling hands. Still weak, the boy wavered when he stood. He stared at the gun in his hands and said, "Wallace?"

A *whir* and a *crack* as a bullet flew by. They'd seen us on the roof and were attacking.

No. We couldn't die here.

"Line up," Wallace told us.

"Wallace, please," I begged him. Chase was dragging me away from the ledge, teeth bared.

"Line up!" Wallace demanded. The other guys faltered, ducking low beneath the ledge for protection. Fearful glances were passed among them. A temporary break in the smoke brought a hailstone of more bullets. Riggins, swearing profusely, grabbed a gun and kneeled behind the barrier, aiming down toward the line of soldiers. Two others followed. Houston's hands were cupped over his ears, but though his lips moved he made no sound.

"Crazy bastards," muttered Tucker.

A jet of flames burst from the stairway and then was sucked back inside. The roof beneath our feet trembled with the strength of an earthquake. Had I a voice, I might have screamed.

A weak voice came from behind me. "Through the other building." I turned, surprised to find Sean sitting upright.

Yes. The office building adjacent to the Wayland Inn was abandoned. The space between them was narrow, maybe three feet. We might be able to jump in through a parallel window.

An instant later Chase and Tucker were running toward the bench where poor Lincoln lay.

They lowered his limp body to the ground, and I had the sudden revolting memory of the base, transporting the dead prisoners in laundry carts to the crematorium. I hadn't known those people, but Lincoln was not a stranger. I knew what his laugh sounded like. I knew how tall he was when I stood next to him. That was when I realized—*really* realized—he was dead.

Tucker and Chase each took an end of the wooden bench. They carried it around the stairway exit, toward the side of the roof that interfaced the office building. I helped Sean up, and we ran to follow. There was a shattered window down a few feet across the gap. I watched as they leveled the bench between the roof's ledge and the windowsill, making a slide into the darkened room below. The curtain of jagged glass above made for an ominous entrance.

When I glanced back four more of the men were gone, maybe back through the smoke-filled stairway. Wallace was shouting, gesturing in wild motions with his arms, and forcing Billy to his knees before the ledge. When Billy tried to get up, Wallace pushed him down.

He'd lost his mind. Billy was like a son to him, and here he was, preparing to sacrifice them both for a fight we'd never win.

Billy was coming with us, and Wallace and the others too, if I could make them.

But as I approached, it hit him, an invisible bullet, slicing through the smoke. It ripped through Wallace's shoulder and threw him to the ground, flat on his back.

I ducked low, hearing Chase bellow my name. I kept going.

"Wallace!" I pulled him up, and then Billy was there, and Wallace, groaning, was seated, blood flowing freely from the blackened shirt just below his collarbone. "We have to go," I said desperately. "Come on! Now!"

"Wait, wait a second," Billy was saying. "Wallace?"

Wallace was shaking his head, regripping the pistol that he'd dropped.

"Billy is going to die," I said flatly. "You are going to kill him."

He met my eyes, and I saw the infection, the fever of insanity circling the whites around his irises. I summoned all my strength to burn clarity through my gaze, and after a moment, he blinked.

"Get to the safe house," he said, voice scratchy. "We'll meet you there. All units are pulled in. You have to get on the road now."

My thoughts turned to Cara, waiting at the checkpoint. How much time had passed?

"Take Billy," Wallace said quietly.

My stomach dropped.

"No!" shouted Billy, grasping his shirt like a child. "You'll burn—"

"Take him!" shouted Wallace, and in a burst of strength stood and shoved Billy at me. Chase was suddenly by my side. He grabbed a struggling Billy around the shoulders, locking his arms down.

"Wallace!" Billy was crying. Wallace shoved his handgun into Billy's pocket.

"Exhale when you pull the trigger, just like we talked

— 168 —

about." His voice cracked, though not from the fire. "You saved my life, kid. Remember that."

And with that Wallace collapsed to his knees. He crawled to the crate and grabbed another gun, loading it with shaking hands.

"Go." It was Riggins who broke the trance, pushing me away. "You have to get out of here." He blocked my view of Wallace and smirked. "The sniper. I should have seen it earlier. I wouldn't have given you such a hard time."

I couldn't make sense of what he meant, or why he was now pushing me away from the ledge. He knelt beside Wallace and the only two other remaining resistance members at the Wayland Inn. And then we were running, back toward the bench and the neighboring building, a blazing inferno just beneath our feet.

CHAPTER
10

TUCKER was the first to try the slide. The bench wobbled beneath his weight, but Chase held it steady. After leaping over the threshold, he grinned wildly back at us and then disappeared, only to return a moment later to clear the overhead glass from the window with a scrap of plywood.

I held Sean's arms to steady him, noting how half of his shirt had been singed off his back. It was hard to tell the damage to his skin through the soot. Tucker grabbed him from the other side and helped him down.

If you hurt him, I'm going to kill you, I thought.

Billy put up a good fight, but tired quickly. As soon as he was subdued, Chase pushed him over the ledge of the roof onto the bowed wood of the bench. We had to keep moving. Short quaking bursts had begun to rock the building, threatening a cave-in.

Tucker reached out from the window, grasped Billy's forearms, and jerked him inside.

"You're up," said Chase, meeting my eyes briefly before

lifting me up onto the bench. He stared across the way at Tucker and swore under his breath.

I looked down and gasped when the thick white smoke clouding around my ankles began to pull at me, screwing up my balance. The board groaned as I adjusted my position and tried not to fall.

"Look at Tucker," Chase said. I did, and with Chase holding one hand, I skated down until Tucker was holding the other.

He pulled me inside the building, where my knees wobbled and the natural darkness shocked my eyes. Billy was kneeling over Sean, who'd sunk down against the wall. The room was empty but for the shards of glass on the floor that gleamed black in reflection of the smoke outside.

I spun around just as Chase came in behind me.

We were bright red and streaked with soot—awfully suspicious to those who waited down on the street.

"Clean off," I said. We flipped our clothing inside out. I wiped my face on my forearms, but it just seemed to smear the black.

"That's it, move out," commanded Chase. Sean was sturdier on his feet now, but not by much.

Chase knew the way from having searched this building a few days ago. We followed him to the dark stairway and began our descent. My muscles gripped with every step, and my throat burned with thirst. I longed to rinse the fire from my eyes, but there was no time.

I watched Billy, worried he might try to bolt. My burned hands knotted in his charred shirtsleeve, but he shook me off and pushed forward to the front.

Finally, we reached the exit.

With my heart jammed up my windpipe, I stepped out onto the narrow, one-way street, desolate with all the action occurring next door. Over my shoulder the civilians were rioting, still attacking the soldiers with their fists and their curses. They'd succeeded in breaking the front lines, as so many soldiers were now dedicated to shooting upward through the smoke toward the roof. It was impossible to tell in all the chaos if our people had hit anyone.

My mind turned to Riggins and his last words, urging me to go. *The sniper. I should have seen it earlier.* The pieces fell into place now that I'd had a moment to breathe, and with them came a prickling dread. He'd changed around me, maybe sacrificed himself for me, because he—like the woman in Tent City—thought I was someone I wasn't.

I glanced back for Chase, and instead saw Tucker. My thoughts shifted. Hardened. I remembered why I hated him, why I could never trust him. But somehow something had changed between us. He'd waited for Sean. He'd pushed me over the burning stairs and possibly saved my life.

Screams stole my focus. The roof of the Wayland Inn was collapsing. The fire had taken over, clawing angrily at the blackened sky.

"Wallace!" Billy shouted.

Chase hauled him to the opposite side of the road, where we could no longer see our fallen headquarters. When we were out of sight from the Wayland Inn, we ran.

"The Red Cross Camp," I heard Sean say to Chase as we caught our breath in an alley.

"Aren't there any more of you?" Tucker asked through labored breaths. "Another base or something?"

"The garage," I said. East End Auto. I didn't like Tucker asking that question, and I didn't like leading him to where the carrier met refugees, but we were out of options. "Cara's waiting there."

I hoped she was still waiting there. I didn't know how much time had passed. More than an hour, at least.

We took side streets, staying away from the Red Cross Camp and the Square. With all patrol cars pulled into the fire, the back roads were clear. The breath seared my sore lungs, but there was no time to rest.

Finally we reached the garage, and without delay, Chase pounded the code—SOS—into the flimsy metal.

Sweat streamed into my eyes. One minute passed. Then another.

She was gone. We'd waited too long.

Frustration consumed me. I was just about to kick the door when the bolt inside released, and the metal rose to hip height. Cara and I came face-to-face as I swooped under the threshold.

Her face lifted in surprise when she registered the group.

"You're all that's left?" she said, glancing between us. Her eyes hardened when no one responded.

"Tell me you have keys to that truck." Chase pointed to the yellow Horizons distribution vehicle. The garage didn't smell damp as it had during the storm. Now it was dry, and cold, like the inside of a tomb.

Cara lifted a key ring from the pocket of her Sisters of

Salvation skirt and held them up for us to see. I nearly cried with relief.

"When's Tubman get back?" Sean's voice was a tempered groan.

"We need to get to the safe house," Chase explained. "All units have pulled into the city to look for resistance. The roads should be clear, at least until we pass city limits."

"I don't know when Tubman's getting back," she said, her voice smaller than I'd expected.

"Weren't you with him?" I nearly shouted.

"We got separated," she said smartly. I wanted to shake her. She turned back to the others. "I know a place, though. A checkpoint in Greeneville. We can hide there if we can get out of the city."

"And past the highway patrol." Tucker siphoned in an impatient breath. I watched his face change from speculation to acceptance, and wondered what his angle was.

Cara rolled on. "Tubman makes a stop there. We meet up with him, we get our ride to the safe house."

The blood was still pumping through me. It was as good a plan as we were going to get.

"Find me a delivery uniform," Sean said. "I'll drive. Cara can sit up front and give me directions. We'll tell them we're going to a soup kitchen." I winced as he pulled the remnants of his T-shirt over his head. He blinked for several seconds, placing a hand on the bumper for support as Cara disappeared down the stairs.

Chase jerked the back of the truck open; it clacked against its rickety metal runners.

"I'll drive," he said. "You can barely sit up."

"No." Billy was shaking his head. "We can't leave Wallace here. We can't. He'll come, just wait a minute." His track was stuck on repeat.

Chase tried to force him into the compartment, but Billy lashed out and shoved him back hard. The move was so forecasted, I was sure even I could have evaded it, but Chase didn't. Maybe he wanted Billy to hit him, I don't know.

Then Billy crumbled, tears carving bright tracks down the filth on his cheeks. I crouched by his side and held him tightly against me. "Come on, Billy. If he's made it, he can't wait for us here. We're going together, okay? You and me. Come on." Telling Billy this made me feel stronger somehow.

Finally, he lifted his head, and without another word climbed into the truck. His eyes stayed pinned on the garage door, as though Wallace might appear at any second.

When I turned back around, Chase and Tucker had squared off, staring at each other, an unspoken, lethal hatred balancing on the edge of control. The red on Tucker's face had faded everywhere but the side of his jaw where Chase had punched him.

I'd been caught up in the momentum of our flight, but reality finally tackled me. Tucker was with us now. Without thinking, we'd even arranged his transportation out of the city.

I stepped beside Chase, and when Tucker glanced down at me, he faltered, as though I was somehow betraying him.

"Did you start the fire?" I heard myself ask.

He didn't answer. Maybe he thought his obvious resentment was enough.

"He was with me all morning," Sean wheezed.

"We've got to move!" Cara slapped the side of the truck.

For one beat no one said a word, and in that silence Tucker turned and began walking toward the exit. There was no gun in his waistband.

"Morris, wait," called Sean. He shook his head at Chase. "Come on, man. I don't know what he did to you two, but it's over. It's not like you haven't screwed up before."

Chase grunted. Tucker stopped.

Since Sean had heard my side of what had happened with Rebecca, he hadn't once made me feel guilty, but I felt it now. It stabbed into my gut as I remembered exactly what the soldier's baton had sounded like falling over her small body. Still, I speculated that Sean would not be so forgiving if confronted with *his* mother's killer.

My heart beat out every second. Time was wasting.

"Promise you won't hurt anyone while you're with us," I said.

It went against everything that felt right in my body, like swimming straight into a current. But Cara was right, we had to go. And as much as I hated it, Sean was right, too— we'd all done things, myself included, for which we could be judged.

"Ember," Chase said under his breath.

"I don't trust you," I continued as Tucker turned. "I won't ever trust you. I don't know what you were doing in that building, or why you helped Sean and me. But if you promise not to screw this up, I'll believe you."

"And if you do screw this up, I'll kill you," added Chase quietly.

Tucker approached. Nodded once soberly.

"I guess that's fair," he said. "Fine. I promise."

"Sean, you're driving," said Chase bluntly, never taking his eyes off Tucker. Sean nodded, stepping into the beige, button-up uniform.

Without further pause we loaded into the back. Cara tossed up a flashlight, a bottle of water, and a first-aid kit, and slammed the sliding door down. It occurred to me that we'd lost the backpack somewhere. Our only possessions, my letters to Chase included, had likely burned to ashes. All evidence of the past was gone.

It was nearly dark; the only light cut in from a high line of vents along the roof. An icy panic gripped my chest as my eyes adjusted. I was five feet away from Tucker Morris, and I could barely see to defend myself.

He gave his word.

He's a liar.

I heard the metallic slide of Sean locking the gate in place. There was nothing to do now but wait and be ready.

The engine started, and a moment later the truck lurched forward.

I perched, ready, between Chase and Billy on one of the wooden crates that lined the metal compartment's interior. Tucker sat directly across from us. The tension was as palpable as the smoke inside the Wayland Inn.

Wedging the flashlight between his cheek and his shoulder, Chase inspected the throbbing blisters that ran from my thumb across the fleshy part of my palm. He opened the tin first-aid kit and began cleaning the burn with an antibacterial swab that might as well have been steel wool. Not once did he meet my gaze. He hadn't since he'd yelled at me on the roof.

With my opposite hand I took a small sip of water from our only bottle and passed it to Billy. Sharing had been understood in the resistance, and traditions had to be maintained. As far as we knew, we were all that was left.

"Who has a firearm?" Chase asked. His voice was still raw from the smoke.

Billy glanced around the cabin before timidly revealing the 9mm Wallace had given him. "I guess that leaves me, huh?"

"Have you ever fired that piece, kid?" asked Tucker.

"I'm fourteen," said Billy. Wallace called him kid. Not Tucker.

"I didn't mean any disrespect."

"I bet you didn't," I muttered. In a clinical, detached way, Chase wrapped my hand with a small roll of gauze and told me to keep it elevated.

"I'm just saying he should give it to one of us who has a little more . . ." Tucker paused, shifting his gaze toward the metal ceiling. ". . . experience," he finished, almost inaudibly.

I couldn't swallow.

"Keep the light on," I told Chase when he lowered the flashlight. I wanted to keep Tucker in my sight.

The truck stopped and we held our breath. I pictured Sean in the front seat, and wished I could see what he was seeing. I hoped he was okay.

Just a traffic light. We moved on, gripping the edges of the crates to steady ourselves against the sway. Billy deliberately placed the gun between us; a sign of trust I did not take lightly.

"What's in these boxes anyway?" he said.

He crouched, picking at the nails embedded into his makeshift seat. Tucker beat him to it; a loud *crack* resounded as he ripped the top off the crate beside him with his uncasted arm.

"Now *this* is more like it." I watched warily as he removed a glass bottle filled with brown liquid. Dust from the packing straw floated through the air like snow.

"Whiskey," said Chase, removing the lid off another box. Horizons manufactured alcohol? Since it was contraband to civilians, this must have been for one of the MM parties Sarah had talked about. I felt the sudden urge to break every bottle.

Chase palmed the glass neck like a baton. The makeshift weapons were stacked at our feet in preparation. Something was better than nothing.

"Wallace brought back some of this once," said Billy, laughing suddenly. "We got trashed. It was awesome."

I returned to the crate beside him, thinking of how much he reminded me of a high school boy just then. Of a life that seemed so far gone I could barely discern the details of it. How long had it been since I had seen Beth or Ryan? Only a couple months, but it felt like years.

"How'd you meet that guy anyway?" Tucker asked.

I winced; his question was like salt in a fresh wound, and I resented him for speaking to Billy at all, but that didn't mean I wasn't curious, too. Billy began peeling the label off a bottle.

"It was when he was still a soldier," he said. "My mom, she . . . turned me in as a runaway for some cash." His shoulder jerked awkwardly, and all of his attention focused on peeling splinters from the lid of the crate.

Tucker snorted. "I guess we know where you rank."

Billy laughed forcefully and said, "She took me out for a cheeseburger first." As if this somehow made it okay.

I couldn't remember the last time I'd had a cheeseburger. Rations vouchers weren't redeemable at restaurants.

"We were eating when this soldier showed up. A fat guy. I knew what she'd been up to then, so I ran—straight into his partner, who'd been looking for him down around the corner. He was quick for an old guy. Tripped me with his nightstick and smashed the burgers all up. I was so pissed I told him he could go screw himself."

"Must have been some burger," said Chase.

"What'd he say?" I prompted.

"He . . . he told me to play nice."

A collective silence fell over us. *Play nice or we don't play at all* was Wallace's number one rule. Behind my closed lids I could see the roof of the Wayland Inn crashing down.

"And I said that you don't get to play nice when you don't got any food. And then he asked how old I was and I said sixteen, even though I was really just eleven, and where my dad was and I told him that he died in the War. That's when his partner caught up to us, and before he said a word I hear this *bang*! And the fat guy dropped dead. Right there. Right in front of me."

All the air seemed to suck out of the compartment

through the vents. I willed myself not to think of the carrier on Rudy Lane, murdered before us. I willed myself not to think of my mother. Chase had become motionless, and so, surprisingly, had Tucker.

"Wallace killed his partner?" clarified Tucker. "That's cold."

"He had it coming," said Billy. "That's what Wallace said."

I looked across at Tucker, staring at Chase, who was staring back. I shifted. "Wallace and Riggins and . . . the rest of 'em, they're probably already on their way to the safe house. Wallace always said that was the plan." Billy's voice cracked.

The heaviness in the compartment increased. I rubbed my chest with the heel of my hand but the tightness would not loosen.

Lincoln was dead. I could see him perfectly. Tall and wiry. Black freckles. I wondered how Houston was taking it; I'd never seen them apart. I wondered if Houston was even alive.

Wallace. Riggins. The brothers. All the guys who risked their lives and came home to play poker. Burned to ashes. Burned in a motel-sized crematorium.

"People do stupid things when they're desperate," I told Billy quietly. He was hunched over, digging into the crate between his calves.

"She wasn't stupid," he said. "You don't know anything about her."

Billy had never talked to me like that before.

"I didn't mean . . ."

"She always got what she wanted. Always."

I swallowed, the revolt churning inside of me. Clearly this

wasn't the first time Billy's mom had "turned him in." Wallace was more than family to Billy. Wallace had saved his life. Or maybe they had both saved each other.

"I just wish my cat didn't have to die, you know?" he said, by way of an apology.

The truck turned, and we all held on until it was righted. The pace picked up. The whir of the tires on the road made it hard to concentrate on anything but the danger outside.

"We're getting on the highway," said Chase.

When Billy's head fell, I placed my arm over his shoulders. Tentatively, like I'd once seen Wallace do. Billy didn't make a sound. I think I was the only one who knew he was crying.

THE minutes passed, each lacing my muscles more tightly together. It was exhausting to be so on-edge, so powerless.

In the dim glow of the flashlight I could see the shadowed outlines of my companions. Billy, curled into a ball on the floor, fast asleep. Chase, hunched over his knees. Tucker, shifting positions every few minutes, unable to sit still. Which was more dangerous? The killer inside this box, or outside?

A half hour passed and my neck began to cramp. I rolled my head on my shoulders. We ran out of water, and the friction inside my throat felt like sandpaper.

An hour. No one wanted to jinx us, but collectively we'd begun thinking we might be in the clear after all.

As my breathing grew less shallow, I became excruciatingly aware of the sharp scents of sweat and blood and heavy smoke that filled the truck. With such little ventilation, the stifling air made me nauseous. I leaned against the cool metal walls, letting the reverberations from the road rattle my bones.

A plan began to take shape. Tubman would meet us at the checkpoint, but we weren't going to the safe house. Rebecca was still somewhere in Chicago and I couldn't rest until she was found. I wasn't sure how Chase was going to take the news, but he wouldn't be able to change my mind. He, of all people, knew the importance of keeping promises. He'd promised my mother he'd find me, after all.

I stared at Tucker, wondering what he would do. He'd fooled the others; he wasn't the dream recruit Wallace and Sean had talked about. I couldn't imagine him fighting against the precious organization he'd been so proud to be a part of. No, he was only out for himself, to progress in rank, to shoot down anyone who got in his way, and it seemed a terrible mistake to give him the location of the safe house.

And yet I kept seeing him on the third floor of the Wayland Inn, surrounded by smoke, desperately attempting to rescue an unconscious Sean. As much as I tried, I could not think of a reason why he would start a fire and then stay in the building, why he would risk his own life to make others believe he was good. It left only the possibility that he was absolutely insane—which I hadn't yet ruled out—or that he *had* changed.

The box containing us seemed to tighten.

He shifted positions, and in the low light I caught the reflection of metal. I straightened and grabbed the flashlight to shine in his direction. In his hand was a small red pocketknife; he'd already succeeded in sawing his cast halfway off.

My stomach turned. Freed from that cast, he'd have full use of both hands and would be even more dangerous.

"Shouldn't you leave that on?" I asked flatly. "See a doctor or something."

"She's right," said Chase. "You only need one arm to stab me in the back."

Tucker shook his head. I thought I could hear him chuckling.

"It's sweet you two are worried." He didn't even look up.

"Oh, I'm worried," I said between my teeth.

The tires continued their consistent rotation on the highway.

"Don't be," said Tucker. "I've got nowhere else to go." He cast a languid but deliberate look my way. For an instant I saw my own hatred mirrored back at me. I saw how Tucker blamed me for ruining his career and his life. And then the look was gone. The cast came off with a tear, and he groaned in relief, scratching one forearm, then the other.

"You, on the other hand, are off to Chicago, I hear," he said.

"Maybe I am," I said, crossing my arms over my chest.

I could feel Chase's eyes boring a hole through me, but didn't dare look away from Tucker. He leaned back against the ribbed metal siding, as though it were as comfortable as a couch.

"Your pal Sean told me. You're lucky to have such good friends. Especially considering that reward on your life."

Riggins flashed again in my mind and brought with him

a twinge of guilt. He hadn't protected me because we were friends, but because he thought I was the sniper.

I hadn't noticed that I'd moved to the edge of my seat until Chase placed his left hand on my knee, and when he felt the energy making my leg tremble, he spread his fingers and pressed down, holding me in place.

"She's luckier than you'll be," said Chase.

Tucker's teeth flashed in a quick smile. "Come on," he said. "I think you can cut me a break. After everything we've shared."

My eyes widened as Tucker's gaze lowered over me. The memory of kissing him in the Knoxville detention cells, trading my integrity for information, was sticky and sour in the back of my mouth. *"God, I wish Jennings could have seen that,"* he'd said. *"We wouldn't even have to kill him. He'd off himself."*

Chase's hand gripped my leg so hard I nearly winced.

"You've shared nothing," I said, fury making my voice shake.

And then I turned to Chase and kissed him.

His mouth wasn't soft, as it usually was, or even heated and demanding, like the night we'd clung to each other. His lips parted in surprise, but he barely responded, not even to touch me.

I grasped his face in my hands and kissed him again, keeping my eyes tightly closed, all but bruising our lips. I couldn't stand his confusion, or the grim realization that followed as he tightened his jaw. All I wanted was for Tucker to know that Chase was mine, and that nothing, not even my mother's killer, could tear us apart.

His hands cupped mine. Slowly, he pulled back. A sideways glance revealed that Tucker wasn't even looking; he was back to digging through the whiskey crates.

My whole body heated in a sick, ugly way, and the space between Chase and me suddenly seemed too close. I looked down before he could say anything. I wished I could disappear.

Tucker had kissed me to hurt Chase, and now I'd done the same to hurt Tucker. I'd wanted us to have nothing in common, and yet, here we were.

"Em . . ." But before Chase could finish the truck shifted gears. I braced myself on my crated seat.

"Are we there?" Billy rolled to his knees, the motion having woken him. His cough was like the crackling of dry leaves—we hadn't had water in a long time.

"The coast is four hundred miles away," said Chase. "We've got a few more hours at least." He clicked off the flashlight, bathing the compartment in darkness.

"We're stopping," I said. I could feel the steady pull of the breaks. A cold line of sweat dribbled between my shoulder blades.

"Someone's following us." Billy's voice was ripe with fear.

"Might just be giving us a break," said Tucker, but he didn't sound hopeful.

"Ember, take Billy to the back," murmured Chase.

My place was beside him, but if I didn't hide, neither would Billy. I reached for his hand and pulled him up. As the truck ground down to a lower gear, I sank low behind a row of boxes, skin prickling with a familiar sensation that I hadn't felt since the holding cells. The detached insight that I might very soon be dead.

Before Billy knelt beside me, I heard Chase tell him something. Their voices mixed with the hum of the motor and I couldn't make out what they were saying, but soon Billy nodded and handed Chase his gun.

"Don't be scared," Billy said tremulously when he melted into the shadows beside me. "I'm gonna protect you."

I stared at Chase's back, a sharp ache tearing through me. The truck came to a stop.

Tucker and Chase had positioned themselves side by side at the exit. They seemed to be having some unspoken conversation that hadn't yet evolved to manslaughter.

Please let us live through this, I thought.

Chase chambered the cartridge on the 9mm. Tucker lifted a bottle over his shoulder.

"Nine to twelve," said Chase.

"Check. Twelve to three," answered Tucker grimly. "Just like the good old days."

"What are they talking about?" I whispered. The adrenaline pounded in my ears.

The bottle Billy was holding scraped against the metal floor as he shifted closer.

"Chase'll take out anyone on the left side, Tucker anyone

on the right," he said. "Wallace taught me that. It's like numbers on a clock."

So they were partners again. I closed my eyes and listened, praying that Tucker would keep his word.

A knock on the side of the truck nearly made me scream. Billy grabbed my arm and pulled me back down, but my muscles quivered. We couldn't run. We were trapped.

Chase. We couldn't end like this. We needed more time.

Male voices outside the truck. I strained my ears, but the words were muffled, like we were underwater.

Someone knocked on the sliding metal door at the rear of the compartment, where Chase aimed the gun down on whoever waited outside. Tucker angled his body so that his back was to his partner.

"I'm opening the back," came an intentional call from Sean outside. "If one of you shoots me I'm not going to be happy."

I sobbed with relief, but covered my mouth. We weren't in the clear yet.

The back latch of the door squealed as it was unlocked. As Sean opened the gate, a slice of florescent light highlighted the bottom of the cab. He stumbled back.

"What a way to greet a guy," he said, coughing to hide the hitch in his voice.

Neither Chase nor Tucker lowered their weapons. There, behind Sean, waited two uniformed soldiers; one African American with buggy eyes, the other pale with a hooked nose, balding prematurely. Both were in their late twenties and in good shape, and neither reached for the firearms holstered in their belts.

"Look." Billy pointed to the neatly painted sign on the back wall of what appeared to be a printing factory of some kind. One Whole Family.

Resistance.

CHAPTER
11

"THEY'RE the good guys," assured Sean.

Slowly, Chase brought the gun down. He and Tucker jumped to the concrete floor and did a quick search before the rest of us followed.

"Welcome to Greeneville," said the man with dark skin. "Or what's left of it anyway. I'm Marco, and this is my esteemed colleague, Polo."

I scoffed, noticing that their name badges had been removed.

Some of the boys at the Wayland Inn had talked about Greeneville. As with most of the smaller U.S. cities, the town's population had dwindled during the War—no jobs. People had forsaken their homes for the larger cities where they could at least access resources like soup kitchens.

As I looked around I found my earlier assessment had been correct. We'd been brought in through the loading docks to a factory floor, where several monstrous silver machines waited, dormant. A black rubber belt stuck out like a tongue from a gaping hole in the machine on the left, and upon it at even intervals rested neat stacks of paper, waiting to be loaded into various sized boxes near where we'd parked.

"The lovely Sister has informed us that y'all are taking the Tubman express to the safe house," said Polo. "Feel free to use the amenities, grab a delightful Horizons bottled water, and make yourself at home."

"Such hosts." Cara winked at Marco as she slid by them into a small office where the water was located. Polo whistled, an appreciative gaze trailing after her.

"How long until the carrier returns?" asked Chase.

Marco's shoulders fell. "They're in such a hurry to leave, Polo."

Polo nodded somberly. "Is it me? Am I unlikeable, Marco?"

"You do smell a bit . . ."

"Later today?" Chase pressed.

"Oh no." Marco shook his head. "He was just through. Tomorrow morning at the earliest. Besides, you can't make it across the Red Zone border before curfew. Such an attempt would mean certain death."

"So dramatic," chided Polo.

Chase and I shared a glance; we'd tried to cross into a Red Zone once, and nearly been arrested. If not for Chase's smooth talking, we might not have made it through.

I stepped closer to the black belt, leaning over the nearest stack of papers.

"Look," I whispered to Chase. Statute Circulars. We had come to an MM Statute Printing Plant. I thought of all the times I'd seen them—at school, on the windows of businesses, even on my own front door when my mother and I had been arrested. I wondered if they'd all come from here.

"We're spending the night?" Tucker asked with a sigh.

"I can try to find you a pillow," offered Marco.

"I'm not staying the night," said Sean. "I'm taking the truck to Chicago."

"*We're* taking the truck to Chicago," I corrected.

A small grin fought its way through his exhaustion. His face was paler than usual, and his eyes were bloodshot. When he turned to the side, I could see the copper streaks that had soaked through the back of his uniform—he hadn't yet attended to his burns from the fire. Feeling the weight of Chase's stare, I climbed back into the truck and searched for the first-aid kit.

"Wrong," sang Polo. "You won't make Chicago before nightfall and Horizons drivers have to obey the curfew. Only soldiers can go out after dark." He popped his collar importantly.

Sean blinked, obviously having forgotten this information. He sighed in frustration. I found the first-aid kit behind one of the boxes and sat on the bumper, motioning for him to sit beside me.

"Since we're all sharing," said Cara, returning from the office with several plastic bottles cradled in her arms, "I'm cutting out. I've got family in town. My cousin lives here."

My brows knitted together. I'd never heard she had family here, but then, I didn't know she had family *anywhere*—we'd never talked about that. I worried the circular medallion around my neck, feeling the smooth, puckered flesh beneath it had seared into my skin. It stung fiercely, and reminded me of how she'd disappeared from the Wayland Inn during the fire, how she and Tubman had separated sometime after they'd left with the truck full of refugees. Like Tucker, I had a grim feeling she wasn't telling us everything.

She passed me a bottle of water, which I guzzled, spilling streams of it down my chin. I wasn't sure anything had ever tasted so good. The others followed Marco and Polo, who announced that there was food in their office.

Sean had a hard time removing his arms from the Horizons uniform, so I helped, cringing when the fabric stuck to his back. He sat bolt upright, the heat wafting off his skin.

"I can clean it, but we don't have a big enough bandage," I said, fighting the nausea. An angry red welt spanned from his shoulder to the opposite side of his waist, surrounded by smaller cuts and burns. Some of the skin had already been sloughed away when he'd removed his shirt.

"It looks like something fell on you." I could still feel the burst of flames when the ceiling had nearly toppled on my head.

"Honestly I don't remember. I guess that's probably better." With effort that had nothing to do with physical pain, he twisted so that he could look into my face.

"I never should have let you guys leave without me," he said.

Gently, I cleaned his back with a damp rag. The black film wiped away, making his injuries less monstrous. I couldn't help but think about how Chase's shoulders were wider, how he, too, had a scar, one I didn't know the origin of, that looked like the swipe of a giant set of claws from the side of his ribs to his spine.

"I know why you did." Tucker had information on Rebecca—at least that was what Sean thought. If I'd thought someone had information on Chase, I would have stayed, too.

Sean looked through the glass office window at my mother's killer. "Can I trust him?"

I opened my mouth, but nothing came out.

"I don't know," I said finally, apologizing when he winced.

Chase came up beside us. His gaze flickered to mine, just for a moment, but I concentrated on the task. "Hell of a burn," he commented.

"Thanks," Sean said tightly. "I hadn't noticed."

Chase stood silently for some time, watching me work, and I chewed my lip, remembering how stupid I'd been to kiss him in the truck.

Finally he said, "We should change the plates on the truck first thing tomorrow."

I smiled as he walked away.

"WHOA." Billy's voice came from within the office, just as I was helping Sean back into his shirt. "They hooked you up! I had to build a machine out of spare parts and cruiser panels to access the mainframe."

As I approached, I saw the source of Billy's fascination: a computer, scanning equipment, and a printer atop a wooden desk. A shoulder-high gun safe was in the back corner, beneath a flat window revealing the bright blue afternoon sky. I shied away from the open area instinctively.

"Only the best for the FBR," said Marco. Several people chuckled. It took a few seconds to realize he wasn't joking.

"Don't freak out." Cara smirked. "They're still on the payroll."

"Soldiers *and* resistance?" I clarified.

"Article Nine, at your service," said Polo, referencing the new Statute that would punish rebels to the full extent of the law.

"Turncoats," grumbled Tucker. He snorted when every eye shot to him, and raised his hands in surrender. "Tough crowd. Not like any of us are any better."

"Then why are you here?"

Sean laughed uncomfortably from the doorway. Obviously Tucker had told him nothing of why we hated each other.

"It was a joke," he said. "A bad one."

Was it just a joke? Directing Tucker to the largest safe house on the Eastern Seaboard felt like pulling the pin out of a grenade and throwing it into a playground. I felt a wave of responsibility that I should somehow stop him, but how could I, after he'd saved Sean and me in the fire?

Marco was eyeing me curiously. "You look familiar," he said, taking a seat behind the desk.

"A lot of people say that." I twisted the gold band around my ring finger.

"Well, I'll be damned," said Marco. "Hey, Polo, come look

at this." Needing to see exactly what they did, I skirted around the desk for a better look at the screen.

It was my picture from the reformatory that had been posted around the Square. My eyes were red and swollen from crying after the arrest, and my hair was a natural brown and long past my shoulders. I still had stretches in my school uniform from where Beth had tried to pull me away from the soldiers. I read the caption just below it, but it didn't scare me as it had before. I guess the shock had worn off.

Ember Miller, it said. ARTICLE 5. *Wanted in association with Region Two-fifteen sniper murders.* My stats and charges were listed below.

"I figured they'd already closed your case," said Polo conversationally.

"Oh, don't play coy," said Marco, big eyes bugging at me. "If I print out your photo, will you give me your autograph?"

I couldn't help but laugh at how genuinely awestruck he sounded.

"Make sure you sign it *Love, Sniper,*" said Cara. The chill in her tone melted my smile.

"She's not the sniper," Chase insisted. "She doesn't know the sniper. She's being framed."

He was right to put a stop to it; I'd seen what happened to the people who gave the MM information about me and it was no laughing matter.

"Told you," said Polo, resigned. He shoved Marco's shoulder. "You know, I met him once," he added.

"Here we go," groaned Marco.

"What?" Polo looked injured.

"He met this guy in Chicago like, ten years ago who said the way to break down the FBR was to go to a public place and take out one soldier at a time," explained Marco. "As if no one's ever had that idea before."

"It was like . . . four . . . or five years ago," Polo pointed out. "And anyway, he was tough. He'd fought overseas, before the War. He showed up at the FBR enlistment office in old army fatigues, spouting all this stuff about how President Scarboro and his Restart America buddies were behind the attacks."

"What?" I stole another bottle of water. "Insurgents were behind the attacks." I'd memorized the word from the news reports we'd watched in my living room, but it wasn't until high school that I learned what it actually meant.

The people who had bombed the major cities weren't terrorists from a foreign land, though many suspected that's where they'd gotten their support. They were American citizens. They were born and raised in our towns, in our schools, and held jobs that weren't particularly special.

But they were poor, even though they were educated, and even though they worked. They lived like my mother and I did, paycheck to paycheck, and when the money wasn't coming in, on what assistance they could find. One of the Insurgents was the manager of a restaurant—a normal looking guy with a receding hairline—and when he gave his statement before execution he said that he was tired of sleeping in the back of the kitchen, feeding his kids rich people's scraps. He just wanted to level the playing field.

My mother told me once that the world was like her

favorite singer, an overly busty blonde with a tiny waist. It was just a matter of time before her middle was stretched too thin and she broke in half.

And that's what the Insurgents had done. They'd broken the world in half. They'd hit every major city on the coasts, and some of the big ones in the middle, too—like Chicago and Dallas—and when it was done, nobody was rich, and nobody trusted anyone.

That was when Scarboro became president. Maybe before people thought his rigid stance on government control was a joke, but they didn't anymore. It wasn't two months after he'd taken office that the military branches—what were left of them—were relieved of duty, and the Reformation Act came into effect. It was said that Reinhardt, the man he'd named the Chief of Reformation—the man who had nearly been assassinated while we'd been in Knoxville—was responsible for the changes, including the creation of the Moral Statutes.

Polo leaned forward, rubbing his hands together. "Yes, but how did the Insurgents get their bombs?"

"Same way we get our guns," said Sean, although he didn't sound so sure. "They stole them. Or bought them on the underground."

"That's a lot of firepower," said Polo, conspiracy brightening his eyes. "I'm not saying it's true, but this guy—he had a point. Scarboro and his pal Reinhardt were backed by Restart, and Restart had money. Tons of money. Lots of people believed in their cause, too—getting rid of the division between religion and the government, bringing back those old-fashioned values. Think about it. He sets up the crash, then swoops in to save the day."

"Ridiculous," said Tucker dismissively.

Polo laughed. "The Insurgents effectively brought down our nation. I've yet to see Three make that kind of stand."

"What do you know about Three?" I asked.

"What does anyone know about Three?" Cara said cynically.

"Heard they operate out of the safe house." Polo winked at me. "Sure you don't want to wait for Tubman?"

I did feel the sudden urge to wait for the carrier and find out more about these elusive resistance leaders. Beside me, Chase made a noise halfway between a groan and a sigh. He'd thought the safe house would be safe, but if the largest resistance organization in the country was there, it couldn't possibly be. I glanced back at him, noting how quiet he'd been through this conversation.

"I heard they operate from a Bureau base," said Billy.

"No one knows," said Marco. "Honestly, they're probably the ones that started this whole sniper rumor anyway."

I felt my eyes narrow. Had he been in the Square during the last attack, I doubted he'd be referring to it as a rumor.

"Marco's a skeptic," said Polo, waving him off. "He thinks the whole thing's a crock. That those soldiers were done by their own troops and the Chief of Reformation's just looking to cover it up."

"Which is more likely than the sniper being some random tattooed protester," argued Marco.

"He did have a tattoo on his neck," Polo admitted. "I mean, who does that?"

"The sniper, apparently," said Sean.

Polo pointed at him. "Exactly."

"What kind of tattoo?" asked Chase suddenly. "A snake?"

His uncle had a snake tattoo on his neck, and he had been in the military. That Chase would speculate the man could be responsible for a string of murders made me even more cynical of the time Chase had spent with him before the War.

Polo frowned. "I don't remember. Maybe. Why, you've met him?" Sudden excitement lit his eyes.

"There are a lot of guys with tattoos out there," evaded Chase.

"No way it was soldiers. It had to be a sniper," Billy interrupted. "Cara was at the draft in Knoxville when he hit. Tell them, Cara."

One blond brow arched. "They're saying it was someone in a uniform, you know," she said. "A mole. Sort of like you boys. I'd be careful if I were you."

Marco and Polo were speechless.

"I think we've had enough bedtime stories to give everyone nightmares," Marco announced finally, his eyes even buggier than before. With that, he stepped on the office chair and lifted a slat from the ceiling. Hidden in the rafters was a lumpy trash bag, which he tossed down to his partner.

"Santa Claus has arrived," announced Polo. Clothes were doled out from within, and I was given some old dusty jeans and a sweatshirt. Both were big enough to fit two of me, but I was glad to get out of my smoke-drenched wardrobe.

Tucker pulled off his shirt right in front of everyone, and I immediately looked away. I had no desire to see what he looked like under his clothes, nor did I want him to see me change. It didn't help when Chase checked to see if I was watching.

I retreated into the single-stall bathroom. The light flickered, and the door didn't lock, so I pushed the trash can in front of it. My mind was still spinning with Marco's and Polo's claims—about the War, and the president, and the mysterious Three. When I peeled off my singed pants something clattered to the floor. I crouched beneath the sink to see what had fallen and retrieved the copper cartridge I'd found under the front seat of the Horizons truck at East End Auto. With everything that had happened, I'd forgotten all about it.

Someone knocked, and I jumped up, stuffing my legs into the borrowed jeans.

"Just a second!" I called, but Cara was already forcing her way in. Apparently the trash can wasn't enough of a hint that I'd wanted some privacy.

"Girls only," she called over her shoulder to whoever waited behind, then slammed the door. "What do you got there?" she asked, pointing to the fist I'd clenched to my chest.

"Oh." I opened my hand reluctantly. "Just something I found."

Cara's mouth rounded in surprise.

"Where'd you get that?"

I shrugged, and when my hand moved, her eyes followed.

"Riggins thought it was you," she said in a strange voice. "He told me, at the garage in Knoxville. After you went missing on the mission."

I winced. "Yeah, I know." He'd died thinking it was me.

"He says you've gone missing a lot."

I balked at that. *She* went missing a lot. Chase and I had been pulled apart in the Square during the attack, but she'd been separated from Lincoln and Houston as well. And yet no one, not even paranoid Riggins, questioned *her* whereabouts.

She plucked the bullet from my palm, holding it close to her body as she admired it. Again I considered how much larger it was than the standard rounds the resistance and the soldiers used.

"Why aren't you at the safe house?" I asked, something inside telling me to tread carefully. "I thought you said Sisters could get through the highway lockdown."

She turned her hips, still mesmerized by the cartridge. Her blue woolen skirt fanned from side to side.

"Looks like I was wrong."

"I'm serious," I said. "Sarah and that family with the baby needed a doctor. Did they get caught?"

Her tongue skimmed along the edge of her teeth. "Are you suggesting I jumped ship?"

My blood heated. "You didn't exactly stick around to help when the motel was burning to the ground."

She laughed, but it felt forced. "Self-preservation. Not all of us are martyrs."

"If it was self-preservation, what were you doing talking to that soldier?" I pictured her standing before the flames, the man in uniform urging her to back up.

For a moment she seemed confused, and then shrugged one shoulder. "Maybe he was looking for a date."

"Why can't you just answer the question?"

She smiled coldly, eyes like blue crystals. "Look, the soldier at the fire thought I was a Sister, and asked me to help clear the area. As for Tubman, we made it to the roadblock and saw a sign that only FBR would be allowed past. I bailed before anyone saw me. But since you're so concerned about your precious little party favor, relax. I hid off the side of the highway and watched Tubman drive that FBR truck straight through."

I was relieved, but no less irritated. "Why do you have to cut her down like that?"

Her look turned to exasperation as she began to disrobe.

"Please. Did you see her? She had it coming. You can't put wrapping paper on a present and expect no one to rip it off."

"You're *blaming* her?"

"I would if she wore that dress to a social."

A *social*. That was what Sarah had called it, too, back in Tent City. A party for all the lonely soldiers who'd dedicated themselves to the cause.

I kept my arms pinned to my sides so I didn't throttle her. Blaming Sarah for what others had done to her was like saying my mother deserved death because she'd broken a Statute. Like saying Billy's mom had been right in selling her own son for cash.

She pulled off her Sisters of Salvation blouse, and as she

slipped into a faded black sweatshirt, I caught sight of three parallel scars just below her collarbone—scars not unlike those I had given Tucker. She made a point of quickly hiding them, and despite myself, I suddenly found myself feeling sorry for her. Apparently she wasn't made of steel. Someone, at some point, had been able to hurt her.

"Hey," she said as I placed my hand on the door in preparation to leave. "Thank you. For what you've done."

I turned back to face her, surprised by the smallness in her voice. It took a full beat to realize what she was talking about, and when I did I nearly groaned.

"Cara, Riggins was wrong. I'm not who he thought I was. I didn't shoot anybody."

"I know," she said. But I wasn't sure she believed me.

I had more important reasons to be on the defensive. I gathered my clothes and returned to the factory floor, and Tucker Morris.

WHEN I emerged, Chase was leaning against the wall outside the door, arms crossed, scowling across the station at the Horizons truck. I smoothed down the sweatshirt and cuffed the ends of the pants four times before they finally reached my heels. I'd forgotten my arms were still smeared with dried blood and soot, and while I examined them he combed a tentative hand through my hair. Instinct had me leaning into his touch, but I frowned when he revealed a fistful of ash. I would have given my next meal for a shower.

"Billy's checking the mainframe for new arrests," he said,

crossing his arms again as Tucker's shadow appeared in the back of the truck.

"Has he found anything yet?" It seemed callous, but if Wallace hadn't made it out of Knoxville, I hoped he'd gone down with the Wayland Inn. I knew what awaited him in the holding cells should he have been captured.

"Nothing new." Chase hesitated. "Lincoln's name was Anthony Sullivan. I never knew that."

The room silenced. Sean looked up from where he stood with Marco and Polo outside a small storage room across from the truck. From the look on his face, he, too, was surprised. Some people went by nicknames so we couldn't get too close, but Chase had just torn that down. He'd made Lincoln more human, his loss even more devastating.

The mood, already tense, turned somber fast.

Tucker, hopping down from the back of the truck, lifted two bottles of whiskey. "Might as well make the most of being stranded."

No one objected.

Cara, who'd emerged from the bathroom behind me, said, "You boys got any cups?"

Marco disappeared into the storage room and returned with a tower of paper cups. Tucker popped the top on a bottle of whiskey and poured a liberal amount into each. While we formed a circle behind the truck, I contemplated how the one and only drink I'd ever had was when Beth and I had snuck some wine from my mother's contraband supply in the ninth grade. I wasn't sure how I was going to manage a half cup of whiskey on a nearly empty stomach.

"Someone should say something," mumbled Sean.

The others looked at Chase expectantly. Not Cara, who had known Lincoln longer, but Chase.

Wallace's voice echoed through my head. *You had it, Jennings. You had it, and you threw it away.* I'd thought at the time he was just disappointed to lose a good soldier, but it was more than that. He'd seen Chase as a leader.

I sloshed the amber liquid around the cup. Wallace was right; Chase was good in times of crisis. All the time I'd spent fighting him after he'd rescued me from reform school seemed like wasted energy now.

As Chase raised his cup, I felt a wave of uncertainty. What were you supposed to say at funerals? We didn't even know if Lincoln had family.

"To Lin—Anthony," Chase said, clearing his throat. "He was a good soldier in . . . in the fights that mattered."

This is the only fight that matters. The one we fight today.

"To anyone else stuck in that building, too," he added. "Cats included."

Billy gave a wet hiccup, his shoulders rounding. Cara wiped her eyes on her sleeve and leaned against Sean, who patted her shoulder, looking grim. Marco bowed his head, lips moving in a silent prayer.

The air within the printing plant grew heavy. Loss after loss surrounded us, so that the space seemed to thicken with their ghosts. We remembered our loved ones—those we weren't strong enough to name. We remembered why we were fighting back.

I missed my mother so much it hurt.

My gaze found Tucker's across the circle. His shoulders were heaving, like he'd just run a mile, and all I knew in that moment was that I didn't want to know what he was thinking. Anticipating the taste with a cringe, I brought the cup to my lips.

"Wait," said Tucker. "While we're on it. To . . . to the people we . . . the person I . . ." His head rolled back and he looked up, of all places, for inspiration.

I lowered the cup. A clock from the office ticked by each second.

"Tucker," Chase warned. "Don't."

My whole body tensed in anticipation. Tucker stole a quick breath and met my gaze.

"I'm sorry, Ember."

The peace and power of the moment shattered, and I was horrified. *How dare you.* That was all I could think. *How dare you.*

"You're sorry," I repeated. I saw him, only him, as a haze of red blocked the others out.

In one quick motion he downed the shot, hissing at the sting. I hadn't realized I'd dropped mine until Billy bent down to pick up the cup.

"Ember." I shook Chase's hand off my shoulder. I was closer to Tucker now, though I hadn't even felt my feet move.

"You want to *apologize?*"

I couldn't have heard him right. He was incapable of re-morse. *I'm a good soldier,* he told me after he'd admitted his crime. *I did what needed to be done.*

Tucker stepped back, tapped the empty cup against his leg. His cheeks were flushed.

"You want to drink to her, Tucker? Is that what you were thinking?"

"Easy, girl," said Cara.

"Say her name," I demanded. "If you're so sorry."

He didn't.

"You don't even know it, do you? You don't even know her name."

I pushed him hard, and he staggered into the bumper of the truck. I wanted to kill him with my bare hands.

"That's enough." Chase was between us now, trying to block me from Tucker.

"Her name was *Lori Whittman!*" I shouted. "That was her name! That was my mother's name!"

I saw Tucker's face, sallow and shocked, for one instant before Chase caught me around the waist and hoisted me over his shoulder.

"Let go of me!"

"Cool off," he said.

I kicked him and punched his back and only when my teeth sunk into his shoulder did he toss me down. We were in the storage room, surrounded by weak metal shelves hold-ing tool boxes and printer paper and boxes of ink. He wheeled around and slammed the door shut.

"If you value your life at all, you'd better turn right back around," I hissed, fists clenched.

"I'm not leaving." To make his point, he placed both hands on the shelves on either side of the door. He'd taught me to always keep my exits open, and here he was, blocking them off.

A noise snuck up my throat, halfway between a groan and a growl. I paced around the tight circle, keeping out of reach, so furious at Tucker, at Cara, at *everything*, I couldn't even speak.

He blocked out the single overhead bulb, and all that remained were the shadows silhouetting his face.

"You can't let him get to you," he said.

I slammed to a halt. "So you're on his side now?"

A vein on his neck jumped.

"I'm on your side," he said. "I'm *always* on your side."

"Doesn't feel that way." I regretted it even as I said it, and resumed my pace.

He shook his head. "I don't know what Tucker's doing here, but it can't be an accident. This is what he does. He digs his way in and gets under your skin. And before you know it, he's ripped your life apart."

My shoulders jerked back, tall and defiant.

"You think I don't know that?"

But my voice shook because even though I did, I'd still fallen into the Tucker trap. I'd kissed Chase to hurt him. I'd gotten information about Rebecca in the holding cells, but at his price. He'd been discharged now, but what if this was all part of the plan? What if *this*—the carriers, the safe house, the soldiers fighting for the resistance—was what he'd wanted?

"I didn't." Chase jammed a hand through his hair. "I trusted him once, and it cost me everything. I have to live with that, but you don't."

I staggered back, needing to put some distance between us. He never spoke of what he'd witnessed with my mother—not since he'd first told me—but how obvious that burden was now. I hadn't been there for him because it hurt too much, and in doing so I'd left him alone.

I missed her. But I missed Chase, too, and somehow that was worse, having him here and missing him. Seeing him every day and feeling a world apart.

"You didn't lose everything," I said.

He looked up, and moved toward me slowly, and the look of surprise in his face was enough to break my heart.

"Neither did you," he said quietly.

The tears came at last. Salty and hot, yet somehow cool and cleansing, too. He didn't wipe them away, but traced them gently with his fingertips.

Someone knocked at the door.

I was jolted back to reality, to the checkpoint, and Tucker Morris, and the things I'd said to him outside. Chase was right; Tucker *had* gotten under my skin, and it wouldn't happen again.

When my eyes were dry, Chase opened the door.

Sean was standing outside, looking sheepish.

"So." He scratched his neck. "I didn't know it was him—Tucker—that, you know. You believe me, right?"

I nodded.

"You could have said something," he added, a little injured. He was too far away to have this kind of conversation, which made him feel all the more distant.

"I'm not going to freak out and stab you or anything," I muttered.

"Oh, good." As if waiting for permission, he stepped forward and pulled me into his arms. I tucked my chin over his shoulder, careful not to touch his burned back. I felt stronger with both Chase and him at my side.

"Notice how my hands are above the waist," I heard him say to Chase, who snorted in response.

Before pulling away, he said, "Something's come up."

"What?" Chase edged beside me.

"It's weird. Probably nothing, but you'll want to hear it."

We moved wordlessly past the printing machines toward the office, not running into Cara or Tucker. Maybe Cara really had left to see her cousin. Maybe Tucker had magically disappeared. That would be fine by me.

Billy was sitting on the desk with Marco and Polo. When he saw me, he jumped off, glancing between us as though one of us might combust. I forced my chin up, but wanted badly to blend in with the walls.

"I can't believe—"

"What happened?" interrupted Chase. I gave him a small, grateful smile.

"Okay, so here's the thing," began Marco. "You say *Lori Whittman*, and I say to Polo here, 'Lori Whittman. Sounds familiar, right?'"

"And I say, 'Yes, Marco, sounds real familiar.' And so we come back to the office, and I remember. Last week the carrier from Chicago comes through, saying he's stopped at a new checkpoint on the way."

My heart was beating hard, anxious to know where this was going.

"And your friend Sean here remembers that you're from Louisville," said Marco. "And I say, 'That's where the carrier stopped!'"

"How does Lori Whittman tie into it?" Chase asked when I couldn't find the words.

"She's the one!" said Billy, picking up a scrap of paper. "She's the one that set up the checkpoint in Louisville. The Chicago carrier even wrote down the address so Marco and Polo could see if it was being scouted by the Bureau. Fourteen-fifty Ewing Avenue."

My knees gave way. I barely registered the hard feel of the floor beneath me. Chase was as pale as death itself. He was right to be. He knew that place all too well.

Fourteen-fifty Ewing Avenue was my address.

CHAPTER
12

"THAT'S not possible," Chase choked out.

Could it be possible? Who else could it be, in *my* home? If she had survived, she would have perfect motive to set up a checkpoint. No one would better understand the need for a safe house.

She's alive. She doesn't know I'm alive. She's looking for me. She's putting herself in danger.

She needs me.

My hands covered my mouth, as though I'd been speaking my stream of panicked thoughts aloud. I couldn't do that. I couldn't make them real. Hope was a dangerous thing. Too much hope in a time like this could destroy a person. Set up unrealistic expectations. Yes. Best to proceed with caution.

"It's a trap," Sean said. "Think about it. Why else would a checkpoint in her name come up now, while the Bureau's hunting for the sniper? They're baiting you."

My heart sank like a stone. Sean's assessment seemed far

more likely than the alternative that my mother was actually alive.

"The Chicago carrier had us look up the name and address a week ago. *Before* they framed you," said Polo. "The mainframe does say that Lori Whittman's deceased," he added, looking sorry.

"But it says that about Chase, too," said Billy helpfully. "I checked."

"Are you sure she was dead?" I asked, but my words were so quiet that no one heard me. I repeated myself.

"Yes," Chase said. "I saw her die."

"But you got in a fight with Tucker, right? You told me you don't remember what happened."

"Whoa," I heard Billy say.

"Someone hit me," Chase admitted. "I woke up in a holding cell." His hands hung slack at his sides. His shoulders bowed. He looked like an old man, and for the first time since before her death, I wanted to comfort *him*.

Marco, Polo, and Billy were glancing back and forth between us.

"Maybe she was just hurt," I said. "Maybe . . ." I covered my mouth again. *Don't hope don't hope don't hope.*

"I guess there's only one person that knows for sure," said Sean cautiously.

Chase was far away. My insides, when I could feel them again, were tight as a drum. I whispered his name, needing him to come back.

He looked up, remembering the rest of the room. He coughed. "Right. Tucker."

"And I told him to leave," finished Sean.

Chase spun on him. *"What?"*

"How was I supposed to sit here with him knowing . . ." Sean looked away, like he was afraid of upsetting me again. "Cara was leaving for her cousin's anyway, so he went with her."

My heart rate kicked up a notch. What had Sean done? At the worst, he'd given Tucker an out to go straight to the MM. At best, Cara and Tucker would be out in the community, close to curfew, attracting a lot of attention as an unwed couple. One glance at Chase and I could tell he was thinking the same.

"When? When did they go?" I asked.

"I don't know . . . twenty minutes maybe," said Polo. "Marco and I were still looking for the address the carrier left."

Chase's hand gripped mine so hard I winced.

"We need to leave," he said urgently. "We all need to get out. He's turning us in."

"Hold up, big guy," said Polo. "Who's turning us in?"

Chase zeroed in on Sean. "We have to risk the roads tonight."

Sean gave him a sober nod and left the office.

"What about the safe house?" Billy said. "Wallace said . . ."

But Chase was already following Sean toward the truck. I snagged his sleeve as he barreled past.

"I have to go," I said.

"I know. We are." Chase's tone was clipped.

"I have to go *home*."

His eyes brightened with caution. Hands on my shoulders, he leaned down to make sure I understood his next words.

"Em, she's gone. I know what I saw." He stopped when he registered the determination on my face. "What if Sean's right, and it is a trap?" He sounded frightened. Not of the MM, but of what he might find. Of hoping, just like me, that she was alive.

"I have to know," I said.

He glanced over my shoulder, staring at nothing. Then, with a short, muttered curse, he swung back into the office.

Marco and Polo had already set out water and food for our trip, and Sean was preparing to load it in the back of the truck. I raced to help him, finding Cara's folded Sisters of Salvation uniform on one of the dismantled crates.

I broached the silence. "We have to make a detour."

To my relief, he only sighed and said, "I figured."

Low voices rumbled within the office, and then I heard Billy's cracking voice yell, "You're doing *what?*"

"Oh no." I reached the threshold just in time to see Polo place a set of car keys in Chase's open palm.

"You're going to get caught." Billy's face had gone ashy.

"Our shift is up at eight A.M.," said Polo. "That's when we're reporting it stolen."

"Unless you get caught before then, in which case we're reporting it stolen early," added Marco. "You're all right, Jennings, but a lot of people count on us working this angle."

"Thanks," said Chase.

"Don't thank us yet," said Marco reluctantly.

The adrenaline was already kicking through my veins.

The only vehicles that couldn't be caught breaking curfew were the ones enforcing it. FBR cruisers. Like the one we were about to steal.

Still reeling from our whirlwind plan, I turned to Billy. "You'll come with us, right?"

He pulled a string from the frayed hem of his shirt, frowning.

Chase put his hand on my arm, as if suspecting I might try to drag him with us.

"What's it going to be, Billy? It's your call," he said.

I held my breath. *Please come with us.* I felt a gnawing inside of me, like I had in the days after they'd arrested my mother. I didn't want to let Billy out of my sight.

Billy swallowed audibly, shoving his mop of dark hair out of his eyes. He transferred his weight from foot to foot. Chase was right, it was important that Billy make this choice for himself. He hadn't gotten a say before.

"I'm waiting for the carrier," he said at last. "Wallace is going to meet me at the safe house."

Silence seeped across the room. No one knew how to say the words Billy would never believe, not unless he saw it for himself.

Wallace is dead.

"If Tucker brings back soldiers . . ." I couldn't finish.

"We'll take care of it," said Polo. Beside him, Marco nodded.

Something pinched deep inside of me. If we didn't deliver Billy all the way to South Carolina, we'd let Wallace down, but short of forcing him into the cruiser, there was nothing we could do. Decisions had to be made, and quickly. I grabbed him then, squeezing him tightly, despite his awkward, adolescent stance, and kissed him on the cheek.

"Take care of yourself, Billy. I hope I'll see you again soon."

He blinked rapidly and muttered a good-bye under his breath.

In less than ten minutes we were ready. Outside the loading dock was a single gas pump, meant for the delivery trucks on their distribution routes, and Marco filled three red plastic canisters with fuel so that we wouldn't have to stop in public. The cruiser was parked in a single parking spot beside the building's generator, just beside the high chain-link fence that surrounded the plant. When he placed the sloshing drums in the trunk I had the fleeting fear that hauling around that much gasoline was dangerous, but figured combustion was the least of our concerns.

With Chase and Sean in borrowed uniforms, and me in the Sisters of Salvation skirt and blouse that Cara had abandoned, we rolled down the ramp onto the highway and gunned it home.

WE watched the images on the television, horrified. The ground was crowded with hunks of concrete and fallen streetlamps. The dust was powdered chalk, thick as fog. People, coated in white, ran from it, screaming, coughing, like it was a living creature chasing after them, not another building crashing to the ground. Our living room crackled with static.

The camera shook. The guy taping the scene was running. And then the screen went black and returned to the newsroom.

Chicago had been bombed. Like Baltimore and San Francisco. Washington and New York. But so much closer.

"Baby, come here." Mom reached out her hand and I slid beneath her arm, feeling how she was damp and trembling. I pinched my eyes closed. Outside, kids were playing. A car drove down the street. How could people be so unafraid?

Chase, I thought. Just his name, over and over. I didn't know where his uncle lived. I prayed it wasn't in the heart of the city.

"Ember, if something like this happens, you come straight home, okay?" Her voice cracked. I wrapped my arms around her waist to make her stronger. "I'll meet you here, and we'll figure out what to do."

I HAD a hard time sitting back in the leather seat. Between the lingering fear of driving after curfew in a borrowed cruiser, the daunting computer panel beside the steering wheel, and the glass partition behind my back, I had a hard time calming down.

My mind wasn't helping. The thoughts slapped one atop the next. Flashes of my mom, her hair in clips, wearing clothes from my closet. The similarities in our faces. What did she look like now? Only a couple months had passed, but I knew I looked different. Hardened. Wary. Was she the same? If she'd survived the gunshot, how badly was she injured? Was she getting enough medical treatment? Or was she being forced, like the woman with her son in the square, to scare others into compliance?

Stop, I thought. Stop. She's dead. Stop fantasizing she's not. Stop hoping.

My heels hammered the vacuumed rubber floor mats. Cara's wool skirt made my legs itch.

I turned back to check on Sean. We'd opened the vent in the partition between the seats, but couldn't hear each other without yelling. He looked out the window, content in the silence. It had been a long time since I'd seen that small, peaceful smile. That was Becca's smile.

"Talk about something," Chase said, startling me. His eyes stayed glued to the road.

"What about?" I asked.

"Anything. Your voice . . . helps." His thumbs drummed on the steering wheel.

"Do you think we'll ever see him again?" I asked. "Billy, I mean." Not Tucker.

"If Tucker doesn't get to him first." The way he said that name—it was like he was tearing something with his teeth.

I rubbed my temples. "I keep thinking it's my fault," I said quickly. "That I could have stopped all of it—whatever he's doing—that day at the base. If I'd have shot him he never would have shown up at the Wayland Inn, he wouldn't have come with us to the checkpoint, he wouldn't know anything about the safe house. But I couldn't, you know? I messed up. I was a coward, and now . . . now something even worse is going to happen, I can feel it."

It had burst out in one breath—things I'd been hiding from him because I'd hated to admit they were true, even to myself.

"Wait," he said. "*Not* killing someone makes you a coward?"

I shrugged. I didn't like him turning this around on me. He rubbed the back of his neck.

"Em, what you did that day, it makes you better," he said. "If you'd given me the gun that day, I would have done it. I almost did at the Wayland Inn. And killing someone—even if it's *him*—that changes everything. It makes all the good things wrong and all the wrong things seem okay. And it gets easier. To do again, I mean. I've seen it." He took a slow breath. "Look at Wallace. He's got nothing but Billy and the cause, and when it came down to it, he could only hold on to one."

In the silence I remembered the Wayland Inn, purged by fire. Remembered how Wallace had forgotten what was most important.

"Be glad you didn't kill him," Chase said gently. "Holding back, that was brave."

I shifted, because *brave* didn't fit right against my skin. When it came to Tucker and what I hadn't done, *coward* felt right, and *failure* felt right. At least they had. Now, I wasn't so sure.

"I wish I knew what he and Cara were doing in Greeneville," I said.

"You didn't buy the cousin story either, huh?"

I glanced behind me, but Sean was still blissfully ignorant to our conversation. It wasn't that I didn't want his opinion, I just felt more comfortable discussing some things with Chase alone.

"All I know is that she's hiding something," I said, picking at my fingernails, frustrated that I didn't have the answers. Thinking of Cara suddenly reminded me of the copper cartridge I'd shown her in Greeneville. I'd been so distracted by the things she'd said about Sarah and the scars on her chest, I'd forgotten she'd been the last to hold it. Now who knew where it was.

I needed to change the subject.

"It's strange going home after everything, isn't it?" In my mind it was preserved, just as it had been when I left, but maybe it was different. I knew *I* was different. "I doubt anyone would even recognize me."

"I would," he said.

I laughed and combed my fingers through my short, dyed hair, catching a new waft of smoke. "Right. I look just like I did when I left."

"You look beautiful," he said. "And anyway, I'm not planning on running into anyone we used to know." He cleared his throat, fixing his eyes on the road. "Why are you looking at me like that?"

All the hard edges within me had shimmered and gone soft.

"You said I was beautiful."

He smirked and settled back in his seat. "I guess I did."

I hid the smile in my shoulder.

CHASE drove fast, simply because he could. We passed no one on the highway. Not a soul. It was desolate, a half-pipe with trash and forest debris and the occasional stiffened roadkill arcing up against the side partitions. We were mostly silent, each lost in our own thoughts. My guarded hope, and his fearful dread.

Three hours in, just after we'd passed the turnoff for Frankfort on I-64, we pulled off for gas. It was dark, and the cold scent of rotten leaves filled my nostrils. Chase removed one of the canisters from the trunk and tipped the yellow nozzle into the fuel tank while Sean and I stretched our legs.

"So this is home," he said, rolling his shoulders.

"It's close." I hesitated. "It's weird coming back. Not knowing who is going to be there."

"Yeah," he said with a strange, strangled sigh. "Sometimes it's better not to know."

I frowned. Sean shook his head. "It's good to check, though," he added as an afterthought.

My thoughts returned to Tent City, to Sean's confession that he had lived in such a place, and I wondered if he had family somewhere. He never talked about them. He didn't look like he wanted to start now.

"What did you find out about Chicago?" I asked. His head bobbed gratefully.

"Marco told me we rendezvous with the resistance at an old airfield in the Wreckage."

I shivered. During the War, the first places the Insurgents attacked were the airports. I'd seen what remained of them on the news: demolished buildings, concrete dust storms, but never a plane. Not since air travel had been banned at the beginning of the War. Chase shifted nearby. These weren't just television scenes to him. He'd been there.

"He says it's a rough bunch up North," continued Sean when neither Chase nor I commented. "Says they're crazy. Too much time in the field or something."

"Will they help?" I asked speculatively.

"Sure. We just shouldn't expect any hospitality."

I frowned, wondering what this meant, but imagined that little in our line of work rivaled Marco and Polo's generosity. They had let us steal their car, after all.

When the tank was full again we moved out.

THE lights from the old basketball arena, which had been converted to a Horizons manufacturing plant after the War, were the first signs of home. Cold and yellow, they lit the night like a warning rather than a welcome. The rest of the city was black, but for the gleam in the distance from the hospital— the first place I'd been taken during the overhaul. I returned to the edge of my seat, absently tugging at the knot in the uniform handkerchief around my neck.

The roads had been completely empty, but as we approached the Kennedy Bridge another cruiser came careening from the south, going fast enough to jump the Ohio River.

My heart clutched in my chest.

"No," I whispered. *"Don't stop don't stop don't stop."*

I sank in the seat. Sean remained motionless behind us, sleeping.

It sped by without a hint at braking. Chase exhaled loudly and continued on.

"So, I guess we know what the MM does after curfew," I said shakily. I wondered if the soldiers inside just liked to drive fast, or if they were drunk on whiskey like the kind in the back of the Horizons truck. Or if actually, there were two people inside just like us.

It helped to think that.

The clock on the dashboard flashed 2:27 A.M. as we crossed the dark waters of the Ohio on the high metal bridge. There were only four hours until curfew was up, until any nosy civilian could recognize our faces and make a report. The pressure made my muscles tense. We hadn't said it out loud, but it would be better all around if we were out of here before dawn.

The cruiser rolled over the cracked pavement, headlights shining on landmarks like we were historians excavating some ancient tomb. There was the stop sign halfway between Beth's house and mine. We used to meet there before we walked to school. Back when I used to go to school. Trees I recognized, dogwoods, already turning pink with blossoms. Tall, overgrown grass and weeds in front of every home. I remembered before the War when people had used lawnmowers. What a waste those things were. That much gas could power a generator for hours.

I'd tripped there and skinned my knee on the sidewalk. On that corner, a girl once set up a lemonade stand for a quarter a glass. And right beneath that tall brick wall was where I'd been standing when I'd fallen in love with Chase. I was nine, and he'd just won a race against Matt Epstein. He was the fastest boy in the whole world.

So many Statute circulars glued to so many doors. How many people had been taken since my overhaul?

We reached Ewing Avenue—my street—and a small whimper came from my throat.

I looked up a steep embankment on the right, but the old,

abandoned house where I'd met Chase for the first time was now hidden by shadow. Hidden, like the children we used to be.

My house had come into view. Small and boxy, white. A sister to its next-door neighbor, the Jennings's home.

"No fast moves," Chase hissed. Two headlights came over the swell at the top of the street and caused my heart to stutter. The FBR cruiser eased by Mrs. Crowley's house, right across the way from mine.

"They're already here!" Bands of tension ratcheted around my lungs. I bit my lip so I wouldn't scream, so hard it bled.

"It's just a curfew patrol," he muttered as we rolled past. "Just like us."

The tinted windows were too dark to see inside. As Sean continued to snore, the patrol car continued to the intersection and disappeared around the block.

We approached my house. The familiar L-shaped walkway led to the front door where a Statute circular, the same that had been placed there during my arrest, still hung. A single tear slid down my cheek and I hurriedly wiped it away.

"Look." I pointed. Below the living room window someone had tagged my house with black spray paint. One Whole Country, One Whole Family.

Someone was here after all. Someone fighting back. My pulse ran a mile a minute.

Chase buttoned the top of his collar, which he'd left slack

in the car, with one hand. "We'll park off the street and go through my backyard. Check your house from mine."

I had to get in there as soon as possible, but was petrified of what we'd find.

We parked two streets down, in a cul-de-sac overrun by trash the city workers had missed and storm debris from the surrounding trees. I recognized this place, though barely. Chase and I had played here as children. Hide-and-seek. It was close enough we could still hear our parents calling us home to dinner.

It was disheartening how much the place had changed. Now it was dark and silent. Those who hadn't moved away were hidden inside for curfew. Those who caught a glimpse through their closed curtains of our stolen FBR cruiser were afraid.

Chase killed the engine. Behind us, Sean woke and took in our surroundings.

Time to go, I told myself. But my legs wouldn't move.

Sean got out. Chase followed, and I heard them conversing in low voices. Sean took off around the block, moving stealthily through the shadows. He was going to keep watch from up the street.

Get up. Still nothing.

Chase returned to the car. He rubbed his forehead with the heel of his hand and we sat in the dark. One minute. Two. We didn't have time to waste; sunrise was coming, we had to move on to Chicago, but even though I told myself this, I could not summon the courage to open that door.

Slowly, he leaned over the center console and unbuckled my seat belt. I still felt where his hand had touched my stomach even after it drew away.

I could tell there were things he wanted to say. Chase things. Things like, *we don't have to do this*, or *why don't I look and you can stay here.* He didn't say any of them though. Maybe he knew what my response would be. Likely he knew just as deeply as I did that this was something we *had* to do. This mystery, left unsolved, would haunt us the rest of our likely short lives.

He stayed close, and the warmth from his body flowed across the inches between us. I could hear him breathing. His uniform jacket shifted, and in the moonlight I saw the raised half circle of skin where the cords of his neck met the muscles of his shoulder. Teeth marks, from where I'd bitten him when I'd been so furious at Tucker. Shame heated my cheeks. Chase hadn't been the intended target for my rage, but all the same, he always seemed to get the brunt of it.

Tentatively, I closed the space between us and kissed that spot. I could fix it, I thought. I could reverse all the harsh words if he gave me the chance.

His skin was soft, but the muscles just beneath were taut and strong. My lips stayed against his neck as his breath quickened in my hair. I closed my eyes.

"It's time," he said, voice heavy. "Let's go, Em."

We stepped outside the stolen FBR cruiser, knowing we left all uncertainty, and the safety that came with our once-believed truths, behind. There was no going back now. Hope, and all her terrible consequences, had struck. In minutes we would learn the truth.

Either my mother was alive, or someone was playing a very dangerous game.

WE snuck between two weathered garage units and through the yard behind Chase's house. The dose of adrenaline coursing through my veins gave me the resolve to scramble up and over the privacy fence, but left me twitchy.

I waited in the wild tangle of grass beside the back door while he rummaged quietly through the bushes for a large rock. Beneath it, to my surprise, was a dirty plastic bag holding a key, and though it grabbed as he slid it home, the door opened in virtual silence.

"Stay here," he whispered as we slipped inside.

I remained low, leaning against the wall just inside his living room, waiting for my eyes to adjust to the dark. He carried a flashlight and a gun, holding them stacked atop each other but aimed low so that the glare wouldn't reflect off the front windows. I breathed in, thinking the place might smell of comforting memories, but it didn't. It smelled stale, cold, nothing like the home where I'd spent half of my childhood.

Chase returned after a thorough check of each room. The

flashlight was off, tucked into his pocket, and he'd holstered his gun as well, though I noticed he hadn't snapped the latch closed. There was still the chance a passing patrol could come to check things out.

"It's empty," he said with a mixture of relief and regret.

I stood slowly. It was so dark I could only see degrees of shadow, but it was enough to tell that the room had been cleared of furniture. After his parents had died, his uncle had hired someone to sell most of their things at a garage sale. Some pieces remained—those that couldn't even be given away. A wicker plant stand that leaned to one side. A couple lawn chairs against the dining room wall. I tiptoed around the corner into the kitchen and saw the wire dish rack on the counter; the last remaining evidence of a woman who used to make us cookies after school.

"It's still weird in here without all your things." I hugged my elbows to my body. "It's sad."

"It's just a house," he said, keeping his eyes fixed on the living room window. I recognized that flattened tone. It only came up when he was swallowing down his feelings.

"We can watch your place from my room, but we're not going over there until we're sure they haven't posted anyone inside," he added.

I didn't like this; I wanted to see if she was there, and if not, search my house for clues. I wanted to sit on my bed, cuddle in my comforter, touch my books. I wanted to get my clothes, get a bra that actually fit and jeans that were my own. But Chase had a point. None of those things would happen if we walked into an ambush.

I followed him down the empty hallway, and even in the dark I could see the faint glowing outlines on the wall where pictures had once hung. His room was the first on the left, and the second we entered it, my stomach clenched. There were no curtains or blinds to hide my bedroom, ten feet beyond his window.

My house was dark.

Disappointment scored through me. It could have been made a checkpoint and then abandoned when the MM had accused me of supporting the sniper. If that had happened, who knew where the inhabitants were. In another neighborhood. Another city. Arrested. My hands fisted tightly in my skirt.

Chase took a low position beside the sill, angling toward the street where he could see any potential movement.

"Let's go look," I whispered.

He considered this, but shook his head. "We'll wait. If someone's there, they'll rotate through."

There was no use arguing with him.

The minutes passed. While I stared out the window, he knocked down cobwebs. I remembered with a regretful pang what his room had looked like when we were kids. Clothing strewn across the floor. Empty Coke cans under his twin bed. A jar on his dresser for whatever bugs he managed to sneak past his mom. He was such a boy.

Crack! Automatically I fell to my knees, but it was just Chase in the corner of his closet, peeling back a floorboard beneath a loose scrap of carpet.

"What are you *doing?*"

He shined the flashlight on a small wooden container, half the size of a shoebox. When he blew on it, dust sprayed across the room.

"I left some things here before I was drafted," he said.

With one eye on the darkened window, I watched him pull open the squeaky lid and rummage through the contents inside with one finger. He removed a school picture of a pretty mixed girl with jet-black hair bobbed to her chin. Rachel, his sister, when she'd been in high school. Intrigued now, I sat beside him on the floor, ears still perked toward the window. The sudden sensation slid over me that we'd done this before—hunched over a flashlight and buried treasure while trying not to get caught.

He shuffled through forty dollars cash, a dinged-up matchbox car, a couple baseball cards from teams before the War, and a wedding picture of his parents, folded in the middle. The white crease across the center of the page was so thick it nearly split in half.

Something fluttered in my stomach. I thought of the letters I'd written that he'd carried in our backpack for so long. He didn't have much, but his small collection of memories kept him grounded. It was touching, and somehow profound that so little could represent so much to him.

What did I have to remind me of home? Of my mother? Of Beth, just blocks away sleeping in her bed? All I had was this stupid necklace that was supposed to have been for my protection. And it wasn't even really mine. Suddenly Chase, with all his loss, seemed rich beyond belief.

The box shifted, and something metallic slid across the

bottom. He placed it in his hand. A tiny circle in the broad expanse of his calloused palm. Braided silver, colliding into a single black stone, as dark as Chase's eyes.

His mother's wedding ring.

"Maybe you should switch yours out for this one," he suggested. There was a thin quality to his voice. He was trying too hard to sound casual.

I gulped, but a solid lump had formed in my throat that I could not push down. Nervously, I twisted the ring he'd stolen for me from the Loftons' ranch. I kept it as a disguise—there were Statutes about unmarried girls staying out alone with men. *Indecent*, the MM said. *Scandalous*. Like nail polish and hair dye and all the other contraband items deemed *immoral* in Article 2. But if I wore Chase's mother's wedding band, it wouldn't just be for my safety. It would be for other reasons, too.

Two memories collided simultaneously. One, just a flash of Chase's mom and dad kissing. I'd been young enough to run away shrieking, and old enough to wonder what it was like.

The other of me standing in line at the pawn shop, cashing in my mom's engagement ring.

We'd both lost our families. We could die, just like them, at any moment. We were living on borrowed time already. What if he was captured? Executed? What if he just disappeared?

I stood, looking anywhere but at him. The heel of my hand rubbed forcefully at the tightness in my chest.

"It's not like it would mean anything. Not really." He

scratched his head, and chuckled dryly, but his eyes were dark and brooding.

My hand fell to my side.

"It wouldn't?"

He shrugged, too carelessly.

"We're not even valid citizens. It's not how it was for my parents. I'm just saying it wouldn't be real, that's all." He laughed again. "Forget I said anything."

But I didn't want to forget. A deep ache had filled me, a longing for something more. For a future, one with him, one that shimmered in the distance like a mirage.

I stopped him before he could shove the ring into his pocket. I didn't care if the MM thought I was a valid citizen, or recognized our relationship. We had each other, now, and if *we* knew it that was all that really mattered.

I reached for his fist, curled around his mother's ring, and brought it to my lips. Gently, I kissed the inside of his wrist. I heard his breath change tempo, quicken.

"Does that feel real?"

He nodded.

"Then who cares what they say?"

A warm, relieved smile spread across his face.

"Someday," I promised.

But instead of saying something more, his expression flattened, and he shoved the ring in his pocket. For a moment I was humiliated, until I realized his gaze had narrowed on a point behind me.

"We've got incoming," he said quietly.

I spun toward the window, ducking when I saw a shadowed

shape. Had someone just come in? Or had they been inside the whole time?

"Sean?" I whispered.

"Too small."

"Too small for a man?" I clarified. He didn't answer.

My heart pounded out of my chest. In that moment I knew that she was here. I could feel her, just feet away. I would have her back in seconds.

"We're going."

He couldn't tell me no, because now he had to find out, too.

"I can break through the lock in the back," he said.

"I don't care if you throw a rock through the damn window," I said even as he shushed me. "I'm getting in that house *right now.*"

He placed a steadying hand on my arm and I forced myself to take a deep breath.

We snuck out his back door, onto his patio. He locked the door while I bounced from heel to heel. He didn't waste any time with good-byes. It was a house. Just a house, like he'd said.

We exited the side gate, sneaking as quietly as we could across the grass divide between our two houses, then edged along the building, careful to stay out of the moonlight, and to roll our feet from heel to toe to make as little noise as possible as we crossed into my small backyard and stood on the single step that led into the kitchen.

My home. We were home. Everything, *everything* was going to be okay. The tears were already filling my eyes. My whole body was trembling and ready to hold her and squeeze her until her ribs cracked. We would take her to the cruiser. She couldn't stay here and do this. We'd take her to Chicago. And then, after we figured out how to free Rebecca, we'd all go to the safe house.

Chase jimmied the back lock using a knife from his belt, and after a few painfully slow moments, it clicked open. He raised his weapon. I wanted to tell him to put the gun down; he didn't want to accidently shoot her after everything she'd been through.

He pushed inside.

Despite my bubbling excitement, the scurrying of feet across the carpet spiked my awareness, and my body, trained to react with caution these last weeks, braced.

"Soldiers!" I heard a male voice whisper fearfully.

A scuffle sounded across the carpet beyond the kitchen.

I ran toward them, petrified that they would try to escape out of the front and run right into a passing cruiser on cur-few patrol. I jerked around where the kitchen table should have been and slid, rounding the corner too fast.

Chase was right on my heels. He grabbed my shoulder and shoved me bodily into the wall, pinning me against it. A moment later my heart rebounded, its cadence slamming through my eardrums.

"No soldiers here," Chase called loudly enough for some-one in the next room to hear. We waited behind the wall that separated the kitchen from the living room and the front of the house.

Hurried footsteps, and then silence.

"We won't hurt you!" I said against Chase's tightening grip. "Don't go out the front! There was a patrol car passing through earlier."

Silence.

"I'm not a soldier," Chase said again. "It's just a disguise."

"Yeah, right!" returned a male's voice. "How'm I s'pposed to believe you?"

"I'm putting down my gun," said Chase. He cast me a warning look before releasing me, and then, to my shock, knelt and leaned the weapon against my foot. I scooped it up, but kept it lowered.

"I'm not putting down mine!" the man responded.

"We both know you don't have one," said Chase calmly.

"We're looking for a woman—Lori Whittman," I said. "That's all. We don't want any trouble, we just want to talk to her."

"She's here," said a female voice. "I'm Lori Whittman."

My stomach turned. *No, no, no, no, no.* That was not my mother's voice.

"I'm coming out," I said.

Chase blocked my path. He flipped on the flashlight and stepped out into the hall with me right behind him. I tucked the gun in the back of the skirt's waistband and pushed, trying to get him out of my way, but he was as solid as a brick wall.

"Who gave you my name?" the girl inquired.

"A friend . . ." Chase trailed off. He stiffened before me.

"It's . . . you," she responded. "*You!*" she screeched. She knew him. And he knew her.

I finally succeeded in shoving Chase aside.

There before me, highlighted in the beam of the flashlight, was a girl with a wild thicket of red hair, pale cheeks, and dark freckles. Her thin mouth was pulled back into a sneer, and the green eyes I'd known since my childhood hardened with fury, and then blinked, confused.

"*Beth?*"

"*Ember?*"

My knees began to knock. This wasn't right: Beth, here in this condemned house, using my mother's name. She couldn't be running a checkpoint, she was just . . . Beth. Just Beth, my best friend. She didn't know this world. She knew high school and who was dating who and what assignment was coming up in English class. She knew what size pants I wore and that I hated tomatoes. This was all wrong.

But I didn't think any more about it, because the next second her arms were around my neck and she was hugging me, and I was hugging her back, and she was blubbering and bawling like I'd only seen her do when we were thirteen and her cat Mars had died.

She smelled like Beth, and she felt like Beth, all hard joints and long skinny limbs. She was wearing a turtleneck sweater and jeans and cute slip-on flats and all I could think was how impossible those would be to run in.

"*Ohmygoodness* I thought you were dead! What are you doing here? What are you *wearing*? Are you a Sister now? And your hair. . . . Are you going back to school? Wait, that's silly, I don't know what I'm talking about I'm just glad you're alive!"

She said it all so quickly I couldn't get a word in edgewise. It was better that way. If I had opened my mouth, the disappointment would have come flooding out, and I couldn't do that because this was Beth, my best friend, and I was supposed to be as overjoyed as she was.

A second later she pulled back, and I caught a glimpse of a short guy in his late twenties with a goatee and circular glasses. Before I could ask who he was, or what Beth was even doing here, she released me, and pounced on Chase, claws out like a redheaded wildcat.

"Beth!" I grabbed her around the waist and heaved her off of him. He stumbled back into the kitchen, arms raised in surrender, and stalled against the stove. It clanged loudly, the metal scratching metal. He stilled it with lightning fast reflexes.

"What are *you* doing here?" she sneered at him. Beth always had a mean temper, even when we were kids.

"We heard my mom was here," I said. I didn't let go of her skinny waist.

"You have some nerve coming back here after what you did to them!"

"He's okay," I told her. "He helped me escape from rehab! He's not a soldier."

"He sure looks like one."

"He's not."

"He can't talk for himself?"

"Beth, *please*."

"I'm not a soldier," said Chase in a low voice. Beth had her own flashlight and shined it accusingly on his face.

"Then where'd you get that uniform, huh? And why were you with the soldiers when they took my best friend?" I could practically see the steam coming off of her.

"Keep it down!" said the guy behind Beth.

"Beth, stop it," I said, instantly exhausted. Where were the kitchen chairs? I had to sit down. Where was the table for that matter?

"She waited forever for you, you know that?" Beth rolled on, a year of pent-up best-friend aggression letting loose. "When you left it *killed* her. I've never seen her that sad in my whole life."

A wave of guilt crashed over me, followed closely by embarrassment. I didn't want her making Chase feel bad with that stuff. He already felt bad enough.

"I mean seriously, what kind of boyfriend doesn't even write a letter to say he's okay?"

"Not a very good one," said Chase.

"And then you come back and *arrest* them?"

I backed into the wall.

"Beth, please."

"Well, he should know," she said haughtily.

"Where are the chairs?" I asked.

She shined the flashlight in my face. "Oh God, you look like you're going to throw up. You're not going to throw up, are you? Stephen, get a trash can!"

"There aren't any," said the guy behind her.

"Ah, hell. The MM took all your stuff, Ember. They cleaned you out. I got a couple things before they finished, but all the furniture and everything, it's all gone."

I slid down the wall to the floor. In a second, Chase was at my side, helping to settle me on the dusty linoleum. The moment I was down, he released me and backed away. I didn't want him to go. I needed him close. Beth eyed him reproachfully and knelt at my side.

"You're not going to puke?"

I had yesterday, outside the Wayland Inn during the fire. No one had balked at me then, like Beth was doing now.

I shook my head.

"Beth, what are you doing?" I asked.

"What do you mean—"

"This," I said, throwing my arms out to the side. "My house. My mom's name. In the middle of the night!"

"Quiet!" said Stephen again.

Beth took a quick breath. "Okay. It's kind of complicated, so just hang tight. There's this thing called a *safe house*," she said the term slowly, as if I'd never heard of it. "And people who are in trouble go there, but they have to wait at more remote places, *checkpoints*, for—"

"I know what a checkpoint is!" I shouted.

"Alert the neighborhood." Stephen's footsteps clacked against the floor as he marched into the next room. I tracked him with my eyes, wondered where this stranger thought he was going in *my* house.

"You do?" Beth tucked her hair behind her ears. "Did they teach you that in Sister school?" She pointed at my blouse.

"I'm not a Sister," I said, face falling into my hands. "It's a disguise, just like Chase's uniform."

She chewed her lip. "Maybe I need a disguise."

I groaned. "This isn't a joke!"

"Of course it's not." She looked wounded. "I help people here. I helped Mrs. Crowley across the street. The MM was coming after her, and I told her to hide here, and since then four more people have hidden here, too. People we know, Ember. And now they never have to get arrested." She sniffled a little and wiped her eyes.

I felt like I'd been punched in the gut.

She'd grown quiet, waiting for me to answer. I said the only thing I could think to say.

"Mom's gone, Beth."

I closed my eyes, not caring that we were in my house anymore, or that there were patrol cars outside, or that Beth's yelling had probably alerted half the city to my presence. I was so tired of it, all of it. The running and the sneaking around and the cruel games that the world played.

"That's what Harmony's brother said. I . . ." She sniffled. "I was really hoping it wasn't true." Her eyes shifted to Chase. "Did he know?"

He was crouched near my feet, watching me, never turning to glance at anyone else. There was just enough light to glint off his eyes.

"He knows," I said weakly. "How did Harmony's brother tell you?" Harmony, our friend from school, came slowly to mind. Long dark hair, almond-shaped eyes. I wondered absently if she was still dating Marcus Woodford.

"He joined last Thanksgiving, remember?"

"I remember. He's playing both sides?" I pictured Marco and Polo.

She twirled a lock of hair around her finger. "Kind of. He's not supposed to talk to Harmony, isn't that crazy? But apparently he can talk to me without breaking the rules. Anyhow, he followed me home one night and wanted news about his family. I told him I would tell him if he'd tell me what they did with you."

"You must have freaked," I said.

"Was it your friend's brother that told you to start a checkpoint?" Chase asked, diverting the conversation.

She glared at him, still angry.

"He doesn't order me around," she said stubbornly. "If anything, it's the opposite. He wants to know about his family, he's got to help me out."

It occurred to me that Beth had no idea that she was playing with fire. If Harmony's brother tired of her blackmail he could instantly turn the tables and send her to rehab or worse.

"He told you about the carriers?" I asked.

Beth nodded. "He told me about this guy in Chicago that takes people somewhere safe, and sent him this top secret radio message."

"Beth . . ." I started, feeling the sudden urge to throttle her. "What you're doing is really dangerous. *Seriously.*"

She cast me a hurt look.

"She's saying the soldier could turn you in if he wanted," explained Chase. "And if he knows about the safe house, and gets enough pressure from above to talk, a lot of people could die, not just you."

"*Die?*"

It was as if she'd never considered that she could be killed. I felt very sorry, and very worried for her just then.

"What did he tell you about the safe house?" I asked.

Beth was frowning now.

"Nothing besides a guy comes and takes you there. He came last week and tagged your house all up with spray paint, I hope you don't mind. He says all the places like this have that on them. He calls himself Truck ''cause I drive the truck,'" she quoted in a manly voice. "Stephen heard from someone at the soup kitchen where . . . where your mom used to work that I'd opened shop here."

She leaned forward and whispered, "He's got a warrant. For an Article Three."

Article 3. Whole families are to be considered one man, one woman, and children. I could still see the Statutes we read over and over in the reformatory as though they were right in front of my face.

I looked into Beth's puffy eyes, and all of a sudden everything—all my fear for her, and the anger at how naïve she was being, and the relief at seeing her, but also the crushing disappointment that she wasn't who I'd wanted her to be—collided into one big black pit inside of me. It festered when I thought of how stupid I'd been, fooled into thinking my mother was still alive. How once again I'd thrown Chase and myself into the eye of the storm for the same naïveté I saw in Beth.

She was chewing on her lower lip, and flipping the flashlight from hand to hand.

"It was my idea to go by your mom's name," she said. "I figured since Lori was already . . . I figured it couldn't do much harm since she wasn't going to be coming back here. She was always so brave. It's like she wasn't scared of anything." She hiccupped, then wiped her eyes again. "I figured this place could be, like, dedicated to her or something."

Before she could say anything further, I scrambled up off the floor and escaped down the hallway toward my bedroom.

CHAPTER
14

"GO back to bed. This is between your mother and me."

He stood over her—this man she'd said would complete our family. His shadow blanketed her body on the floor, where she was trying to pull herself up by one of the dresser drawers. When she saw me standing behind him, she gave a small, pained gasp, and covered her cheek with both hands.

She was too late; I'd already seen the mark.

Somehow, I was beside her, helping her up, telling myself she'd fallen. That was all. It was an accident. My mother didn't let anyone hit her. My mother was the bravest woman I'd ever met.

And then it was tearing through me, all the rage and disappointment and disgust.

"Get out." I blocked him as he reached toward her, already apologizing for the red welt on her cheek, and the tears that made it glisten. I jumped up and snatched the lamp, hefting it over my shoulder. "Get out!"

"Ember, stop it." My mom was standing now. "Go back to your room."

I couldn't believe she'd said that.

"You know I'd never hurt you." Roy's voice broke. He put his hands on his hips. He started crying.

"You did!" I screamed.

His shoulders bobbed as he cried, but I had no pity for him. Only relief as he walked out. The front door slammed, rattling the pictures on the wall.

She pushed past me and raced after him, but he was already driving away, tires screeching around the corner. I met her at the door, the lamp still gripped in one hand, its power cord tailing after me like a snake. I was shaking. I wanted to scream.

"Why'd you do that?" She grabbed my shoulders and shook me. "That was none of your business, Ember. None of your business! What goes on in my—"

I didn't wait for her to say any more. I ran to my room, hid under the covers, and cried until the power shut off and the sky outside turned black. Until the floor groaned under her weight and she curled up next to me.

"You're not scared of anything, are you?" she whispered.

THERE was nothing inside my bedroom. All my things, the bed I'd slept in since I was old enough to have a bed, my bookshelves filled with worn novels, the dresser with the gold handles that my mother had found at a garage sale, they were all gone. Had they tossed them into a junkyard? Given them to a donation center? These were *my* things. These were the only pieces I had left of my mother. Of my life. Why did they have to take *everything*?

"Do you have any surveillance, Stephen?" I heard Chase say, leading him back toward the kitchen.

I turned to see Beth holding a paper bag just inside the door. I'd never seen her look timid in my life, and realizing I'd scared her made me feel awful. I couldn't blame her for not being my mother. I couldn't even blame her for not knowing the danger she was in. It was definitely something one had to experience to believe.

"Em-Ember," she stammered. "Why've you got a gun?"

I'd forgotten it was in the back of my waistband. She would have seen it, standing behind me now.

"It's nothing," I said quickly. "It's not even mine. It's Chase's."

"Oh," she said slowly. I could see the whites of her eyes reflected in the glow from her flashlight. "I, um, I brought, like, a ton of food over for Stephen in case some more people came, but no one else has come in the past couple days." She set the bag on the floor between us like she was offering a scrap of meat to a wild animal.

I knelt, and tore into a package of crackers and peanut butter. I hadn't realized how famished I was.

Beth inched back toward the door. "I heard the craziest thing. Did you know that they're saying you know this guy that, like, *killed* all these people?" The way she said it made me wonder if she really thought it was all that crazy.

"I heard something about that." I forced myself to put the crackers down.

"They posted your photo at the mini-mart two days ago with four other guys," she said. "There's a big sign right underneath that says *Have you seen this person?* No one at school believes it. Well, Marty Steiner and her bunch do, but you know them, they're just a bunch of gossip queens."

I could barely picture Marty Steiner. I couldn't remember a world where the power of gossip queens outweighed the brutality of armed soldiers.

I realized I needed to tell Beth something to ease her fears, but I wasn't sure what to say. If she was caught, forced by the MM to talk, she'd know too many things she shouldn't. I thought of Tubman, the carrier in Knoxville. He had it right, avoiding people's names. I almost wished we hadn't seen Beth, but the selfish part of me was glad we did.

"I can't tell you everything," I said honestly.

"You're my best friend," she frowned. "At least you were. You're acting really weird."

"I know." But I didn't. Weird had become my baseline. Whatever sense of calm I held now was actually a reprieve from the emotional roller coaster I usually rode.

"Did you kill those people?"

"No!" I stepped forward and she stepped back. She lifted the flashlight like a sword and I felt a sob choke off my windpipe.

"No, I haven't killed anyone," I said more slowly, in the kind of tone Chase used when I was scared. "You know me, I wouldn't do that."

"You're wearing a Sisters of Salvation uniform. I would have *never* thought you'd join them. You'd say it was too pro-government. Like it fed the invasion or something."

I sighed. She had a point. "When did they come here anyway?"

"Two weeks ago. They're teaching classes now."

"At Western?" I asked incredulously.

"Yup. They're all over town, too. At soup kitchens and stuff. People say they came from some Sisterhood Training Center in Dallas."

I pictured a manufacturing warehouse. Normal girls entering through one door, and coming out another in full, conservative uniform. For a brief instant I thought of Rebecca. What a zombie she'd been, or at least *pretended* to be, when I'd first met her.

"Well, I'm not a Sister. The uniform's borrowed, just like the gun."

"Why do you need the gun if you're not shooting people?"

"I was framed, okay?" I said, frustrated. "It's . . . for my protection."

"Stop me if I'm wrong," she said, "but doesn't packing heat generally make you *less* safe?"

I snickered. "I'm not *packing heat,* loser, I'm . . . I don't know."

"You're packing heat," she asserted. "You're like some crazy secret agent now."

I laughed despite myself. "I've missed you. A lot."

"Yeah, yeah." But she half smiled.

"We're trying to get to a safe house." *Eventually.*

"Like the one Truck goes to?" she asked, referring to the Chicago carrier.

"He didn't tell you where it is?" I asked. She shook her head. She had no idea what she was doing. But again, maybe it was better if she didn't know.

"Yeah, we're going somewhere like that. And you should too."

"Um, sort of got responsibilities here," she said, sounding more like herself again.

I shook my head, feeling a sharp pang of regret. "I wanted to graduate, too, but . . ."

She scoffed and crossed her arms over her chest. She only did that when her feelings were hurt.

"This?" I realized. "*This* is your responsibility? You need to stop doing this. You should get out of town. Take your parents and your brother and go somewhere."

"Ember, you're freaking me out."

I grabbed her shoulders and she flinched. "You should be freaked out!"

She stared at me unknowingly for a second before whipping away.

"It was for you!" she said, crying again. "I wanted to make sure what happened to you never happened again!"

I fell back, stung. *Never again?* It was like trying to explain to a child why bad things happened. I couldn't make her understand. And worse, I thought in her shoes I wouldn't have understood either.

"I . . . I know, I'm sorry. But, see, I'm okay. So you don't have to worry about me. And you've got your family and yourself to look out for. Let people with less to lose risk it all." *People like me.*

"Less to lose?" she said, an edge to her voice. "They took my best friend and killed her mom! What more excuse do I need to try to help?"

As much as I didn't want to, I got that.

"How's Ryan?" I asked, diverting her for a moment while I thought of a way to get her to see reason.

She turned toward a shadowed corner and knelt. A shine of the flashlight revealed a moving box.

"I don't know," she said petulantly. "I don't care either."

"You two broke up?" Ryan, with his studious jacket and school uniform, had had a crush on Beth since our freshman year. I had a hard time believing he wasn't in the picture.

"Yup."

"Wow. Why? He didn't get drafted, did he?"

She shook her head. "He's not a big fan of me hanging out here."

I ignored the sharp stab of betrayal. Ryan had been my friend, too. He was there when I'd been arrested, but he wasn't as brave, or as stupid, as Beth. He was smart. He was *right*.

I collapsed beside her on the floor.

"See, that's what I'm talking about! You *shouldn't* be here! I doubt your parents know or they'd have padlocked your door. What happens if Harmony's brother turns you in? You don't want to go to rehab, Beth, I'm serious." *If they even bring you that far.*

"I'm older than you by four months," she said sharply. "Stop lecturing me."

I snorted. The truth was she didn't feel older anymore. I

felt older. Years and years older. I'd experienced things Beth hopefully wouldn't for a long time, if ever.

"Here," she said, softer now. "This is all I could save for you."

She shoved the box into my knees, and I saw a full outfit, bra included, some silverware, half-used shampoo, a nail file, and a pre-War magazine. My fingers slid down the crinkled, waterlogged pages. My mom had liked to read these. She traded them with the ladies that volunteered at the soup kitchen. Knowing her hands had been on this, just as mine were now, provided me a small bit of comfort. I thought of the pictures Chase had, and his mother's ring, but I wasn't jealous. This was who she was. Someone who broke little rules she didn't deem necessary. Someone who preferred to focus on the good and interesting things in life rather than the bleakness of our future.

"How'd you get all these clothes?" I asked.

"You left them at my house."

Yes, I remembered now. I sometimes borrowed Beth's washing machine and left some spare clothes to wear while the others were being cleaned. The jeans and sweatshirt weren't my favorite, but they would fit, and so would the bra.

I gathered the clothes and the magazine and carefully tied them inside the body of the sweatshirt for later.

"He really bailed you out of reform school?" she asked, tipping her head down the hallway.

"That and a lot more."

She sighed. "The way he looks at you . . . like if I twisted your arm, his would fall off or something. Ryan never looked at me like that."

"He's sort of protective." I wasn't sure what else to say.

"Obviously." She snorted. "You still love him, don't you?"

I nodded. A reluctant smile spread across her face.

"Are you still a virgin?"

"Yes. *Jeez.*" I looked at the window at his empty house and wished he still lived there, and I still lived here, and things were as simple as him sneaking over after curfew.

"Oh. Good. Me too." A quick laugh snuck out.

We settled into a tentative conversation, one which encroached on our old selves, but never quite reached them. I was afraid of getting too close because inevitably I'd lose her again. I wondered if on some level she felt the same.

Our time was running low. I could feel the *tick, tick, tick* of the clock with each beat of my heart.

"I'm sorry about Ryan."

She bit her lip. "Yeah. It sucks."

"You can't tell him I was here."

"I figured."

"You can't tell anyone."

"I know."

"Not even your parents."

"I *know.*"

There was a knock on the doorframe.

"We need to get going," Chase said, appearing in the threshold. I'd heard him walking from room to room, checking our exits while Beth and I talked.

"Already? But you just got here!" Beth said.

I felt it, too. The strain, the roots that bound my feet to the floor. I couldn't stay, but I wanted to. I had to remind myself that my life wouldn't be normal if I stayed. This, right now, was as good as it was going to get.

"Beth," Chase cleared his throat. "You can come with us."

"No, I can't. I've got to do this. For Lori and for Ember." Her tone was so resolute I knew we couldn't argue with her.

"Do you have a way to get out of town?" he asked, obviously having expected this answer.

"My dad has a car he saves for emergencies," she said. "But we never drive it."

"Does it work?"

"Yeah. He starts it up about once a month when he's having a my-life-sucks-so-bad-I-can't-even-drive crisis."

Chase removed the forty dollars cash from his pocket and handed it to her.

"Go to the fill station and get a can of gas and some food, something nonperishable. Leave them in the trunk with a few changes of clothes for you and your family. If you have to get out quickly, you'll be ready that way."

He was protecting her, even when she'd thrashed him earlier.

"Change your name and your hair," I said. "And look for places that have a hand-painted sign outside: One Whole Country, One Whole Family. If you can't find one, ask around for a carrier at a soup kitchen. But don't talk to soldiers and don't talk to Sisters. You have to keep a low profile."

"O-okay," she said. "But really guys, I think I'll be fine."

I rubbed my temples. Just then a knock came from the front door, and a moment later we heard it push inward. Unbelievable. The door wasn't even locked.

Chase and I were on our feet instantly. He'd pulled the gun from the back of my waistband and aimed it low before him. I gripped my clothing and my mother's magazine hard to my chest.

"It's just Harmony's brother," said Beth uneasily, keeping her eyes trained on the weapon. "He always knocks at the front door. I told you, he's okay."

I didn't like it.

"Don't tell him we're here," ordered Chase.

"All *right* already. Let me go see what he wants."

She made to leave the room, but I grabbed her arm frantically.

"Beth, be careful. The second you think someone's watching, go. Promise me you'll do that."

"But—"

"Promise me!" My whispered voice hitched. A tear slid down her freckled cheek.

"I promise," she said, voice pained. "I'll be right back. Stay here."

As she left the room, I fought the urge to follow and make sure she was safe. Chase motioned toward the window, but I shook my head. We had to wait. What if she was wrong and that patrol car had swung back around? We needed to be here to protect her.

I listened from the door, but could only hear muffled voices. Needing reassurance, I snuck into the hallway and caught a glimpse of Beth's back. She was talking to a soldier, presumably Harmony's brother, though I couldn't see his face. *See? I told myself. No need to panic,* and yet somehow the pressure of Chase's hand encompassing mine, squeezing as if to say, *time to go,* sent a wave of skepticism through me.

Then I turned my head, and at last peered into my mother's bedroom.

It was empty, just like all the other rooms, the scent of mildew permeating the stagnant space. Her bed was gone, and her dresser and nightstand, along with her framed pictures atop it of me growing up. Vaguely, I was aware of a small pop inside of me, a pinch, as all the remaining strings binding me together were severed. And then I was unraveling, spinning faster and faster.

"Mom, that music's contraband!"

She jumped on the bed, pulling me up, where we jumped and twisted and danced. It was like melting. I was an ice cube and she was the sun and I was powerless to stand against her.

"We used to do this when you were little, remember? I would hold your hands and spin you, and you'd giggle and shout 'Faster!'"

The chill started in my bones and worked its way out to my skin, and soon I was shivering so hard I could barely stand. Maybe she wasn't perfect, maybe things weren't always easy, but she was my mom, and she was dead. Erased. As though she'd never existed. And nothing, *nothing* was left of her but an old magazine rolled up in my sweatshirt.

"Get me out of here," I said quietly.

Chase gently pulled me back into the bedroom, gathering the bag of food beside the window.

"Stop!" I heard Beth yell.

In a snap I'd detached Chase's grip and was running back

toward the front of the house. One step into the entryway and I ran smack into Sean.

"Ember!" His breath hitched, but he recomposed quickly. "We've got a problem."

Chase had succeeded in grabbing my arm and jerked me to his side. "What is it?"

"I told him not to come back here!" Beth said.

"You talked to a soldier you didn't know?" I shrieked.

"I recognized his friend from your arrest," she said indignantly. "I thought they were with you."

And there, from the shadows, stepped Tucker Morris.

I couldn't think of a word to say. Not one word.

"I'm sorry," Tucker croaked. "I didn't know what to do."

"What the hell are you doing here?" Chase asked in a low, dangerous voice. His weapon was drawn, but Tucker didn't seem to notice it. Distantly I registered the sound of Beth crying.

"We got hit." Tucker's voice was strained. "Cara and me. We got hit outside Greeneville on the way to see her cousin." He scratched his neck nervously. "Before we left they said something about your house. That a driver came here. It was right before he kicked me out." He pointed at Sean, then gulped down a deep breath. "And then . . . then everything fell apart. I went back to the printing plant, but everyone was gone. I thought maybe you'd try to come here. I didn't know where else to go!"

I hadn't even considered that my mother's name had been spoken while Tucker and Cara were still in the building. But it had. I'd gotten lazy. I'd put Beth in even more danger.

My stomach turned to water. "Billy?" I asked. "Billy was gone?"

"They were all gone!" Tucker responded. "Lights off. Empty."

"Oh no." I reached for the wall for support.

"Where is Cara?" demanded Sean.

"She's dead, man. She's dead. They hit her."

It took a second for Tucker's words to sink in. Cara was dead. Billy was missing, probably captured. A silent scream filled my body.

"Turn around," Chase said. Tucker complied. Chase patted down the back of his shirt and his pockets, but found no weapons. "Did you turn us in? Is that what you did?"

"No! I went with Cara. That's all." Tucker's face twisted.

"Get out of this house!" I shouted suddenly.

"Keep it quiet!" warned Stephen in the background.

"You can't be here! Have you brought soldiers here? Are they following you?"

"No!" Tucker shook his head. "No, I got rid of them in Tennessee. But I didn't know where to go. I don't know the other check station . . . things. *I don't know!*"

His fingers twined before him, as if he were praying, and for the first time since I'd known him he looked genuinely panicked.

"How did you get here?" asked Chase. His pacing was getting faster. I began to feel my heart keep time with the cadence of his voice.

"A car . . . I took a car. Her cousin's car."

"Where is it now?"

"I parked it at a dump a few neighborhoods over. Hid it, you know? So no one would look twice. And then . . . then I started walking. I remembered this place from the overhaul but couldn't get the street right. I didn't know where else to go. Man, she's dead."

"Shut up," said Chase coldly. "It's not your first time."

My spine zipped straight up my back.

"We have to leave," I said. "Right now. Right this second. He can't be in this house."

"We'll get the other car," said Sean.

"No." I wouldn't leave here knowing that Tucker could come back for Beth.

"No," Chase agreed. "He's coming with us. He doesn't leave my sight until we clear the area."

Tucker nodded gratefully.

"Thank you," he said quietly. I felt sick. First an apology and now a thank-you? It felt all wrong.

"Beth, get out of here," I said. "Go home. *Now.*"

That was all there was. I pushed her out the back door and she ran, and I hoped she would never, *never* come back to this place. Stephen watched on blankly, but I had nothing to offer him.

"Good-bye," I said quietly, watching the spot in the black hole of night where she'd vanished. I hadn't even told her to her face. I wasn't going to say how much I loved her and how the memories of her kept me sane. It was just the same as it had been with my mother, only now, I was the one disappearing.

Good-bye, I said. To the little girl with the crooked eyebrows who cut her hair with her mom's scissors. To the smell of vanilla candles after curfew. To the drooping plants on the kitchen windowsill, the shared hairbrush on the bathroom sink, and all the *goodnights* before bed.

Good-bye, Mom.

We passed through Chase's yard, running in silence on numb feet. My head felt muddled. Cloudy. A sense of disillusionment filled the night air. I knew without a doubt that I would never come home again.

It's just a house, Chase had said. Just a house, not a home. Just a shell. A vessel. I wanted it buried, just like I wanted my mother's body buried. So that it could rest. So that I didn't have to wonder what happened to it after its life had passed. I wanted Beth to be safe and alive. For tonight she was, and I guessed that was all we could ask for.

I didn't know why Tucker was here. I didn't know how Cara had been killed, or why he'd driven all these miles to find us, of all people, for help. One second I wondered if he'd murdered her. The next I was sure he'd been telling the truth. Whatever the case, we had to get him out of town fast. He was a grenade. He was poison.

We got to the car and once inside, Chase started the engine. He made Tucker sit behind the partition, right behind me, so that he could always see Tucker in his peripheral vision.

We drove away from our houses, from the haunted apartments where we'd met, from the wall where I'd watched him run faster than Matt Epstein. Past Beth's street. Past the turn to Western High. Onto the highway where the black night before us blended with the black asphalt in defiance of the cruiser's high beams.

"Don't stop," I said.

Chase didn't answer. He didn't even look at me.

TUCKER and Sean talked some. I tried my best to listen, but it was too muffled through the glass. I hated that he was right behind me. I felt like there was a loaded gun aimed at my back. I sat at an angle with my back to the window so I could see all of them. Tucker kept his eyes down.

The atmosphere grew increasingly tense. Chase was starting to worry me. The long hours without sleep were wearing on him, but it wasn't just fatigue that tightened his jaw and the cords on his neck. He'd been deeply upset by Tucker's presence in my home; I could feel his anger crackle between us. And we weren't going anywhere that might offer comfort. Chicago had not been kind to him; its presence represented War, scavenging for food and shelter, and later, the FBR. It was not a place of happy memories.

Signs started cropping up for Indy. CLEARED, they said in big spray-painted letters. Indianapolis had been evacuated during the Chicago bombings. It was thought the Insurgents would hit there next. I'd heard rumors that people had tried to return, but the MM had barred them because they'd intended on making it a Yellow Zone, occupied by soldiers.

A cautious glance out the window revealed nothing but the sickle moon and the silver-streaked long grass that had overgrown on the side of the road. The highway was down to two lanes here, and quite suddenly Chase slammed on the brakes and parked just off the pavement at a slant. There was no forethought, not the usual care he'd take to hide the car or limit attention. No, he was in a hurry. My eyes scanned the night to see if I'd missed some obvious danger.

Chase jerked open the car door and unlocked the back.

"Stay here," he growled.

I didn't.

He rounded toward the back where Tucker was getting out, and slammed him into the side of the car.

"Hey!" Sean raced around the trunk and attempted to separate them, but Chase was almost five inches taller and outweighed him by a good thirty pounds.

"Stay out of this," Chase warned. Sean took a step back.

"Give me your firearm," he said. "That's all I'm asking."

Tucker gasped, the breath knocked out of his lungs. He tried to stand again but Chase shoved him back down and kicked him hard in the gut.

"Chase!" I yelped.

He seemed to register the sound of my voice through his fury. Though he didn't face me, I saw his shoulders roll back.

I didn't know what he was thinking. We couldn't stop here. The roads were mostly empty, but we were closing in on a base. What if a cruiser drove by?

At the same time I wanted this. I wanted him to hurt Tucker, to beat the truth out of him. But Tucker was unarmed, and Chase in his rage could kill him. He would carry that blood on his hands for rest of his life, and I would, too, because I'd stood by. This couldn't happen. This was wrong.

"I saved your life!" Tucker gasped. "The woman in the holding cells—Delilah—she was going to tell them she'd seen you alive! I couldn't hide that Ember escaped, but I covered for you! I made her disappear!"

"You did have her killed." I felt sick. Her death was my fault. If I hadn't escaped, she would still be alive.

His green eyes stayed on Chase. "I just . . . scared her. That's all. So she wouldn't talk." He was on his knees. Begging.

"Why," said Chase.

"I don't know," Tucker spat. "We were partners."

Chase laughed, a low, frightening sound. He leaned down, so that his face was right in front of Tucker's. "You ratted me out to CO, and let them crucify me in the ring night after night, and killed someone I cared about. No. We were never partners."

"Don't you want to get into that facility?" Tucker shouted. He rubbed the back of his head, where it had connected to the metal above the window when he'd tried to get out. The other hand was braced before him in defense.

"What facility?" Sean asked.

"The one where they're holding your girlfriend." He siphoned in a deep breath. "It's right next to the hospital. I did a rotation there after they discharged Jennings. Training for the Knoxville holding cells. I know a guy there. He'll let me in."

A long beat of silence passed.

"If you knew all this, why didn't you say something before?" Sean's voice was raised. "I've asked you a dozen times if you knew anything else about Rebecca!"

"I didn't know if I could trust you!" Tucker pleaded. "I didn't know who to trust."

There was fire in his petulant green eyes, but Sean didn't see it. He swore softly, and then his hands unclenched, and he said, "All right. I get it."

"Sean," I warned.

Chase's words from Greeneville echoed in my head: *This is what he does. He digs his way in and gets under your skin. And before you know it, he's ripped your life apart.*

"I'll make it up to you," Tucker told Sean. "I'll get you in. From here on out, I've got your back. That goes for all of you."

I was about to tell him to shove it, but Sean had shifted and, to my disgust, held out his hand to help Tucker up.

Chase very deliberately removed his gun from the holster. I held my breath and squeezed the skirt in my fists.

"Chase," Sean's voice quaked. "Come on, man. He knows how to get Becca. . . ."

Chase handed the gun to Sean.

"Talk," he told Tucker.

With pressured speech, Tucker explained how he and Cara had walked across Greeneville toward her cousin's. She'd pointed out the house; a small place with a white sedan out front. Tucker had guessed that they were wealthy, and Cara had told him her cousin's husband worked for Horizons Weapons Manufacturing. As they'd gotten closer, they'd noticed the squad car tracking them a block back.

"It was close to curfew," he said. "I thought they were going to give us a citation for an Article Four."

I shook my head, crossing my arms over my chest. Chase

and I were always careful to portray ourselves as married in order to avoid a citation for indecency, but a couple walking the streets so close to curfew was bound to draw attention. Maybe Tucker was still too impenetrable to anticipate this, but Cara should have known.

In order not to endanger Cara's cousin, they'd passed the house and ducked into a nearby ditch.

"But the patrol hit the sirens," said Tucker. "So we ran."

They'd hidden in a large, tubular cement drain packed with trash and waited for the MM to lose them. *Thirty minutes,* Tucker said. Until the rats got used to their presence and came to visit.

After a while Cara had ventured out, but Tucker had gotten a cramp in his leg. He'd stayed under cover while shaking it out.

"It happened fast, man. *Fast.* I heard someone on the road overhead, and I looked over at her and she fell. Just like that. Shot in the shoulder, straight through the heart. Done before she hit the ground. I went out the opposite side of the drain and hit the road running."

"Coward," muttered Chase.

"*I'm* the coward?" said Tucker in disbelief. "It was a code one, Jennings. No arrest, no questioning. They're killing any girl they think might be Miller. *They're* the cowards."

For a moment Tucker's words made no sense. It was like he was speaking another language. And then their meaning set in.

Code One, Chase had told me. *They can fire on suspicion alone.*

It had happened. Someone had been killed in my name. Someone had died as the sniper. A girl I'd known. I didn't feel relief—my name wouldn't be cleared once they realized it wasn't me. I felt like I was going to throw up.

I didn't kill her, I told myself. But I didn't believe it. She was dead because I'd escaped those holding cells, because I lived. Because my death was the death the MM wanted. What kind of world was this where people had to die for others to live?

I backed away. I couldn't listen anymore. Not just because I'd known Cara, because I'd worked beside her in the resistance and now she was gone, but because of the sincere pain in Tucker's voice. He hadn't hurt so much when he'd killed my mother, whom *he'd* shot in cold blood. When *he'd* been the coward. What was it that made Cara so much better than her? What made him care? Why could he feel remorse now, but not then?

And Billy. We'd left him alone with Marco and Polo, and now he was gone.

I wandered back into the grass, until I came to a wooden fence, glowing silver in the moonlight, cracked and splintered just like me. I tilted my head back and stared at the sky and felt the exhaustion bend me and weaken me and make my knees tremble. I hadn't slept in almost twenty-four hours, but I was too afraid to close my eyes.

My hands filled the deep pockets of the uniform skirt Cara had worn, and I felt it. A copper bullet, caught in the wool folds. The one I'd shown her that I'd found. She must have put it in her pocket and forgotten it when we were changing.

I heard Chase before I saw him. I recognized the way his boots rolled on the grass. That tentative step when he thought I might bolt like a rabbit. I released the bullet, but felt it, solid against my leg.

"It's not your fault," he said quietly.

"I know." I grasped the fence hard.

"No, you don't."

I punched the fence hard enough to break the rotted wood. My hand stung, but my breath came more steadily. He didn't crowd me, but stayed close, knowing exactly the kind of comfort I needed.

"Let's go," I said.

We returned to the car, and drove north.

CHAPTER
15

I JARRED into consciousness in the cold silence, with the acute awareness that I was alone in the car. An eerie intuition crept over my skin. The others were in trouble. Something had happened.

These thoughts had me out of the door before I drew another breath. It was frigid, but not so much that the puddles on the asphalt had frozen. The air cooled my knuckles, heated and swollen from hitting the fence. I clutched my elbows and scanned the shadowed parking garage, heart racing, furious at myself that I'd fallen asleep. Dawn cracked through the pewter thunderheads outside—I'd been out for *three hours* at least.

The stolen cruiser was parked beside a tarp-covered vehicle on the bottom floor of the structure. Sinister pieces of rebar and fallen chunks of cement cut jagged angles down the open frame to my side, where the natural light was brighter. Mountains of gravel and rocks outside blocked my visibility, and the breeze blew an instant film of dust over my clothing and hair. It was one thing to see the Wreckage on the news, but another entirely to stand among it, a soft body of flesh and bones. I had the sudden sensation that I had awoken in the mouth of some giant beast; shortly it would crush me in its concrete teeth and swallow me whole.

A huge metallic sign lay strewn across the ground just beyond the exit. It was bent and scratched, but still readable. CHICAGO MIDWAY INTERNATIONAL AIRPORT.

"Chase!" I whisper-shouted. No answer. Panic gripped the base of my neck.

Sean appeared around the entrance. He was back in civilian clothes but for the gun holstered in the belt at his hip, and his face was warped with edgy frustration. He was closer to Rebecca than he'd been in weeks, but she was still just beyond his grasp.

"Good, you're up," he said. He tracked my gaze as it rose behind him to the heap of gray rock that was once an airport terminal. "This is where Marco said we're supposed to wait for a pickup, but the place is a graveyard. Literally," he added.

I knew he didn't want to wait for the resistance. I didn't either. I wanted to get Rebecca and get out, but we weren't prepared. Tucker had offered some intel on the schematics of the rehab building and the placement of the guards, but Chicago ran this area. We couldn't encroach on their turf without a formal introduction; Wallace would have called that *bad form*. And if they really were rough like Marco and Polo had said, we didn't want to get off on the wrong foot.

"Where is he?" I asked quickly. "Where are *they*?" I corrected.

Sean pointed around the corner to where Tucker was leaning against the outer wall of the parking garage, sleeping in the dirt with his chin on his chest. The skyline weighed heavily upon us; rain was coming.

"Chase," I pressed.

"Relax. He's on point. Over that hill." Sean motioned toward a rock heap on the opposite side of the building. "He asked me to keep my eye on you a while. I told him I had the first shift, but you know him. . . ."

I did know him. When his mind was set on something, no one could tell him otherwise. But I sensed something was wrong; he wouldn't have drifted so far from Tucker otherwise.

I took off in the direction Sean had indicated, noting all the fallen concrete blocking our view. There were walls of it, stained with weather and anti-MM graffiti. Shattered glass was sprinkled across the ground. A hundred eyes could be watching us here and we'd never know; there was just too much to hide behind.

"Chase?" I called quietly, knowing my voice was muffled by the environment, but too wary on this foreign soil to speak any louder. My pulse quickened when I didn't see him around the first bend. Long grass had grown here, covering the rough road and cushioning my steps.

I held my breath, listening for any noise that might direct me to him.

Gasps, ten yards away. My heart clutched. I surged through the foliage toward the sound without thinking. I found him alone on his hands and knees on the ground, his breathing strained, ragged. One arm locked around his midsection, as though he'd been shot.

"Chase!"

I ran to him. He heard me and jerked up, but not all the way. One hand motioned for me to stop.

"Get back in the car," he ordered weakly.

I paused, ducking reactively and scanning the field. There was danger here, I could smell it in the electric air.

"Get back in the car!" he said more forcefully.

Scared, I kept looking but saw nothing. I listened, but only the breeze on the grass filtered through my heartbeats. It was just us. We were alone.

"I . . . don't understand."

"*Please,*" he begged, and fell to his hands and knees again. His back rounded in his struggle, like a dying animal, and I did understand then. There was no threat here but himself.

The fear in his voice was so thick it shook me to the core. He was always so strong, but not now. Now he was falling apart. Like Wallace, on the roof of a burning building, he was pushing me away.

I would not go.

I approached him gingerly, each frenzied breath from his throat striking me like a punch.

His pain hurt me in a way I'd never felt before. It was worse than my own pain. My strength wavered. I felt completely powerless.

I imagined him in the car, acting calm as I fell asleep in the seat beside him, hiding that choking panic until I was no longer conscious. The thoughts that must have filled his head in my silence. My mother, murdered before him. Chasing me to the holding cells, then into the fire at the Wayland Inn. One close call after the next, finally culminating with a chance to reverse it all that had instantly fallen through.

And so he'd made it to the meeting point, changed into his civilian clothes quietly enough not to disturb me, and escaped to battle his demons alone.

I knelt beside him, placing one cautious hand on his back. Sweat had soaked clean through his sweater. My arm rose and fell as he swallowed what air he could, and I hurt, so completely, for him that the tears filled my eyes.

"Can't . . . breathe. . . ." he ground out. He scratched at the stretched neck of his T-shirt.

"Yes you can," I said. My voice was low and even.

Instinctively I wrapped my arms around his waist and leaned over him so that my chest rested on his back and my face pressed against his neck, sticky with sweat. I took a long breath, hoping he could feel my heart slow through the barriers of our clothes and skin.

He tried to match my tempo but began to shake. His hand clutched mine over his flexing abdominals and squeezed so tightly I thought my fingers would break.

"I'm here," I said. "I'm not letting go."

I breathed again, and he moved with me, a low, strangled moan seeping out his throat.

In. Out.

Again.

Again.

The terror passed quickly, leaving him exhausted and

drenched. There was water in the car, in the bag Beth had given us, but I didn't dare leave him even for a minute. I used the Sister of Salvation handkerchief to blot at his neck and forehead while he gripped my other hand, and when he fell back onto his heels, I somehow ended up shifting in front of him, so that I straddled his lap.

My breath caught. Our eyes locked, both of us waiting for what would come next. His fingers slowly spread over my back, his thumbs grazing my ribs. I ran my hands through his damp hair, feeling his gaze, somehow staggered, linger on my face. Feeling our bodies warmly connected. Finally, his head came to rest on my heart and I held him, willing him to know that he was not alone.

"WAS I like Beth?" I asked, frowning. "When you came back. Did I seem so young?"

I sat on the ground across from him, arms encircling my knees, chin resting on the crook in my elbow. He mirrored my position, watching the way our boots overlapped, but refusing, like me, to back away. The second we had separated he'd become shy, though not cold, and my mind drifted back to what had happened at my house.

A small smile graced the corners of his mouth. "Maybe a little bit."

I thought of how naïve Beth had sounded, how idealistic that she was doing the right thing, so impenetrable to consequences.

"I must have driven you crazy."

"You drive me crazy on a pretty regular basis."

I stomped on his toes. He grinned, and then blinked and rubbed his eyes.

"You're tired," I said.

"Yes."

He wouldn't sleep until he was ready, but I wished I could do something to help him.

"There's food in the car," I said. "Come on. You can eat something at least."

He reached for my hands and I pulled myself up, and then used all my remaining strength to hoist him off the ground.

The pendant-shaped burn below my collar had begun to throb again, and I prodded it gently, thinking of Cara and how she'd needed St. Michael's protection more than me. The lump grew inside of my throat. I still wasn't sure what to feel. Anger that she'd been so cruel, so secretive. Guilt that she was killed by people trying to kill me. Pain, though we hadn't been friends.

We began slowly walking back toward the cruiser.

"Listen, back there . . ." he started, then paused.

I waited while he sorted through his thoughts. I hoped he didn't try to apologize. What had happened out here had bound us closer, and it would have stung had he regretted it.

"It just gets heavy sometimes," he finished, with a great heave of breath.

He didn't have to explain further. I knew exactly what he meant.

A muffled whisper diverted our attention, driving my heart into my throat. Chase's hand was immediately at his back, where he'd placed the gun Polo had given him, but he didn't draw.

Tucker jerked out from behind a cement blockade just to our left. "Scared me." He was wearing the same jeans and sweat-stained thermal he'd been in earlier, though now I noticed a streak of burnt copper down his left side. Was that his blood, or Cara's?

"Who were you talking to?" I asked.

"No one," he said. "I was looking for you."

"Where's Sean?" Chase didn't bother to hide the accusation in his tone.

"Still on guard," Tucker answered. "But he didn't rotate back. I thought maybe he came to find you."

My shoulder blades tightened. I glanced around, as if Sean might appear, too, but there was no sign of him. Somewhere closer to the heart of the old city, the clouds began to groan.

"So you thought it was a good idea to leave post, too, huh?" said Chase.

Tucker didn't lower his gaze. "In case you haven't noticed, this isn't the FBR anymore, Jennings. It's every man for himself out here."

"Actually it's not," I said flatly. "Come on, let's find him."

Chase held me back, tilting his head toward Tucker as if to say, *after you*. Tucker hesitated only briefly before turning and walking quickly back toward the parking garage. Though I searched the entire time for Sean, Chase, just to my side, did not once turn his head away from his old partner.

"Do you think Tucker's telling the truth?" I whispered to Chase. I reached into my pocket to feel the copper bullet once again. I wanted to show him, but not with Tucker around.

"No."

"Do you think Cara's really dead?"

He nodded once.

So it wasn't her death that he questioned, but the manner in which she'd died. I felt the shiver run through me. Tucker had seemed genuinely affected by the sequence of events that had led him to my door. But what if he'd lied? What if he'd reported us, and somehow turned Cara in? And then turned Billy in, just after?

And now Sean, wherever he was, was willing to risk his life on Tucker's supposed contact in the MM. If Chicago didn't offer any better options—and I really hoped they did—Chase and I would, too.

We were seriously considering placing our safety in the hands of the one person I trusted least in this world.

We searched the garage and the outlying area, calling for Sean only as loudly as we dared. As the minutes passed, my dread began to build, until Tucker finally admitted he'd last seen Sean near the terminal. With a harsh word, Chase took off immediately in that direction, and I followed closely behind, feeling Tucker clinging to my shadow.

We crossed what had once been a street and went left around a large base of construction waste. We found him there, just beyond the bend, facing the opposite direction.

"Sean!" called Chase. "What are you doing out here?"

Sean jumped at the sound. "Thought I saw someone. Over there, behind . . ."

Three men in ragged clothes emerged from the asphalt and concrete dunes, twenty feet away. Two were in their thirties, and handled their rifles with an unsettling degree of confidence. The third man was younger, close to Chase's age, with a massive muscular torso, and a baseball bat resting over one shoulder. He looked like the type that might bulldoze anyone that got in his way.

Resistance. They had to be. But if they were, Marco and Polo were right. They did *not* look friendly.

Chase deliberately placed himself in front of me.

"You lost, strangers?" asked the man in front with a rifle. He had a crisp, city accent. His dark hair was tussled and he hunched slightly to hide his immense height.

"I doubt it," said Chase.

My pulse quickened.

"Then how may I be of service?" The tall man grinned.

"Knoxville sent us," said Chase. "Before the FBR burned it to the ground."

The man snickered. "Any weapons?"

"Possibly," said Chase.

"Yes," confessed Sean. "But I'm sure as hell not giving it to you."

The tall stranger's smirk dissipated, ratcheting up the silence to a tighter, tenser level of unease as he clicked his dirty fingernails along the rifle shaft. He was clearly trying to intimidate us.

I was tired of being intimidated.

"Stop," I said. "We've come a long way, so if you're not planning on shooting us, put your gun down. Please."

My words hung in the air. All eyes locked upon me; all but Chase's, as he was still watching the tall man. Someone began to chuckle. I turned toward the bulldozer with the baseball bat; he was missing one of his top K-9 teeth.

The leader lowered his gun. "You got a name, Sister? Or should I just call you the Mouth?"

I *really* didn't like him. I wasn't sure if he bought my disguise, or if he was simply mocking me, but my legs itched within the wool skirt, flexing and ready to run, and my jaw snapped shut.

"No? Shame. How about you?" He turned to Chase. "Wouldn't be Jennings, would it?"

Chase stilled. My eyes widened. They had recognized Chase, not me, even with my photo posted. How did they know him? He didn't seem to recognize them. He didn't say a word.

"Told you," said Toothless. "Didn't I tell you, Jack?"

Jack grinned sadistically. "Maybe you can test out your theory."

"What theory?" I asked. No one answered.

The third guard searched Sean and Tucker while Toothless came to pat me down. He was surprisingly appropriate—maybe because Chase watched him like a hawk. Still, there was too much pressure in the air. Something was wrong. The three shared too many knowing glances, too many sly smirks.

They took our weapons. Two guns, and a screwdriver Tucker had stolen from Greeneville.

Jack whistled. It was a piercing noise, one that pinpointed the back of my jaw and made me cringe. Toothless chuckled again.

In moments we were surrounded.

They came from every hidden corner of the graveled battlefield, encircling us, blocking us in. Thirty or more of the scariest people I'd ever seen. Brawny and sneering, tattooed and scarred, the type you'd find in a prison gang. Those closest were shooting hard stares our direction, making the hairs on the back of my neck prickle. No one smiled except the guy with the baseball bat.

My breath came faster. I glanced from side to side, suddenly aware of how close Chase had become. Sean drew in as well, blocking my right side.

"See, we've got a problem," hollered Jack, loudly enough for everyone to hear. "We've been watching you all morning. Watched you drive up in your little MM cruiser and park in our garage. Watched you change out of your uniforms into street clothes—well, all except the Sister here. And the thing is," he said, and smiled, stepping back to join the ring. "The thing is, we *really* don't like snitches."

"I guess that's one thing we have in common," said Chase darkly.

"Don't piss him off, Jack," chuckled Toothless. He seemed as relaxed as could be despite the tension.

"Don't think I can take him?" quipped Jack.

"That's over," said Tucker. It was the first time he'd spoken since the arrival of the others. He almost looked humble with his hands in his pockets and his shoulders drawn forward. "He doesn't do that anymore."

It finally occurred to me what was happening. These guys had been soldiers when Chase was. They'd seen him fight when the MM had forced him into the ring, trying to break him. A defensive wave rose within me. My fists bunched. I didn't like this Chicago bunch, and I definitely did not like Tucker standing up for Chase.

"Ladies and gentlemen, Chicago boxing legend Chase Jennings!" Toothless trumpeted. Several people laughed, the anxious, strained sounds of hyenas. A few even cheered. The breath came fast and shallow in my throat.

Tucker swore under his breath. "Here we go."

"They're stolen uniforms," I said, trying to keep my voice even. "We're resistance, too. We're from Knoxville."

"You sure?" asked Jack. "Because I have a hunch you got friends somewhere close, watching us right now. I think you're acting big and bad because you know they won't let you get hurt."

My palms itched. A line of cold sweat dribbled between my shoulder blades. The circle had gone from bawdy to whispers in just seconds, and a crater formed around us, locking us in the center.

They thought we were MM. They thought we were here to break into their camp. And they were willing to hurt us, just to see if any soldiers came to our rescue.

If this many people were here, how many more were lying in wait?

I thought of Wallace's first rule. *Play nice or we don't play at all.* These boys had dialed it up a notch. Grimly, I realized there was probably a reason for their paranoia.

"It's not like that," Sean objected.

We both watched Chase. A veil of very controlled hostility had fallen over him. His head sunk, his shoulders loosened. A slight bend in his elbows, a slight crouch. He was ready to spring, and we were cornered.

"We don't want trouble." Chase's voice was harder than I'd ever heard it.

"Hear that? *He* doesn't want trouble! I saw him almost beat a guy's head in at the base and *he* doesn't want trouble!" shouted someone from the ring.

I flinched. I'd seen what Chase could do in a fight. What his eyes looked like when they went cold and emotionless. He couldn't go back there.

"Still think you're tough?" Jack sneered at him. I wanted Jack to look my direction instead of putting this all on Chase. My nails pinched into my palms.

"What is your problem!" I shouted at him.

"Sean," said Chase quietly. Sean grabbed my arm and began pulling me back, away from Chase. I tried to jerk out of his grip but he held fast.

"No!" I struggled. "Let go!"

"Don't do this," said Sean nervously. I wasn't sure if he was talking to me, or Chicago.

Toothless let the baseball bat fall to the ground, and it made a terrible clatter that echoed off the concrete pylons. He grinned again, that stupid black hole in his mouth blinking at me. He seemed excited, not petulant like Jack, but primed for a fight.

"You first, huh?" Chase cracked his knuckles. "Thought you were scared."

"Me?" he said innocently. "I'm not scared. Stupid maybe, but not scared."

I thought this was probably a pretty accurate assessment. He laughed, and several others around him laughed, too. What was wrong with these people? Didn't they get enough fighting with the MM? They were like a pack of wild dogs.

Sean had brought me almost all the way to the edge of the circle when a hand snaked out and pinched my side. I yelped and kicked out reactively, connecting to the shin of a gaunt-faced boy with a shaved head. This evoked a mocking roar from the closest spectators.

Chase pointed a menacing finger his direction.

"Touch her again and you're next."

Several of them cheered. My heart, my nerves, the blood running through my veins, it all clamped down now. There was certainly going to be a fight, but there were at least thirty here to our four. I wasn't convinced they didn't want to kill us, which kept my fear, and its dueling resentment, alive.

Sean's fist was latched around my biceps. Tucker and Chase turned so that they were back to back. I hated that Chase was still in the center, while Sean was pinning me on the outside of the circle. I should have been beside him.

There was no further warning. Two guys came immediately from the side and went for Tucker. Another came for Chase, grasping his torso like a flailing fish while Toothless took his first swing. Chase ducked at the last second, and the fist collided with the guy behind him.

"Stop!" I screamed. But no one heard me, they were all cheering.

Sean released me suddenly, and my whole body recoiled when I heard him cry out against a swipe to his burned back. I barreled into his attacker and we all fell to the rough ground. In the shuffle to stand, I grabbed Sean's collar and jerked him toward where I'd last seen Chase. We had to stand together; it was the only way we'd get through this.

The circle hadn't closed in; Chicago had created a fluctuating barrier, shoving anyone who got too close to the edge back inside. It was like being thrown into a water bottle and shaken. I stumbled, and when I rose, someone's hand slid across my chest. It was a guy with chin-length greasy hair and a giddy smile on his face. With blood behind my eyes, I punched him hard, right in the nose, and then gasped when the pain ricocheted up my shoulder. Something cracked. The sound stirred a sick feeling of satisfaction in the pit of my stomach. He swore at me and immediately disappeared behind the first row.

My eyes locked on Chase. He was pressed close to Toothless, almost like they were embracing, except that Chase was wheeling back and planting several sharp successive jabs into his side. Someone ran up behind Chase, grabbed him by the shoulders, and heaved him off: the third guard. I was relieved to see the rifle gone. I sprinted toward them, dragging Sean by the shirtsleeve, but we were intercepted. Tucker jutted in front of us and tackled Chase's attacker. They flew across the ground, now splattered with blood.

Sean was down again. My body reeled when I saw some-one's leg swing like a pendulum and kick him in the gut. He arched, taking the blow with full force in order to protect his back. I reached for him, but someone grabbed me from be-hind, his forearm slamming up against my windpipe. A burst of stars appeared in my vision, blocking Sean, blocking everything.

I dug my nails into his skin, tucked my chin, and threw my hips back hard, just as Chase had taught me.

The hold released, and I sputtered for breath, hitting my knees. Jack had fallen beside me, shocked that I'd been able to shake him off. As I tried to stand, I slipped and nearly toppled over the baseball bat. In a blind fury, I swooped it up and charged him.

I lunged, a puppet to my anger, and landed on his chest, knees pinning his shoulders down. He gave me a twisted smile and bucked his hips, nearly tossing me over his head.

Go for soft spots, Chase had said.

I shoved the bat beneath Jack's chin and pressed down on his throat.

"Call them off!" I screamed.

He gasped, but managed a small shake of his head. There was blood on his teeth.

"Call them *off!*" I ordered again, pressing down harder. All that rage inside of me burned for this moment. His face seemed too familiar then. Soulless green eyes. A calculating smile. *Tucker.* I was hurting Tucker. My eyes stung. *You killed her. How dare you.*

I blinked. *Jack*, not Tucker. But still the rage whipped

through my veins, leaving me unable to release him. Someone had to be accountable for all these disappointments.

"You're no better than they are!" I shouted into Jack's face.

"Neither"—he breathed—"are . . . you."

Something twisted inside of me, almost as though I'd been punched, but this bite emanated from the inside, within my ribcage. The line between right and wrong had never felt so fragile, and here I was, crossing it. No, not just crossing it, but trampling it, consumed by a dark and furious thrill.

Still pressing the bat to his throat, I reached in my pocket and removed the copper bullet. I held it right before his eyes.

"Do you know what this is?" I said as acknowledgment registered in his eyes. "Do you know who I am?" I released the bat, disgusted with myself, but kept my eyes on Jack and didn't move. He just kept smiling. Red on white.

"Let me up," he said.

I rose fast and ready. He snatched the bullet from my hand, grabbed my arm, and led me through the wall of resistance to a woman, older than Wallace if I had to guess, wearing men's fatigues complete with lace-up boots. She had short, spiked black hair and a sharp, jutting chin. There was a severe look in her eyes, like someone who was used to living hard.

Jack leaned down and whispered something in her ear, his arm still clamped down on mine. He revealed the bullet, and she scanned my face. After several beats, she smiled.

"Enough!" Her voice, low but piercing, carried over the others.

I spun to see Chase behind me; three fighters, Toothless included, were on the ground groaning at his feet. Chase, clutching his side, turned and spat, wiping the blood from his mouth on the back of his hand. The skin around his right eye was red, and his shirt was ripped, revealing most of his shoulder.

He glanced down over my body for injuries. There was a hard glint in his eyes, but no apathy. He was still there.

Coughing, and groaning, some extraneous cheers, but mostly silence. I surveyed the damage. Sean's hands were on his knees, a line of blood dribbling down his chin. Tucker's face was crimson from the exertion.

"I said enough!" She looked to me as they silenced, and shoved me forward. "Tell us who you are. Say it loud, so everyone can hear, otherwise I let the boys pound you into the dust."

I glanced at Chase and Sean, then back to Tucker. What had I done?

"My name is Ember Miller," I said. I swallowed down the tremor that was building inside of me.

"I can't hear you," she prompted. Chase tried to move beside me, but was stopped by Toothless. "Tell them why they should believe you aren't snitches."

I tried to breathe, but couldn't find enough air. They all watched me expectantly.

I'm sorry, Chase.

"My name is Ember Miller!" I shouted. "I'm the one they're looking for! I'm the sniper!"

CHAPTER
16

"YEAH right!" shouted someone. "I'm the sniper, too, Mags!"

People laughed. The woman—Mags, I assumed—smirked.

"And why should we believe you?" challenged Mags. All voices silenced when she spoke. "How do we know you're not lying?"

"Check the mainframe," I said. "Pull up my photo. I'll verify anything you want." My body felt rigid, strung too tight. There were murmurs from the crowd.

"Mm . . ." Mags gave me an evaluating look. "You do look like the picture. Not so soft though."

"Give her a gun." I braced at Tucker's voice. "See what she can do if you don't believe her."

We both knew the only thing I could do with a rifle was prove myself a liar.

"Let's not," muttered Jack. Mags laughed.

"They stopped running that report," a guy near Mags said speculatively. "They must've verified that that Greeneville girl was Miller."

"It wasn't," Tucker said, staring at me with the clear message not to screw this up. "I don't know who that was. Just a code one victim. But that's good news, isn't it, Ember? I guess you're off the hook."

The fact that he could even pretend to be indifferent made me sick.

I was frozen, unable to jump for joy that my name was cleared because it had meant Cara's demise. But if he was right, how was it possible? Cara and I looked similar from afar, but the MM couldn't possibly think she was me after a good look at her poor, lifeless face.

Still, if these people here had heard that the sniper— *Ember Miller*—was killed, then I had a few moments reprieve. Moments to get Rebecca. To deliver her to the safe house. If we survived the day.

"They're lying!" shouted someone. "They're just trying to skip a beating!"

"Ask him," I said, pointing to Sean. He shot a worried glance in Chase's direction. "He was my guard at reform school. There's got to be some records in the mainframe that prove that."

My heart thundered in my chest as we waited. Waited. Mags walked a slow circle around me.

Chicago is going to turn me in. They're going to shoot me right here.

But no one looked angry. It slowly occurred to me that these people weren't mad at me at all. Like the woman in the square who'd given me the medallion, they'd been supporting me. They'd been *cheering* for me.

Or rather, for who they thought I was.

"How'd you do it?" someone called out. "How'd you get so close to all those uniforms?"

I closed my eyes, just for a moment, and summoned Cara's cool exterior.

"Do I look like a threat to you?" I smiled sweetly.

"What kind of gun? Was it an M40?"

"Oh, I don't know," I said, fixing my hair. "It was a big one."

Someone laughed. It was contagious, and soon the others were nodding and smiling as though they'd never intended to harm us. I could hardly believe it. Was it really so easy to evade the truth? To be someone else?

"I like it," said a guy wearing a cockeyed knit cap. "A patriot if you ask me."

The adrenaline was humming through me. I had no idea what would come next, but at least I'd stopped them from killing us.

As the copper cartridge was passed around the whispering crowd, Chase and I locked eyes. His betrayed nothing, though I knew he feared what I had done, and what would happen when Chicago realized my lie. Would it just be a fight then? Or would Chicago skip the beating and eliminate the problem?

"Who do you work for?" Mags asked. "Let's just say you are the sniper. No one could have gotten half those hits without some protection."

I stiffened. Tried to swallow, but couldn't.

"Everyone reports to someone," she said, testing me.

I closed my eyes, and tried to remember what Sean had told me at the Wayland Inn, how Marco and Polo had only added to the mystery.

"Everyone reports to Three," I answered, immediately regretting my words. How far did Three's power extend? How much trouble would I stir for dropping their name?

Before me, Mags had stopped her pace. Her brows had lifted. I prayed that she didn't ask anything more direct.

"Indeed," she said. "I've heard rumors that something big's about to go down. Is that why you're here?"

I wanted to ask what she'd heard—was Three planning some kind of revolution?—but I couldn't break from the story now.

"Our friend was sent to rehab," I said. "We need to find her."

Everyone had gone very quiet. They were watching Mags, who wore authority just as she wore those battle-beaten boots.

"Rehab . . . you mean the circus?"

I glanced at Tucker, who appeared just as clueless as the rest of us. This was not a term soldiers used.

"Find her and what?" Mags added. "Extract her? Waste of time."

A vein on Sean's forehead bulged. "Hold on—"

"It's our time to waste, ma'am," Chase interjected. He moved beside me. "But we'd waste less of it with your help."

I held my breath as Mags's eyes traveled over the four of us. A frown pulled at the corners of her small mouth, but she regarded us with less suspicion now. When she spoke, her tone was flat.

"We have a plant inside at the base who can get an updated roster for the circus. You'll brief me tonight at *eighteen hundred*"—she articulated the words so there would be no confusion—"with a full report of your plans before you make a move up top. You may have immunity according to Three, but this is still my territory. Not one trigger pulled without my go-ahead. Is that understood?"

"Yes, ma'am," said Chase.

She turned to her people. "I don't want to hear about anyone roughing them up."

Jack nodded. "Yes, ma'am."

"Thank you," I said.

"Thank *you*," answered Mags. "For your service to the cause." She fixed my collar, and I fought the urge to jerk back. "But just so you know, I have zero tolerance for vigilantes and cocky hotshots who can't follow orders." My gaze turned down from her harsh stare, and I felt her smile, twice as cool as Cara's.

"Got it," I said.

"Good. Now clean that blood off your face and get some sleep." She smirked as she walked away. "You people look like hell."

AFTER gathering our belongings at the car, we followed Jack around the dunes toward the airfield. Chase was beginning to stumble. The adrenaline was wearing off and I worried protectively that these new people would see him weakened and attempt another attack. I didn't trust Mags's peace decree; their actions would have to prove it.

The other soldiers pestered me with questions. Most of them I deflected like Cara had done, and in response, Tucker had taken to filling in the blanks. I'd never seen someone so pleased to be the accomplice of a serial killer. How much he seemed to know about the sniper murders was just starting to worry me when Chase leaned down and whispered, "Do you have any idea what you're doing?"

I watched the others. No one seemed to have heard.

"What do you think?" I said. "I'm getting us in."

"That's when we decided on the roof across the City Square. It was a clear shot to the draft tables." Tucker was just behind us, surrounded by fighters Mags hadn't detailed to surveillance. I pinched the bridge of my nose.

"They're eating this up," I said. Chase nodded.

Toothless, the bat back over his shoulder, jogged to catch up with us.

"I saw you fight a couple times before they kicked me out. Always thought I could take you, but you're meaner than you look, Jennings." He stuck out his hand, and when Chase reluctantly offered his own, Toothless shook it enthusiastically.

"Truck," he said. " 'Cause I drive the truck."

Chase closed his eyes momentarily, looking utterly disappointed.

"*You're* the carrier?" I asked.

"You've heard of me!" He looked delighted. "Jack, she's heard of me."

"That's real sweet, Truck," said Jack from the front of the line. I glared at him.

"We have a mutual . . . friend," I settled on, though that

didn't seem right. There was no way Beth could have trusted this person, even if she was naïve. Though now that the fight was over he did seem surprisingly benign.

I could almost hear Chase's teeth grinding. The plan was to get Rebecca and go to the safe house, but Chase wasn't about to put our lives in the hands of a carrier who took nothing—not even a punch to the face—seriously.

"So wow," said Truck in awe, standing a little too close to me for comfort. "You and Jennings really did break out of the base. Nice."

I almost laughed. He'd chosen the one accusation that was actually true.

"I suppose you had a little help from Three . . . ?" he asked. I forced a smile, and this was answer enough for him. Beside me, Chase's jaw twitched.

"This contact that's checking on our friend," I said. "Would he be able to check on someone else, too?"

Truck shrugged. "Don't see why not."

"His name is Billy. Or . . . William," I said, suddenly unsure. I realized I didn't even know his last name. "He disappeared in Greeneville yesterday, at the checkpoint, about the time the girl was shot there." I stumbled over the last part.

Truck scratched a hand over his clipped, flaxen hair. "I didn't hear anything about a raid on a checkpoint. I'll ask around though."

Some of the tense muscles behind my neck eased. Marco and Polo could have taken Billy somewhere. He might still be safe. "Thanks."

"Anything for Three," he said with a wink. Chase coughed into his hand.

"Whoa," Sean interrupted. "Look at that."

It was a plane—at least, what was left of one. The big jumbo jet balanced precariously on one broken wing while the other reached into the sky like the arm of a dying man. The tail end was missing completely, but the hull was still largely in one piece. Its smooth, silver metal was tarnished by black burn smudges. It filled me with both awe and a kind of sad nostalgia. There was so little left from the time before.

"Strange that there's only one," Chase said.

I scanned the debris-covered field, but he was right. This was the only plane. If the airport had been attacked during the War surely more of them should have found their graves here.

I didn't consider it further. At that moment we turned toward a mausoleum-like hole in one particularly large pile of rubble. Three armed guards hunkered nearby. They'd been expecting us, based on their lack of affect.

"Welcome to Chicago," said Jack. As Sean went to move past him, Jack slapped a hard hand in the middle of his chest. "You scram and squeal, we hunt you down." He grinned viciously.

"Good to know," grumbled Sean.

Jack pulled back a large piece of sheet metal—the hatch on the side of a plane—and descended a ladder secured to the wall. We all followed.

It was dark, *cave* dark, when the last man in closed the hatch. The fear contracted in my belly as we dove deeper into the well, rung after rung, feeling our way blindly toward the bottom. Sweat slickened my grasp, and the bars groaned under our combined weight. Just as my arms were beginning to shake, my feet found solid ground. I listened for Tucker, more wary of him than all these strangers and their dark tunnels combined. There was a whirring noise, and then the light built steadily from a wind-up lantern. Tucker was still feeling his way down the ladder.

"Guess you all aren't too concerned about heatstroke down here." Sean's voice echoed off the low, dome-shaped ceiling. He was right. My skin alighted with goose bumps. It was easily fifteen degrees cooler than the surface.

"What is this place?" I asked. "The sewers or something?" I wrapped my arms around my body. The dark was like a palpable thing; everywhere the light didn't stretch seemed to stroke my skin with its icy tendrils.

"The tunnels," corrected Jack. He shined his lantern down a long corridor that faded to black. My foot bumped against a metal rail, and when I looked down I saw two parallel lines of steel.

"I thought the subways were blown up," said Chase.

"They were," said Jack. "And it must have shaken something loose, 'cause that's how Mags found this place. The Bureau never thought to check that something might exist below the subway."

Black cords ran overhead, breaking into a fray of dusty wires at every crack in the cement ceiling. The air was stale, and brittle, as though a fresh breeze hadn't swept through in a hundred years.

"How old is this place?" I asked.

"Older than you and me," said Jack.

While he and the other rifleman led the way, Truck recounted the gory details of some of Chase's fights to anyone close enough to hear. I eavesdropped with morbid curiosity. This wasn't something Chase liked discussing, and though I wanted the guy to shut up, I couldn't bring myself to stop him.

What I heard sounded brutal. Broken limbs. Blood, dripping from wounds gouged by fists and teeth. Matches that weren't called off, even when they should have been. My heart broke for the little boy within him that was afraid of haunted houses, who kept pictures of his family in a box beneath the floorboards. I was the only witness of his existence. These people only knew a fighter.

Chase walked just before me, back straight, eyes flicking from side to side. I wondered what was going through his head. He didn't like places where he couldn't readily access an exit.

"Those stories aren't all true," he said quietly to me, and then swallowed.

"Neither are mine," I said. His shoulders lowered a full inch.

We walked what felt like a long way before we came to a raised, open area. Up atop the platform, I saw what had happened to the other planes. Luggage racks had been rigged into bunk beds and bolted to the walls. Below them on the chipped tile floor were army cots, lined up like those at the Red Cross Camp. A dozen or more people were laid out sleeping as we passed. There was at least one girl in the mix.

"Barracks," said the third guard, who hadn't spoken very much. A rusted tin sign on the platform wall said CHICAGO TUNNEL COMPANY. Beside it was a metal door, and the words BOILER ROOM—EXIT could barely be deciphered through the corrosion. We were heading right underneath the city. I began to feel claustrophobic. What was above us? Burned-down buildings? The base? Rebecca?

Our path widened as other tracks converged with the central line. Small hanging lanterns were rigged to the cords that ran along the ceiling, low enough that Truck could wind them up as we approached. Chase had to weave around them to avoid hitting his head.

We continued on past the latrines—airplane lavatories taken straight from the planes. They were pressed against the wall of the tunnel, but not particularly evenly. A shovel was leaning against the last open stall, and when I glanced in I saw my distorted reflection in the shadowed aluminum mirror.

I tried to picture the resistance dismantling planes, lowering piece by piece of scrap metal down to the tunnels, but the task seemed too daunting. They were *planes*, thousands of pounds. And yet, the proof was all around us.

"When will we have the roster for the rehab facility?" I heard Sean ask.

"When you stop whining like a little girl," answered Jack. Apparently association with Three didn't buy us good manners from everyone. Sean fell into place beside Chase and me.

We walked farther. A mile, it felt like. My eyes were already adjusting to this grade of darkness. I began to see details more clearly, even without the assistance of a flashlight or the lanterns hanging from the low ceilings. There was graffiti on the walls here. One Whole Country, One Whole Family, but other signs, too. The flag and the cross—the insignia of the MM—X'd out. Swear words. The names of the deceased with the dates they died.

And three hash marks. Someone from Three had been here. I hoped they weren't here now to call me out.

We came upon another station, which our tour guide named sick bay. Several train cars sat dormant on the tracks, crowded with towels, gauze, and medical supplies. Lanterns hung in the last compartment and a dirty-faced boy about my age sat on a large wooden stool and hugged his bleeding arm against his body. He hollered when a medic doused it with peroxide. The medic laughed. I cringed and jogged past a stack of white buckets to keep up with Chase.

The next stop on our tour—the Receiving Station, going by the faded paint on the wall—was much more open, and packed with people. Fifty at least. They sat in blue wool plane seats, using the trays from the row in front of them to hold plates of food. I could smell the warmth and the salt above the cold, dank mold and dirt of the tunnels.

Their glances turned to stares. Their conversations turned to whispers. Truck told anyone who lifted a brow my direction that I was the sniper. I reminded myself to stay aloof, but the lie had grown beyond my control, and I hated myself for ever mentioning it.

"How many people live here?" I found myself asking.

"About a hundred, give or take a few," said Truck.

I cleared my throat against the rasp of cold air. We'd only had thirty in Knoxville, and who knew how many of those were left.

"If you keep going that way, you'll hit the Loop," said Truck. "That's where the briefing is. Make sure you leave early, it's a hike."

We climbed out of the trench, and a full kitchen was revealed. A cafeteria-style counter, made of welded pieces of plane hull, ran along the length of the far wall. Behind it were a steadily humming generator and three mismatched refrigerators. Five workers, one of them a thick girl with cropped hair, were serving tubs of Horizons instant mashed potatoes and cooking burger patties—real meat—over a grill atop a flaming metal trash can. The smoke was wafted down the tunnels by some unperceivable current.

I thought of how much cereal and canned corn we'd eaten at the Wayland Inn. Food we'd stolen from the MM. These people had someone working inside at Horizons, that much was obvious.

Truck was kind enough to get us some food and damp rags with which to clean ourselves before leading us behind the mess hall. Despite my anxiety I was beginning to see double again. I thought if I closed my eyes, I could be asleep in seconds.

The farther we moved away from the tracks, the more debris cluttered the area, and the stronger the scent of rust and concrete dust became. Truck explained that the bombings during the War had taken out the city above us, but that the deeper tunnels, and some of the old elevator shafts to the surface, were still clear. When I pointed out the large crack in the ceiling, he only raised his lantern and shrugged like it wasn't a big deal.

He led us around a cramped area with smaller rail carts filled with what looked like coal, toward a room that said ENGINEERING on the door. Inside were two young men, one with spiky blue hair, the other with porcelain skin and almond-shaped eyes. Their guarded demeanors turned eager as soon as Truck informed them they were in the presence of celebrities, and I was bombarded with questions again.

I pawned off their enthusiasm on Tucker while I explored the room. It was like someone had gone Dumpster diving in a Contraband Items bin. The walls were lined with stacks of clothing, both uniforms and otherwise, linens, and boxes of hair dye and electric clippers. Everything from jewelry to batteries to religious items, including crucifixes and menorahs, were laid out across three sturdy tables. Behind all this was an emergency exit sign, hanging pathetically on wires from the ceiling.

"Is that still a way out?" Chase asked. We all followed his line of sight to the back of the room, where a corridor stretched into darkness.

"Yeah," said the guy with the almond eyes. "That's where they bring supplies down. Guards keep watch up top to make sure no one unapproved gets in."

Chase nodded and took a deep breath. This settled him only minutely.

"We've still got five hours until curfew," Sean whispered to me while the others were rifling the inventory for stolen uniforms and blankets. "If we wait until the meeting, we'll be stuck here until morning."

I felt his urgency. The time had begun ticking through my bloodstream, weighing me down, but we *had* to play it safe. We weren't going to get to Rebecca any faster if we broke the rules and got kicked out of the resistance. I should know.

"We'll get her out, okay?" I said, trying to summon patience. "We need a plan and before we can do that, we need to crash."

"All this attention wearing you out?"

His cynicism surprised me.

"You're not the only one who wants her back," I said, waving when one of the supply boys continued to stare at me.

He sighed. "I know. Sorry. It's just, we're so close."

"We'll get the roster soon," said Tucker, inserting himself in the conversation. "And then I'll get us in. Trust me."

"Trust you. Great idea," I muttered.

EXHAUSTION was taking over by the time we'd taken turns in the "showers"—nozzled bags of undrinkable water—and returned to the barracks. Chase chose two empty cots near the back where he could face the rest of the platoon. The glow of our flashlight revealed a steady vein of water leaking from the ceiling that disappeared into a mound of mud wedged against the wall.

I didn't like separating from Sean and Tucker, but Sean

couldn't rest until he knew more about Rebecca, and there was no way I could sleep if Tucker was anywhere near.

"Turn that light out," someone groaned. I clicked off the flashlight, glad for the first time to be made anonymous by darkness.

What had I been thinking, declaring myself the sniper? I'd gotten us in, sure, but it was just a matter of time before Chicago poked a hole in my lie. We'd better make sure we were gone by the time they figured it out.

Was this how Cara had felt? Always deflecting the truth— whatever that truth actually was. I pictured her pretty face, her cold, sparkling eyes, her mouth curved up in a flirtatious smile. It made me sick to think about, and even sicker that I felt thankful to be alive. Not glad she was dead, but relieved that I was still here. And that was just the same as being glad, wasn't it?

I collapsed on the edge of my makeshift bed and it squeaked. The next cot over felt miles away, too far from him, and in this place, surrounded by people I didn't know, people who thought me someone else, I didn't want to be alone.

I grabbed his hand, urging him down to sit beside me. When my cheek brushed against his shoulder, his chin came to rest on the top of my head. We still smelled vaguely of smoke.

"Don't go," I whispered.

He exhaled slowly, then shifted. I heard the slide of fabric as he removed his boots, and then his warm breath on my knee as he removed mine. I scanned the blinding darkness of the room. I couldn't see anyone. Which meant they couldn't see us.

He lay back. I remembered the way he'd clutched his side after the fight, and tentatively pushed back his shirt. My fingertips skimmed over the rise and fall of his abs and the lean, quivering muscles sweeping around his ribcage. There were bruises here; even in the dark I could imagine them. Purple blossoms tinged with yellow. I swallowed thickly.

"Does it hurt?" I whispered.

He hesitated. "That doesn't."

His skin was so smooth I couldn't take my hands off of it. I briefly wondered what he would do if I kissed that spot, right near the base of his sternum. Thoughts of Cara gave me pause. Cara, who would never touch anyone this way again.

"Lay down with me," he said. The metal frame of the cot whined as he pulled me close. I fit into the cradle of his hips, my back flush against his chest, my knees bending over his. My head found a pillow on his biceps, and I trembled when his other hand rose up my hip, beneath the hem of my shirt, and his fingers spread over my bare stomach and wrapped around my waist. He held me tightly, until the warmth of his body melded with mine. Until I couldn't tell where he ended and I began.

In the peace that followed, I thought of Jack and Truck and Mags, how heavy the weight from the surface pressed down on the shoulders of the soldiers beneath. How it made them brutal and callous, and how much more familiar that felt than Beth's innocence, even after such a short time.

Even hardened, there were still moments like this. Soft spaces in time. Moments that made everything else matter.

That was when I finally realized that though I may have changed, I wasn't broken at all.

I AWOKE to passing footsteps and the dim glow of a lantern. My limbs were tangled with Chase's, reminding me how tall he was when my socked feet only reached his shins. One heavy arm locked me against his firm chest and his warm breath tickled my ear.

Home, he'd told me once. I was his home. He was mine, too. Had my mind not already begun churning with what the next hours would bring, I could have stayed right there forever.

He had obviously been hurting for sleep. Normally up at the slightest sound, he barely stirred when I wiggled away. Carefully, I slipped on my boots and meandered toward the muted light of the main tunnel, trying not to bump into anyone sleeping on a cot or luggage rack.

I needed to find Sean—hopefully he'd learned more about Rebecca's situation while I'd been asleep. Now that I was more alert I felt it. She was close, and we were wasting time until the meeting not attempting a rescue.

I heard footsteps again, and a light appeared thirty feet down the tunnel in the direction of sick bay. I squinted, and in the dim glow caught a head of golden hair hurriedly walking away.

It could have been any number of people I hadn't met, but

I was certain it was Tucker. The knot in my gut was proof enough.

Heart pumping, I ran after him. I should have waited for Chase—I knew that. But I also knew that whatever Tucker was doing, he was doing in secret. I wasn't going to miss the opportunity to bust him. If he caused trouble here on Chicago's turf, all of us were going down.

The light disappeared as I rounded the bend in the tunnel. My feet kept between the dull blue tracks, but reactively slowed when the path before me lay empty. The clatter of my steps echoed like mocking laughter, drawing a prickling sensation down the back of my neck. I was surrounded by shadows and corridors that disappeared into the black. Tucker could be hiding anywhere.

There was a rustling to my left, and I gripped the long metal handle of the flashlight as though it were a weapon. The sound came from the line of temporary showers down a tile-encased corridor. As I tiptoed toward it I heard Sean's voice from the medical car twenty feet away and told myself to relax. He would hear me if I ran into trouble.

I pushed back the trash bag curtain, but there was no one standing on the wet tile floor. *Drip, drip, drip,* went the steady, ear-shattering leak from the doorway. The IV shower bags with their attached spray nozzles hung limply on their wall hooks. I stared so long into the shadows that I began to see shapes. Hear things that didn't exist—creaking, moaning, *whispers.*

"You get used to it."

I spun, already swinging the flashlight, and watched Truck stagger back into the wall, surprise painted all over his simple face.

"*What?*" I bent, hands on my knees, trying to catch my breath.

"The dark," he said, and then began to laugh. "You get used to the dark after a while." He leaned close and whispered, "Saw you sneaking around. It gets to you quick, doesn't it?"

His blond hair gleamed in the glow of the flashlight. He was the one I'd seen, not Tucker. I shook my head to clear my thoughts.

"Yeah, I guess so," I said.

He walked with me to sick bay to meet Sean, who was sitting on a wooden stool in the train car, talking to Jack, and the medic I'd seen earlier; a short, bawdy man with a bald spot on the back of his head.

There was no sign of Tucker.

I stepped inside guardedly, remembering how Jack had looked below me as I pressed a baseball bat into his throat.

"I guess we're all friends now, huh?" I said.

"No sense of humor," said Jack. He flashed a condescending grin from across the car, and I caught the thick red mark across his neck. "Guys, we forgive and forget, but not a chick, man."

"Find a bat and I'll remind you," I said.

"Ooh!" Truck gave me a high five, which I reluctantly returned. Here, under the wind-up lanterns, it was obvious that his left eye was swollen from the fight. He was sitting beside a cardboard box with the word *morefeen* scribbled on it. The medic laughed as Truck playfully shoved a sullen Jack off his perch.

"Shut up!" Sean shouted, slamming his hand against the wall. I stiffened. "The report's wrong. Your man screwed up," he said.

"The roster," I realized, deflating. "She's not here." We had the wrong town. I hated myself for ever believing Tucker Morris would tell the truth.

"He's never wrong—" began the medic.

"He's wrong," interrupted Sean. There were shadows of disbelief under his eyes.

"If you didn't want to know, why'd you come?" asked Jack.

"What's going on?" I said. "Is Rebecca at the reformatory or not?"

"Good news, she's there," said Truck. "Bad news, it's not a reformatory."

"*What?*"

"It's a *physical* rehabilitation center," the medic said. "Attached to the hospital. We don't go there—not because it's packed with soldiers or anything," he qualified. "There's only a skeleton staff of uniforms and it's mostly manned by Sisters and doctors. But it's . . . bad luck."

"What does that mean?" I was beginning to feel that cold hand of panic walk down my spine.

"The place is a circus," said Truck. Mags had said this earlier, but Truck's tone held far more disgust. "A freak factory. They're all over. You seriously haven't heard of a circus?" I shook my head. "All right, look. It's a place where they patch up the injured just enough that they can put them on tour and . . . what did they call it? Deter something . . ."

"Deter noncompliance," finished Jack.

"Right," said Truck. "All the people the Bureau messes up get sent there. Civvies and ex-soldiers and Sisters. They're kept in enough pain so that they're dependent, you know? So they can't run away."

I saw the burned boy in the Square, whose mother had held him up for everyone to see.

Advertising, Chase had said. *Nothing puts people in their place like the threat of pain.* He'd seen this first while he'd lived here, in Chicago. Had he suspected?

"One of our guys got caught," said Jack. "They beat him pretty bad. Kept him on a breathing machine in that rehab facility and toured him around the base. Wanted to show off what happens when you bite back."

It was the first time I'd seen him without his tough front. Even Truck was quiet. The cold air around us grew thin and brittle.

My anger for Tucker was scalding. How could he have neglected to mention this? If he'd really been inside that building, he would have known what went on there. Unless his supposed training—and his contact on the inside—were just more lies.

"What happened to him?" I asked weakly.

"Mags," said Truck. "Mags went topside with a team, to this old abandoned high-rise across the street. From the top floor you can see down onto the courtyard on their roof. When they brought him outside, she took him out."

"Mercy kill," added the medic. It was the first time I'd heard the term used with something other than a bird with a broken wing, and it sunk into my body like fangs. "Mags is tough as nails. She could probably teach you a thing or two, Sniper."

It took me a moment to remember my role, but when I did, all I managed was a one-shouldered shrug.

Now I knew why the gang outside had silenced when we'd mentioned where we needed to go. Why they'd all waited for Mags's reaction. She'd killed one of her own men there, and instead of being horrified, they'd been reverent.

It occurred to me the sniper could have been in Chicago all along. It made perfect sense. Mags was cold, protected by a legion of ex-soldiers who could defend her if needed. I wished Chase was here. I wondered if he'd woken yet; if he was looking for me.

My mind turned back to Rebecca, my fear for her swelling. "Why couldn't the team break into the facility and get him? You said there aren't many soldiers."

The three Chicago boys glanced at one another warily.

"A Sister has to accompany any soldier into the building," Truck told me. "And it's not that Mags couldn't rig that, but what were we supposed to do with him once we got him out? We can't support that kind of care down here."

Sean had had enough. He tore out of the car into the darkened passage.

I shook my head, wishing I could replay this conversation with a different outcome. But we'd come here for answers, and we'd gotten them.

I left the car and found Sean just outside, pacing.

"Sean," I said. He didn't stop. I stood in front of him. "Sean!"

"I still have to go. I have to see." He crouched, hands on his head.

"Sean, stop it," I said, grabbing his shoulders. "We'll figure this out."

"How? How are we going to do that?"

"I . . . I don't know. Yet. I don't know *yet*, okay? But we'll think of something."

He stood, shaking his head. "I should have gotten her out of there years ago."

"Sean, it's not your fault. If anyone's, it's mine."

"No." He shook his head. "No, I was supposed to look out for her."

"Sean . . ."

"Chase got you out!" His voice was powerful enough to push me back a step. "Chase didn't wait, but I waited. I kept waiting, thinking that there'd be a better time. She'd age out, and then I'd go AWOL . . ."

Sean was losing his control, and as he did, mine returned. My hands had captured his wrists, and squeezed when he tried to brush me off.

"Sean, listen to me."

"I swear, if they've been towing her around the base . . ."

"Stop. They said it's run by Sisters. I promise, if I have to go in there by myself and get her, I will, okay?"

"I should have—"

"We'll tell Mags tonight we're going to try Tucker's contact." I couldn't believe what I was saying, but we had no other options. "We'll see her tomorrow, okay?"

Finally, he blew out a strained breath.

"Dawn," he said.

WHILE Sean stayed in sick bay to question the Chicago resistance for more information, I ran back to the barracks to wake Chase. Now that I didn't have to be strong for Sean, I became aware of the fear, rooting deep inside me. Rebecca was in more danger than I'd ever suspected. She'd been hurt—badly—and now they were torturing her, showing her off like that poor boy in the Square. I thought of Mags, cold and hard, standing in that window and shooting her own man. *Mercy kill,* the medic had said. We couldn't do that to Rebecca, even if her life had become what they'd described.

Chase was not in the barracks.

I ran back past the showers, but he didn't answer when I called his name.

I returned to sick bay. He wasn't there either. Neither was Sean, or the Chicago guys.

We still had an hour until the meeting, but clusters of people were already filtering out of their respective stations and funneling toward what Truck had called the Loop, just beyond the mess hall. Sharp-smelling bodies surrounded me, bumping me, reminding me of the tight quarters in the Knoxville Square.

I searched for Chase, but would have settled for Sean or even Tucker. It made sense for Chase to go on to the meeting site without me; it's where I would go if I'd woken unable to find him. But moving through the crowd of muscled arms and dismissing faces was about as easy as wading through quicksand; I kept getting stuck. Finally we passed the mess hall, where everyone who had just eaten was filtering out into the tunnel.

I saw the tall, athletic build and the golden hair, and staggered only momentarily before pursuing. I was sure it was Tucker this time. He was heading to the supply room—the opposite direction from the meeting. I lunged onto the platform and sprinted past the refrigerators and the counter made of shiny plane hull, to the back of the mess hall. Only a few stragglers remained. Most had left for the meeting.

A flash of movement near the coal carts caught my eye and I dashed after it, but the supply room was empty when I entered.

"Where's the sniper fan club?"

At the sound of Tucker's voice I spun back to the entrance that he now was framed within, the shadows over his face sending a chill straight to my bones. His eyes, pinched around the corners, looked edgy—like they had when he'd told us how Cara was killed.

I became acutely aware that it was just the two of us. My hand gripped the flashlight. When his head tilted curiously to the side I gritted my teeth.

"Not still worried about being alone with me, are you?"

He took a step toward me, and I moved back like the wrong end of a magnet.

"Guess that answers that question," he said.

Laughter filtered through from the platform, not too far away. If Tucker tried anything, I could scream, and they'd be close enough to hear me.

"What are you doing here?" I asked.

"Stealing."

I twitched.

"Relax," he said. "My arm hurts."

He rolled up his sleeve and revealed the pink, swollen forearm that until yesterday had been hidden within a cast.

"Looks traumatic," I said. "Why don't you go see the medic?"

"I don't need to see the medic." He regarded me with too much familiarity, the way a big brother shuns his annoying little sister. He began to sort through a box atop one of the tables. "I get the feeling there's something you want to say." He didn't sound particularly pleased to hear whatever it was.

I gripped the flashlight harder.

"Apparently there's a little problem with your rehab facility," I said. "You neglected to mention that it was a *physical* rehab, not a girls' reformatory."

His golden brows arched. "I didn't know a distinction was needed."

He was incapable of honesty. Slippery as an eel.

"Is she even there?"

"Yes. Unless she ran away. Which I doubt. Where does one run in a town full of soldiers?" he mused when I narrowed my eyes.

"What really happened with Cara?"

The lines of his mouth drew tight. "I told you what happened."

"Sorry if I don't exactly trust you."

He shook his head and glanced up at the exit sign. I had the fleeting fear that he was planning on bolting. He was going to escape and we would take the heat when he didn't show up to report to Mags. She'd probably ground us so we couldn't break Rebecca free.

"Believe it or not, I thought Cara was all right," he said. That look of regret was back, and it made my spine tingle. I believed Chase could change, I could change, *everyone* could change, but not Tucker. "She had it bad," he continued. "She told me she used to host at FBR socials. They didn't always treat those girls so well."

Cara? She may have been flirty, but not desperate.

I thought of how harsh she'd been to Sarah when we'd found her in Tent City, and then later, when she'd called her nothing more than a party favor. Then, strangely, I found myself picturing Cara in the pretty dress. Cara chatting with soldiers. Cara doing what she had to in order to stay alive.

"You mean *you* didn't treat those girls well," I countered.

A dark speculation filled me as the pieces slid into place—Chicago was quick to believe that the cartridge came from a sniper's rifle, and Cara had been a part of the team that had hijacked the Horizons truck, the very place I'd found it to begin with. The other guys at the Wayland Inn had said she'd disappeared more than once; she'd even been in the Square during the last two shootings.

It seemed so clear now, I didn't know how I'd missed it before.

Unless I hadn't wanted to believe it.

Wallace had to have known what Cara had been doing. He'd sent me out into the streets knowing I'd been accused of a crime she committed. They'd used me as her cover, so that she could keep killing soldiers.

Thank you for what you've done, she'd told me. *Thank you for taking the fall* is what she should have said.

I felt ill.

I lifted my eyes to Tucker, doubting his story more than ever, suspecting that he knew, as I so certainly did now, that Cara was the sniper. But gone was his arrogance from the base, stripped away like his blue uniform.

"Hey, Sniper!" someone shouted from outside the room. "Come on, the meeting's getting ready to start!"

"You should go," he said.

"I'll be right behind you."

He moved toward the door, hesitating near the entrance, as though he expected me to join him. When I didn't, he walked away.

Every muscle within me was shaking. Wallace had lied. Cara had lied. Tucker was lying. Everyone was hiding some truth my life relied upon.

I hated secrets.

I removed the St. Michael medallion from my neck. It couldn't touch my skin anymore. It was for the sniper. It had been given to me right in front of the sniper. I'd been her cover all this time. Even in death.

It slid from my trembling hand and bounced on the floor with a fragile metal *click*.

I don't know why, but amid the pounding revelations my mind found Chase. Clearly I saw him, sitting beside me on the tailgate of Tubman's truck, telling me about St. Michael, and the spirit world, and his hope that my mother had found peace.

Before another thought entered my head I was on my hands and knees, retrieving the coin from where it had fallen, beneath one of the long tables covered with hodgepodge supplies. I needed it. It had kept me alive. I couldn't let it go.

That's when it happened: a deafening, thundering crash. The walls shook. Dust spilled down from the ceiling. It was a short burst of an earthquake, over in seconds that felt like a lifetime.

I was still on the floor, halfway beneath the table with the necklace locked in my fist. Terror had seized my muscles. I couldn't move. I couldn't even breathe.

A high screech of twisting, tearing metal filled my ears. The flashlight's beam vibrated against the wall. The sounds were coming from deeper in the tunnels. Somewhere closer to the remains of downtown. Somewhere near the Loop, where the meeting was to be held.

Where Chase and Sean and Tucker were all headed.

One more explosion, and I watched the ceiling crack open like it was paper torn down the center. I heard it grumble angrily and whine, and then vomit rock and dust. The walls, so solid in appearance, bowed, the racks broke and spit supplies into the center of the room.

The world went bright white, and then black.

THE pain receded. Not immediately, but in stages, like I had slipped into a hot, healing bath. My muscles relaxed. The fear dissipated. Soon the darkness seemed as natural as nighttime.

And then she was there. I don't know how, or even when she came exactly. All I knew was that she was there, as real as I was. She crouched on her knees and then laid down close beside me, so that we were both staring up into the black.

"Hi, Mom."

"Hi, baby." Her delicate fingers wove between mine and our joined hands came to rest on the soft T-shirt covering her stomach.

"So I'm dead then," I said. It didn't seem so bad; I wasn't scared. I wasn't tired or angry or hungry. But even though she was here, I still had the strange sensation that something was missing. Some crucial part of me.

"I don't *think* you're dead," she said.

I snorted at her uncertainty. Of all people, she should know.

She hummed quietly, running her fingers over the back of my hand. I sighed. For the first time in a long time, my mind was quiet, peaceful. I turned my face and smiled, and she smiled back, and I thought of how we had the same mouth. I liked that.

"I've missed you," I said.

She was warm, but when I tried to snuggle up to her side a rock embedded into my ribcage. What was that doing here? Just a moment ago the ground had been soft. I released her hand to pull the rock out, but though I felt the rough edges, I couldn't see it. I couldn't even see my hand. All I could see was her.

My head began to throb, building to a hammering in the base of my skull that sent waves crashing behind my eyes. There was something in my other hand. A flat and round piece of metal. It was wet, and my fingers hurt from squeezing it so hard.

It reminded me of something. A silver ring, with a pretty black stone. But it wasn't a ring, it was a coin.

"I knew he'd find you. He's always been a good boy. Came from good people," she said.

A sharp pain exploded at the front of my brain. Streaks of light appeared before my eyes, blocking her out for seconds at a time.

I remembered. I remembered everything. His black hair and calloused hands. His dark eyes, always watching me.

Please don't be dead. Please.

"Mom, is he . . ." I couldn't say it out loud.

"I don't know," she said with a small frown.

That little expression did it. I was torn. Ripped clean in half. I had to find out if he was dead so that he could be with us, but I couldn't leave her. Not for a second. I'd never let her out of my sight again.

"Ember, *sweetheart*," she soothed, pulling me close. But she wasn't soft and warm. She was cold, and the light inside of her was growing dim. When I grasped for her she wasn't there. My fingers connected with something hard and flat above me. Splinters dug into the beds of my nails.

"No, wait . . ." I sobbed. "Mom. Please. Stay."

"You can't have us both," she said, her face pale. "But it's okay. You know why?"

I gasped for breath. Pain jolted from my left wrist to my elbow.

"It's okay because I got almost eighteen years with you. The best eighteen years of my life."

"Mom . . ."

"Hush. Listen now. I need to say a couple mom things."

Chase and I were sitting on the truck bed at East End Auto. He was telling me about his mother. About the spirit world. He was right. He was always right.

"Listen, because this is important. Eat more—you're getting too skinny. And smile. Oh, and don't believe anyone who says they'll pay you back later; they never do."

The pain in my arm was like fire in the bone. It whipped through my body to my spine, to my ankles, to the back of my head.

"And one more thing," she said. "I have never loved one single thing in my life more than you. You were worth living for, and Ember, you were worth dying for."

And then she was gone. And it didn't matter how much I cried that I loved her back, or not to go, she was simply gone. There was only the black, and the rubble, and the walls of my silent tomb.

WHEN I woke again, it was with the acute understanding that I was alone. The rest returned slowly—the tunnels, the supply room, crawling under the table to retrieve the St. Michael pendant. My mother.

I screamed for help, but the sound slapped against the walls of the enclosure and made my ears ring. I reached up, feeling the underside of a flat board, less than a foot above my face. It angled down over the length of my body, trapping my shins and ankles. My left wrist seared with pain, and sent my fingers into spasms of prickling numbness. With my right hand and left elbow, I pushed upward on the barrier as hard as I could. It didn't move.

I was trapped.

Okay, I thought. I forced myself to breathe, to try again. But the board didn't budge.

A sudden panic seized me, and I twisted, throwing my shoulder against the board. My knees cracked against it. My cries were met with silence.

Nobody was going to come.

Nobody was left alive.

Everyone had died in the earthquake, or whatever it was. I didn't even know how long I'd been down here.

After a while I became still, too scared to move. The

seconds passed, one by one. I tried to count them, anything to quiet the scalding horror. When I passed one hundred, I stopped, realizing that I'd begun the countdown to the end.

I was going to die here.

I wasn't even going to get to tell Chase good-bye.

I tried to hold on to what I could in my last moments. His rough, strong fingers intertwined with mine. His mouth tightening to hold back angry words, and the way his shoulders hunched when he'd gone too long without sleep. I knew the exact angle in which I had to lift my chin in order to kiss him, and what his laugh sounded like, and how a nightmare could make him, of all people, feel small.

I held his memories. Of when he'd gotten all As on his seventh-grade report card, and when he'd gotten grounded for fighting Jackson Pruitt in the sixth grade. Of how he fit into his family. Of how he fit into mine.

When I was gone, who would remember who he really was?

Stop, I told myself. *I've lived through rehabilitation. I've escaped an MM base. I've survived a fire.*

I am not dead yet.

"Help!" I whispered. And then my whispers turned louder, and louder, and my cry for help became his name. I shouted it twenty times. Thirty. All the while, I resumed my attack on that unmovable board.

My voice grew hoarse. My throat was on fire, closing with each frantic second. I would have sold my soul for some water.

I am not dead yet.

I summoned every fiber of strength in my entire body. I called upon every bit of determination within me. And I pushed.

The board tilted above me, and dust rained down on my face. I coughed and squeezed my eyes closed. My good arm had succeeded in dislodging the barrier. Now that I had enough room to move I added my knee. Every muscle in my abdominals and back contracted. Whispered screams of exertion belted through my locked jaw.

And then I heard something.

I held my breath, fighting off the sudden burst of faintness.

"... *think someone's down there!*"

A frenzied state of urgency took me, and as the light filtered in from the window I'd loosened, I fought like an animal. Every thought cleared from my head. I had to get out of here *now*.

I shimmied out before my rescuer pulled the board all the way off of me. Sweating and exhausted, I stared into the face of a green-eyed ghost. Not a ghost. His flawless skin was covered with white concrete dust.

Not you, I thought. *Anyone but you.*

Tucker shined a flashlight into my face. I wasn't ready for the brightness. It burned straight through to my brain.

"Help me up!" My mouth moved, but no sound came out.

"She's alive!" he shouted to someone behind him.

I shoved to my knees and jerked up too quickly, stars exploding in my vision. Tucker grasped my waist for support.

My legs wobbled, but could still support my weight. There didn't appear to be any real damage to them, but the bruises must have gone straight through; they throbbed to the marrow. My wrist was another story. It was contorted to the side, and nearly made me vomit to look at. Had it not been so numb, I was sure it would have been killing me.

"That table saved your life," Tucker said. "Good thinking getting under it."

There was an absent, distant feel to him. The kind Chase sometimes got when he'd been left alone too long with his thoughts.

I glanced down to where he pointed. The table from the supply room had been tossed aside. The legs were broken on one end: where my ankles had been trapped. I shuddered; not allowing myself to consider what might have happened should the opposite legs—those on either side of my head— have collapsed.

Our half of the room was still standing, but the cave-in had taken out most of the opposite wall. All that remained was a landslide of rock, some pieces bigger than my body.

The exit was wiped out.

A dozen people were close, assisting the injured or shoveling away the debris. Crying voices. Moaning. A scream. I didn't know why they weren't running.

"Chase," I demanded. *Please let him be alive.*

He shook his head. "I don't know."

I spun, coming face-to-face with the boy with almond eyes from the supply room. He held a canteen, and taken by a force beyond my control, I snatched it from his hands.

I tried to drink only a little, but it soothed my aching throat, and I couldn't stop. Soon more than half the canteen was gone. He didn't seem to care that I gasped and sputtered, or that half the water dribbled down my shirt.

I grabbed his shoulder with my good hand and pulled myself close to his ear.

"Chase Jennings," I whispered. "He came with me from Knoxville."

The boy blinked.

"I haven't seen him in the last hour, but he lived through the blast."

Alive. But my stomach stayed knotted. I'd been down in that hole for more than an hour. Because of a *blast.* Had we been bombed?

"Where is he?" I mouthed.

"Sick bay." He pointed in the direction of the airfield.

I shoved by him, still unsteady on my feet. I half walked, half ran through the gravel, tripping only once and then catching myself. I peered into every face, but no raven hair. No wolf eyes. My head was throbbing, and the lights from the hand-cranked lanterns and flashlights left comet trails across my vision.

The main tunnel was mostly empty, but I could see lights down the way where the train car with the medical supplies still stood. My eyes landed on someone thick, muscular: *Truck.*

I blinked, and kept moving toward them, pushing the St. Michael medallion that had saved my life into my pocket.

Truck was holding someone around the waist, struggling to contain him while his arms flailed. I recognized Sean off to the side. He looked so tired; his hands were on the knees of his dust-skinned pants and he was shaking his head.

And there, the person Truck was fighting. Chase.

Truck was hauling him away from the wreckage: the passage where the shower bags had hung had been consumed by a concrete avalanche.

"She's not there!" I heard Truck yell.

Chase twisted and elbowed him in the side of the head.

"Chase!" Sean shouted. But he wasn't looking at Chase, he was looking at me.

Chase turned. Our gazes locked. The voices, the crackling of rock, it all faded.

I ran forward, sobbing, limping, latching my busted wrist to my chest. He took three steps toward me and stumbled to his knees, as if his legs had lost their strength.

I collapsed before him, inches away. Blood was smeared across his cheek. Dirt and what looked like oil marked his clothes and skin. Sweat carved jagged lines down the dust coating his jaw. Until that moment I hadn't thought what I must have looked like. I didn't much care.

His hand lifted slowly toward my cheek, his eyes deep and afraid, his cracked lips open slightly. I longed for that touch, I craved it, knowing it would make me real again instead of some player in my waking nightmare. But he didn't touch me. He couldn't. When I glanced to the side, his bloodied hand was trembling, and he lowered it, wiping it on his jeans.

I could almost hear his thoughts. Or maybe they were mine.

Please be real.

With no more hesitation I grabbed that hand and kissed his palm and watched it dampen and fill with my tears. A strangled sob came from his throat, and then he grabbed me firmly by the waist and crushed me into his body so hard I gasped. Finally, *finally* I was back, locked within his sheltering arms, hidden within his bones.

"I thought you were dead." His voice broke.

I closed my eyes for a moment, thankful to be alive.

"I saw my mom," I whispered. "Maybe I was dead."

His chest rumbled with a short, wet chuckle. "How did she look?"

"She looked like my mom," I said with a smile. "You know, short hair. Big eyes. Little." It was the same literal translation he'd once given me when I asked the same question. "I thought you went to the meeting."

His breath whistled through his teeth. "I did," he said, his voice still unsteady. "But you weren't there. I ran into Sean on the way back. He said he'd seen you at sick bay."

A sudden wave of drowsiness crashed over me. "I think my wrist might be broken."

He jerked me back immediately, nearly giving me whiplash, and then cradled my arm with the gentleness that only a big person can summon. Sean crouched beside us.

"We ended hide-and-seek an hour ago," he said. "Maybe you missed it."

A smile cracked my lips.

He grinned reluctantly. "Glad you're not dead."

"Me, too."

"Get the medic." At Chase's order, Sean rose and darted away.

"What happened?" I rasped.

He'd begun a full inspection, feeling my arms, forcing me to sit back, and then lifting my pant legs and cringing at the bloody bruises on my shins. He shifted to feel his way down my back. Any other time I might have laughed at the diligent expression on his face.

"Bombs," he muttered. "I'm starting to feel unwelcome."

Once was enough, but Chase had been here during the War, too, when the Insurgents had flattened the city.

Truck took a knee, wiping his brow with the back of his hand. "Someone gave us up. They bombed it from topside, sent the ceiling down near the Loop. Got fifty people, maybe more. Mags was there."

His once carefree face filled with sorrow. The number was staggering, and somehow unreal at the same time. So many people gone, so fast. And Mags, their leader, wiped away just like Wallace.

"We have to go," I said, suddenly aware of the still-prevalent danger.

Chase's expression was grim. "We're blocked. There's an exit near the barracks that lets out near the lake. Scouts are working on clearing it now."

No way out. I shuddered.

"But what about the others?" I said. "I was trapped under a table, who knows how many people are still alive!"

"We'll find them," said Truck dutifully. "It's not like the

Bureau's going to come down here anyway when the ceiling might buckle."

In response to his words, I looked up, noting the way the dust sprinkled down like snow. We didn't have much time.

The medic arrived a moment later, carrying a blue canvas FBR bag over one shoulder. He looked flustered.

"Thought you were toast," he said. He felt around the back of my head and I hissed as a new bright pain ricocheted behind my brows.

"Keep the wound clean," he said. "Let's see that wrist."

I held it out, and Chase's jaw tightened.

"Look at that!" the medic shouted, staring over my shoulder behind us. The moment I turned my head he grabbed my hand and jerked it toward him, hard.

A crack as the bones in my wrist realigned. I gasped, then blinked, feeling nauseous and a little faint again. Chase supported my back. My fingers regained movement, although they now tingled painfully.

"Well, it's not dislocated anymore," the medic said, then disappeared without another word.

Chase held me for a moment while my vision cleared, and the sounds from the tunnels filtered back through the ringing in my ears. Then he pulled me up, sending a challenging glare toward the creaking ceiling. Truck left to help another group digging into the collapsed side of the mess hall with Sean.

"Can you stand?" he asked, the conflict playing over his face. And when I nodded, he said, "Then let's get these people out."

CHAPTER
18

MOST people were clustered together. I moved from group to group, hastening them to carry the injured toward the exit route immediately. That way when it was cleared, we'd be ready to evacuate the city. They grabbed what provisions they could carry—weapons mostly, but uniforms, blankets, and medical supplies, too. The thick scent of mud and sewer water hung in the air, gagging me in some of the more stagnant spaces.

Some recognized me, and those that didn't followed those that did. They believed me when I told them Truck, the carrier, would be ready to transport them to a nearby checkpoint. They believed me because they thought I was the sniper, and how could the sniper lead them astray? But my confidence was as hollow as my identity. I was deceiving them even now, when they were most frightened. I didn't know if any of us would live through the night.

I moved toward the cave-in that blocked the mess hall

from everything behind it, and raised the lantern I'd picked up off the ground. The sight before me stole my breath.

The way was blocked completely by a wall of concrete and pipe. Water sprayed from one corner. On the opposite side, several guys were struggling to put out a fire, but every time they got close, the rock base they climbed upon gave way, and they all crashed back into one another. Those that were digging nearby had to abandon the area on account of the heat.

A boy about Billy's age was screaming. His leg was trapped beneath a hollow pipe with a greater circumference than his core. Sitting against the wall in the shadows I spotted a tall, slender man and shouted my plea for help. He stared into space, unmoving.

"Clear!" shouted someone. The call was infectious. "Clear! The exit's clear!"

I wanted to run, follow them toward the tunnel that led to the lake, but couldn't. Not with this boy here, staring at me through pain-glazed eyes. Trapped, as I had been.

Sean, having been close at the cave-in, came sprinting toward me. He assessed the situation with a tight grimace and bent down to help.

I planted my shoulder against the pipe, favoring my sore wrist against my chest.

"On three," he said.

The boy began to pant. "Wait," he begged. "Just wait . . ."

On three we pushed. The boy passed out, but we got the pipe off of him. His leg was bent at an awkward angle. A sharp piece of bone from his shin stuck out through his denim pants.

I covered my mouth, biting back the bile climbing my throat. Sean hoisted him over one shoulder. The boy's head bobbled limply to the side.

When I hesitated, Sean glanced toward our exit. "We've got to go."

I caught sight of Chase then, digging into the rock with his bare hands, calling out orders to those around him. Something about the desperation in his movements finally brought reality home. The MM had done this. They weren't just skulking around prison cells taking out defenseless individuals. They were attacking on a large scale now. Like with the fire, they meant to destroy us all. Today, they'd done a pretty good job.

Get out, I heard with each thump of my heart. *Get out, get out, get out.*

Sean followed my gaze. "Hurry up," he said, and took off.

I limped toward Chase, but on the way tripped over a man's long legs, splayed out from where he sat against the tunnel wall. His arms were down loosely at his sides. His face was almost completely blackened by dirt.

"Jack?"

I touched his knee, unsure if he was dead or in a trance.

"Jack!" I shouted. He clawed at his ears, smearing the trickle of blood that veined down his neck. He couldn't hear me.

I moved closer to his face. "Jack! It's me, Ember. We need to go, okay? We've got to get out of here!"

He blinked. His mouth was moving slightly. I leaned close to hear him.

"Run," he whispered. "We've been hit. Mags is down. Run."

I touched his hand. It was ice-cold. Vaguely, I recalled someone once telling me this was a sign of shock. I rubbed his arms rapidly, hoping this would help. My swollen wrist sparked with pain. I pulled him to a stand and he sagged back against the wall.

Finally a sound interrupted his mumblings. He began to laugh. It was a highly disturbing sound given the shouts and moans of pain.

"The sniper," he said. And then laughed again. "The sniper, from Knoxville."

"Okay," I said. "You're right. It's hilarious."

He stopped laughing and shook his head as if to clear it. "We need to evacuate."

"Yup," I said, shoving him down the hallway. "I'm two steps ahead of you."

WORD traveled fast down the tunnel. Thirty minutes after I'd emerged from the rubble, a scout up top radioed down a sighting of soldiers on the airfield. They were combing the area looking for a safe entrance to the tunnels. The signal didn't need much interpretation: they knew how we got in, which meant that someone had snitched, like Truck had said, or been followed. I hoped that it had not been us.

After I'd sent off Jack, I went for Chase, but he was already barreling in my direction. He grabbed my uninjured hand,

- 335 -

and I could feel the slick sweat and blood between our palms. Without another word we ran, hearts in our throats, fate on our heels. His grip never faltered.

The way became less cluttered by rock and debris as we approached the barracks and the exit route, but the ceiling had begun to rumble again. Another collapse was imminent. We could not move fast enough.

A crash came from behind us—an aftershock of the original bombing that had weakened the whole infrastructure. The roar of the rock and hiss of broken pipes shattered my eardrums, the repercussion reverberating in my chest like the smack of a bass drum. The floor trembled, then seemed to lift and pitch, and we were on an ocean of sand and rock, clinging to each other, fighting to stay upright.

I willed myself not to look back, but I knew the landslide was coming. It swallowed each remaining lantern, until behind us was only black, and all that remained ahead was the wreckage that appeared in the bouncing beams of our flashlights.

Finally the barracks came into view, and Truck darted through a metal door that said BOILER ROOM—EXIT. Sean had been waiting; he motioned us to hurry. We passed him, colliding into the bodies that were stacked inside.

"Stop! It's this way!" I heard Sean yell behind me. I turned in time to see Tucker staring farther down the hall, toward the airfield exit where we had entered the tunnels, a desperate look on his face.

Sean grabbed his sleeve and jerked him back toward us, just as the cave-in reached the barracks. The crunch and squeal of the medical car dissipated in seconds beneath the rubble; any visual of the tunnel was suddenly blocked behind the slamming metal door. Tucker stumbled, pale panic stretching his features thin.

This hallway was damp and dark, and my eyes watered from the acrid fumes of gasoline. I remembered the flames beside the cave-in; there were probably multiple gas leaks. My breath felt dense and palpable in my throat as the tunnels outside collapsed.

"Eyes open!" Truck yelled, and ran on.

He shoved through a door on the opposite end of the corridor to a stairway and we ascended five levels, exiting into a room filled with rusted pipes and human-sized cobwebs. Rats scurried across the floor. For the first time in my life, I welcomed the sight of them: we were heading toward the living. Below us, the collapse had halted, and though we knew the reprieve wouldn't hold, the air wafted with the shudder of one collective breath.

We emerged on the other side into a women's restroom, like those in the old department stores we'd visited when I was a kid.

"No joke," Truck laughed thinly. "My biggest nightmare in high school was accidentally walking into the girl's bathroom."

Chase's hand came around the back of my neck. "You okay?" He was breathing hard.

I nodded, checking him and then Sean for injuries.

"Where are we?" asked Tucker.

"Near the lake. We're on the dark side of town—there's

no standardized power over here," Truck said. "The Bureau doesn't come out this way. The worst we've got to watch for is flooding."

"They never replaced the levee after the War," Chase explained at our blank looks.

When Chicago had been bombed, the flood walls had been destroyed, bringing Lake Michigan's shore a block farther inland. The fallen buildings had pushed the waterline even higher. On the news I'd once seen a woman's furniture floating away with the current.

Truck led the way into an open lobby, where at least thirty people were crammed onto the left side of the broken tile floors. The ceiling on the right half had collapsed. Broken wires, fluorescent lights, and fluffs of insulation hung down to the damp linoleum.

I'd thought the underground had looked bad. In our urgency, I'd temporarily forgotten what the War had done to the top half of the city.

It was past curfew, but only just; I felt like I could finally breathe when the muted colors and shadows became decipherable through the cracks in the ceiling. If I never went underground again it would be just fine by me.

The medic was triaging those most injured, giving his approved list to Jack, who boarded them into an FBR supply truck outside. From the looks of it, he'd come back to his senses, but now seemed too embarrassed to acknowledge me.

"What are *they* doing here?"

I stiffened. My eyes found the boy who'd been crushed beneath the pipe. His leg was wrapped now with a wool blanket tied off with bungee cords, and he slouched against the back wall, clearly a recipient of a high dose of *morefeen*.

"Shut up already," grumbled Jack. "They weren't followed."

So this wasn't the first time this boy had made this accusation. I hoped no one else shared his views.

"You think *we* did this?" Sean asked.

"Odd timing," the boy slurred. "Sniper shows up and they bomb the tunnels all to Hell."

"We didn't have to roll that pipe off your leg, you know!" I wanted to confess everything then, to tell them I wasn't the sniper, Cara was, and now that she was dead, there was no sniper. But those people in the tunnels had listened to me because they thought I was important, and maybe that had saved their lives. I couldn't take it back.

On some level I understood that Chicago needed someone to blame. But we were the last to leave the tunnels. We had sweat and bled beside them. Didn't that mean anything?

Chase seethed beside me. The indecipherable muttering from the survivors rose in volume.

Truck, who had gone outside to check the vehicle, returned and cut the tension with his trademark missing-tooth grin.

"Sit tight, ladies," he said. "Checkpoint express is pulling out of station. I'll be back as soon as I can to get the rest of you."

A communal groan. At least half would be left behind, some badly injured.

"I'm not going."

All eyes turned toward Tucker, mine included.

"I won't be further trouble," he continued. "If they meant

to smoke out the sniper like that kid says, we'll be putting the convoy in further danger. I'll stay back. Draw them away from the transports."

What a hero, I thought.

"We'll all stay," said Chase, a wary eye on his ex-partner. "We came here for someone. We're not leaving without her."

My heart pounded in my chest. Beside me, Sean exhaled.

THE first batch left for the Indiana checkpoint, and though I'd made my decision to stay, I couldn't bring myself to watch them leave. For the first time since I'd learned the truth about my mother, I wanted to go to the coast. I wanted peace.

In Truck's absence, a grim anticipation settled over us. It thickened, until someone finally joked about how a guy named Stripes had cried like a baby when the bombs went off.

"You think that's bad," a bald man with a goatee responded, "you should have seen Boston sprint for the exit. You'd have thought his boots were on fire."

Some nervous chuckles.

They called one another girls' names. Sally. Mary. They laughed about who pissed their pants and who broke down. It was sexist and crass, but I didn't even care. You said what you could to pull yourself out.

I thought of how Jack had laughed in the tunnels after the blast, and wondered if he'd had it right. When things got really bad, the horror came full circle, and even violence got to be funny again. It didn't have to make sense.

We inventoried the supplies, ate salvaged rations of crackers and canned mix-meat, and waited for cover of darkness to sneak to Rebecca's rehab. In our quest to stay, we'd been granted a break from the accusations and were donated fatigues, rations, and two handguns. The boy from the supply room, still lightly dusted and streaked with sweat, approached me shyly and handed me a Sister uniform he'd salvaged from the supply room.

"Thought you might need this again," he said, face filled with hope.

I paid him a guilty thank-you, knowing it was far too late to say anything to the contrary.

THERE were two water drums from the delivery truck that were brought inside the hideout to make more room, and since the water was too dirty to drink, we used it to clean the grime and blood from our bodies.

As I waited in line, Chase's presence pulled at me, drawing my attention to where he and Sean had removed themselves from the others. Against the wall, behind a ripped curtain of gray insulation hanging from the ceiling, they conspired. Though I couldn't hear what they were saying, Sean's movements were animated, as if he were trying to make a point, and curiosity had me leaving my place in line to see what had set Chase's shoulders in a defensive hunch and his thumb tapping against his thigh. Before I reached them, Chase broke the conversation and stalked away.

"What was that about?" Sean's head jerked up as I spoke. He glanced after Chase, then, in a low voice, explained how we were to break into the facility.

When he was done, my head was throbbing even harder than before.

No one removed a patient from the premises without the presence of a Sister, so Tucker and Sean would claim that they were assisting me with transporting Rebecca to a Sisters of Salvation home, where she could dedicate her life to service. Tucker knew the soldier managing the facility and felt confident he'd let us through. Just as long as he hadn't heard about the dishonorable discharge.

Chase was not going to be coming in with us.

"It took twenty seconds for an AWOL to make him," Sean tried to reason. "Don't you think there are soldiers at the base who still remember him?"

So now Chase was the liability, and the rescue plan depended on me.

He was going to love that.

Without a word, I sought refuge in the women's bathroom. The minutes lost their meaning as I stood before a sink, knees locked, eyes unseeing. A blank expression fixed itself onto my face, and it was no lie. I felt nothing. Not rage. Not despair. Nothing. I'd placed a bucket of water in the bowl, and absently washed my hands, my arms, my hair, now crunchy with dried blood, and watched as droplets of red and black splashed the old, forgotten porcelain.

The mirror before me was marred by black, mutated roses of corrosion, and within one of them something moved— a reflection from the empty stalls at my back. I spun, and the world spun with me, forcing me to grip the sink behind with white knuckles.

Tucker sat on the floor, his legs bent at sharp angles, his hands clasped between his knees. He leaned back against a stall door, shrouded by shadow and so still he could have been a fixture in the room. Still, I couldn't believe I hadn't noticed him.

We stared at each other for a long moment, until I finally asked the question ringing through my skull.

"What are you doing here?"

His shoulders rose with a long, drawn-out sigh, but his voice was weak. Defeated. "Same thing as you. Taking some much-needed me time."

"What are you doing here?" I repeated. And when he didn't answer, I asked again.

He looked down, and his legs fell straight.

"I don't know."

He crumbled forward, folding over himself like a discarded marionette, and began to shake. At once, conflicting desires rose within me. To leave. To force him, however I could, to tell the truth. To crouch down, and lower my voice, and say something soothing. And because they were all equally strong, I didn't dare let go of the sink.

He is a liar.

He was with us in the tunnels.

I slowly dropped down, careful that I could rise quickly if necessary.

"Tell me something you do know then."

He looked up, his eyes red and his face stained, and for a moment he looked so young I barely recognized him. He wiped his nose with the back of his hand.

"They cut me," he said with a weak laugh. "I was everything they wanted, and they cut me."

"The FBR," I realized.

"Every test. Every level. I was perfect. But all they saw was Jennings. They wanted him. He screwed up everything, on *purpose*, and they still wanted him. It was unbelievable."

Chase had told me he bucked the system trying to get home, but that had made his officers even more intent to break him. When he finally did comply, it was for my protection. It was unsettling to hear Tucker speak of it now.

"You know I enlisted early? Before my senior year," he continued. "The first day I could. I was waiting for that day. I'd been waiting since I was nine years old."

"What happened when you were nine?" I found myself asking.

"The War," he said bitterly. He rolled his ankle in a slow circle, winced. "My dad managed a grocery store. It was a small place, not one of the chains, one of the first to go under when the economy tanked. We lost everything." He looked up. "My dad's car. Then our stuff. The house. My mom lost her job, too. We had to get rations vouchers and stand in lines for food we used to sell."

My calves were falling asleep, and reluctantly I kneeled, feeling a strange connection to his story.

"It takes a toll," he said, and his jaw twitched. "That's what my mom used to say. *It takes a toll, Tuck.* That's why he drinks so much. That's why he beats the crap out of us. Because it takes a toll."

I didn't want to hear this. I didn't want to feel sorry for *him*, of all people.

"And then the soldiers came to town." He was wistful now. "And Dad got a job with Horizons, and things got all right after that. His boss knew a recruiter, and he'd come over to the house and talk to me about joining up. It made sense, you know? This officer, he had everything we used to have. Cars and a house and nobody screaming at each other. I made up my mind right then that that's what I was going to do."

"And when you saw what they did? What *you* did?"

His eyes blazed into mine with a sudden sharpness, and he stood, as if suddenly remembering who we both were.

I stood, too, and asked one more time. "Why are you here?"

He looked uncertain. "Because I'm a soldier," he said. "If I'm out there, I'm not anything."

The door swung open, making us both jump. Chase walked toward me, hands clasped behind his neck. They dropped when his gaze flicked to his old partner.

Without a word, Tucker left the room, but the doubt remained, deep in my chest.

"Everything all right?" Chase asked.

I nodded, but he stared at the closed door as if willing my answer to be different.

By now he'd have heard the plan. I knew he was going to argue. Say we couldn't do this. Say that I wasn't going without him. He was going to fight tooth and nail until we found another way, and I was going to tell him there *was* no other way. This was our window. It was a matter of time before the MM figured out I wasn't dead.

I placed my hand on his chest, steeling myself for a fight, but when our gazes met, I faltered. I remembered those minutes trapped beneath the table; how the question of his survival drove me to live. How panic and despair stalked just beyond the border of our memories. Maybe he was thinking of the same things, because he cast his gaze away, as though he couldn't look at me any longer.

He pulled a silver key from his pocket. "Chicago keeps a spare key to an FBR van at the hospital. Truck gave it to Jack before he left in case they needed a set of wheels before he got back." He shoved the key back into his pocket. "Looks like we've got our getaway car."

"Okay," I said.

Without further discussion, we left.

REFORMATION Parkway was only nine blocks west from where we'd left the others. The hospital was easy enough to find; it was right beside the FBR Recruit Barracks, where Chase and Tucker had lived during basic training.

I'd known our stakeout would be there before I saw it. I'd known because Truck, Jack, and the Chicago medic had told Sean and me about it in sick bay. This abandoned building, just across the street from the hospital and rehab center, was where Mags had been when she'd sniped off her own man.

We entered through a weakly boarded door in the back and climbed to the seventh floor, where we could spy on the five-story facility below without anyone catching a lateral glimpse of us across the street. As the hours passed we kept watch on that building, as if Rebecca might appear in any window, hip cocked, arms crossed, wondering what was taking so long.

Tucker sketched a layout of the building on one of the walls with a jagged piece of glass, identifying all exits and stairways. We split our meager rations. We slept in shifts. Chase woke me every half hour to check my pupils; it was like when we'd first joined the resistance, when he'd been healing from a concussion, only now our positions had been reversed. The disruptions didn't matter; after a couple hours I couldn't fall back asleep anyway. No one could. When Sean got too restless, Tucker agreed to relocate with him to the bottom floor to watch the rehab's entrance, leaving Chase and me alone.

"YOU'LL be fine. Tucker can't do anything to you once you're inside, not with all those soldiers standing around. He was right; he's got nowhere else to go if he screws this up."

Chase was already in uniform, methodically taking apart the gun Jack had given us, and cleaning it with the ripped remains of his T-shirt. I turned back to face the window, because it wouldn't do much good to mention he'd already cleaned it twice, or that we'd reviewed tomorrow's plan double that. I let him talk because he needed to, and I needed it, too. It eased the pounding in my head.

It was well after curfew, but the power across the street remained on at the hospital and rehabilitation center, as it did at the massive base behind it to the west. The triangle was completed by the prison across town. Three twinkling lights in the darkness. Their glow filtered in enough light to throw long, condemning shadows across the room.

I gazed down at the stone entranceway of the facility, wondering what lurked inside. I found myself imagining the strangest things—if the floor was tiled or linoleum, what color the walls were painted—grasping for something.

Did my mother know, walking into that jail cell, that she would never again come out? It seemed impossible that she couldn't have felt mortality breathing down her neck, as I did now. I wondered if she'd felt brave. I wondered if tomorrow I would be.

A chill took me despite the warm temperature in the room.

Before I realized what I was doing, I'd begun a list. An inventory of all the things I wanted to do before I died. There were trivial things, of course. Take a hot shower. Eat ice cream, like in the days before standardized power. But there were more important things, too. Find Billy, and if I could, get him to the safe house. Put up a memorial for my mother.

Be with Chase.

Hold his hand without keeping the other on a weapon. Have long talks about nothing important, but everything essential, like we used to. Not just fight, but *live*. We had to live fast these days, because we died fast, too.

I slid the uniform scarf over my head and let it fall to the floor, then opened the top buttons of my blouse, finding it suddenly too tight around my neck. I took a deep breath, then another.

Chase trailed off, and for an instant I thought he might

be preoccupied by the weapon, but then I heard the click of the metal atop the table and the rustle of clothing when he stood.

He approached slowly, like a stalking wolf, or maybe it was the nerves burning low in my belly that seemed to exaggerate each second. Before he reached me he stopped, close enough that I could feel his warmth. Feel his eyes traveling over my reflection in the window, more intimate than any touch.

He shook his head and glanced back at the table, as if he'd forgotten how he'd arrived here. Then he swallowed. Raked a hand through his hair. Tried to conceal an embarrassed smile behind a serious mask.

"Are you paying attention? Or just trying to distract me?"

"Trying to distract you," I said. *"Obviously."*

His amusement swelled, then faded, leaving me anxiously awaiting his next move. It came slowly: his tentative fingertips found the back of my jaw and trailed down the nape of my neck, stopping right before my collarbone. Making me aware of nothing but the feel of him.

"I remember you used to like to be kissed here," he said, voice thick. "Do you still?"

I had to concentrate in order to respond.

"I don't know," I whispered. "No one has since you."

In the reflection I saw his lips part slightly. My heart beat so loudly in my chest I wondered if he could hear it. If he knew it beat that way for him, and no one else.

He leaned down, the tip of his nose skimming my earlobe and lowering, until his lips found that spot, *his* spot, that made my knees weak and my whole body tremble.

He turned me slowly, fingers weaving through my hair. He came closer, until we shared the same breath. His lips were warm and soft and full of restraint, but as the seconds melted together his arms pulled me tighter, and his mouth became more urgent, hot breath and grazing teeth, and the firm, soft feel of his lower lip between mine. He felt it, as I did. The moments counting down, pulling us apart, and if we didn't hold on to each other fate would beat us, separate us, and we would be lost to each other forever.

His large, calloused hands surrounded my ribs, untucking the coarse blouse, sliding gently down to my hips. Each place he touched lit with goose bumps and sparks of heat. *Remember that,* I told myself. *How his hands feel right now. Remember every second with him.*

Our breathing became ragged and uneven. I grabbed the hem of my blouse and pulled it over my head, expecting to feel self-conscious or too skinny or too plain, but his lips parted, and his eyes grew round, and all of those thoughts disappeared. His fingertip slid just under the waistband of my skirt, circling my belly, and I grasped at the round wooden buttons of his canvas jacket, feeling an unquenchable thirst to be close to him. When my injured wrist made the task cumbersome, he tried to help, but our nervous hands fumbled. We laughed at our lack of grace.

Then, I took a step back and laid his jacket on the floor,

spreading it out like a blanket. He watched, silently realizing the weight of my intentions.

He didn't respond at first, but then nodded once, seemingly at a loss for words.

I sat down on our clothing and he kneeled before me, holding my face in his hands, his bruised thumbs stroking my cheekbones. *This is it,* I thought, swallowing. And I didn't even have to remind myself to remember this, because I knew without a doubt, I would.

But his eyes drifted over my bare shoulder, to the floor and his coat, and his brows pulled together.

I covered my chest with one arm. "What's wrong?"

"Is this okay?" The vulnerability in his gaze startled me. Made me realize he wasn't asking if I was okay with this dusty room, but with him.

"Yes."

He said nothing for a moment, then blinked. "You wouldn't regret . . ."

"No," I said. My eyes lowered.

He hesitated. "I've screwed up so much already. If you had second thoughts . . ."

"I wouldn't," I said.

He sighed through his teeth. "You say that now." But he was already leaning back over me, brushing my hair out of my eyes and skimming his fingertips along my jaw.

"I wouldn't," I whispered again. "This might be our only chance."

He stopped. "What?"

"Nothing," I said hurriedly.

He sat back. "What do you mean?"

I pulled his jacket over my shoulders, feeling very exposed suddenly.

"We don't have much time left in case . . . you know. In case something happens tomorrow."

His jaw fell slack. "You're not planning on coming back."

"I am. I mean, I want to." *As if dying were a choice?* I stared at my feet. "You haven't thought about it?"

He jolted up and began to pace, leaving me alone on the floor.

"Of course I've thought about it," he said roughly.

"Then what is it?"

"I'll find you. If something happens I'll find you. We'll be okay. We're going to South Carolina." He sounded so desperate to believe that truth that I knew it was thin enough to shatter.

"And if it's not okay?"

"It will be!" he shouted, making my back straighten. He inhaled sharply, trying to recompose himself.

"You're not going."

"*Chase*—"

"*You* don't even think you're going to live through this! What was I thinking?"

I stood as tall as I could, the tears threatening to spill over. My heart was breaking. I could feel it tearing apart inside of me. He knew, he *had* to know what this felt like, this guilt-punched hole inside of me.

"You were thinking that if *you* could change things, you would," I said.

My mother's spirit filled the room. Without blame or accusation, but she was there nonetheless.

He stopped suddenly and stared out the window, not at the facility, but down the street at the barracks where he'd lived when we'd been apart.

A minute passed. Two.

"I would do anything to bring her back," he murmured.

"I love you."

The words were out before I'd even thought to say them, released by some force beyond my control. Instantly they consumed me, overwhelmed me, like the fact of my love was the only truth I'd ever known. The only truth there was. *Chase Jennings, I love you. I love the boy you were and the man that you've become and even when I don't like you at all I still love you because you are you, kind and safe and good, because you understand me and are not afraid.*

As the honesty of my words sunk in, he became very still. Statue still. And I waited, more raw and vulnerable than ever.

He took a long shaking breath, and in it, my heart clutched.

"You don't fight fair."

"Yeah, well, neither do you," I said. It was true. Risks weren't so risky when you had no one to lose.

With a short, dry chuckle he came to me and wrapped his arms around my waist and lowered his forehead to mine, closing his eyes. My fingers traced the pink corkscrew scar across his biceps, and I was reminded of a day he'd nearly died for my protection.

"Now's where you say it back," I prompted.

"Say what?" When I hit him he grabbed my hand and pressed it against his chest. "I love you, Em. I've loved you since I was eight years old, and I'll love you my whole life."

His smile was so unguarded, so true. The tears clouded my vision, and my chest hurt, and I didn't know how it was possible to feel so happy and so terrified at the same time.

"What happens now?" My hands flattened over his chest.

"Now I go find Tucker," he said reluctantly.

Of all the things I'd hoped he'd say, this was not one of them.

"*Why?*"

He kissed my temple, letting his lips linger there while he continued. "Because tomorrow, I need him to do what I can't."

CHASE came back an hour later looking edgy. I didn't know what he'd said to Tucker, and he didn't offer it. Instead we sat beside each other, watching the rehab center, and talked, *really* talked. About everything else.

We talked about Cara, about Wallace and Billy, about Sean and Tucker and Rebecca. About the guys from Chicago, and how I'd found Jack, in shock, on the tunnel floor, and seen my mother in some concussion-induced vision. We talked about Beth and the place we'd once called home, knowing that history carried itself in the body and soul, not a physical location, not in letters burned in a fire or a magazine trapped beneath the rubble, and that now we had each other when we needed to remember. And we kissed. Sometimes gently, sometimes with the same frenzied passion as before. Sometimes in the middle of our sentences, when we'd simply forget what we were talking about. In those short hours we purged our secrets and held each other and prayed that time would both slow and hasten because just like the night before he was drafted, we knew tomorrow would leave us forever changed.

Eventually, I fell asleep on the floor with my head on his thigh. The last thing I remembered was the feel of his fingers combing through my hair.

BEFORE dawn he snuck across the street to the hospital parking garage with the spare key given to us by Chicago. I bit my nails to nubs until light, when he pulled out onto the street like any other driver, and appeared around the backside of the abandoned building in an FBR van. Tucker sat in the front, and Sean and I slipped silently into the middle row of seats, where I rubbed the St. Michael pendant around my neck and hoped that I hadn't used up all its luck.

"I wouldn't blame you if you backed out." It took me a moment to realize Sean was talking to me, not Tucker.

Was he crazy? Our plan was contingent on my presence. "I'm not going to back out."

He nodded out the window, as if expecting this answer.

"What if I said I didn't want you to come?"

"I'd say good luck getting Rebecca without me."

He shrugged. "I'd figure something out."

"Well you don't have to," I said. "I'm coming."

He was quiet for a several seconds. "Don't do anything stupid, okay? I'm not losing you, too."

"Sean." I forced a smile, but it might have looked a little scary. "When have I ever done anything stupid?"

"Perfect," he muttered.

It took less than five minutes to reach an intersection with Reformation Parkway. My pulse thrummed with the engine motor as we weaved through other FBR vehicles onto the main street. Chase slowly veered across the lane to park in front of Horizons Physical Rehabilitation.

The sidewalk was crowded with people. Most of them wore navy FBR uniforms. I spotted a couple other Sisters, hustling to their destinations with their heads down. They didn't exude the same confidence in this setting that the men did.

The sideling patches of grass were all manicured. There were trees planted, too, surrounded by little wrought-iron fences and landscaped flowers. The stone face of the building was graffiti-free, with high glass windows and a trash can to the right that wasn't overflowing with garbage. I felt like we'd driven into the past. It looked like someplace from before the War.

We're coming, Rebecca.

Anticipation dripped through me. Here, at last, was my chance to make things right. To fix what I'd broken when I'd blackmailed her and Sean into helping me escape. Here was my chance for redemption.

"Hopefully this won't take long," said Tucker.

Sean was out of the car first. Tucker followed, and then

Chase and I were alone. He stayed in the front seat and kept his head down, so as not to attract the attention of the passersby. We hadn't said good-bye and we wouldn't now.

I pulled off the gold band he'd stolen from the Loftons' and reached for his hand, pushing it onto his pinky finger. His fist began to shake as soon as I let it go.

"Thirty minutes," he said. "And then I'm coming in."

I nodded and stepped outside, knowing I would rather die than have Chase follow me into that building.

CHAPTER
19

I WENT over the plan in my head as we walked up to the entrance. Most of it relied on Tucker. It still seemed beyond surreal that I was putting my life in the hands of my mother's murderer. I reminded myself that he'd helped us out of the fire at the Wayland Inn. That he'd stayed to evacuate the tunnels, and seemed almost human when he'd told me about his family.

He hasn't killed me so far, I told myself. But it was small consolation.

There was a glass-covered posting of the Statutes near the entrance, but I couldn't see the five most wanted in conjunction with the sniper shootings. Maybe the FBR still thought that Ember Miller had died two days ago in Greeneville. Still, I kept my head bowed, just in case.

Tucker walked straight up to the front door and pulled it open, allowing me to step into a brightly lit lobby with a black-and-white checkered floor. A Sister of Salvation sat behind a glass window, smiling in a plastic way. She had a broad forehead and flat hair, pulled back in a pencil-thin braid. By the time we reached her, my nerves had settled into that same eerie calm I remembered from my escape from the base. I was glad for it. I needed a clear head now.

"Welcome to Horizons Physical Rehabilitation. How may I help you?" she chimed.

"Patient transfer," said Tucker.

"I'll need a copy of your orders, please." She reached her hand under the bottom of the glass expectantly.

My fists clenched. Tucker hadn't said we'd need paperwork.

"Is Sprewell here?" Tucker asked irritably, as though he couldn't be bothered with this girl and her silly rules. I wasn't entirely sure the sentiment wasn't genuine.

"Um . . . yes, sir. Do you have an appointment?" she asked, her mouth now drawn tight at the corners.

"We'll wait."

He stared at her until she stood up and walked away.

"You don't have to be so rude," I whispered.

"Not now," snapped Sean. Tucker smirked.

The Sister returned and sat back down. "Sergeant Sprewell will be with you in just a moment."

"Thank you," said Tucker, not particularly kindly.

Church of America music was piped in through the speakers. The soprano singing struck a note that gave me the chills. I nursed my sore wrist and tried to focus on relaxing the bundled muscles in my neck, but the Sister kept staring at me.

"We've met, haven't we?" she finally asked.

I dropped my chin and looked away. "I don't think so."

"Oh, I'm sure of it," she said. "I recognize your face. . . ."

For several blank seconds the words caught in my throat and I seriously contemplated running. Then I remembered what Beth had said about the arrival of the Sisters in Louisville.

"Dallas," I said. "I trained at the center in Dallas."

"That's it," she said. "I trained there, too." She smiled again, in her hollow way.

An atrocious buzzer sounded and I jumped to attention. A moment later, a ruddy-faced guard with beady eyes— SPREWELL, according to his name badge—pushed through the locked door on the left side of the check-in window.

His eyes drew to me first, with a look so slimy I felt the need to take a shower. I instantly despised him.

"Still guarding cripples, huh, Sprewell?" chided Tucker.

I bristled at the word *cripple*, thinking of the Chicago fighter that Mags had shot. Then I held my breath, praying that Tucker hadn't been too bold. Thankfully the guard recognized him and laughed.

"Miss me that much, Morris?"

Something in his mannerisms reminded me of how Tucker had been at the Knoxville base. Cocky. Too clever for his own good.

He shook Tucker's hand, and Tucker smiled, like he belonged in this world. I shifted, moving closer to Sean and the handgun in his belt.

"What brings you back this way?" asked Sprewell.

"Transfer. The Sisters put in a request to bring one of your girls to their order in Knoxville."

"So that's why you're in mixed company." The guard's brows went flat with indifference. "Any gimp in particular?"

"Her name is Rebecca Lansing," said Sean, sweat beading on his forehead.

I tensed. My heart hammered against my ribcage.

Sprewell's chin lifted. "This a pal of yours, Morris?"

I was done talking to Sprewell. I wanted to see Rebecca *now.*

"Ms. Lansing is to set an example for the other Sisters," I said. "To steer them away from a life of sin."

Truck had said this is what they'd done to that poor Chicago soldier with the broken neck. Toured him around the base. I hoped it wasn't too unreasonable that the Sisters of Salvation would do the same thing.

Sprewell glanced at Tucker, as if to verify that I'd spoken out of turn. I hid the irritated sigh that threatened to sneak out. It seemed men could only address men these days.

"They're a little bold down south, aren't they, Morris?" he said with a ghost of a smile. "The ones here are . . . what's it called . . . like those bugs that don't have any male or female parts. *Asexual,* that's it."

"We *are* on a time crunch, Sprewell," said Tucker.

He sighed. "Fine, all right. Come on back and we'll run your IDs."

The three of us froze, refusing to look at one another. Had Tucker forgotten this crucial step? Was this an accidental omission, or a deliberate one? I looked out the front window, seeing the van still parked on the curb. There was still a chance to run for it.

But I couldn't run. Any doubt that Rebecca was here had been erased. Anyway, I wouldn't make it ten feet before Sprewell had shot me in the back.

I followed the boys through the locked entry. There was no turning back now.

ON the opposite side of the door was a long counter, where a Sister sat beside a young soldier doing paperwork. He had a strained look on his face, and averted his eyes from Sprewell, out of fear or aversion, I didn't know.

"ID checks," said Tucker, trying to sound casual. "That's new since I trained here."

"Is it?" asked Sprewell, but he wasn't particularly interested.

"Name?" asked the soldier behind the desk. He pushed nervously at his dirty blond hair as though he was used to it being longer than the short soldier's clip. It was a move that reminded me of Billy. It made him seem younger, and elicited a pang of worry for my friend.

Sean hesitated.

"Randolph. James," he lied. I shot him a quick glance and then looked away. Randolph had been another guard at the reformatory. One I didn't regard fondly.

"Where are your name badges?" asked Sprewell skeptically. "That's a disciplinary action if your CO finds out."

My hands fisted.

"Not today," lied Tucker. "Cleaning Services lost them."

Sprewell snorted. "Women."

"Come on," said Tucker. "You know me, that's ID check enough. Let me get this girl so we can get back on the road."

The soldier was still searching the mainframe for Sean's alias.

"Yeah, fine. Having a tough time, New Guy?" chided Sprewell, then snorted. "Harper couldn't count to ten with his shoes off."

The soldier's—Harper's—face reddened. He glanced at me quickly, but I looked away.

"It's the whole class of new recruits," said Tucker conversationally, as though Harper wasn't sitting right there. "We got two in Knoxville—neither one can read."

Sprewell smirked. "Digging up the bottom feeders, that's what it's come to. Pathetic, but I guess we need the manpower. I'm sure you've heard all that talk about evacuating the rat nests. Now that we've got those heat-seeking missiles it's cake; fifty warm bodies within fifty yards of one another, that's all it takes to burn the house down. Those things just need a point in the right direction and BOOM!"

My throat grew too dry to swallow.

"LDEDs," said Tucker. "Yeah, I've heard about those."

"Too bad you weren't here yesterday. Got a tip that a whole load of violators were hiding out in the sewers. Right under our feet." Sprewell stomped one boot. "We sent the roof down on 'em. Whole damn compound shook when they blew the place." He snickered as he retrieved a clipboard from behind the desk. "Let's see. Just a rental, right? You're bringing her back sometime next week?"

My teeth had clenched so hard I thought they might break.

"Sure," said Tucker thinly. "If that's all you can part with her."

Sprewell laughed and looked up a patient chart while Tucker signed the paperwork.

"Lansing, let's see . . . Fourth floor. Room 408," he said.

I was already walking to the elevator.

"Peace be with you," called the Sister.

"And also with you," I responded over my shoulder with a smile.

"YOU'RE welcome," said Tucker as soon as the three of us were alone in the elevator.

"Don't jinx it," I told him. He laughed. Sean wiped the sweat from his brow on the sleeve of his stolen uniform jacket.

"Come on, come on, come on," he said as each floor lit up on the board.

I bounced on my heels, willing the elevator to go faster. How long had we been in this building? Ten minutes? Fifteen? Chase was going to follow soon if we didn't hurry up.

LDEDs. Long Distance Explosive Devices. I'd heard of these once before; one of the other four who'd been wanted for the sniper shootings had been protesting a demonstration of the bombs. Sprewell and Tucker had said the heat-seeking missiles just needed to be aimed in the right direction, toward fifty warm bodies. Who had told them that the resistance would gather at that time beneath the city?

The elevator opened, revealing a cream-colored hallway and a nurse's station, manned by Sisters and a middle-aged doctor in a white medical coat who didn't seem affected one way or another by our presence. A quick survey revealed that Sean and Tucker were the only soldiers on the floor. Truck had been right about the security here, but my relief dissolved as quickly as it had arrived.

A man sat in a wheelchair against the wall wearing only his underwear. His legs had been amputated just above the knees, capped by bandages that were soaking through with blood. Branching up his bare white thighs were the red fingers of infection. His torso and face were flushed with fever. His eyes stared through us with no registration.

I wondered if he were a soldier who tried to escape or disobeyed an order, or a civilian who'd crossed the wrong officer. I couldn't let myself think of it. We only had time for Rebecca. The tension in the air ratcheted up a notch.

Our shoes squeaked over the newly waxed floors. *Don't rush, don't draw attention*, I told myself. Sean beat me to 408, but there was no one inside.

As we returned to the attendants' station the elevators dinged and opened again. Sprewell appeared, a look of consternation on his face. He was holding a paper in his hand. A computer printout. Was it my photo? Had the soldier downstairs remembered my face from the Missing Persons report? Involuntarily, I glanced at the gun on his belt, thinking of the code one.

"Morris, I need to speak with you."

Tucker stiffened and walked slowly back toward his old friend.

My brain was reeling. What did they have to talk about? An instant filter through the possibilities left me with two options: either Sprewell had scanned Tucker's name anyway and figured out he'd been dishonorably discharged, or Tucker had set us up.

I tilted my head, trying not to eavesdrop too obviously. The chalky music grated down my spine.

"You're kidding," I heard Tucker say in a shocked tone. He called to Sean: "Get the girl. I have to take care of something."

Tucker was going somewhere with Sprewell alone. He was going to rat us out. I opened my mouth to say something, *anything* to make him stay, but my throat tied in knots, like Rebecca herself was gripping my vocal cords. We couldn't follow Tucker. We had to find her.

I met Tucker's eyes once as he entered the elevator. The concern in them was evident enough to spray me with doubt. Maybe he wasn't turning me in. Maybe he really was the one in trouble.

Either way we were running out of time.

Sean sped back to the nurse's station and harshly stated Rebecca's name. The Sister looked frightened.

"Yes, sir. She's either in physical therapy at the end of the hall"—she pointed to the right—"or in the rec room, that way." She pointed the opposite direction.

Sean took off toward physical therapy, and I went the other way.

Slow down, I told myself.

I passed several patient rooms. Most of the doors were closed. All but Room 408, and its neighbor, 409. Inside, a withered man laid on the plastic covered mattress, staring blankly at the ceiling, his mouth open and crusting white. He was crying softly.

I shoved through the door at the end of the hall.

The room was empty but for a table in the center holding a ceramic pot and a plastic tray of pansies. There was a girl in yellow scrubs sitting in a plastic chair facing the side window. Her blond locks, once so long and beautiful, had been shorn to a tight cap around her skull.

Rebecca.

Suddenly, I was bombarded with memories. The first time I'd seen her, with her springy hair and plastic smile. Her unstoppable love for the sandy-haired guard, Sean Banks. Sitting beside her on my bed late into the night strategizing my escape. The night I'd told her about Chase.

She was not a friend at first, and she might not be now, but for a time, she was all I had.

I took a step forward, feeling a cool drip of nerves slide down my spine. If the Sisters were so casual in their supervision, there had to be another security measure in place. Maybe there were cameras, or another posted guard that I'd missed. . . . They were insane if they thought a girl who'd snuck out of her room at the reformatory every single night would stay, unguarded, in a space like this.

"Rebecca," I said cautiously.

Ahead of me, I saw her slender body grow rigid.

"I don't want to pray today." She did not turn around.

My heart cracked at the sound of her voice.

When I rounded the table, Rebecca's nose was down. Even though she wasn't looking at me, I could see a bitter expression pulling at her once angelic face. She was repotting the pansies. Her fingers were black from the soil.

But she looked okay. No broken neck. No feeding tube. With the exception of her hair, she looked exactly as she had when we'd parted. A single wave of cool relief washed over me.

"Let's go," I said, focused again.

Her head shot up, and her pretty blue eyes went round with shock. The mustard-colored remnants of a bruise along her chin and jaw became apparent and elicited a strong twinge of guilt.

"*Ember?*" She kept the flowers on her lap.

"We're getting you out of here," I whispered.

"What? You . . . wait . . . no."

I must have looked surprised, because that's what I felt. "What do you mean *no*? We've got to hurry. Sean is—"

"Not Sean," she said firmly, but there was an edge to her voice. "Ember, you have to leave."

"What?" She was mad at me, that was the only explanation for why she was acting this way. She had good reason, but still, I was here, I was going to get her out. Surely she had to see that.

I realized she was probably afraid, but this seemed crazy. She'd attacked Brock and the guards with her bare hands for what they'd done to Sean, and now she was too scared to leave a hospital?

"You're not taking me anywhere. You're leaving. *Now.*"
Her voice hitched. If she kept this up, the Sisters were going
to hear her.

My brain couldn't wrap around this. "You don't *want* to
leave?"

"No. I want to stay," she said resolutely.

"We can't talk about this now. There's no time." I glanced
over my shoulder. No one was coming. Yet. I snatched the
flowerpot off her lap.

"No! You don't understand!" Her voice cracked. "He can't
see me like this!" Her perfect cheeks were splotchy red now.
They stood out in sharp contrast to her yellow jumpsuit.

"Like what? With short hair? Rebecca, he won't care."

"That's not what I mean!"

Sean burst through the door at the same time I jerked Rebecca to a stand.

Only she didn't stand. She fell flat on her face.

"What the . . ." I knelt to the ground to pick her up.

"I told you!" She was crying now.

Time slowed, and everything became crystal clear.

There was absolutely no concern that Rebecca was going
to run because she *couldn't* run. That explained the limited
military presence. That was why Sisters ran this place.

I closed my eyes and saw it happen, just as it did at the
reformatory. Rebecca in her gray uniform charging Ms. Brock,
the headmistress. The guards trying to contain her. Then
crack! A baton colliding into Rebecca's back. Her sharp cry
of pain. We'd been separated. I'd never known the extent of
Rebecca's injuries.

"Sean!" I snapped. "I need your help!" I tried to pull Rebecca up, but she couldn't support herself. Nothing below her knees moved. Her thin legs splayed limply to the side. *Paralyzed.* I heard the word in my head but it was wrong. It had to be wrong. She could walk, she just wasn't trying.

Rebecca moaned softly, a terrifying, desolate sound, and I knew then that she could try all she wanted; she'd never walk again.

At that moment the fire alarm went off.

"Becca?" Sean asked, confused. He knelt beside her.

"G-get a wheelchair. Where is it, Rebecca?" The blood had drained from my head and extremities, and I felt very cold. The siren bit into my eardrums, and a bright light from above the door began to flash. Fear of another kind filled me. I had had about enough burning buildings to last a lifetime.

"She doesn't need a wheelchair," said Sean. "Get up, Becca."

She didn't get up. She was wailing softly into her hands. He reached for her arm but didn't touch her. Like he couldn't. Like there was an invisible wall between them.

I scanned the room, landing on a pair of crutches and leg braces against a cabinet on the opposite side of the room. Whoever had brought her here had left them far out of her reach. A surge of fury rose within me so immediately that I nearly screamed.

I sprinted toward them, gathering the intricate black plastic braces and the modified crutches, and returned to the floor.

"How do I put these on?" I demanded.

"Becca, look at me," said Sean.

A Sister, about my age, pushed through the door.

"Oh dear!" she said. "Did she have a fall?"

"Back off," I growled at her. She stopped short.

"There's a fire drill," she said cautiously, as if we couldn't hear it. "We've got to move everyone we can outside."

I shuddered to think about the people that couldn't be moved.

"How do I put these braces on?" I demanded of the Sister.

Sean didn't wait for an explanation. He scooped Rebecca up off the floor and carried her out of the room.

"She's being transported to another facility," I said between my teeth. The Sister's mouth had formed a small o.

The siren was much louder in the hall. I stuffed Rebecca's crutches under my arm and clapped my hands to my ears. Girls darted into rooms, shouting directions at one another. I inspected the chaos, convinced that this was some ploy to catch us.

Tucker was nowhere to be seen.

"The stairs are that way!" shouted the doctor over the noise. "The elevators shut down when the alarm is pulled!" He was pushing a man in a wheelchair toward the emergency exit. The patient cried out in pain, pressing his hands to his ears.

My breath was coming fast, raking my throat. We hurried to the emergency exit and joined the crowd of Sisters assisting amputees and wheelchair-bound patients down the stairs. Two girls had dropped their sweet Sister façade and were snapping at each other about how to get a patient's walker out of a crack in the handrail. I prayed that this was simply a drill; they were leaving a lot of people behind.

"Blend in," I told Sean unnecessarily. I might be able to do so, but not him. He was the only soldier in sight.

It didn't matter what I told him anyway. He wasn't listening.

Rebecca's hands remained over her face, a shield from Sean's blank stare. Her legs hung over his arm. I could not swallow the lump in my throat.

Truck's words from before the blast kept echoing in my head. *What were we supposed to do with him once we got him out? We can't support that kind of care down here.*

She's okay, I told myself. *We'll make her safe. We'll take care of her. She'll be fine.*

Please let her be fine.

We'd made it to the landing of the third floor when I saw the other soldier. He was running up the stairs, shoving through the crowds of Sisters into the second floor hallway.

My heart stopped cold.

Chase.

We'd taken too long. He'd come in after me. He'd probably been the one to pull the alarm. And now he had no idea where to look, and was going the wrong way. I opened my mouth to shout for his attention, but he had already disappeared behind the heavy silver door.

"I'll meet you at the car," I shouted in Sean's ear, throwing the braces and crutches onto Rebecca's lap. Without another word I shoved down the last flight of stairs toward the second floor.

My heart was racing as I burst through the heavy door. There were no Sisters here, no doctors either. I heard the weakened call of one of the patients left behind in his room and fought the urge to follow his voice.

"Hello?" I screamed over the siren. I didn't want to say his name if I didn't have to. Eerie worship music rang between the blasts of the siren. My blood burned in frustration. How was he supposed to hear me with all of this racket? How could I hear him?

"Hello!" I shouted again, this time running around the nurse's station. I slid on the slick linoleum floor, grasping the circular desk for balance and sending papers flying through the air.

We saw each other at the same time. He didn't hesitate. He ran toward me from the far side of the hallway. As he drew near I could see the fear creasing his forehead. We collided; he grabbed my hand and whipped me after him.

Our way was blocked.

We stopped short, and I slid again, righting myself just before I fell. A soldier stood before the door ten feet away, his face drawn with anxiety and fear, his gun raised at Chase's chest. I didn't have to glance at his gold name badge to know it read HARPER.

In a flash, Chase had drawn his weapon and jerked me behind him.

Nothing happened. No one fired.

I felt every part of me extending like roots down my legs, through my heels, and into the slick linoleum. I couldn't move. I was frozen. Stuck. It was like a nightmare, when the monster is chasing you down, and you are helpless to defend yourself.

"I know who you are!" Harper yelled over the noise. "Jennings and Miller. We followed your case in basic training. Put down your weapon and come with me."

He was new on the job; I'd figured that downstairs. If he'd followed our story in training, he must have just been sent to work in the past few weeks.

More blaring siren. More church music. I willed my body to move, to do *anything*, but it was like I was shoving through wet concrete.

"We're leaving," Chase responded. "You can let us leave. You can let us walk through the door. No one has to know."

Chase lowered the gun a fraction of an inch. Every beat of my heart felt like an explosion in my chest.

No, Chase, I thought. *Don't trust him.* But gone was the soldier who'd rescued me from the reformatory, the cold, fragmented soul who knew death too intimately. Back was Chase—*my* Chase—who believed in change.

The soldier's hand was visibly shaking. Beads of sweat blossomed on his hairline and dripped down his jaw. I watched his Adam's apple bob as he attempted to swallow. His fear was all around us, choking us, more potent than my fear, which only demanded survival. His fear weighed options. Weighed the consequences of Chase's proposal.

If the MM knew he'd let us escape, they would kill him.

"Lower your weapon!" Harper repeated again, his voice breaking.

I thought of Billy, and how his voice broke because he

was only fourteen. This soldier was only a few years older. He could be the same age as me. We could have sat next to each other in high school. We could have taken the same tests, and stood in line to punch our meal passes in the cafeteria. We could have been friends in a different life.

"It doesn't have to be this way," Chase said.

"Do it or I'll shoot you!" he shouted.

A frightened cry snuck out between my lips. The soldier's weapon jerked toward me, and I saw, straight on down the barrel of his gun, how the whites of his eyes surrounded his brown irises.

My still body grew hard and fragile like glass. If he fired, I would shatter.

"Look at me," Chase said firmly. "Don't look at her. Look at me."

I begged my body to move. I tried to breathe, but I couldn't. The soldier aimed back at Chase's chest.

"I'm taking you in," he said. "I'm giving you five seconds to lower your weapon."

"They taught me that one, too," Chase said. "Back in Negotiations. I trained here, too, did you know that?"

"Four seconds," said the soldier. His hands were still shaking.

The breath shuddered out of my body. My heels moved at last. My fists gripped. The freeze had passed.

"Come with us!" I heard myself say.

His gaze jerked my way, but Chase blocked his path.

"Three."

"She's right," Chase said, the urgency now clear in his voice. "Come with us. We can protect you."

"Lower it! Two seconds!"

"Please!" I begged.

"You don't want to shoot me," Chase said rapidly. "I don't want to shoot you either. I promise, we can help you. We can protect your family."

The soldier twitched. Chase lowered his weapon slowly, aiming it at Harper's knees.

"We can keep your family safe," continued Chase. "I know what it's like. They hurt someone I cared about, too. They threatened to hurt her more if I didn't follow orders, but I got out and you can do the same."

"You don't know that!" Harper choked on the words. The tears blurred my vision.

"I got her away from them," Chase said. He removed one hand from the firearm, and held it up for Harper to see.

The soldier's gun dropped an inch. Then another. A wave of dizziness came on, and I felt my knees begin to buckle.

"Come with us." Chase took a tentative step forward.

"I can't . . ." the soldier was crying now, that heaving, snot-filled crying that wracked spasms through his body. I couldn't hear him over the sirens, but I saw it, and that was enough.

"You can," said Chase. "Let's go."

One more step forward.

The soldier's chin shot up, and he burned Chase with an agonized, distrustful stare.

"You're not going anywhere," he said.

Everything slowed.

I saw Harper's gun lift, as if pulling through water. I saw his eyes change, the lights in them go dark. Chase lunged for his arm, hitting him hard in the break at the elbow, and then they were locked together, chest to chest. They hit the ground in a streak of blue. Chase's gun slid out, bumping against my foot. Before I could bend to retrieve it, the sound of gunfire ripped through my body, and I screamed.

Chase scrambled back.

We sat in stunned silence for a full beat, watching the blood pool on the floor from Harper's chest. He didn't cough or choke, he didn't rasp words like the carrier in Harrisonburg. He died instantly.

And then, in a flood, everything within me burst into motion. My ears rang, my pulse scrambled. Even my muscles burned to run.

Chase felt Harper's neck for a pulse. He grabbed the dead boy's uniform and shook him. "No!" he shouted. And then, "Get up, man. Come on. Get *up!*"

I grabbed Chase around the waist, feeling the quake echo through my body. He was still shaking the dead soldier; both guns were lying to the side.

"Chase!" I grasped his face, turned it toward me. His face was blank with shock.

"Look at me!" I shouted, just as he'd told the soldier moments before. "Look at me, Chase! We need to go! We need to get out of here!"

His breath came in one haggard gasp, and as his eyes readjusted, his hands cupped mine, and he staggered to a stand.

And then he was back. He grabbed my hand, scooped his weapon off the floor, and together we skirted around the body through the exit.

CHAPTER
20

THE chaos in the stairway was thinning, but the way was still blocked by Sisters guiding patients down the steps. They hadn't heard the gunshot over the alarm. They didn't know what we'd done.

Chase released my hand so we wouldn't draw attention. The loss of his touch felt like something breaking off of me. My airway tightened, made it hard to breathe.

Put it away, I told myself. *Lock it up.* That was the only way to get out of here alive.

Finally we reached the bottom of the stairs. I kept my head down, peering through my fringed curtain of black hair as we entered the foyer, where we'd nearly had ID scans, and then through the buzzing door, into the lobby.

It wasn't hard to find Tucker. He was alone, and a foot taller than the Sisters. His brows lifted in surprise when he recognized Chase, but he had the good sense to flatten his expression. As he steadily shoved toward us, my gaze darted from side to side in search of an ambush in these last twenty feet before our freedom.

There was a bottleneck effect near the door. We packed in tighter. When Tucker got close enough, I fought the urge to punch him in the face. He'd been the one to tell me Rebecca was here. He'd known she'd been transported to this facility, so he had to have known why, and he hadn't once mentioned her injuries.

But he'd also gotten us inside.

"Have you seen Sean?" I asked him.

"I saw him carry her outside," he answered. "She can't walk?"

"Don't pretend you didn't know," I whipped back, too quietly for anyone to hear above the chaos. His eyes changed then. From that haughty, hateful edge to something different. Something I'd never seen before.

"Would it have mattered if I did?"

It was honest, maybe the first honest thing he'd said to me. And if I were being honest with myself, too, I would have said *no*. It wouldn't have mattered. I would still have come here.

Each shuffling step filled my head with more crazy thoughts: Harper wasn't dead; he was chasing us, blood oozing from that anemone-shaped hole in his chest. Others were coming, too. Maybe the siren had created too much interference for the radio, but he could have called us in before that.

We had to get out of here. I wanted to push them all out of my way and run, but I couldn't. We were packed like sardines; I couldn't lift my arms, much less shove someone.

Finally we toppled out the exit and onto the sidewalk. The van was still there, ready to go. My chest tightened when I saw how Sean struggled to load Rebecca in the backseat.

Chase and I walked as calmly as we could around the hood, but once I was seated in the middle row he slammed the door behind me. Tucker was already in the passenger seat. Sisters and patients filtered onto Reformation Parkway, blocking our path.

My fingers tapped on my thighs as Chase eased onto the main drag.

"Get out of the way," Tucker told the crowd. His voice angered me. Why had he helped us? Good deeds didn't erase evil, even if they did even things out a little. Did he think he could make up for what he'd done?

Did I think I could make up for what *I'd* done? My friend might never walk again. Harper certainly wouldn't.

I glanced to the backseat. Rebecca was sitting on one side, hunched over her knees. Sean was on the other, his face pale. They were not touching.

"Sean," I said between chattering teeth. He looked over slowly, as though there was a delay in his hearing. What was he doing? She was broken and frightened, and his distance only reinforced that she was damaged.

"I didn't know you couldn't walk," he said. His stare returned out the window.

"Sean!" I snapped. Rebecca sobbed loudly.

Tucker fell back in the seat, hollering excitedly. The path had cleared, and soon Chase was speeding down Reformation Parkway away from the hospital.

"What happened to Sprewell?" I demanded.

"We had a *disagreement* about my discharge status," Tucker answered, high on adrenaline. "He'll be sleeping it off in the elevator while they clear the building. Good thing the place isn't really burning, huh?"

"*You* pulled the fire alarm?" I asked incredulously. I thought it had been Chase, but it made sense. Chase wouldn't have been able to get past the front desk if not for the commotion.

"Go ahead and thank me," he answered.

I didn't. But for the first time, I felt a glimmer of respect for him. For the person who'd let us believe Rebecca was healthy and the last person to see Cara alive. For my mother's killer.

Like a blow it hit me. We'd killed someone, too. We'd crossed a line today—one we could never take back.

Tucker kicked back in his seat. "What a rush. I get why you like it."

"Shut up," said Chase coldly.

"Come on, Jennings," he said, obviously unfazed by the impenetrable tension in the car. "I thought we were pals again."

"Shut up!" Chase roared. His knuckles were white on the steering wheel.

I felt a sob bubble up in my throat.

No. Not yet.

We passed a line of supply trucks, all blue with the FBR logo and motto on the side. So much blue. Blue everywhere. Watching.

"Where are we going?" My voice trembled.

"To the waterfront." Chase tapped the radio on his belt. "Truck is waiting."

My heart took a momentary leap from its fear. If ever we needed a safe house, it was now.

THE bruised sky was high, leaving the air beneath chilly. In the morning light it was easier to see the devastation from the War. Most of the area looked like the airfield. Piles of debris and obtuse rebar, mountains of cinder blocks, and everywhere, the fuzzy peach-skin dust. My eyes drew to a thirty-story building behind the tunnel exit that was somehow still standing, even though it looked like a giant monster had taken a bite out of its waist. It went on like this for miles, until the lake consumed the horizon.

I had the sudden recollection of talking with Chase so long ago, listening to his story about when the bombs had hit Chicago. He'd been evacuated with the other students, and then hitchhiked to a town outside the city limits to meet his uncle.

The uncle who'd later abandoned him.

The uncle we would soon see if we made it to the safe house alive.

We all watched vigilantly for shadows, but no one had tracked us from the base. It seemed insane to me that we'd made it this far without being followed, but with so many uniforms around it was easier to melt into the crowds.

Chase took a hard left and the van descended into a dark abandoned parking garage. The tires sloshed through the water coating the floor. In the headlights I saw the FBR two-ton truck that had made its return from the Indiana checkpoint last night.

There were only eleven people left. Truck was outside, waving giddily. Jack and the supply boy with the almond eyes were among the others. I was glad not to see anyone who had been suspicious of us earlier.

Chase parked, and I stepped out into ankle-deep, freezing flood water.

"Change of heart, Sniper?" Truck asked me. The others were staring at us with a mixture of awe and concern. The medic had told us the rehab facility was bad luck, and as I touched the pendant around my neck, I couldn't balk. Superstition was an acquired skill in the resistance.

"We've got to get out of town," Chase said before I could answer.

They didn't ask if we'd been followed, or why we had to move. They knew what it was like to be hunted. With businesslike intensity, they began loading into the back of the truck. It was then that I noticed that Sean and Rebecca were still in the car.

I splashed back toward the van, Chase just behind me. They were just as we left them: staring blankly, straight ahead.

"We've got to get in the truck, Rebecca," I said. "We're going to take you somewhere safe. You won't have to worry about the MM anymore."

I hoped she couldn't hear my doubt. I hadn't been to the safe house. I didn't know what it was like, or if we'd truly be protected. It was a place of hopes and dreams, and for all I knew, nothing but a fairy tale.

Neither of them moved.

"We have to go," pressed Chase. "*Sean.*"

Sean's hands gripped the seat in front of them. He looked at Chase for a long moment and nodded.

"Becca," he said, without turning her direction. "Do you want me to take you back?"

What was he doing? We couldn't go back now. We couldn't stay in this town another second.

Rebecca didn't answer.

"We're not far," he said. "If you want me to, I'll take you back. But you need to know that I'm not going to leave you there alone. I'm not leaving you again."

A soft whimpering came from Rebecca's side of the car.

"I've got a brother, Becca. Matt. He was nine when I joined up. I never told you about him because I left him there, in St. Louis, in this two-man tent my dad got for us when we were kids." Sean's voice broke. He wiped his eyes with the back of his hand. "He was sleeping when I left. My dad had been gone over a week, and I knew he wasn't coming back this time, and I couldn't do it. I couldn't take care of him. So I enlisted. I went back once, but he was gone. A caseworker got him, is what the neighbors said. Put him in foster care. I told myself it was better than him dying with me, but that was a lie. He was my brother, and I left him, and I'm not going to make that mistake again."

I felt Chase's eyes on me.

"Just give me an answer," said Sean. "We'll go to a safe

house together, or we'll go back to the hospital together. Which is it going to be? Do you want to go back?"

He wasn't kidding himself. He knew exactly what would happen if he went back to that hospital. But he didn't care.

I felt a hot, guilty tear slide down my cheek.

"No," whispered Rebecca.

Too quickly, Sean grabbed her, and pulled her into a hard embrace. She fought him, writhing within his grasp, but he didn't release her, even when she punched his burned back. I meant to intercede, but Chase pulled me away from the car. His arms encircled my waist and I sagged back into him, hating that she was hurt and hating that I couldn't fix it.

After a moment, the punching stopped. I glanced up hopefully, but saw that Rebecca had simply succumbed to exhaustion. Her head hung slack against Sean's shoulder.

He took that moment to lift her in his arms, like a child who'd fallen asleep on the couch. He carried her to the truck and set her delicately on the tailgate. When he was inside he lifted her again, and carried her into the dark interior.

I looked around at the faces from Chicago, daring someone to laugh, even crack a smile, but nobody said a word. It could be any one of us, and they knew it.

There were no boxes to sit on inside, and the metal floor was serrated and unyielding. I sat close beside Rebecca, and Chase sat close beside me.

"Nighty night, ladies," said Truck as he slammed the rolling door down.

Like when we'd traveled in the back of the Horizons delivery truck, I felt my brow dew with sweat and a sudden panic sear my lungs. But for the first time it wasn't because I thought Tucker might attack me. There were now bigger things to worry about than my mother's killer.

The truck jostled and bumped, and we all grabbed one another to keep from sliding. Someone was praying in Spanish. I could hear Jack mumbling that we shouldn't go. There were still people in the tunnels. People we could save.

We had nothing. Not a change of clothes, not the letters I'd written Chase, or my mother's magazine; they'd all been lost along the way. We would start a new life with only what we carried.

I felt through the dark for Rebecca's hand, and then Chase's, on the other side. *My family.*

And then Rebecca's head fell to my shoulder, and I wept.

"YOU'RE going to love it, you know." Mom zipped up my back-pack, having checked to make sure my lunch pass was tucked safely in the inside pocket. "Seventh grade is a big deal."

I wished she'd stop saying that. I knew it was a big deal. All new kids and all new teachers and a school I'd only been to once before. I shuffled my feet to the door when the knock came.

Chase stood outside, skinny as a pole and almost a foot taller than he had been at the start of the summer. His black hair had grown shaggy again, and he pushed it back with one hand. Though he was starting high school today, he didn't look nervous at all. He never looked nervous.

They said their good mornings, and Mom told him he looked handsome in his new shirt, which I was pretty sure she did just to embarrass me. I couldn't even look at him after that.

"You'll walk her all the way to the front doors?"

"Yes, ma'am," Chase said seriously. We were meeting Beth at the corner; she and I could handle walking to school ourselves. But for some reason I didn't tell them so.

Mom leaned down and kissed me on the forehead. I hugged her then, for a long time. After school seemed a long ways away. But when we separated, she smiled, and it wasn't so hard to say good-bye.

"I'm proud of you, baby. I'll be here when you get home."

WE stopped at a checkpoint in Indiana, a small farm, where we reconvened with the remaining Chicago resistance. The elderly couple that ran the place greeted us with buckets of fresh scrambled eggs and canned meat, which we passed around in famished silence. I tried not to think about the fact that if they were caught, they'd be executed for an Article 9 violation alongside us.

Rebecca was still wearing the yellow scrubs from the hospital, but had finally agreed to place her braces on beneath them. They allowed her to walk independently, though she relied heavily on the two canes, not yet accustomed to the spacing and weight distribution of each step.

She denied my assistance at every turn. It was better than her despair, but it made me feel useless. When I told Sean this he just smiled.

"That's Becca," he said. "Only worry if she starts asking for help."

I began to object, but he said, "We got her out, Ember. The worst of it's over."

I hoped he was right. Before we could talk more, Rebecca stumbled on her way to the food line and he jumped up to give her a hand. When she shot him down the same as she'd done to me—with a glare and a sharp "I'm fine"—he turned back to me and winked, and I couldn't help but feel encouraged.

We weren't there long before help arrived. It was a smaller truck, less than twenty feet long, but blue like its brother, with the FBR logo painted on the side. I choked on my water when I saw the carrier greet Truck like an old friend.

Tubman wasn't wearing his loud Hawaiian shirt—he was still in the uniform Riggins had traded him back at East End Auto. The puckered scar on his right cheek drew my gaze from ten feet away. The last time I'd seen him, he and Cara were leaving the Knoxville checkpoint for the safe house.

"Well, well, well," he said, giving me a devilish smile as he approached. "Sounds like you been up to some trouble."

From out of the back of his truck jumped a lanky teenager with a greasy mat of hair hanging in front of his eyes. A laugh bubbled up as I pushed by the carrier.

"Billy!" We collided, my arms wrapping around his bony shoulders. "You made it."

"Marco and Polo took me to another checkpoint to see Tubman," he said. He backed up a step, scratching his head when he saw Tucker. "He didn't turn us in?"

"No," I said, watching Tucker interact with a few of the Chicago guys. "He's . . . all right." I couldn't believe what I was saying.

Billy looked confused, but let it go. "You haven't heard anything about Wallace?"

I shook my head.

A grin spread from ear to ear. "He's at the safe house then. He has to be."

I didn't disagree, because maybe he was right, maybe we would find Wallace. If we could pull Rebecca out of rehab, and find Billy after all we'd been through, anything was possible.

We loaded the trucks—a tighter fit even with Tubman's storage capacity—and moved on toward the Red Zone.

WE drove through the night.

Truck's compartment, which had seated only ten before, now held almost thirty, with the back area dedicated to Rebecca, the medic, and the other injured soldiers. The rest of us took turns standing and sitting, sleeping, and passing around water and bland cookies the woman had baked us. We smelled wretched, like body odor and antiseptic.

In the darkness it was impossible not to think about the tunnels, and the crushing weight of the landslide that had buried me under the table. Claustrophobia tightened our anxiety. Tensions rose, like the mercury on a thermometer, and then returned the speculations about the bombings: who had been followed? Who, as some were brave enough to mutter, betrayed us?

Only Sean, Tucker, and I knew the truth: that someone had sold out the resistance. Someone internal had tipped off the MM. I wondered if he'd already been completed in some jail cell, or if he, like Mags and so many others, had died in the tunnels.

Or if he were in this truck right now.

Some broke the pressure by talking about the safe house. A few of them had been there, and nearly everyone had sent family that direction.

"If every other person's mama lives there," asked someone from the other side of the compartment. "How big *is* this place?"

"Big," said someone.

"Real big," said another.

"It's a town, man. They've taken over a whole town."

At first I struggled, trying to place something like the Wayland Inn or the tunnels in the context of a beachfront property. But then my mind relaxed, and I saw houses on stilts, like I'd seen in pictures long ago. Homes filled with people, bustling with life. A soup kitchen line, like at home, where rations were given out. Yellow sand and the ocean, deep and everlasting.

Marco and Polo had suspected it wasn't just refugees that inhabited the safe house, but the mysterious Three as well. Would their presence make us safer? Or put us in more danger? Finally the vehicle jostled to a stop, and we all braced for what might wait outside.

Trees. That was what I saw first. Tall and leafy, overgrown with ivy and spindly webs that reflected the face of the moon. The air seeped into my pores, so much fresher than the suffocating interior of the truck. My whole body lifted. We were going to be safe at last.

I listened as hard as I could, but couldn't hear the waves. Some of the people from Chicago had talked about that—hearing the ocean, smelling the salt. But I couldn't.

I couldn't hear soldiers either. We were far away from the road, far away from any bases or patrol cars. Miles and miles from the FBR.

We were free.

Truck helped me down, carting me from the tailgate like I weighed no more than a small child. Up close I could see that his eyes were sunken with fatigue, and his huge muscular neck was the same width as his jaw.

"Where's the ocean?" I asked, frowning.

"Six miles east," he said, his face falling into shadow. "Usually there's a scout here to lead us into camp. I tried to radio ahead to them we were coming, but the lines are down."

I frowned, and he play-punched my arm. "No worries," he said. "They probably just ran out of batteries. I know the way in."

The injured were carried, or loaded on stretchers made from blankets. Though Rebecca had tried to walk unassisted, the soft, mossy soil was too uneven for her dragging feet, and she reluctantly agreed to let Sean carry her piggyback.

Truck led us on a narrow path through the darkness. With my good arm, I carried a bucket of medical supplies that had been salvaged from the tunnels, and Chase hauled a flat of ammunition. Despite the added weight, the weariness lifted off my shoulders and my body hummed with excitement.

We stopped at a stream to rest the injured and refill our canteens. My worries about Tucker, about Harper, about the rat who'd sold out the Chicago resistance, drifted downstream with the current. I let the cool water wash over my hands and my sore wrist and my face, and breathed in deeply.

When I opened my eyes, I found Chase watching me. His face was momentarily void of the worry he'd been carrying since the hospital, his eyes clear of the horror we'd seen there. Now a small smile lifted his mouth, and he settled back on his heels. It took me a full beat to realize that he looked relieved.

I don't know what it was, the fresh air, or the freedom of movement after hours in a cattle car. Maybe it was that we finally knew Rebecca was safe and that we were so close to security, or just the way he looked at me, with all the secrets stripped away. Whatever it was tipped something inside, and I splashed him, soaking the front of his shirt and his shins. His mouth fell open in shock.

Then, just like when we were kids, I ran.

I raced away from the group, darting around trees and over bushes, hearing his footsteps hot on my heels. His hand grasped at my waist once, but I evaded him with a stifled scream and ran on. We were in a Red Zone, off the road, close to the safe house—we would not be less in danger than we were right now.

He caught me before the lights from the stream had disappeared. His strong arms closed around my waist and hoisted me up and I kicked through the air and giggled. He smiled into my neck, and I smiled, too, because this, *this* was joy. This, at last, was the leap beyond escape, beyond the shaking threshold of survival.

"Come on," Chase said, taking my hand. "We're close. I

can hear the water." We'd come back for the supplies we'd left at the creek.

I listened, but I couldn't hear what he had yet. Still, I raced after him, faster and faster in the direction of the coast.

The smell hit us first. Pungent wood smoke, oil and dust. Something metallic, too, overriding the salt in the air. I heard it then, the sound of the ocean. The waves. But everything within me had clamped down, and excitement could not penetrate the foreboding sense of danger.

The trees cleared, and the grass grew long, almost to my shoulders. We shoved through, cresting a sand dune.

My heart tripped in my chest.

"No," Chase said weakly.

There before us were the remains of a town. Houses were burned to the ground; some still smoking. Black and charred like the night. Brick and concrete had been blown away, decimated, like the buildings in Chicago. Piles of fresh rubble, yet untouched by moss and weeds, blocked out whole city streets. The hood of a car rested on the ground near us, warped and bent by the explosion that had catapulted it thirty feet away from its overturned body. Beyond it all lapped the silver ocean, constant and deep, unable to voice the horrors that had taken place here.

My knees weakened, and I pitched forward, succumbing to the weight of our hope as it crashed down upon us.

The safe house had been destroyed.

CHAPTER
21

THE ashes clung to my boots, to the legs of my pants. To my arms and my hair, to the sweat of my neck. To the empty cavity in my chest, where joy and hope had both been carved away.

Fifty warm bodies within fifty yards of one another; that was what Sprewell had said. There had been more than fifty people at the safe house, all gathered close for their mutual protection. Heat-seeking missiles had leveled them. LDEDs. That was the only explanation; soldiers on foot would have needed an evacuation route, and there was simply too much demolition to be anything but bombs.

When we'd mobilized enough strength to return to the group, I'd told Jack and Truck this, and Sean and Tucker, intent to see the damage for themselves, had been brought in to corroborate what we'd learned in the rehab hospital. Those still with their wits about them were immediately tasked with rounding up the group for a roll call. With chaos erupting and fear running rampant, this was no easy task, but after a while they fell in line.

There were forty-seven of us in all, counting Rebecca, the Knoxville contingency, and Tubman. Not fifty, but close enough.

Chase was the one to suggest we split up to survey the damage. Rebecca and the others injured in the tunnels were assisted back into the cover of the woods by Sean, the medic, and three other soldiers. There was a wildlife station in the marshes, a dingy shack filled with mosquitoes and stagnant pond water, but it had a roof, and could hold ten bodies laid out on the concrete floor.

Truck and Tubman, our drivers, formed another team.

"Someone's got to warn the other branches," said Truck. "Quick. So they don't send anyone else out this way." It was something I imagined Three would have done, but if they still existed, they would leave no directions for the carriers here.

"I'll go."

I turned sharply to find Tucker Morris. His face, cast downward, was stripped of all emotion.

"I don't know all your bases, but I know where the FBR will be. I can keep us off their radar."

I had to remind myself that he'd proven his loyalties.

Chase said nothing, but the corner of his eye twitched. He hadn't said it, but I knew he wanted to stay and look for signs of his uncle.

If he was staying, I was staying.

Truck's team left without hesitation, promising to return as soon as they'd found a safe place for us to hide. Tucker and I did not say good-bye, and as I watched his back as he disappeared through the tall grass, it occurred to me that I should have felt relieved to finally be rid of him, but maybe there was no room left for such a thing.

The rest of us drew what weapons we had, and sorted through the smoke and the wood and the glass. We overturned doors and crumbled stones and pieces of drywall. And we found bodies. Burned to black. Burned so badly, you couldn't even tell they were human.

Someone who knew of this place had done this. Had pointed the MM in the right direction, had sent those long-distance explosive devices flying through the air, and killed our families and friends. Our chance at peace.

At dawn, Jack pointed out the ruins of a house that had days ago served as a medical clinic. Chase threw himself into excavating it, so savagely that his arms bled and his shirt soaked through with the same salty sweat that hid any tears that dared escape.

His uncle is dead, I thought as I watched. *I am all he has left*. And though I knew this feeling intimately, my heart broke for him.

I stumbled away, winding around the littered trinkets of an old souvenir shop, ears perked to the skies like in the old days when we'd watched the planes. I thought of Sarah, pregnant and scared when her life had been cut short. Of Rebecca, who could barely walk on cement, much less an uneven sandy floor, and Truck's words in the tunnel: *What were we supposed to do with him once we got him out? We can't support that kind of care down here.* Of Sean, who would never leave her side again.

I was secretly glad my mother had never made it to this doomed place.

Snow globes were broken across the ground, little shattered memories of a happier time. I picked up a few tattered beach towels that had survived the blasts, but they were impossibly heavy on my injured wrist.

My eyes fixed on a figure in the distance, sitting atop the hood of a car that had been shoved into the middle of the street. His arms and hair were streaked black, and his shadow stretched thin behind him.

My legs ached as I approached, bruised to the bone from the explosion in the tunnels, but he didn't so much as turn his head.

"Billy," I said cautiously. He stared a thousand yards behind me, past the house that lay in ruins at our feet, to the gray sea. His body slumped, like an empty puppet, and when he stood, he didn't fully straighten.

"He's dead, Ember. Wallace is dead."

Another of us orphaned. Made old before our time.

"Billy, I'm sorry." I reached for his hand, but it was cold as ice.

"I feel like I should tell someone—is that weird? But there's no one left to tell."

His hand squeezed mine, and before I knew what was happening, he was hugging me, and I was hugging him back, and we were both crying.

Below him, my gaze landed on three white lines, etched into the hood of the car where he'd been sitting. Three scars, just like I'd seen below Cara's collarbone when we'd changed in Greeneville.

Three had been here. Maybe Cara had been working for them. It didn't matter. Now Cara, and Three, were gone.

We were all that was left.

"There are people to tell," I heard myself say, the words forming truth in my mouth. "We have to tell people what happened, Billy. What happed to my mom, and to Wallace. We'll tell everyone. Everyone needs to know. That's how we stop it."

I was shaking now, feeling like the world was quaking beneath my feet, and I knew then that it better, because soon everything would be different. I didn't know how, but I would tell my mother's story. I would tell mine, too, and maybe, *maybe* that would shift the tides.

Someone was approaching, and when he saw Chase, Billy turned away, and wiped his eyes with the back of his hand.

I went to him, needing to be close, but the look on his face gave me pause. The hairs on the back of my neck lifted.

"Tracks," he said, voice hoarse. "Some of the guys found tracks leading south."

Survivors.

He was thinking of his uncle; I could see it on his face.

Instantly, I was burning again, only this time with hope. My hand slid into Chase's, and we glanced one more time at the charred, ruined pits of safety, at the last remaining embers that smoldered even after the flames had died. And something told me this was not the end, that there was a reason we had persevered.

Without another word, we ran south.

ACKNOWLEDGMENTS

Now is the point where I get to reflect on how truly lucky I am. As if, with each step further into this writing world, I could ever forget.

This book would not have been possible without the encouragement, advice, and superhero powers of my agent, Joanna MacKenzie, or without Danielle Egan-Miller's and Shelbey Campbell's excellent organization and efforts to advocate. I am so grateful to have the Browne and Miller team in my corner.

Breaking Point would still be locked in my laptop if not for my editor, Melissa Frain. Thank you for your patience and kindness, for your brilliant comments, and for always making me laugh. I would not trade knowing you for anything. Thank you to Kathleen Doherty for being an amazing publisher and for taking a chance on a debut author, to Alexis Saarela for organizing Chase and Ember's social calendar, and to Seth Lerner's art team for making this cover super cool.

A special thank-you to Officer Hernandez, who allowed me to join him through the Ride Along program at the local police department, and showed me just a hint of the risks he takes each night keeping the city safe.

An author is only as good as her support team. Thank you to my friends and family for knowing me and loving me anyway, to the great authors, booksellers, and librarians I have met on this journey, and to the bloggers who have been absolutely integral in spreading the word about ARTICLE 5. Thank you to those who have shared their stories of struggle and triumph with me over the past year—you are truly an inspiration. Thank you to Katie Mc-Garry, who I refuse to call a crit partner or a first reader because she is so, so much more than that. Whatever stars aligned for us to meet, I will forever sing their praises.

And thank you to my husband, Jason. I just don't work without you.